SON, MOON AND STAR

Tyler Scott has written a must-read book for anyone interested in a detailed, scriptural, and historically based story concerning the message of Jesus and His transforming power. Scott's characters adequately convert others through the witnessing of God's Word and good old-fashioned Southern hospitality that transcends race and religion. Scott's book does a very unique job of amalgamating the ideologies of different religions, cultures, and ethnicities into the common thread of Brotherhood. His story brings alive the emotions of a small-town community haunted by its past of racial injustices. Each of the characters comes alive by the carefully chosen words that can easily be identified as a member of any small-town community. I strongly endorse and recommend this book, though fictional, it has transformed my thinking towards forgiveness and evangelism.

—**Dr. Rickey Van O'Quinn** Senior Pastor of *St. Mark Baptist Church* & Dean of Religion at *Kingdom Theological Seminary*

***

An exciting new book from one of Mississippi's premier Christian authors. R. Tyler Scott takes his readers on an adventure that will keep the reader guessing until the very end.

If you enjoy Christian fiction, you need to read this book. I had trouble putting it down and am looking forward to a sequel.

—**Dr. Darby L. Combs**, Senior Pastor of *Bethel Baptist church Brandon, Mississippi.*

***

I have had the privilege of knowing Tyler Scott for the past thirty-five years or so. I know a lot of good things about him but I did not know what a great writer he is until I read his most recent book, "Son, Moon, and Stars". The story, set in rural Southwest Mississippi, is a "page-turner" in the genre of a "who-done-it". Woven into the story is an exploration of many southern stereotypes that have persisted well into the twenty-first century. Mr. Scott deals forthrightly with the ones that still linger. He also does a good job of dispelling many of the negative stereotypes that do not define life in the south. There are several main characters from different religious and ethnic backgrounds. The author skillfully and convincingly develops each character. When I finished the book I felt as if I knew them personally. If you are looking for a great read that quickly pulls you in and then hits you with many biblical truths, including several clear presentations of the Gospel, then you will not be disappointed with "Son, Moon, and Stars". It is also a wonderful book to give to an unbeliever as a witnessing tool.

—**Marvin Howard**, Pastor *Mt. Zion Baptist Church Franklin County, MS*

Son, Moon, and Star

R. Tyler Scott

Published by KHARIS PUBLISHING, imprint of KHARIS MEDIA LLC.

Copyright © 2020 R. Tyler Scott

ISBN-13: **978-1-946277-84-8**
ISBN-10: 1-946277-84-3

Library of Congress Control Number: 2020952032

Unless otherwise noted, Scripture taken from the *King James Version*® Used by permission.

All KHARIS PUBLISHING products are available at special quantity discounts for bulk purchase for sales promotions, premiums, fund-raising, and educational needs. For details, contact:

Kharis Media LLC
Tel: 1-479-599-8657
support@kharispublishing.com
www.kharispublishing.com

CONTENTS

Thank You Letter

When God called me to write, he didn't say I would do it on my own. Glenda, my wife of going on thirty-two years has always been my biggest supporter as well as my best critic. I don't submit anything that she doesn't see first. After Jesus, she is the most important part of my life. I also want to thank all my girls, my two sons in laws and my four grandchildren for their support.

I dedicate this book to the memory of my mentor and friend the late Reverend Bendon Ginn. Several years ago when he and I served together at Philadelphia Baptist Church, he told me I needed to write something that would be controversial but could bring people together and show them Jesus on top of everything else. He went home to be with Jesus before I got this book published, but I was able to tell him about it right before he passed. His friendship and counsel were priceless.

I also want to thank two women who helped me in the early edits. Mrs. Ethyl Dillon and Mrs. Mary Alice Higgs. One of them taught me English and the other taught my children, but both read and gave great insight and kind criticism of the book. They were both Instrumental in getting the project over the finish line. I also would like to thank the editor from Kharis Press Ms. Karen Herceg. She was very complimentary in her editing style as well as her suggestions. She makes her alma mater, Columbia University proud.

Finally, I want to thank my Lord and Savior Jesus Christ. You see, he is the reason that there is even a book to be written. I am not worthy to write and proclaim his goodness. I am not qualified to even write. But just like with his disciples, Jesus doesn't always call the qualified, but he always qualifies the called. I pray that I never write anything that doesn't glorify God and give him praise because he is worthy of more than I can ever give. All He asks is my best. I pray that you see God in this book and if you don't know Jesus as your Savior, you will accept him because it will be the greatest decision you will ever make.

Ain't God Good

CHAPTER 1

Fish out of Water

Looking down at her phone, Aggie wondered if she should ignore the call like she usually did or do something really wild and answer it. The call was from a number she didn't recognize, and most people never answer calls from numbers they don't recognize. But Aggie knew that didn't mean anything to her. If she was a gambler, Aggie would bet money the voice she would hear, if she answered, would be that of HyramSharosh, her father. He called her from random numbers around this time every afternoon. He didn't have a set work schedule, but every day at 1:00 p.m. New York time, he would call to check in on her from wherever he was. The calls came from random offices and businesses, because he didn't believe in cell phones. He believed in computers and the internet. Even though he was one of the richest men in New York, her father felt that cell phones weren't something he could explain to God. He felt that wireless communication was something that should be reserved for praying. "The Jewish people have endured for more than four thousand years without this kind of technology. I don't see the need for it now." He was famous for saying this time and again. This came from a man who made his millions owning television stations around the country and the world.

When the phone finally stopped ringing and the voice mail tone went off, Aggie pondered if she was going to listen to the message now or later. Since she wouldn't answer the call when it came through, it seemed ridiculous to immediately listen to the message. If she had anything else in the world that she could do at this moment, Aggie would do it. Unfortunately, she was standing on the corner of First and Main Streets in Bude, Mississippi. Quite possibly the most po-dunk town she had ever seen. That was saying something because, in the last three weeks, she had seen and been in some extremely rural areas. But from what she had seen in the last few minutes, Bude was probably the one place in the world where watching paint dry was an exciting experience. Looking down what would be considered the downtown area and seeing more dogs than people, Aggie decided that listening to her father's message would be as close as she would come to excitement today.

"Hello, Agnes, this is your father." Aggie hated that he thought she wouldn't recognize his voice and had to tell her that it was him on the phone.

1

The only thing she hated more was the name Agnes. "I was wondering how your day was going and if you have found a synagogue to attend Saturday. I hope you do well with the story you are working on. I will be home this evening around ten if you have time to call. Remember, down there you are not just a girl, you are a Jewish girl. I'm not sure if those people are over Hitler's defeat. Anyway, I hope to hear from you this evening." He never said goodbye when he ended a phone call. He just hung up because there was nothing else for him to say.

Although she had been gone from her New York home for three weeks, this was her first day in Mississippi. She had decided on this small town because it was where she found the most recent story about a civil rights era case. Something about some man who had tortured two young African American boys and had thrown them out of an airplane. Somehow, he had just been convicted for something that happened forty years earlier. Her ethics professor was well known for saying, "crimes against humanity don't have an expiration date."

The reason she came to the South was something that many people in her circle of friends at Rutgers had not understood. Her college newspaper was having a contest among all the journalism students for the most interesting and intriguing article on civil rights, then and now. Some rich alumnus family had given ten million dollars to the college's School of Journalism, and the school had to use a portion of the money for scholarships to be given to students who cared about the civil rights struggle. The dean of the Journalism School, Michael Ozwald, had come up with the idea of giving the scholarship to the student who wrote the most compelling exposé on civil rights from the past to the present. All of Aggie's friends had talked about all the information on the Internet, and the people their parents knew who had gone to the South and fought the good fight. Aggie had never considered writing her article from any other perspective than to come down and get her hands dirty. She believed if she could come to the places where these heinous incidents had happened, then the racial struggle would be more understandable to her. It wasn't that she had not heard about being punished and ridiculed for being something that she couldn't do anything about. Her father had made it his life's ambition to make sure that she, as his only child, would be well-informed of the indignities the world had put on the Jewish people since the days of Father Abraham. He had funded a special teacher in their synagogue to teach the young people about the atrocities the Jews have faced. His comment about Hitler was his fallback position on anyone from south of Coney Island. He felt no one truly grasped the plight of the Jewish people, and it was his job to inform them. The last three weeks were a blur, but the day she left was as clear as crystal in her mind.

That was the day that she saw how much her father wanted to control her and her thoughts.

"Why don't you do a story about the wrongs that have been heaped on our people," he had said on the day she was supposed to leave.

"But Father, the scholarship doesn't come to the person who can understand anti- Semitism. It is supposed to be about racism and the civil rights of African Americans."

"Civil rights? Is there any bigger story of the taking away of civil rights than the killing of six million Jews in the Holocaust? Not to mention all the enemies of Israel who want to kill them right now as we speak. I wonder who made this giant donation? I consider it a slight to all the Jewish community for this scholarship to only go to someone who writes a story about black civil rights. I may make an informal complaint through the Anti-Defamation League.

"I don't need you to make any complaints whatsoever Father. I'm sure the ADL has enough to worry about without being involved in something like this. I can write a great story, but I need to go down and walk the streets where these civil rights were trampled on. Not just in Birmingham, Montgomery, and Atlanta, but in Mississippi and other places where civil rights were and still are a dirty word. Father, this could be the most important thing I ever do, not counting the financial benefits. If I get this scholarship, I won't have to add any more student loans to what I have to pay back. The scholarship is for three years' tuition and, with the publicity I get, I will be able to work for any newspaper or magazine I choose."

"But Agnes, why must you do this on your own? If you will just say the word, I will have a check written that will pay for whatever you need." When he said this, HyramSharosh had put his arm around his daughter and smiled.

"Dad, you have made your position very clear. If you pay for my college, I am required to work for you until I am thirty-five. I love you, but I don't want to work for you."

"Agnes, I own twelve newspapers and seven television stations. You could go to work at

any one of them and write whatever you want. I just want you to be happy and successful."

"I will be successful, but I will be successful where I am happy, not where you want me to be happy."

"I have made millions of dollars convincing people that I know what is best for them, but I can't make my daughter believe it."

"I believe you think you know what's best for everyone. I think you want what's best for you, and I want what's best for me. I am going south and that's final."

Aggie walked to her room and packed her bags. She had her route picked out already and knew where she was going first and how long it was going to take. She had six weeks to get the information she wanted and then write the article. She walked down the stairs past her father and didn't say a word. Aggie put her bag in her car and wished her mother was there to kiss good-bye. She had died three years earlier, and Aggie still cried when she thought about her.

"I am proud you are going to let me provide a car and expense money for this little escapade you are going on," her father said as he stood beside the car. "I don't know how many 2012 Porsches there are down there, so please be careful with this one."

"Daddy, Mom promised me this car before she died. I don't feel guilty about it because she made you get it for me. If the money is a problem, then keep a count of how much I spend and when I get out of college, I will pay you back."

He stood there smiling that smile she hated because he knew Aggie was mad and just saying things. She had worked several jobs her freshman year in college but always needed money from him to tide her over. She desperately wanted to be free of that knowing smirk he was giving her right now. The one that said he really didn't think she could make it without him. With that thought in my mind, Aggie turned the engine on and headed south to write her story and continue her journey to independence from her father and his life.

"Wow, what an awesome car. Can I have a ride?" The voice brought Aggie out of her daydream and back to the reality of Bude.

"I'm sorry. I wasn't paying attention. What were you saying?" The young boy, who looked to be about twelve, was smiling and looking at the car. He was almost as tall as Aggie with brown hair and the darkest brown eyes she had ever seen. He could have been wearing nothing but a sheet, and those eyes would have been the first thing Aggie would have noticed.

"I asked if you would give me a ride in your car? I've seen a Porsche on television but never in person. Walt told me there was one in town, but I

4

didn't believe him until I saw you standing beside it. It is your car, isn't it?"

"What's your name?" Aggie asked. She wasn't going to give him a ride in her car but learning his name would be a nice gesture. It was always easier to say no to someone if you called them by their name. At least that is what her philosophy teacher had said.

"My name's Archie Walker, but my friends call me Jughead." "Oh, after the comic books?" He looked at her and scratched his head.

"I don't know anything about a comic book. When I was two, I got my head stuck in a

jug, and they had to take me to the hospital to get it off. Dr. Bill told me that he broke the jar and my head just popped out. Since then I've been called Jughead.

"Okay, Jughead. I'm sorry, but I don't give rides in my car to strangers, even if they are cute young men. I am just arriving in town and I don't know anyone."

"Well, now you know someone. You know me. Can I ride in your car now?"

"No, Archie, or do you want me to call you Jughead?"

"Nobody but my grandparents and my momma call me Archie."

"Very well then, Jughead, I'm on my way to the newspaper, but I'm not sure where it is."

"Wow. This is your lucky day. My grandparents live right beside the paper. I was supposed to go see them tonight. You can give me a ride and I won't have to wait on my momma to drive me. You get what you want and I get what I want."

The dark brown eyes and the innocent face melted any defense Aggie had. "You drive a hard bargain. Get in and I'll take you to your grandparents."

"All right. Will it go fast? Can we see what it will do in the quarter?"

"No, we can't see what it will do in the quarter. I don't drive fast and neither should you when you get your license. Now are you going to help me get to the paper or not?"

"You betcha."

5

As she opened the door of the car, Aggie noticed a man and a woman standing on the porch of their house staring at her. *They must not see many people from out-of-town around here*, Aggie thought. When she opened the passenger side door, Archie jumped into the seat.

"Wow. This leather feels so good. I've got to take a picture so Walt and Freddie will believe me when I tell them about this." He took out his phone and took pictures of the entire car with him smiling in each one.

Aggie laughed at his excitement. "Which way do we go?"

"Go down to the end of the street and turn right. At the stop sign turn left and just stay straight till we get to Meadville."

"You mean the newspaper's in another town? How far away is it? I can't be responsible for taking you to another town. You better get out, and I will find someone else to give me directions."

"It's another town, but it's only three or four miles. Meadville's where the high school is. Besides, I'm already in the car and Walt is expecting us to drive by any minute. If you come through without me, they will think I'm a big liar."

Aggie smiled at how important not being called a liar was to this young man. "Okay, but I don't want to hear anything about going fast, do you hear me?"

"Yes ma'am, you have my word."

As she drove down the road, Aggie saw buildings that looked like they had seen their better days. The train tracks were a good sign because that meant the world hadn't totally forgotten this area. As they passed every house, Archie waved and told her who lived there. It was apparent that this young man knew everyone and everyone knew him because they all waved back.

"That's the grocery store," Archie said as they came to a three-way stop. "My mom takes me there every day after school to get an Icee."

"What's an Icee?" Aggie asked.
"You don't know what an Icee is? What planet did you come from?" Aggie chuckled. "I'm from New York, and right now I think this is another planet."

Up ahead, she saw that the road became a four-lane highway. "Are you sure this is right? We are getting on a highway."

"Naw, this is the regular road. It will go back to two lanes in just a little while."

As they passed across the bridge over the highway, Archie looked down the road. "That's Highway 84. If you go right, you go to Brookhaven, but if you go left, you go to Natchez. My grandpa used to work in Natchez at the paper plant before they closed it down."

"I'm sorry to hear about that."

"It's okay. He said the unions and the Jews had ruined the company anyway. Can we go a little faster? I don't want anyone to know that I rode in a Porsche that would only go thirty-five miles an hour."

The comment he made about the Jews caught Aggie off-guard. It made her mad that there were still people who thought Jews were the source of all the world's problems. The innocence of this young boy made it even more frustrating. One of the ways she let her anger show when she got mad while driving was to push harder on the accelerator. As the car began to accelerate, Jughead sat up in his seat. "Yeah, that's what I'm talking about. Give it some gas." The Porsche had reacted quickly and in just a moment, Aggie looked down and saw that she was doing sixty miles an hour.

"I better slow down. I didn't mean to speed up, but your comment upset me."
"What comment?" Archie asked.

Before Aggie could answer, she saw a car behind her with blue lights and a siren blaring. Wonderful. I am in town one day and already I am going to get a ticket. Looking up she saw that there wasn't much shoulder to pull onto, but on the left side there was some sort of VFW building with a cannon in front of it. Aggie decided to pull into the parking lot and take her medicine. Besides, she had talked herself out of tickets before, and those were tough New York policemen. These country police officers shouldn't be as hard to convince of her innocence. As she pulled in, Aggie saw another police car come sliding up in front of her. Wow. They take their speeding seriously around here, Aggie thought.

Without any warning, the policeman that had stopped in front of her opened the door and got out. He didn't just get out of the car. He got out with a large shotgun, and it was pointed straight at her.

"These people don't need to point their guns at me," Aggie said. "I know my rights, and I don't have to be treated like this." She opened the door, but before she could get out of the seat, the officer who had come up behind

7

them, grabbed her by the arm, pulled her out of the car, and threw her against the hood.

"Keep your gun on her Billy," the second officer said as he jerked Aggie's arms behind her and put handcuffs on her wrists.

"Don't you worry Bobby. She'll think twice before she tries to kidnap a little boy again."

"Kidnap a little boy? What're you talking about?" Aggie asked.

"Keep quiet ma'am. You have the right to do that. Anything you say can be used against you in a court of law," he said. Bobby McCoy, according to his name badge, must be the ranking deputy of the Sheriff's Department, because he was doing all the talking. As he frisked her, Aggie wondered if she could have fit a gun in the places he was searching.

"Excuse me guys, but I usually have a man buy me dinner before we go this far." Aggie was scared but also confused. When she got scared, she tried to make jokes to calm herself and deflect the situation. What could they possibly think she had done wrong?

"Ma'am, I have advised you of your right to remain silent, and I think you should take advantage of it. Billy, come on over while I get her in the car. You can put your weapon away now. She's not going anywhere."

"Bobby, you have to let her go. She didn't do anything. I begged her to take me to Mammaw's house." Archie had gotten out of the car and was pulling on the deputy's leg.

"Jughead, get back," the other deputy, Billy Henderson, replied. Since he had been the security guard at the school, Billy knew all the kids by name, even their nicknames. It also helped that he had lived in Franklin County his entire life.

"Jughead, you need to get on back," Bobby said.

"If you two would just hear what he is saying, this could be taken care of in just a few minutes," Aggie said.

"Ma'am, I don't know what people in New York do, if that's really where you are from, but when a stranger in a possibly stolen sports car comes along and picks up a twelve-year-old boy, people get skeptical about your intentions."

"Have you run the tag on the car? Have you looked at my driver's license?

Have you done anything except put me in handcuffs and treat me like a criminal?"

"No ma'am we haven't, but we're about to, aren't you Bobby?" The voice belonged to a heavy-set man with a brown shirt and a cowboy hat.

"Sheriff, I was just trying to make sure the prisoner didn't do anything stupid," Bobby said.

"Bobby, I don't think this one-hundred-and fifteen-pound young lady is a threat. Now please remove the handcuffs and do some investigating. I know Jughead is your nephew and you were worried, but I am willing to bet that everything is not what it seems, at least to you."

Bobby turned to argue with the Sheriff but decided against it. He didn't like being reprimanded in front of people, but he was not going to make a bigger scene than it already was. Though it wasn't what he wanted to do, he took the handcuffs off. He was much rougher than he needed to be, but finally the cuffs came off and he stepped back.

Aggie rubbed her wrists and tried to compose herself. Her father always said most people make mistakes because they act out their anger after a confrontation, instead of taking a few moments to catch their breath and get composed. She also tried to look angry but had a hard time doing it, because her heart was beating so loud it felt like someone was playing drums in her ears. The man they had called Sheriff came over to Aggie and smiled.

"Ma'am, my name is Henry Wactor, and I'm the Sheriff of Franklin County. I heard that Bobby told you that you had the right to remain silent but, as you said, this will probably all go away if you talk to me."

"Thank you so much, Sheriff. My name is Aggie Sharosh."

"This is a very nice car, Ms. Sharosh. Do you have any identification and registration papers?"

"They are in my purse and in the glove compartment." Aggie was beginning to calm down and the excitement of the situation was changing into genuine anger. It was not only at the deputies, but at herself for getting into this mess.

As she walked over to her car, Aggie saw that several cars had stopped on the side of the road, and some had even driven into the parking lot around them. *Well, I'm proud to put some excitement into your boring lives*, Aggie thought. When she handed the Sheriff her license and registration, she noticed the two deputies who had stopped her were standing together talking to Archie. Both of them were keeping their heads down and wouldn't look at her. As everyone watched, the Sheriff took out his walkie talkie.

"S.O. 1 to S.O., I need you to run license number 548754874. I also need you to run a tag, New York plates, AGGIE 1." He then looked over at Archie. "Jughead, can you come over here?"

"I can't make myself call him Jughead," Aggie said.

"I can," said the Sheriff. "I think it's the funniest story I've ever heard. Did he tell you how he got the name?" Before Aggie could say anything, a voice came over the radio.

"License comes back to Agnes Sharosh. No prior records or violations that I can see. The car registered to HyramSharosh of New York, New York. Is this the car that kidnapped Archie?"

"This is the car Jughead was in, but I don't think he was kidnapped. Please keep your questions off the air, Sharon." He then looked over at the crowd that was standing around. "Okay everyone the show is over. Please disperse before I allow Officers Henderson and McCoy to get rid of some of the tension and embarrassment, I'm sure they are feeling."

As the people began to get into their cars and drive away, Sheriff Wactor handed Aggie her license. "Ms. Sharosh, now that we have a quiet moment, would you please tell me your side of the story?"

"Sheriff, I tried," Archie began to say.

"Jughead, you stand there and keep quiet until I ask you something. All right, Ms. Sharosh, you have my attention."

"Sheriff, I stopped on the street looking for the newspaper office and I got a call from my father. I listened to it and got a little angry, but that isn't important. When I got to my car, Jug, I mean Archie was standing there looking at it. I talked to him and he asked me for a ride because he had never been in a Porsche. I should have paid attention to my first inclination, but I have been driving all morning and I guess I was swayed by this cute little kid. He told me he knew where the newspaper office was because his grandparents live next to it. He said he was supposed to go see them, and I got swept into some sort of stupidity that made me think it was a good idea to be nice to a little kid. I was on my way when these two storm troopers stopped me and almost shot me. Did you know that the black officer pointed his gun at me?"

"The way the deputies handled themselves will be something we can talk about in a few minutes. Jughead is that what happened? Now don't lie to me because you know I can tell if you are lying."

"Yes sir, that's exactly what happened. I guess it's my fault, but I just wanted Walt and them to see me in this cool car."

"Did you ever think to call your momma and tell her what you were doing? No, you didn't, because when Mr. Osborne called and asked her if she knew someone in a black car with New York plates, she called the precinct and said someone had kidnapped her child. She is waiting on you at the house. Bobby is going to take you home, and I would suggest you take the time between here and there to call her and let her know everything is all right. She also said that she tried to call you but you didn't answer. I think she is going to want to discuss that with you also."

"Yes sir," Archie said. "See you around, Aggie."

"I very much doubt that," Aggie said. "I am going to get the information I need, and I am headed out of here as fast as I can go."

"What information are you looking for?" Sheriff Wactor asked. "Maybe I can help you, and that will take the bad taste out of your mouth for Franklin County."

"I came here to get some first-hand information about the Civil Rights Movement and the deaths that happened here. I am writing a story for my school paper, and I want to get my hands dirty."

"If you want to get down and dirty, you have come to the right place. Did you say you were headed to the newspaper before all this unpleasantness occurred?"

"Yes, sir, that is where Archie was taking me. Is he going to be all right? I heard you say that his mother was angry that he didn't call." Despite the problems that had arisen from their short time together, there was something about Archie that Aggie liked.

"He may get his behind popped and have his phone taken away, but nothing that will scar him for life. I think you should know the reason that Bobby and Billy reacted so forcefully."

"Let me guess. They had a Cops television show marathon on last night?" Aggie couldn't resist being a smart aleck sometimes.

Sheriff Wactor chuckled. "No, but that's a funny answer. You see, we had

11

a young girl who was kidnapped a couple of years ago. She was walking home after getting off the school bus and was never seen again. There were some stories that a black car picked her up, but by the time her parents realized she was missing, there was nothing we could do. Contrary to what you see on television, it is tough to catch a smart criminal. Bobby took it the hardest because he and the girl's father were best friends. Now he doesn't take any chances with reported kidnappings and neither do I. He should have handled himself better, but I hope you can appreciate the situation. Why don't you follow me, and I will take you over to the newspaper? After you get through talking to Mr. Benjamin, you can go over to the library. There are hundreds of articles on microfiche that you can look at. Most of that stuff was before computers were ever thought about, so it won't be on Google search."

"Thanks Sheriff, that would be a great help."

"Then just follow me and I will even get you an introduction."

Aggie got back into her car and leaned against the head rest. While she waited for the sheriff to finish talking to a couple of people who had not left yet, her phone rang.

"Where is area code 601?" Aggie said out loud. Then she realized that was Mississippi's area code. "Who would be calling me from here? I haven't been here long enough to give anyone my number." She hit the accept button and put the phone up to her ear.

"Hello Aggie, are you okay?" A young voice asked.

"Who is this?"

"It's Jughead. I just talked to my mom and she said I had to call and apologize to you forgetting you into trouble."

"Archie, there's no reason for you to apologize. I am as much to blame as anyone. But there's something I have to know. How do you have my number?"

"When Bobby and the others pulled us over and you were outside the car, I sent a text to my phone from your phone so I would have your number. Don't get mad, but I didn't want you to get away without saying goodbye. Also, your father called while you were outside. I told him the Sheriff's deputies had stopped you."

"Why did you answer my phone Archie?"

"Because it was ringing and I couldn't hear what Bobby was saying."

"What did my father say?" Aggie could guess some of what he must have thought.

"He said that you were known to have a heavy foot, and it would serve you right if you got a ticket. He asked me what my name was, and then I saw Bobby putting the handcuffs on you and I told him I had to go. He said he would call you when he got home."

"Did you tell him that they were putting me in handcuffs?"

"No, I told him that you were in trouble, and I needed to go help. Did I do something bad?"

"No, Archie, you didn't. I am going to follow the Sheriff to the newspaper, and then I'm going to the library so I better get off the phone. I hope your mother didn't fuss at you too much."

"Naw, I am probably grounded for a couple of weeks, and when Dad gets home, I will have a class on calling home and telling Momma where I'm going."

"What kind of class is that?" Aggie asked. She had never heard of any discipline like that. "Is your Dad a teacher?"

"Kind of. He says he is teaching me common sense. Now that I have gotten older, instead of getting whippings, unless I do something really bad, he gives me classes to learn to not do something again. Trust me, but I would rather have a whipping."

Aggie was intrigued by this. She had never heard of discipline like this. "Tell me what you think he's going to do?"

"When he gets home, I will have to go outside and walk around the house. Every time I turn the corner, I will have to stop and call my Momma and tell her where I'm at."

"Have you done this before?"

"No, this will be the first time."

"Then how do you know what he is going to do?"

"Because he called me and told me when Bobby was taking me home.'

"How long will this class last?" Aggie was laughing to herself at the image of Archie walking around the house calling his mother every time he turned the corner.

13

"The last class, when I went outside in my socks, lasted two hours. I had to wash the socks by hand in the sink for the entire time. I won't ever go outside in my socks again."

"Well, it sounds like you have a dad who loves you. You take care of yourself and I'll talk to you later. The Sheriff is leaving, and I have to pay attention if I am going to follow him."

"Okay, bye Aggie. See you later."

"Good bye, Archie." Aggie ended the call and put her phone down, saying to herself,

No, Archie, you probably won't see me anymore.

That generated strong emotions. I would eventually come to understand the power of revelation knowledge; however, it would be a long journey, and I had just begun...

CHAPTER 2

The Reason I Came

"Ms. Sharosh, I believe you'll be able to get all the information you need from right in here," Sheriff Wactor said.

The newspaper was called The Franklin County Gazette and was in a two-story building across from what looked like the courthouse.

"That is a really big building," Aggie said. "How long has this paper been here?"

"It has been in existence for more than a hundred and fifty years. It came to Meadville in 1861 right after the beginning of the Civil War. It has been sold a couple of times, but it has always been a local paper. The current publisher has owned it for fifty years. He bought it when he moved to Mississippi and has run it ever since."

Stepping up onto the sidewalk, Aggie was surprised that any town could be quieter than Bude had been, but that was before she came to Meadville. The traffic that came down the street slowed down at the one red light that blinked and very little else happened. There weren't even any dogs on the streets.

"What do you do for excitement around here?" Aggie asked.

"We sit around the scanners and wait for someone from New York to come kidnap our children," a voice said from around the corner. "Is this the little lady that caused the uproar?" The man appeared to be as different from everyone else in this area as anyone she had ever seen. He had a pipe in his mouth and a hound's tooth patterned hat with a matching jacket and pants. To say he looked like he was from another century was an understatement.

"Yes Ben, this is the young lady. Ms. Aggie Sharosh, this is Benjamin Burgdorf."

"A pleasure to meet you, Ms. Sharosh. Lovely necklace you are wearing." Subconsciously, Aggie reached up and put her necklace back inside her shirt. "No need to hide it my dear. This is the twenty first century. There aren't many Jews around here, but those of us that are here aren't scared anymore. Being Jewish doesn't come with all the baggage it used to carry."

15

"That's not what I heard earlier," Aggie said. "I heard the reason the plant closed in Natchez was because of the unions and the Jews."

"That is a common misconception, but things like that happen whether we want it to or not. There are still people who believe the terrorist attacks on 9/11 werean inside job."

"Aggie wants to do some research on the civil rights times, and I told her that you would be the best source of information, along with the library and the microfiche," Sheriff Wactor said.

"Young lady, you follow me and we will have a nice evening. I believe I can get you so much information that you will be able to write a book, much less an article."

"Ben, I thought you were going to write a book," Sheriff Wactor said.

"I was going to, but I like to write things that are current. I don't know how I would do telling stories that either aren't true or happened so long ago no one remembers. No, I've decided to leave the writing to those who are called to it and passionate about writing books. Now come along, young lady, I have lots to show you."

As she walked into the side door, the smell of ink and paper hit her senses all at once.

"Do you print the paper here?" Aggie asked.

"Yes, we still print it here. I got this printing press on the cheap from a magazine company that went out of business. People wanted me to send it to Brookhaven to get it printed, but as long as it's cost effective to print it here in Franklin County, I am going to do it here."

Aggie saw various copies of the newspaper framed and hanging on the walls.

"This place means a lot to you, doesn't it?"

"Yes, it does. I came here fifty years ago and it just bit me, and I have never been the same. Of course, I can say the same thing about my wife and my church. I met her three weeks after I got here. We were married two months later, and I joined the church that same week."

"My father wants me to make sure I find a synagogue for Saturday. Is there one close by?" Aggie asked as she walked up and looked at a paper from nineteen fifty-seven.

"No, my dear, there aren't any synagogues in the proximity. Most of the folks around here are Protestant. There used to be a Catholic church over by the school, but they closed it down. There is a Mormon church in Brookhaven and a Mosque over in Jefferson County."

"Where do you go to worship?" Aggie asked.

"I go to a little Baptist Church in the woods called New Beginnings."

"But I thought you said you were Jewish?" Aggie was surprised at this revelation. "Or do you just go there because it helps your business and there are no Synagogues."

Ben sat down at a desk and took off his hat.

"No, when I came here there was a Synagogue in Brookhaven and McComb. I could have chosen to go to either place and did for weddings and bar mitzvahs. But I worship in a Baptist Church. I am Jewish by birth, but a Christian by choice. What branch of Judaism does your family follow?"

"My father is very orthodox in his ways, so that is how I was raised. He is very wealthy." As the words came out of her mouth, Aggie wondered why she said them. Was she so insecure that she had to brag about her father's wealth?

"That is wonderful," Ben said. "Of course, I guessed as much when I saw your car. They don't give those things away to pretty but poor journalism students."

"I don't know about that pretty part," Aggie said. The blood was rushing into her cheeks, and she couldn't do anything about it. Fortunately for her, Ben was very perceptive and knew that she was beginning to feel uncomfortable.

"Why don't you sit down at the table and I will go and get the scrap book?"

Aggie walked over to the table and sat down in a worn wooden chair. How many people had sat in this very chair to work on this small-town paper?

"Can I get you anything to drink? We have a drink machine in the front foyer. If you'd rather have something else, I can pour you a glass of tea."

"Tea would be fine," Aggie said. "I don't drink a lot of carbonated drinks."

"Good girl," Ben said as he came out from behind a half-wall carrying a

17

large leather- bound folder. "Now these are just some of the highlights from the years fifty-nine to sixty-four. Some of the stories are just local news, but you can pick out the racial stories." He put the dusty folder on the table. "Now you start thumbing through and I will get you a glass of tea."

Sweet tea was not something that was common in her early life, but Aggie promised herself that she would not let that habit continue when she went back home. Over the last three weeks, the sweet goodness of southern iced tea was one of the things she would always remember. Ben had filled her glass and left her alone in the room. He had given her his cell number if she needed something, or if she planned to leave before he returned. Aggie wasn't worried about leaving before he got back. She had already made three pages of notes and was barely a quarter of the way through. Looking through the cut-out articles enclosed in plastic was like walking back in time. The stories were all slanted toward the arrogant Black men who were coming down and trying to change a good place. One story even quoted a local store owner. He said that it was his experience that the Black people like having things separate and to themselves. However, as each story about the trial of the two men who had killed the young man from Virginia was printed, the reporter, Bennie Dorfman, was having a hard time condoning what they had done. Even after the hung jury, the stories were not nearly as biased as they had been in the beginning. Maybe it was because the reporter had to live here and sell advertisements in the paper that he seemed to show partiality toward the accused rather than toward the people that were doing the accusing. At the end of the trial, he had written an opinion piece stating that just because someone wasn't found guilty didn't mean they didn't do something wrong; they just weren't convicted of it.

"Ma'am, can I talk to you for a minute?" a voice said from behind Aggie. She had been so enthralled with what she was reading that she didn't hear anyone come in. Turning around, she saw the deputy who had handcuffed her and treated her like she was a criminal.

"Deputy, I don't think I should be talking to you. My attorney will probably advise me not to have any contact with any of the defendants for the length of my stay here in this quaint little town."

Aggie saw the blood drain from the deputy's face when she mentioned the word "attorney." She knew that the sheriff wasn't so scared, but this guy didn't know whether she was serious or not.

"Ms. Agnes, I am so sorry about what happened. By the way, I didn't introduce myself earlier; my name is Bobby McCoy."

"Mr. McCoy, you need to get one thing through your head. I hate the name Agnes. If I was planning on cutting you any slack, that went out the window when you called me that awful name."

Bobby was completely confused now. "But I thought they said that was your name. What do you want me to call you?"

"My friends call me Aggie, but since you put me in handcuffs and acted like I was a criminal, Ms. Sharosh will be fine." Many times, she had heard her father talk about getting someone on the ropes and not letting go until they cried for their mother. Even though she had tried it with the sheriff, Aggie didn't think he was that concerned about her threats of going to a lawyer. This deputy was a completely different story. She could see the scared and intimidated look on his face.

"Ms. Sharosh, I came over here to explain to you what happened. I have already had one child abducted since I have been on the job. That is one too many. All I got was a call on the radio that Jughead had been picked up by some strange woman in a black car with a New York license plate. Now put yourself in my shoes and see if you might not have acted in the same manner?"

Before she could say how the guarantee of innocent until proven guilty couldn't be taken away just because a crime had been committed prior to the incident, her phone rang. Looking at it, she saw that it was a New York number that, once again, she didn't recognize.

"Deputy, this is an important call from New York. It may be my attorney calling me back, and as much as I would love to hear your excuses for how poorly you acted this afternoon, I really need to take this in private."

Bobby looked as if he wanted to say something back, but Aggie smiled and reached to answer the call. It was then she realized that if she answered this call, she would have to talk to her father and explain everything that he must be thinking. He would have probably tried to call the sheriff to talk to him already. In fact, knowing her father as she did, He would almost certainly follow through with that thought. He would do this so that he would know if his daughter was lying to him. This was another of his tricks Aggie had found out about over the years. If she didn't answer the phone, then her bluff about it being an important call wouldn't work and the deputy would not leave. Sometimes she got so caught up in running bluffs that she got herself into more trouble than it was worth.

"Hello, this is Aggie?"

"Agnes, why must you persist in getting yourself into trouble? Are you in jail? Do I need to send you bail money?"

"Would you please hold on for a moment and I will explain everything," Aggie said. She didn't want Bobby to know that she was only talking to her father and not some big New York trial attorney.

"Officer McCoy, would you shut the door on your way out?"

Bobby turned on his heels and marched toward the door. He was wondering if he'd helped or hurt himself. The sheriff had told him that he needed to go in and apologize for his actions. He was even supposed to apologize for Billy's actions, but she hadn't given him the opportunity. This was because he was the senior officer and Billy was the junior officer.

"Responsibility is a great thing, but with it you have to accept the good and the bad. When you get the praise, you have to be prepared to get the punishment also." This was one of the sheriff's favorite quotes that he used a lot in dealing with his officers.

When the door was closed and Bobby was gone, Aggie took a breath and brought the phone up to her ear. "No, Daddy, I am not in jail. It was a big misunderstanding."

"Why are you riding around with someone named Jughead? I would have thought that a fine young lady like yourself wouldn't be fraternizing with riff raff of that sort. He acted like the two of you were old friends. Is that what you are doing down there, running around with every country bumpkin you can find?"

"Daddy, would you give me a minute to explain. Archie is a twelve-year-old boy. I gave him a ride, but he didn't call his parents. Apparently, there was a child abduction some years ago and everyone is a little on the edge about the kids. Someone saw Archie get into my car, and they called the police." In her mind, Aggie could see the disapproving and perplexed look on her father's face from two thousand miles away.

"You mean to tell me that you and this Jughead fellow were riding around with a twelve- year-old boy? Agnes, I know you have done some frivolous things, but this is on the verge of insanity. Whose idea was it to pick up the young boy? Did Jughead force you to do it, and you are protecting him?"

"Dad, Archie *is* Jughead. There is only one person involved in this story besides me. Archie's nickname is Jughead."

"The Mississippi Highway Patrol office in Jackson has no information about you or anything about an altercation you had with another officer."

"That's because I am not in Jackson. I am in Franklin County Mississippi. There are two towns in this county that I know of, Bude and Meadville. I haven't been anywhere near Jackson."

"I don't know anything about Mississippi, but I have a friend who has a satellite office in Jackson. I called him and he gave me the number to whatever passes for the state police down there. Agnes, why don't you come home. I'm sure you have plenty of civil rights information that will make a wonderful story. Just come home and let's get on with your life."

"Daddy, I appreciate your concern, but I am going to finish what I started. I have found a treasure trove of information just this afternoon. Listen. I have to get back to my research. I'll talk to you soon." Without another word, HyramSharosh hung up the phone.

"Did you apologize?" Sheriff Wactor asked Bobby as he walked back into the sheriff's office.

"I didn't get a chance to. When I started to try, she got all snooty about her lawyers probably not wanting her to talk to the defendants. Sheriff, I may have been a little eager, but I didn't do anything wrong."

"I know you didn't, Bobby. This little lady is full of fight and excitement. I'm sure she has a liberal family who doesn't like the south or conservatives or anything else. I have read that is how most of the Jewish community is in New York."

"How do you know she's Jewish?"

"I saw the Star of David necklace she was wearing and so did Ben. He flat out asked her about it. Of course, since he is Jewish also, she couldn't say that he was making racial remarks." Bobby stopped completely and looked back at the sheriff.

"You mean to tell me that Ben is Jewish? I never knew. He doesn't look Jewish. I remember a couple of years ago he got me a Christmas gift. I thought Jewish people didn't believe in Christmas."

"Bobby, how many times are you going to get bit by the fact that everything is not as it looks?"

Aggie looked at her watch and saw that it was almost six o'clock. Even though Ben had given her a key and said to lock up when she got through, all the adrenaline and pushing had finally started to go away. The thing she was concerned about now, was that according to the app on her phone, the nearest decent motel was thirty miles away. As of right now, the information she had gotten just from this afternoon dwarfed everything she had gotten in Alabama and Georgia. Of course, she had just gone to the local libraries there. She hadn't been given the keys to the kingdom and been told to help herself. Maybe almost getting arrested wasn't the worst thing that could have happened. As she put the folder back onto the shelf, her phone began to ring again. It wasn't her father because he was eating at the Oak Room. She knew this because that was his Thursday night restaurant. He had a different place every weeknight. There were five places, and he stuck to his schedule doggedly. Looking at the phone, she saw that it was another Mississippi number.

"I'm getting really popular around here," Aggie said to the empty room. "Hello, is that you, Archie?"

"No, this is Archie's mother. I'm sorry to call and bother you, but Archie gave me the number. I want to apologize for what you went through this afternoon."

"No ma'am, there's no problem. It was a pure misunderstanding."

"That may be true, but that doesn't excuse Archie from putting you in the situation you were in. I'd like to make it up to you by inviting you over for supper tonight and, if you will allow us, to provide you a room to stay in until you finish whatever you are researching."

"Ms. Archie's mom, that is very kind of you."

"My name is Annette, but you can call me Nette."

"Okay, Ms. Nette."

"And you can drop the Ms. Just Nette will be fine."

"Okay Nette, I appreciate the offer, but I am just going to drive over to Brookhaven and get a room and probably a burger. Tell Archie there are no hard feelings."

"Aggie, I really want to be able to punish Archie in a manner that will stick with him. His father and I have been doing these things and they seem to stay with him longer than a whipping."

"He told me about having to wash his socks, but what could my coming over there

22

matter?"

"You just leave that to me. I know you are a college student. I also know that you're trying to experience different things. And I also know that if you have come to Franklin County, then you are in the perfect place to experience a lot of different things. Please allow us to extend our hospitality and also teach our son a lesson."

Aggie thought for a moment. Though she knew this was probably going to be a great meal with delicious sweet tea, Aggie also knew that she had been very lax on her kosher diet. In fact, the only thing kosher she had found since she gone south of Virginia was a pack of Hebrew National hot dogs. They had been very good, but they were gone, and the idea of not having to eat a burger was appealing.

"Alright Nette, you have a deal. But I don't know how to get to your house."

"I can give you the directions. It will be easy to get here. You are coming to Bude, not New York like you are used to. What is the worst thing that could happen?"

Aggie smiled. "I will take your word for that. I didn't think everything that has happened to me since I got here would happen either."

"Touché. You get a pen and I'll get you here easy-peasy.

There's no way you can get lost in Bude."

CHAPTER 3

Another Night in Paradise

"I can't believe that I am lost in Bude, Mississippi," Aggie shouted in her car. She hadn't thought of putting the address into her GPS because Archie's mother had said it was simple to get to their house. Since Aggie already knew where the main street was, Nette had said to go all the way to the end of the street and then turn right. Aggie had done this without any problem. The problem came when she crossed the tracks and entered into the Harlem of Bude. This was not a big deal, because if she could drive in the real Harlem and run errands for her father, this imposter Harlem shouldn't be any problem. Now that she was turning around for the third time in someone's driveway, that might be the wrong thought process. Aggie's phone had started an automatic update when she left the newspaper and was still in the process. Now she couldn't call anyone, and every time she drove past a certain group of young men, they all looked and smiled at her and her fancy car. If there was any place she could stop and wait for her phone to finish its update, Aggie didn't see it.

She was on her third street, and the only thing she had seen was a run-down baseball field with kids playing all around it. When she got to another stop sign, Aggie found a street sign. It said that she was on D Street. On the corner was a mobile home with lawn mowers and cars strewn all around. Sitting in the front yard was a black man who looked very safe. Aggie decided to ask this man if he could direct her to a pay phone or just how to get back to downtown Bude. She rolled the window down and put on her biggest smile.

"Excuse me sir, could you help me? I got turned around and I need to get out of here. Could you tell me if there is a pay phone or just tell me how to get back to downtown?"

The man got up and walked toward her. He had a noticeable limp but seemed nice enough.

"Boy, that's a nice car you got there. I couldn't hear you earlier. What you need?"

"I'm sorry to bother you, but I got turned around and I can't find my way back to downtown. I'm not from here, but I am supposed to go to dinner at Ms. Annette's house. My phone decided to do an automatic upgrade, so I can't call them. Could you give me some directions?"

"Hee, Hee, Hee," he said. "I've been watching you go 'round in circles. It's a wonder you didn't get stuck or robbed when you went on them back streets. Are you talking about Jughead's momma Annette?" Aggie breathed a sigh of relief. If this man knew Archie, then he must know where they lived.

"Yes, that is the Annette I know. Do you know how to get to their house?"

"My name is Leo White. I worked for Ms. Annette and her husband Jack, so I know exactly where they live. I even know Ms. Annette's brother Bobby. He's a deputy with the Sheriff's Department."

"Wait a minute. Bobby, the big tall deputy is Archie's uncle?"

"Yep, that's him. Him and Ms. Annette's daddy used to be plumbers. That's where I got my start. I'm a plumber too."

"Mr. White that is so good to know but, if you don't mind, could you please just give me directions on how to get to their house? I would be willing to pay you for your kindness." Leo stood up and stepped back.

"Ma'am, I don't need your money. I have money of my own. I know you have an expensive car, but you don't have enough money to pay me off."

Aggie didn't know what to say. Her Daddy always said that if you needed a little grease for the situation, then money always worked. She reached into her purse and grabbed a twenty- dollar bill.

"Mr. White, I am sorry to have offended you. I just wanted to show my appreciation. I meant no disrespect."

"You have got a lot of learning to do about living down here. Folks don't act like that in Franklin County." Then he saw the twenty- dollar bill in her hand and his demeanor changed. "Of course, if it would make you feel better to pay for the information, I guess I could overlook it this time."

Aggie leaned over and held out the twenty. "If you could get me out of here, it will be worth this and much more."

Leo took the money and then smiled a big smile. "You go straight to the next stop sign and take a right. Then you go to the next stop sign and take a left. Follow that street and it will take you back to Main Street. When you cross the railroad tracks, take a right and stay on Railroad Street for three blocks. When you get to the last stop sign, look on the left and they live in that brick house."

"Thank you so much Mr. White. I don't know how much longer I would have wandered around." Aggie could see the first stop sign, so she was close to where she needed to be.

"Okay, you have a safe day, and tell Mr. Jack and Ms. Annette old Leo said hello."

"I sure will, Mr. White. Have a safe day." Looking in her mirror, Aggie saw that a car full of young men had come up behind her, and they were getting out of the car and walking toward her."

"You get on out of here now. These boys are no good who walk around and ride up and down the streets all day. I'll talk to them." As she drove away, Aggie saw Leo walking toward the teenagers. He was talking to them and pointing toward her car. *I'll bet they don't give him a lot of back talk*, Aggie smiled to herself.

When she got to the second stop sign, she realized that this was the road she had come in on originally. She had driven for fifteen minutes within three blocks of where she needed to be. *I will be so happy to get back to familiar New York traffic.*

Leo's directions proved to be spot on. When she got to the brick house, Aggie saw that there were several cars in the driveway. The house was not extravagant, but it had a fair-sized yard and a couple of nice flower beds. It's not what she was used to in New York, but probably upper middle class for this area. As she got out of the car, Aggie thought about her demeanor and had to remind herself that arrogance would not be appreciated by these people. Over the last three weeks, the one constant thing she had seen in the South was that they still distrusted people from the North. One man in Alabama at the library said it was because of the Civil War. That seemed a little far-fetched since the Civil War was over a hundred and fifty years ago.

As she walked up to the door, Aggie could see several people standing in what appeared to be a den. One of them caught sight of her and pointed and waved. Aggie waved back but didn't recognize the person. That wasn't surprising since she had only actually met five people.

"I'd be careful who I waved at," a voice said from behind her. "That guy proposed to the last single girl who waved back at him." Aggie turned around to see Deputy Bobby.

"You scared me. Did you sneak up behind me to see if I was going to terrorize Archie again?"

"Ms. Sharosh, I've got a great idea. How about you and I call a truce? This is my sister's home and Jughead is my nephew. Nette called me and invited me over for supper. From the looks of things, she invited several others. If I am going to be a distraction or problem for you, I will speak to my sister and make my way back to my house."

"Oh, don't do anything special on my part," Aggie said. "Just try not to handcuff any innocent people while you're here. Remember, I am not supposed to have any interaction with you since I will probably be a defendant in a multi-million-dollar civil rights violation case."

Bobby leaned down toward Aggie's face and smiled. "I talked to the sheriff, and he says your threat to sue is full of crap. You may sue us, but you are in Franklin County, and I believe the good people of Franklin County would take the word of a sworn law officer born and raised here over a civil rights hippie who bee-bopped in here from New York to make us look bad about our history of civil rights violations. So, if you want to sue me, crack your whip, 'cause I'm ready." Then with a smile of victory, he opened the door and walked in leaving Aggie standing there with her mouth open, but no words coming out.

"Aggie, come in this house. Bobby, where did you learn your manners?" A very petite woman asked as she walked out of the house. "I'm guessing from the description Archie gave me that you are Aggie. I was beginning to wonder if you had a change of heart and weren't going to come. I'm Annette Walker."

"Hello. I'm Aggie Sharosh. You have a lovely home." Aggie wanted to say something about the jerk she had for a brother, but common decency wouldn't allow it. Either that or she knew he was right and she hated having her bluff called.

"Oh, this place isn't much, but it's paid for. Jack talks about building a new house one day, but I keep telling him that this house is big enough for us. Now you come in and meet everyone. I hope you don't mind, but I decided as part of Archie's lesson, we would have a dinner party."

"Archie's lesson? You mentioned something about teaching him lessons, but I didn't completely understand. Is he going to wash everyone's socks?"

"No, but I may keep that in mind for the future. Of course, with some of the people in Franklin County, I would probably be arrested for cruel and

27

unusual punishment if I made my son touch their nasty feet. But that day he had to wash his socks, that is the best one so far. He won't go out into the yard with his socks on, I don't care what's going on. No, tonight's lesson will be a little more formal."

As she was talking, Aggie looked at the open door to see Archie standing there in a white coat and a weak smile on his face. Mom, I think dinner is ready."

"Thank you, Archie. Now go into the kitchen and wait on me. You will serve everyone when we all sit down."

Aggie chuckled. "Is this part of his lesson?"

"Oh yes. If he is going to go off and not call me or let me know what is going on, then I am going to teach him that serving others is more important than your own happiness. His daddy said I should just beat his butt this time, but I think twelve going on thirteen is too old to be getting whippings. Don't you agree, Aggie?"

Aggie smiled and thought for a moment. She had never been whipped in her entire life. The only thing close to a whipping she had gotten was the time her mother had threatened her with a belt. Just the fear of that had straightened her up. "I don't know what is a good or a bad age. I really don't agree with corporal punishment. I read a study my freshman year in college that hitting a child for failure is just like showing them that losers get struck, and it give them a bullying mentality."

"Girl, you are going to fit in not at all tonight, but I like different points of view. Now come on in and let me introduce you to everyone."

Never in all her life had Aggie ever seen such a different group of people from the ones she grew up around. Everyone had said the South was a different place but, for some reason, she didn't think about it. It wasn't that these people were zombies or anything like that. It was just that they seemed to actually care about each other. There was a saying at school that you could always tell if a tourist was from the South. They would always want to talk and ask questions. The normal New Yorker just wants to be left alone, whether they are on the subway or walking down the street.

As she was introduced to each person, Aggie noticed that they all seemed to care about her and what her plans were. Everyone had a different reaction to her speech and accent. If they could only read her mind and the thoughts that were going through her head listening to their slow country drawl. All the people she had talked within Atlanta and Montgomery had been polished and acted as if they had come to the South from somewhere else. Now that she was meeting what she considered true Southerners, their accent was something she truly enjoyed.

There were eight people standing around in the living room besides Annette and her family, and all of them were very polite. For some reason that Aggie couldn't explain, she could always remember first names, but last names were hard for her to keep up with. There was Brad the pharmacist who said that he was into drugs. This must have been his go-to joke because everyone laughed like they had heard it before. Then there was Johnny, who said he ran the feed mill in town. Vickie the school teacher was very friendly, but Annette whispered to Aggie that she hadn't gotten the principal job at the high school. Everyone knew it now, but no one wanted to tell her. Keith, the architect, was constantly looking at his watch. Aggie thought that maybe he was late for something. Tonya, the lady who worked for the state, smiled and asked Aggie if she planned to have children. Aggie had said she needed to find a husband first. This got a good laugh out of everyone who heard it. Rusty was the county administrator. Annette had said he was good with everyone's numbers but his own. Bobby stood over in the corner and didn't say very much. From time to time he would look over at Aggie, but when they made eye contact, he would look away as if he was still embarrassed. Aggie decided that sometime tonight she would make the effort to talk to him and make him feel comfortable. Since this would be the last time that she would ever see him or any of the other people in the room, there was no sense in having hard feelings about anything.

While everyone stood around and talked, Aggie noticed that there was no alcohol. At all the dinner parties she had ever been to, most of the guests were half toasted before the main course was served.

"Nette, I am not asking for anything, but where is the bar? I assumed since this was a dinner party that there would be drinking. Is it against the law?" Aggie had read about places where alcohol was still illegal just like prohibition.

"Aggie, this is the wettest dry county you will ever find, but in my house, there won't be any drinking of alcohol. Everyone knows this and respects it. If you go to some other houses, some of the people will be drunk before they get there, but not when they come here. My grandfather was a drunk, and I promised myself after seeing his actions that I would never put up with alcohol in my house. That was a stipulation for Jack when he asked me to marry him. I said I could put up with anything except drinking. He agreed and we got married. On top of that though, and the true main reason I don't allow

29

alcohol in my house, is that my relationship with Christ is more important to me than anything. I won't purposefully sully his name if I can help it."

Aggie tried to keep a straight face without showing her discomfort. The one thing she had been taught by her father and all the teachers at synagogue was that all the so-called "Christians" really didn't like the Jews. They had shown images of Klansmen who carried signs saying the Holocaust was a fake and that Jews were the evil instigators. This was one of the many reasons the civil rights era had been such a passion of hers. The fact that the Jews and the Blacks were so hated because of how they were born was unbelievable to her. Then there was the idea that the Jews had killed this Jesus person was one of the excuses different maniacs had been using to terrorize the Jews for the last two thousand years. Hitler was the most vocal, but her father had said that if it hadn't been for 1948 and the formation of the country of Israel, the Jews might have been obliterated by now. Even though she knew her father overly exaggerated things, she also knew that he was one of the most revered historians of Jewish history in their synagogue. She also believed that anyone who was vocal about their Christian beliefs really hated Jews but didn't have the guts to say it.

Annette must have been a better reader of people than Aggie realized because her brow furrowed and she looked at Aggie. "Aggie, do you have a problem with me saying something about Christ? I am very passionate about my beliefs, but I don't force them on anyone. What people do in the world is their business."

For some reason unknown to Aggie, her face began to turn red and she felt hot. "No, nothing like that. Like you said, this is your house and you can say and do what you want to do. Would you excuse me? I need to go outside and make a call."

"You don't have to go outside. Right down that hall, the second door on the right is my bedroom. Go in there and make your call. I'll go see if Archie is ready to do his penance."

"I'm glad you mentioned Archie. I haven't seen him since I got here except when I first arrived."

"He's in the kitchen. When you get done with your call, we should be ready to eat and you will see him."

Aggie walked past the two different groups, each discussing totally different topics. Brad was talking about the upcoming college football season in one group, and Tonya and Vickie were talking about the shortage of money and teachers in the state with another group. All of them smiled as Aggie passed.

When she got into the bedroom, Aggie took her phone and started looking through her numbers. At this very moment what she wanted more than anything else was to talk to someone. It was times like these that she missed her mother the most. She always understood and spoke her language. Aggie could feel tears beginning to well up in her eyes. Why did this suddenly hit her? Since she left New York, she had felt no desire to hear the familiar sounds of her childhood. Now all of a sudden, she yearned to hear the voice of a *guido* or a sharp Brooklyn accent. Looking through her numbers, Aggie wished she had a favorites list. Her father wouldn't allow her to make one on her phone. He said if it was stolen, they could find the people who she had the most information on and either steal their identity or find their homes and rob them. This was very silly to Aggie, but she complied since he still paid her bills and sometimes picked up her phone and looked through it to see if she had an actual favorites list. As she scrolled through her numbers, it hit her who she needed to call: her aunt Rachel. Since her mother's death, Rachel was the one Aggie talked to about the very intimate things that her father didn't understand. Not that he wouldn't have sent her to a good doctor to talk about why her period was late if she wasn't sexually active, but sometimes you needed to talk to someone that would listen to you whether you were paying them or not.

"Hello, is this my favorite journalist?" Rachel asked.

"Hello Rache." As far back as she could remember, Aggie had been forbidden to call her Aunt, or anything else besides Rache. "Have you got a minute to talk?"

"I always have time for my favorite niece. I asked your father if he had heard from you the other day, and he said that he calls you every day, but you don't return his calls every day. I told him I understood because you haven't called me since you went on your pilgrimage. Sowhat happened that has you calling me on a Thursday night? I know that tone in your voice, so don't try to tell me nothing is wrong."

Aggie knew she didn't have time to go into the entire story of her day. Point being, she didn't want to talk about any of those things. She just wanted to hear someone's voice that could reassure her. Someone who believed in the same things she believed in. Aggie didn't admit this to anyone, but since she had been in college, she had developed several questions about her Jewish faith. She knew what she had been taught, she knew all the stories, and she could quote parts of the Torah, but there was something missing. Maybe the passion Annette had expressed when she talked about why she wouldn't allow alcohol in her house had struck a nerve. Either way, hearing her aunt's voice brought back a feeling of calm that she needed.

"No, I am just in the middle of the deep South at a dinner party like you have never seen. I wonder if they are going to show *Deliverance* when the meal is finished." This movie was the only thing her friends and family knew about the South, so it had been a joke since she had decided to come down here. "I miss being at home, and since Daddy is at the Oak Room tonight, I decided to call you. I hope you don't mind."

"I have always said that you can call me any time, day or night. What kind of favorite aunt would I be if I wasn't always available for you?"

"Except for when you have the answering machine on," Aggie said with a giggle. She had called Rache to talk to her during her senior year, and the answering machine was on. Rachel had called her back a few hours later and told her that anytime she called and got the answering machine, that meant there was a gentleman at her home.

"Yes, but lately, the answering machine hasn't been connected a lot. I guess I am beginning to realize that my single life is getting a little humdrum. But you didn't call to hear about my personal life."

"I know you have been all over the world, and I wanted to know how you handle people who don't like Jews?"

"Have you wandered into your own little anti-Semitic area of Mississippi?" Rachel's voice was getting louder, which is what happened right before she let loose a verbal tirade on someone.

"No, it's not that. I just met a woman, and she seems to be one of those big time Christian people we've heard about. You and Dad always told me that those big time Christians secretly hate the Jews. I don't want to be ugly to this woman, so I need to know if this is something I need to run from or just pay close attention to." Aggie heard Rachel take a deep breath.

"Okay that is a little different. I may have agreed with your father when he said those things, because I didn't want to disagree with him in front of people. To be truthful, I haven't had that experience with the Christian people I've run into. Of course, I've never been in the South, except for Orlando, so they may be different where you are. I would suggest you just pay attention and keep that necklace with the star on it inside your shirt just in case they don't like us."

"I've already run into a couple of people who have seen it. I bet if Bobby had seen it, he would have gone ahead and shot me," Aggie said this last statement aloud before realizing that it wasn't just a thought.

"Wait a minute. I noticed a change in your tone when you said the name Bobby. You haven't gone south and fallen head over heels for one of them tall tight country boys, have you? If you find one, ask him if his father is single."

"No, I have developed a sincere hatred for a Southern boy. Never in all my twenty-one years on this earth have I met someone who makes me so angry."

"Wait till they put you in handcuffs, and then you will have something to get angry about, unless, like me, you like that sort of thing."

"Well, we've already done that," Aggie said again without thinking.

"Wait a minute. This guy put you in handcuffs? Were you arrested? Aggie, I can't wait till you get back home to get *this* story! You've got to give me something. You know I live my life vicariously through you anyway." Before Aggie could reply, there was a knock on the door.

"Aggie, I'm sorry to bother you, but we are ready for the guest of honor," Annette said. "It would be horrible southern hospitality to eat without you."

Aggie covered the phone. "I'll be right there, Nette."

"Aggie, you have piqued my curiosity, but I heard that you have been summoned. Tomorrow I expect a call with lots of juicy details. Is that understood?"

"Yes, Rache, I promise. I've got to go now."

As she opened the door, the door to the bathroom across the hall opened and Bobby walked out at the same time.

"Excuse me Agnes. I didn't mean to be in the same area as you." When he said Agnes, he sneered like he was the villain in a cheesy Western.

"No problem, Deputy Bobby. From what I've read today, you Franklin County boys do your best work in the bathroom. There was an article from 1966 alleging your sheriff at that time got a confession from a young black man by taking him in the bathroom and beating him until he confessed." She then pushed past him toward the living room.

Bobby didn't know whether to shout at her or shoot her. In the back of his mind, there was the hint of another feeling, but he wasn't willing to acknowledge that one yet. She was going back to New York tomorrow and he would never see her again.

Aggie was angry from her toes to her nose, and she didn't really know why. This should have been a fun time. As the idea of begging out and leaving came into her mind, she saw Archie standing at the head of the table in his white dinner jacket and a towel over his arm. He was not smiling, and he didn't look like he was having a good time. He was being punished, and it was partly her fault. Aggie put on her best smile and headed into the dining room, determined to be miserable with him, even if it was just a little bit.

"Well there she is," Annette said. "Archie, would you please escort our guest of honor to her chair and seat her?"

Archie walked over to Aggie and offered his arm. Aggie wanted to laugh, but it would only make this harder for the young man. "Why thank you sir, I would be honored to be escorted by such a handsome gentleman."

"I wish she had beaten me into a coma instead of making me do this," Archie said low enough so that only Aggie could hear him. When she got to her seat, Archie pulled the chair back and Aggie sat down as ladylike as she could. He then took a bell and rang it.

"Would everyone please be seated? I will be serving the soup and salad momentarily." Aggie was seated at the head of the table, and Annette and Jack were sitting on her right.

Keith, the architect, was sitting to her left with the others scattered around the table. Bobby was at the end of the table as far away from Aggie as he could get. Aggie looked around and realized that Annette and Jack were the only married couple at the table.

"Nette, where are all the spouses of these people? Everyone I've met has been nice, but they haven't introduced me to their wives or husbands. This isn't some crazy single party is it?"

"No dear, it's nothing like that, but that's a very good observation on your part. I should have thought to give you the heads up on that. I would hate for you to think I hang out with a bunch of lonely losers. Keith, Brad, and Johnny's wives are all on a church retreat for married women. Vicky's husband works the third shift at the saw mill, and Rusty is divorced, but he is dating a woman from Jackson that he is trying to keep secret, but Tonya found out and has been telling everyone. Tonya's husband works out of town, but no one really knows what he does. Some kind of technology salesman, but it is above all our heads. What we do know is that he makes a boatload of money, and she doesn't have to work but does because she says she gets bored sitting at home. My brother, Bobby, down there has never been married, and if he doesn't start looking, he is going to wind up marrying that badge. There now, does that soothe your mind?"

"Yes, it does. I was just curious. Now, about Archie, how long is this punishment going to go on?" Annette nudged Jack who was talking to Brad across the table.

"Our guest of honor wants to know how long Archie's punishment is going to go on?"

Jack looked at his watch and made drawing motions in the air like he was working a math problem. "I think until all the dishes are washed and put up. I expect it to take until somewhere around eleven o'clock tonight."

"I can already tell that he hates this, so I am sure the lesson is being learned," Aggie said as she watched Archie walk around and pour water into each glass.

"When you want your children to grow up to respect authority, you need to show them that our choices have consequences," Brad said. "I think the Scripture that says spare the rod and spoil the child doesn't mean you have to beat your children. I believe that what you are doing is using the rod but in a different way."

"Does every decision you make come from something in the Bible?" Aggie blurted out. Everyone at the table stopped what they were doing and looked at her like she had just passed gas and claimed it.

"You don't believe the Bible is a good resource for life?" Annette asked.

"I'm not sure whether it is good for these current days." Aggie could feel herself getting in over her head, but she was not going to let these people push their beliefs onto her. But why was she being so defensive?"

"What do you think we should do? Should we listen to Dr. Spock and all those liberal book writers?" Tonya asked. Obviously, everyone was going to get involved.

"Don't you think that someone with a PhD in child psychology has more information on how to raise a child than a two-thousand-year-old book written by men who were not born in this century?" As she made the statement, Aggie tried to remember her debate coach's lessons on how to keep your cool when you were alone in your beliefs.

"I'm sure that the reason the crime rate in New York is so high is because all those parents read parenting books by these PhDs you mentioned instead of using biblical truths," Bobby said.

"Now everyone remembers that we're all entitled to our own opinion. Our guest comes to us from a different upbringing, and I don't want her to feel like we are jumping down her throat," Annette said. Aggie calmed down a little when Annette said this.

"I don't mean to be difficult, but what are the crime numbers in Mississippi per capita compared to New York? Bobby, you seem to know about these things." Why did she try to kick Bobby on every turn?

"I don't have them in front of me right now, but I can look them up on this here phone. I know you Yankee folks think we are still talking on cans and strings, but we do have technology."

"Actually, I'm a Mets fan," Aggie said and stared back. Everyone laughed when they saw Bobby getting flustered.

Before anyone else said anything, Archie came out of the kitchen and rang the bell. "Ladies and Gentlemen, before we begin our first course, I would like to ask Mr. Keith to make the blessing on the food."

Keith stood up and smiled at Archie. "I would be happy to pray, Jughead. Everyone please bow your heads."

Aggie looked at everyone at the table bowing their heads and closing their eyes. She had seen things like this on some old television shows, but this was 2019 and she didn't think people did this anymore. But, since she had already stirred up a big controversy before the salad, she decided to go along with them and bow her head too.

"Dear Lord, we thank you for this food. We ask you to bless it to the nourishment of our bodies and our bodies to your service. Bless the hands that prepared it and this home we are receiving it in. And finally, Lord I pray that you will bless Jughead to remember the lessons he is taught by his parents and that he will be the kind of young man you can be pleased with, In Jesus' name, Amen."

"All right Archie, you can bring out the salads," Annette said.

As the plates were passed around, Aggie decided it would be in her best interest to fill her mouth with food so that she wouldn't say anything else that might cause the party to focus on her and her beliefs.

"If I ate like this all the time, I would weigh two hundred pounds," Aggie said as Archie picked up her plate. "Please tell me that Archie didn't fix this. If he did, he has a great career as a chef in his future. I have never eaten roast and gravy that tender. The vegetables were perfect and that chocolate cake is better than any I have ever eaten."

"No, I did the cooking, but he can cook. Mostly eggs and sausage and pancakes, but isn't breakfast all most men can cook?" Annette said as she laid her head on Jack's shoulder.

Since the discussions about religion and child rearing had stopped, Aggie had genuinely enjoyed herself. She had even laughed at a joke Bobby told. Now as she looked at the clock, Aggie decided that she needed to say her goodbyes.

"Annette, I want to thank you so much for your hospitality, but I need to get on the road. I need a hot bath and a bed and I can't impose on you any-more."

"Aggie, I thought we had discussed this. You're staying here is Jack's idea. He said that before you go back to New York, you needed to get the whole treatment. Staying at a complete stranger's home is something I'll bet you wouldn't do up there. Now, if tomorrow you find yourself uncomfortable, then you can spend the night in Brookhaven with no hard feelings. You can't get a better deal than that. Besides, you said yourself earlier that you had some more research at the paper tomorrow. This way, you can get up and get an early start without a thirty- minute drive."

Aggie wasn't normally willing to get close to people that weren't known to her, but for some reason, she liked them.

"Mom, can I come in there and eat?" Archie asked from the kitchen door.

"You sure can dear, but don't forget that when you get through eating you have a kitchen full of dishes to clean. When you get through with that, I'll bet you don't ever go off with someone without calling me or your daddy."

"Yep, and if you do, I don't care how old you are, I'm gonna beat you within an inch of Walt's life," Jack said. "Is that understood?"

"Yes sir. I wish you had done that tonight. I've never worked this hard in my life."

37

Everyone had left and Archie was carrying the dishes back into the kitchen when Aggie walked out to her car to get her overnight bag.

"I got those figures for you," a voice said from behind her. Bobby walked out of the shadows and toward Aggie.

"Wow, you were able to find that all on your own? I would have thought that kind of heavy lifting would take you all night."

"No, I had it in the house at dinner before dessert was served. I just figured you and I had tried to take each other's head off enough for one night. Besides, Nette gave me the evil eye, which meant for me to calm down."

Aggie laughed. "She looks like the type of woman whose looks can have several meanings."

"Okay, now that we are laughing, I'll tell you the numbers. Yes, New York is higher than Mississippi in murders, but not nearly as much as I would have expected. We are ranked thirty-first and New York is ranked twenty-second. That is per capita, not total."

"I guess you are a better police officer than I gave you credit for," Aggie said. "Well, it's getting late and I have a big day tomorrow. If I am going to get on the road headed home, I need to get an early start."

"You be careful, and have a safe trip," Bobby said and then turned around and walked back to his car.

Aggie watched him get in his car and drive away. She wondered if she watched him because she wanted to make sure he left, or if she wanted him to turn around and come back. When his lights went out of sight, she walked back into the house.

"Sweety, I have the guest room set up for you. There's a bathroom in there and clean linen on the bed. Everything you would get at the motels in Brookhaven. There's also a television in case you can't go to sleep."

"Thank you so much, Nette. I enjoyed tonight as much as I have anything since I came South. You and your friends were so gracious. I just hope some of my opinions weren't too radical for them."

"No, I'm one of the few people in Franklin County who is willing to hear any and all opinions. I do want to talk to you about your religious preferences, but that will hold till tomorrow. Now, I am going to go upstairs and see if I can't get some talk time with my husband. That's the one thing I think women and men forget to do these days, is have talk time. They worry about everything except each other. Remember that when you get a husband."

"Thank you, Nette, but I hope my getting a husband will be a long way away. I'm perfectly fine with being single."

"That's good. You wait till the right one comes along and don't settle for just anyone now. If you need anything else, make yourself at home."

After changing into her favorite sweat pants and her Rutgers T-shirt, Aggie sat on the bed and turned on the television. One of the guilty pleasures she had acquired since coming south was eating three chocolate chip cookies and drinking a glass of milk while watching Jimmy Kimmel. She had heard her mother talk about her love of Johnny Carson and that was how Aggie felt about Jimmy Kimmel. Unfortunately, since she thought she was going to be in a town tonight, Aggie had not replenished her supply of cookies. Also, she didn't have any milk. Maybe Annette had some in the kitchen. She had said to make herself at home, so Aggie was going to take her at her word. As she walked down the hall, she heard sounds coming from the kitchen. When she opened the door, she saw Archie standing at the sink washing the pots and pans from dinner. He had his ear buds in and didn't hear her come down the stairs. Aggie walked over and patted him on the shoulder. She scared him so badly that he almost dropped the glass bowl he was washing.

"I'm sorry," Aggie said. "I didn't know you would still be awake."

"You scared the crap out of me. What are you doing in here? I'm not serving anything else." Archie was tired and didn't like the idea of having to wash anymore dishes.

"I know, but I just wanted to get a couple of cookies and some milk. It helps me to go to sleep. You don't have any chocolate chip cookies, do you?"

"They are over in the cupboard behind the oatmeal. Dad likes the chewy chip cookies, so Momma keeps them for him."

Aggie walked over and looked. Sure enough there were chewy chocolate chip cookies. Since she usually got the normal ones, this would be a welcome change.

"Your Dad isn't going to mind me eating his cookies?" Aggie asked as she opened the pack.

"As long as you don't eat all of them, I'm sure you're all right. If you need milk, please don't mess up a glass. Just use a paper cup because I don't want to have to wash anything else."

Aggie saw a red plastic cup in the corner. She got some milk out of the fridge and poured herself a glass of the white goodness. Then, just like she would have done if she were at her home in New York, she hopped up onto the counter.

"I feel like this is partially my fault," Aggie said as she dipped her cookie.

"Naw, you think? I didn't see you volunteering to help tonight. Momma is going to get sick of me calling and telling her what I am doing, but I won't have to go through this again."

"Don't take for granted the opportunity to call and talk to your mother. I wish I could talk to mine every day."

"Doesn't she have a cell phone?" Archie asked innocently.

"No, my mother died a few years ago."

Archie looked back stunned. "I'm so sorry. I didn't think about her being dead. I've never had someone I loved die. I would hate to have sad memories all the time."

"My memories about my mother are never sad. Only the thoughts about her being gone are sad, and I am getting better at dealing with them." Aggie looked at the pile of dishes that were left and then at the clock. There was no way he was going to be through with this any time soon. As she finished off her third cookie, Aggie hopped off the counter and picked up a towel. "Okay, you wash and I'll dry. Maybe we can get you out of here before midnight."

CHAPTER 4

Why Am I Here

Despite everything her father had done to instill in her an appreciation for getting things done early in the day, Aggie was not a morning person. She could stay up until all hours of the night if necessary, but mornings were not her specialty. Unfortunately for her, both Jack and Annette Walker were morning people. She could hear them in the kitchen laughing like it was some comedy club. Annette must be making breakfast because Aggie could hear what sounded like dishes and pots and pans being dropped and used. They were probably the same dishes that she and Archie had spent so much time cleaning last night.

Looking around the room with the sunlight coming through, Aggie liked how cozy it felt. Usually her first night in a strange place, even a motel, she would not sleep very well. But last night there had been no wake-ups wondering where she was. She had slept through without waking up at all. It had been several years since that had happened. When she picked up her phone to check her email, Aggie saw that there was a missed call from a New York number. It probably wasn't her father, because he would have left a voice mail. *I'll call it later*, Aggie thought and then got out of bed. Sounds of life must have been what Annette was waiting for. No sooner than she had had the thought there was a knock on the door.

"Are you awake, Aggie?" Annette asked. "We've got breakfast cooking if you want some."

"Thanks, Nette, I'll be right there." Aggie changed into her other jeans and a tee shirt. She didn't want to wear the same thing she had worn last night. They may be the kind of people who frowned on that sort of thing. When she opened the door, she quickly realized that her clothing decision was not going to be a problem. Jack was wearing the same shirt he had on the night before, and Nette was wearing some kind of sleep pants with holes in the legs and an Atlanta Braves tee shirt.

"Look who's awake and dressed," Annette said. "You look fresh as a daisy. Did you sleep well last night?"

"Yes, I did. I didn't wake up at all. That is the first time I have slept

41

through the night completely in a very long time. It must be all this southern hospitality."

"It might be that I add sleeping pills to my chocolate chip cookies," Jack said with a grin.

"Jack, you stop that this instant. This young lady can eat all your stupid cookies if she wants too."

"How did you know I had some cookies?" Aggie didn't know if he was going to be mad or was just giving her a hard time.

"I told him," Annette said. "I came down last night and saw you sitting on the counter talking to Archie. I didn't want to disturb the two of you because he needed someone to talk to. Anyway, thanks for helping him with the dishes," Annette said as she placed a plate full of pancakes on the table.

"Yes, I did take three of your cookies Mr. Walker, but that was all. Besides, Archie said it was all right as long as I didn't eat all of them."

"You are welcome to all of them if you want, and let's get rid of that Mr. stuff. My name is Jack, or you can call me JW. Mr. Walker is what we call my father. Now come over here and sit down. I've got to go to work and breakfast is the most important meal of the day. Ain't that right Aunt Jemima?"

"Oh, Massah Walker, I sho' hope you enjoy this meal, cause if you call me Aunt Jemima again, your next meal will be with the dogs in the pen."

"Oh, I am very sorry, ma'am. Please forgive me. Is it Uncle Jemima now?" Aggie laughed and milk came out her nose.

"See there what you did?" Annette said. "You have done ruined our guest's breakfast with your crass uncouth humor. Are you okay, Aggie?" She then took her dish towel and hit Jack in the head with it.

"I'm sorry, but that was so funny. You have a great sense of humor Mr...I mean JW."

"Don't you go giving him a big head. He thinks he's the funniest thing in this community anyway. Now, how do you like your eggs cooked?"

"No eggs for me, I'll just have some of these delicious pancakes."

"Are you sure? It won't be any trouble. I usually make them for Jack, but since he has such a smart mouth, he may have to make them himself."

Jack reached and grabbed Annette and pulled her to him. "Now, darling, you know I would never mistake you for an Uncle. Can I please have a couple of eggs?"

"Yeah, you knew you better change that tune. Luckily, I knew you weren't the rat you sounded like in front of our guest, so I already fixed your eggs."

Watching the two of them laugh and giggle, Aggie saw a side of married life that she was not used to. The "have a good time and enjoy each other" side.

The pancakes were good, but the hamburger patties that were also on the table were better than any Aggie had ever eaten. She had never had hamburger patties for breakfast, but she was finding out quickly that food and food items in the South were definitely different from what she was used too.

"What brand are these hamburger patties?" Aggie asked. "When I get back to New York, I've got to have some of these. I have never had hamburger patties for breakfast."

Jack chuckled for a moment then he jerked back. "Don't kick me," he said to Annette between laughs. "Honey, those are not hamburger patties. They are a special blend I don't think you will be able to get in New York City."

"I don't know, I have many different places that can get any kind of food I want. My father owns part of a Kosher deli in midtown, and they get everything we ask for."

"Then I know they won't get that because those are deer sausage you just ate."

"Deer, like in Bambi deer? And you said sausage, like pork sausage?" "Yes, there is some pork in there also but not much. The majority of the meat is fat and deer I killed last year. We don't buy hamburger meat or sausage from the store. I kill five or six deer a year, and we grind it into sausage and hamburger meat. We also have deer roast and deer steaks."

"Darling, are you Jewish?" Annette asked.

"Yes, but what does that have to do with anything?" Aggie asked more defensively than she meant to sound.

"It doesn't have anything to do with anything. I was just wondering. It does explain why you reacted like you did when I mentioned Jesus' name last night. Also, you just said your father owns part of a Kosher deli. I have to

43

admit that I do love their hot dogs."

"Something smells good. Is there a cover charge to get something to eat around here?" Bobby asked as he walked into the room.

"Why, little brother, you are right on time. I made enough because I had a feeling that you would make your usual Friday trip to my breakfast table. Go get a plate and eat with us. Aggie was just telling us about her heritage."

"Come have breakfast with them, I've got to be in Natchez at eight-thirty, and I better get headed that way. Aggie, will you be here tonight?" Jack asked as he started toward the door.

"No, I plan on getting done today and heading back north. I believe I will have more than enough information to write my story. Thank you so much for your hospitality."

"Don't thank me, thank my lovely bride. She does the hospitality; I just make the money she spends to do it. Bobby, you take care of yourself. Are you working the Little League game tonight?"

"As far as I know. They haven't called to tell me any differently. If I don't work it, I will probably go anyway. Everything is very quiet in the county. Nothing happens until some Yankee comes south and tries to kidnap a help-less child."

Aggie knew that Bobby was trying to be charming, and for the most part it was working. Of course, she couldn't let him get away completely with making fun of her.

"Wow. You have to have security at your little league games? I would think those kids wouldn't cause enough trouble to need security," Aggie said.

"We have security, but it is not for the kids. It is for the parents who don't know how to keep their mouths shut. We have more fights at the kids' games than we do at the adult gatherings all over the county. But I don't work se-curity, because I'm an umpire."

"An umpire? I am so much more impressed. Do you take your handcuffs with you, or do you just use them on us Yankees?" Aggie couldn't help her-self.

If she thought she was going to get the best of him this morning, then Aggie was mistaken. Obviously, a night of contemplation gave Bobby more confidence.

"No ma'am, I save the handcuffs for the Yankees. We just shoot the local folks or take them into the bathroom and beat a confession out of them. I researched your little story you mentioned last night. It seems that story wasn't exactly true, but it sold them a bunch of papers."

Before Aggie could reply, Annette put a plate of pancakes on the table and a glass of milk. "Bobby, eat up before this gets any colder. I am not going to make any fresh for you."

"What about Jughead? Doesn't he get fresh breakfast?" Bobby asked between mouthfuls.

"Archie is going to sleep a little late this morning and I'm going to let him. I do believe this is the most exhausted I've ever seen him. Besides, he's got a game tonight too."

Aggie wanted to spar with Bobby some more about the bathroom article, but saw that Annette was growing tired of their bantering back and forth. Aggie also didn't want Bobby to take her good-natured ribbing as flirting. She didn't need him to become attached to her today. She was leaving in a few hours and, if there was anything, she could do about it, Aggie would never come to Franklin County ever again. In fact, if she went ahead and got started, she might get done today and get on the road before it became too late.

"Thanks for breakfast. I'm going to get ready and head down to the paper. Nette, thank you so much for everything."

"Aggie, you make sure you call me before you leave. I would like to stay in touch after you get back home. I'm sure Archie will never forget his time with you."

Bobby put his fork down and looked at Aggie. "He's not the only one."

"Why, Deputy Bobby, I'm flattered that you would remember me," Aggie said.

"I was talking about Sheriff Wactor, but I like how you think," he said with a wide grin.

"Sis, thanks for the breakfast. Tell Jughead I'll see him tonight." Then like a scene from an old cowboy movie, Bobby walked out the door with a swagger that made Aggie watch until he had driven away.

"Don't pay any attention to Bobby. He's my brother, but he can be a real pain in the rear sometimes, if you know what I'm saying."

Aggie turned and looked back at Annette. "Oh, I'm not worried about him. He got me then, but I think I won on points. Now if you'll excuse me, I have to get ready."

It took her a little longer to get ready than she thought it would. Aggie didn't want to come to town looking anything but fabulous. If this was the last time that she would see the people of Franklin County, she wanted them to remember her.

When she finally made it to the newspaper, she was surprised that there was so much activity on the street. Compared to the day before, it was Times Square traffic. Most of the people were making their way toward the courthouse, but a few were headed toward what looked like a bank. The local pharmacy seemed to have a lot of people going in and out also.

"Look who made it through a night in FC," Ben said as Aggie walked through the door. "I am so sorry I couldn't make it to your dinner party. I heard it was a tremendous success. I am planning on doing a story on Jughead's punishment next week. I think it will be something everyone will love."

"I would love to read that. I will give you my email address if you don't mind," Aggie said. "I look forward to telling all my friends, but I'm sure they won't believe it. If they see it in print from someone else, it will make the story a little more believable."

"Did you get some good information?" Ben asked as he poured himself a cup of coffee.

"Yes, I did. I was amazed at the details of the newspaper's coverage. I have to ask you something though. I could see a change in the way the stories were covered at a certain point. Since you were the one writing most of the articles, what changed? You went from being a strong supporter of keeping the blacks in their place, to slowly writing stories about how they were wronged, and that everyone deserved to be equal in the eyes of God no matter what their skin color."

Ben took a swallow of coffee. "Do you want a cup?"

"No, thank you. I have a strict rule about coffee outside of New York. The closest thing I have found is Starbuck's with soy milk. That's not what I drink when I am home, but it's the closest thing I have been able to find down here."

"Well that is one thing I don't think you will ever find in Meadville. For

46

the most part, because these cheap people won't pay four dollars for a cup of coffee. Not when you can make a pot of coffee for less than a dollar. I really think you should try my coffee. Since you and I share the same heritage, I believe you would like its strong flavor. I have the coffee shipped to me from a shop in New York."

This intrigued Aggie. "What store do you get it from?"

"A small coffee house in Chelsea. You probably don't know it or anything about Chelsea. A fine upstanding young woman like you wouldn't spend much time down there."

"That's where you are wrong. I spent almost my entire junior and senior years of high school wandering around Chelsea. I had some friends who had family that lived there. We would go to the clubs and listen to the poets and the music." Just thinking about the music of Chelsea made Aggie even more anxious to get home.

"The name of it is Brew Boys. It's on Twenty-sixth Street a block from Chelsea Studios. The man who owns it is a friend of mine. We graduated from college together."

Aggie put her hands to her mouth. "You have got to be kidding me. That coffee house is where we would go every Monday. He has a stage in the back, and on Mondays they have poets come in and read their material. I even got up there a couple of times, but I quickly found out that poetry is not going to be my career."

"That's a good thing, because poets spend most of their time looking for their next meal. They don't make any money. Now would you like to try my coffee?"

"Yes, I would love to try your coffee. It's not too much to ask if you have any soy milk?"

"As a matter of a fact, I do have some in the refrigerator. I don't like it all the time, but I keep it for the times when I feel like it. You sit down and I will get you some soy milk."

Aggie sat down and watched as Ben walked to the back and got the milk. When he returned, he poured a large cup of coffee and handed it to her along with the milk and sugar.

"I didn't want to add the fixings to your coffee. You may like yours different from the way I like mine."

Aggie took the coffee, and the smell of it brought back the nights of sitting with her friends and listening to the poets. Some of them had been awful, but the atmosphere was amazing.

"This smell delicious." As she poured the milk and finished fixing her coffee, Ben sat down at his desk. "You never answered my question. If I didn't know better, I would think you were avoiding the question."

Ben smiled. "No dear, I'm not avoiding it. I am prouder of my decision on March 19, 1965 than I am of any decision I've ever made."

"Is that the day you decided to take the side of the civil rights pioneers?"

"No, that is the day I became a Christian."

"That's right, you said that you were a Christian. Were your parents Jewish or did they just join the Jewish faith. I know a lot of people who committed to Kabbalah but weren't Jewish."

"No, my parents can trace their lineage all the way back to Jerusalem before the Romans destroyed it in 70 A.D. I am a Jew from top to bottom. My family has stayed true to the faith through many generations. I am the first to leave the faith."

"My father would have a heart attack if I ever considered doing something like that. He even threatened me when I was in high school that if I ever married someone outside of my faith that he would cut me off from my inheritance. I don't know if he would, but he seemed to be very serious when he was telling me."

"If your father is Orthodox, then he is very serious. I have many family members that are Orthodox and they have not spoken to me since I accepted Christ. I am banned from the family gatherings and I am not welcome at Temple unless there is a funeral. But I gained so much more than I lost. Have you ever questioned your faith?"

Aggie sat up straight and placed her coffee cup on the table. How could he have known that?

"No, I've never questioned any of that. I was raised to believe the Torah and live according to its laws."

"I too had the same upbringing but, as a young man, I was always wondering if there was something else besides the rules and regulations. I like kosher as well as anyone, but when that is the only thing you can eat, you begin to question if it is truly correct."

48

"But how did forsaking everything you had ever been taught, and everything your family had fought and died for, make things better? As Jews, we have a responsibility to maintain the faith because without us it will go away."

Ben leaned forward and looked into Aggie's eyes. "I am a really good student of human behavior. I think you just quoted something that either your father or your teacher told you. I don't think you truly believe that."

Aggie held his glance for a few seconds before looking away. "I think you are misinformed. I could never forsake my heritage for something that isn't real. My heritage is real. I have never heard of anything real in this Christianity." Aggie was not on firm ground, but she had to make an argument defending her beliefs or she would look weak.

"I am not going to get into a religious argument with you today. I am just going to say that I am probably one of the few people you will ever meet, especially in the South, that had the same kind of upbringing as you. I had that upbringing, and I found something that was greater than anything the Jewish faith could give me. You wanted to know what changed my point of view? It was Jesus, pure and simple."

Suddenly, there was the sound of a siren coming from across the street. As they looked out the window, two sheriffs' cars came screaming from the back of the courthouse and sped off toward the west with their lights on and sirens blaring.

"What is going on?" Aggie asked. "Do they do that a lot?"

Ben had a grim look on his face. "No, they don't. In fact, they are not allowed to turn their sirens on unless there is a possibility of a life and death situation." He then reached behind his desk and turned the scanner on. "I don't keep it on anymore because, most of the time, I hear about things on my phone as soon as it starts to come over the scanner.

"Deputy Nelson, please be advised, the caller stated the body hanging from the tree was a black male. The crime scene is about a hundred yards off the hospital road. Caller advised that there is already a large group of people beginning to congregate. Sheriff says to use extreme caution, and that he is on the way as soon as he gets through with his calls to the MBI and the Attorney General's office," a voice said over the scanner.

"Did he say what I thought he said?" Aggie asked.

Ben was up getting his camera and a note pad and a pocket tape recorder. "Yes, he did, and I am going to go do some real reporting. Do you want to come along? I need a cameraman, or camera person if you like."

"If you don't mind? I don't want to be in the way." Aggie couldn't hide her excitement. If this body could somehow be related to a racial situation, then this would definitely put her over the top. An eyewitness account of a black man lynched. She might even be able to sell this story to The Times.

"The only thing I ask is that if you come with me you remain unbiased. You can't get caught up in the emotion and make a bad situation worse. We are not there to find anyone innocent or guilty. We are there to report the facts to the best of our ability. Are we clear?"

"Yes sir, completely clear."

Ben tossed the camera to her. "You know how to operate that?"

"Yes, I have one almost exactly like it, but my lens is not this big." Aggie said as she looked at the buttons and settings. Judging by the size of the lens, you could take pictures from a long distance.

"Okay, you take pictures of everything you think is relevant. Don't get in anyone's face. That is what the lens is for. They will set up a perimeter and I will abide by it, but you don't have to. That telescopic lens will reach out and see things. You can get close to someone without being close to them. Do you understand?"

"Yes," Aggie said.

"Then let's go see what in the world has happened."

CHAPTER 5

Like it Came out of a Book

The drive to the crime scene shouldn't have taken more than ten minutes, but they had to pull over twice for emergency vehicles to pass. Along with these vehicles were several cars filled with people, both black and white, who had heard rumors and wanted to see what was going on.

When they finally got to the scene, the reports of a large crowd were grossly exaggerated. Aggie counted fifteen people who weren't law enforcement personnel. That number would grow judging by the number of cars that were behind them.

"Okay, remember what I told you. They haven't set up a perimeter yet, but they will and, when they do, you get behind the tape. Until then, get as close as you can and don't stop shooting pictures until the batteries run down," Ben said as they got out of the car.

Aggie considered herself ready for anything she would ever see. When she got out and turned toward where all the people were walking, that assumption went out the window. It was like a scene from a movie. The body was hanging limply from a limb. His hands were tied behind his back, Aggie assumed it was a male, and there appeared to be a pillow case on his head.

"You okay?" Ben asked her. "You are as white as a sheet. If you need to get back in the car, I can handle this by myself."

Aggie knew she couldn't miss this opportunity. "No, I'm fine. Let's get going."
The dispatcher had said the body was a hundred yards off the road, and it was probably

close to that. Before they got to the body, the deputies stopped them. Bobby was one of them.

"Ben, you can't come any farther. The sheriff wants us to clear the crime scene," Bobby said.

"Can you tell anything from your initial investigation?"

51

"Nothing but the fact that this is a murder and not a suicide. It's pretty hard to hang yourself with your hands tied behind your back. Other than that, we don't know anything. I really need you to move back to the road. I have already had to ask the people who were here when we arrived to move back there."

"Who found the body and reported it?" Ben asked. When he asked this, he touched Aggie on the shoulder and nodded his head at the body.

Aggie understood and immediately began to shoot pictures of the body. This would be as close as they would ever get, so they needed to get as many as they could. As she took the pictures, one of the deputies took the pillow case, or whatever it was, off the victim. Aggie got several shots before they put it back.

"Come on, Ben, take Ms. New York and get back to the road. I'm sure the sheriff will give you whatever information you need."

Aggie started to say something about being called Ms. New York but decided against it. The pressure everyone would be feeling now would make them say lots of things they might not normally say. Besides, she didn't have time to do anything but take pictures.

"Okay, let's go," Ben whispered.

"I don't know how many shots I got, but I did get some when they took the pillow case, or whatever that was, off his head," Aggie said in a lowered voice. She didn't know why they were whispering, but she didn't want to be the one who changed the tone and volume of the conversation.

"Did you zoom in on the clothes? I want to be able to see what kind of clothing he was wearing."

"I did, but what does that have to do with anything? They looked like normal clothes."

"Some of the local gangs have certain clothes that they wear."

"Wait a minute. You have gangs in this little town?"

"You seem surprised. Do you think that gangs and violence are only in the big cities? I have seen communications from New York and Los Angeles gangs in all the counties surrounding us. The school had to ban wearing the color red in the uniforms because of its use in gangs. Now let's hurry and get to the road because there might be trouble any minute now."

Aggie looked around at the building crowd. "What are you talking about? What do you see?"

"You see that man over there wearing the all black suit? That is Maalik Saalam, the Imam from the mosque in Jefferson County. Lots of people around here call him other things, but Imam is his official title. How did he get here so fast? Usually it takes a couple of days for him to make his presence felt away from Fayette."

Aggie got her camera and zoomed in on the man. He looked to be about six feet tall and moderately built. His attire was very different from those Imams she had seen in New York. There were many mosques and many Imams, but this man was dressed in a long black coat with a black tie and black shoes.

"In New York all the Imams I've seen dress in their robes most of the time," Aggie said. "Why is he in a suit?"

"I asked him the same question when he came to Mississippi ten years ago. He told me that he was of the more liberal wing of the faith, and that when he was in hostile territory, he was allowed to wear clothing that didn't bring unnecessary attention. He is a mostly likable guy, but when he thinks he has the upper hand on you, he will become ruthless and overbearing. I heard that even the African American churches are scared of what he is trying to do."

Aggie took a few more pictures and then looked at Ben. "What is he trying to do?"

"Make Sharia Law the rule of all African Americans and, eventually, everyone else. From what I've heard, he's building his congregation very steadily."

Aggie shuddered because she had a friend who did a paper on Sharia Law their sophomore year. The things she said it required of the women still made Aggie's skin crawl. As they made their way over to the perimeter that the deputies were setting up, they saw Sheriff Wactor drive up. When he got out, everyone saw the determined look on his face and gave him plenty of space. Aggie noticed that this was not the happy-go-lucky man she had dealt with less than twenty-four hours ago. This man was on a mission and was not going to be deterred. Ben saw the look also, but he had a job to do and was not going to back away now.

"Sheriff, did you get hold of the AG's office?" Ben asked as Sheriff Wactor walked by.

"Yes, I did. I'll give you an interview after the press conference." He never stopped walking as he talked. The deputy who had finished putting up the yellow police line tape lifted it up to allow him to walk through without stopping.

"Sheriff, I hope you are going to find the devils responsible for cutting this young black man's life short," the Imam said. "It is a horrible tragedy that I hope you take as seriously as I do."

"How did you find out about this so fast Maalik?" Ben said as he offered his hand.

"When a young African American man is hanged, it is the duty of all African Americans to fight the injustice." When he said this, the growing crowd nodded and murmured their agreement.

"They better hope that's not some of my family," a voice said.

"Gonna be hell to pay if that's one of my cousins," another voice said, a little louder.

"Don't you agree my newspaper friend?" Maalik was emboldened by the reaction of the angry crowd.

Ben looked at the growing group and assessed the situation. "I agree that if a crime has happened, then justice should be served. But I also think that until the investigation is completed, everyone should reserve judgment."

"How can we reserve judgment? There is an innocent young man hanging from a tree in a truly racial incident in a racist county. How can we judge it any other way?"

"It is not our job to judge anything. We have people who are tasked with that job so that others like us can feel safe in the justice system." The cool and calm demeanor Ben was exhibiting amazed Aggie. Maalik was on the verge of shouting and Ben was speaking slowly and calmly. This was a man she would like to emulate as a journalist.

"You are a white person. You have the ability to have faith in the justice system. I as a black man do not have that luxury. Too many times I have seen the justice system let my people down. As a leader of my people, I can't allow it to happen while my body still holds breath."

As they were talking, Aggie got the camera and began to shoot pictures of the crowd. She saw many young men and women who were caught up in the moment. The anxiety and anger on their faces were evident even to a novice like herself. As she continued to take pictures, she saw that they were pointing toward the tree the victim was hanging from. Turning around, she saw that they were taking the body down. She zoomed in and saw that Sheriff Wactor had his arms around the body. Bobby had climbed the tree and was getting the rope loose.

"Is there anyone out there who is trained in crime scene management?" Aggie turned around quickly because this voice was not Maalik's? When she turned, she noticed for the first time the young man standing beside the Imam. He was a little taller than the Imam and was dressed in a suit as well. There was a similarity between him and the Imam, but that could just be that he was trying to be like his leader. Ben noticed the change in voices also. He had his tablet out writing down something that Aggie couldn't make out. The only thing she could see was the word son. "Is that his son?" She whispered.

"Yes, but this is the first time he has ever uttered a word in public. He is always around his father, but he never says anything. Looks like someone got promoted, and he is going to let the world know that he's a player. I think Sheriff Wactor was a crime scene investigator when he worked for the highway patrol," Ben said.

"How long ago was that? Did they even have computer profiling and imagery back then?" The bitterness in his voice was even more pronounced than that of his father. His father must have noticed this, because he turned and placed his hand on his son's arm. Not a rebuke, but a noticeable sign to hold it down just a little.

"Who is your assistant?" Maalik asked. "I didn't know you had a photographer on the payroll."

"No, this young lady is not on the payroll. In fact, she is not from here. She, like myself, is a native New Yorker. She's doing some research for an article she is writing for her journalism class."

"New York is my favorite town in the world. What is your name and what part of the city are you from?" Maalik asked with genuine interest. There was no animosity in his voice anymore. It was as if he could turn it on and off with a thought.

"My name is Aggie Sharosh. I was raised on the Upper East Side, but I'm attending Rutgers now."

"Ms. Sharosh, it is nice to meet someone with culture besides this old newspaper man. I am delighted to make your acquaintance. May I introduce my son Aziz. He has been to college and now has joined me to help our people." Aggie stuck out her hand and Aziz did also.

"It is nice to meet you, Aziz. Where did you attend college?" Aggie asked.

"I spent two years at Columbia, but I finished my degree at Alcorn."

"I know about Columbia, it is a great school, but I have never heard of Alcorn." Aziz laughed. "That is because it is just a few miles away in Lorman. It is a predominately African American university. If you aren't a sports fan, most of the world has never heard of Alcorn. We have many famous sports stars who have graduated from Mississippi's HBCUs. Walter Payton, Jerry Rice, and Steve McNair are the three most famous ones."

Aggie was amazed at Aziz's change in tone. He, like his father, was not angry or confrontational like he had been just a moment before. He was cordial and polite.

"I don't know much about football, but I have heard the name Jerry Rice on Dancing With the Stars." Before they could continue the talk fest, the coroner came up to the perimeter pushing the gurney.

"Hello, Ben, how are you?"

"Doing well, Chris. Do you need any help bringing out the body?" Ben asked.

"No, I will get the sheriff to give me a deputy to give me a hand. I may need some protection when I come out." When he said this, he looked at Maalik. The dislike showed all over his face, and Maalik returned it. Obviously these two didn't care for each other.

"Yes, Mr. Jarrett, you may need some protection, especially if you do your job like you normally do."

"Maalik, why don't you make trouble in Jefferson County where you live. I'm sure they need you much more than we do."

"Maybe we have been sent to make sure you do your job," Aziz said. Gone was the pleasant young man and the confrontational one reappeared. The coroner just shook his head and pushed the gurney under the tape and walked toward the crime scene.

"Maalik, do you want to make a statement?" Ben asked. "I don't see any of the other leaders here yet."

"Reverend Matthews just drove up," a voice said from the crowd.

56

"Who is Reverend Matthews?" Aggie asked.

"He is one of the finest men I have ever known," Ben said. "I was hoping he would be here, but sometimes he is out of town. He is the leader of the Ministers' Alliance."

"Of course, you would want a statement from the man who wants to be best friends with the same people who try to kill us," Maalik said.

"There he comes," Ben said. "Maalik, don't worry, I'll get a statement from you, too. I'm just going to get his first. If we were in your county, I would defer to you."

"I understand Ben. As long as we get to speak our piece. Aziz, let's get out of the way so Reverend Matthews can have room."

Aggie wanted to ask why he needed room until she saw the crowd part like the Red Sea. A man came walking through that had to be six feet six inches if he was an inch. His shoulders were broad and his forearms looked like Popeye's arms from the cartoon series.

"Hello, Ben, do you have any idea what's going on?" When he and Ben shook hands, Aggie was shocked at how small his hand made Ben's look. This was a big man.

"I don't have any details Louis, but Sheriff Wactor said he would give me an interview after the press conference. I went out there and from what I could see, he was hanged and his hands were behind his back."

"Oh, my Lord. Did you see who it was?"

"No, there was a cover or pillow case on his head. I got some good pictures to see if it is gang related or something else. One thing I am quite sure of is it wasn't a suicide. Do you want to make a statement?" Ben asked as he took out his tape recorder. Even though it was an audio statement, Reverend Matthews straightened his tie and took off his hat. It was as if he was preparing his physical demeanor to coincide with his audio demeanor. "Just that we need to reserve judgment until we know the facts. Both the black and white community need to wait and let the authorities do their jobs. Franklin County has made too much progress in race relations to let this destroy us. However, I will tell you this, and you may quote me: The Ministers' Alliance is prepared to do whatever needs to be done to make sure that justice is served. You have my word on that."

"I don't believe that for a moment," Maalik said. He was standing beside a car some ten or twelve feet away. "I don't think the alliance has the guts to do whatever is necessary."

"Maalik, thank you for your input. I welcome your ideas and suggestions. Just as soon as you become a Christian minister you can join our group."

"He is a minister of Islam," Aziz said. "He is the true minister and you are the infidel."

Reverend Matthews looked at Aziz and shook his head. "Maalik, please control your son. I have more than enough problems without having to debate religious theologies with your prodigy."

"Louis, you know that sometimes the young speak louder than they need to. Although what he speaks is truth, I agree there is a time and a place for these kinds of discussions." With one sentence, Maalik had rebuked his son without raising his voice. Everyone who could hear the conversation knew what had happened. If they didn't know it by the tone of the words, they could look at Aziz. He was trying to keep his pride, but he was slinking back onto the car. Some of the men who had come with them tried to offer encouragement, but they were rebuffed.

Aggie was taking pictures like she was Jimmy Olsen from the Superman movies. She saw the coroner coming across the field pulling the gurney. The body was completely covered by a sheet, probably to keep anyone from recognizing him and a riot occurring, but she took pictures anyway. Sheriff Wactor was walking beside the body while the other deputies were standing around the tree.

"Ben, here they come," Aggie whispered. Everyone else must have seen it too because several began to shout and curse. Aggie noticed that several of the men who were standing around Maalik were the ones who were moving into the crowd, and they were shouting. Almost like they were inciting the crowd. Reverend Matthews was standing in the road directly in the path they would have to take to get to the coroner's ambulance. When they got to the police tape, Sheriff Wactor walked ahead and raised the tape so that the gurney could come through.

"Sheriff Wactor, I would like a word with you," Reverend Matthews said.

"Louis, I promise, I will meet with you this afternoon. I have some major investigating to do and taking care of public relations is not my priority right now."

"Then you need to make it your priority today because I need to be able to calm these people." He then leaned down and whispered. "There are some people here who aren't concerned with calming anything."

"Did you come alone?" Sheriff Wactor asked.

"No, my wife is in the car."

"Then why don't you ride with me and let her bring your car back to Meadville. That way, we can have some time to ourselves."

"Why can't *I* come ride with you to find out all the inner workings of the department?"

Maalik asked. He had come over close enough to hear the conversation. "Why does the radical reverend get special treatment?"

"Because he is a member of the community and you live in Jefferson County. If you want to be at the press conference in an hour, feel free to make your way to the court house. Now, if you'll excuse me, I have an investigation to run. As the sheriff, coroner, and pastor walked through the crowd, everyone's eyes were fixed on the body they were taking away. Even though they gave hostile looks, no one made any attempts to have a physical confrontation.

"I'll be there Sheriff, and you can count on that. I will be there every step of the way. You are not going to cover this up like Franklin County always does. We are going to hold you accountable." Maalik was shouting now, not for volume, but for effect. From the reactions of the people standing around, it was working. He was now talking to the crowd, and they were eating it up. Once again, Aggie could see that the people who seemed to be with Maalik were the most boisterous and vocal. Aggie knew this and apparently so did Ben because he nodded for her to follow him to the car. When they had gotten into the car, Ben looked over at Aggie. He had a serious look on his face.

"I know you are not wanting to get involved in this and will be gone soon, but I need someone to bounce things off of right now."

"I can listen to you if that's what you need," Aggie said. "You let me take pictures and get involved in something that I never thought I would see, so the least I can do is be a sounding board for you." Aggie didn't want to admit that the adrenaline rush from the excitement was greater than anything she had ever experienced. Ben wished he had his pipe in moments like this.

"Something doesn't sit right with me on this. I've known Maalik since he

59

came to Mississippi. He is very passionate, but he has always taken a subordinate role in situations like this. He has never been out front like this. Why come down here from another county and shout so loudly?"

"Maybe he's planning on getting into politics," Aggie surmised. "I know in New York, the first thing a person does before he puts his name on the ballot is to get some press coverage. It doesn't really matter what kind of coverage, just something. My father calls it the informal announcement when this happens."

"Your father is a very wise man. You may be right, but why do this in Franklin County. He doesn't live here, so he can't run for any county office and, even if he did, he wouldn't have a snowball's chance of getting elected. I'm not sure he can get elected in Jefferson County, but he would have a better chance there." Ben cranked the car and looked around for a way to get out. There were close to a hundred people milling around now that the coroner's car had taken the body away.

Aggie looked toward the tree and saw Bobby walking toward the road. "Sheriff Wactor must have a lot of faith in Bobby to leave him out here at the crime scene alone. Can he handle this without causing a full-fledged riot?"

"Aggie, don't let the events of yesterday cloud your judgment of Bobby. He is one of the finest young officers I know. He could and probably will be sheriff when Henry retires, if he wants to be. I know Henry is grooming him for that."

As they started to move, Aziz walked in front of the car. He was looking down and not paying attention to anything around him. When Ben stopped the car, Aziz realized he had walked in front of someone and looked up. He had an angry look on his face, but when he saw Ben and Aggie in the car, he smiled and waved. "He seems to like you," Aggie said.

Ben gave a little chuckle. "I don't think he was waving at me."

CHAPTER 6

The Identity

I f she thought there was a lot going on earlier, Aggie was shocked at how many more people were standing around the courthouse. Someone had even parked in Ben's spot at the paper. They had to park up the street at the grocery store. "Is this normal?" Aggie asked as they walked down the street. "How did this news get around so fast? Did CNN have a news alert?"

"My dear, you are a child of the digital age. Folks don't always depend on television for everything. Even though we are a small county, we have Internet and cell phones. I would guess that the news was all around the county before we got out to the crime scene. When we get to the office, I need you to do a web search to see if anyone has uploaded any pictures of the crime scene. If they did, we need to get ahead of them. Getting the story out fast is nice, but it is more important to get the story right. Sometimes as a journalist, we can figure out things faster than the law officers. There are many more ways to identify people than just their faces. Not from luck, but from hard work, we have the best pictures of the crime scene not taken by law enforcement." Ben sat down at his desk and took the memory card out of the camera.

"This is the reason I asked you to take the pictures of the body. We can go back and look at things and see if we can find something useful. Besides, two pairs of eyes are always better than one. The hospital won't do anything for a couple of hours. If Henry keeps to his usual pattern, he will wait for Chris to do an initial examination. Even if the boy's wallet is in his pocket, Henry will wait until there is concrete proof of identity. He doesn't want to tell a family that their child is dead until he knows for sure the name of the victim. He won't tell anyone until he is sure." As he talked, Ben was busy loading pictures from the memory card onto his computer. "I can be fast and right. We can get the story right and work to keep our town and our county from becoming a battleground. I wish school was going on though. It would cut down on the kids standing around. They are the prime targets for rabble rousers. Did you notice Maalik's friends? They were dispersing through the crowd shouting and stirring up trouble."

61

"I saw that, but I didn't know if it was my imagination or if it was true," Aggie said.

"Come over here and help me look at these first pictures of the body."

Aggie pulled a chair over to the desk. As she began to look at the pictures, the notion of getting on the road and leaving Franklin County in the rearview mirror was the farthest thing from her mind.

Standing back at the crime scene, Bobby wondered why this had to happen here. It was true that there was a lot of racial disharmony over the years in Franklin County, but it was the twenty-first century, and things like this shouldn't be happening. Before Sheriff Wactor had left with the body, he had said that if anything was ever going to be handled by the book, this case had to be it. Not just because of the racial overtones, but because it was their job. What he didn't say was that Marcus Baker's family was going to get the worst news of their life. At least that was what his identification had said his name was. His address said he was from Fayette, but that didn't tell them a lot. Many young people moved around to live with different family members. His license also said that he was about to turn seventeen years old. What a waste.

Most of the people who had been standing around were gone now. Only a couple of cars and a few stragglers were still out by the road. The crime scene was pretty well trampled, but Bobby had secured it the best way he knew when he got there. Now he had to try and make sense of what had happened with very little to go on. The call that had come into the sheriff's office was from a cell phone, and the person didn't give their name. They would run the number and find out who it belonged to unless it was a burner phone. From what he could tell while the body was still hanging, there was no doubt this was a lynching. The young man's hands had been tied and his face was beat up so badly that, even if they had known him, they would not have been able to recognize him. That was the reason they couldn't trust the identification in the wallet because there was no way to make a facial recognition.

"Bobby, what exactly are we looking for?" Billy asked. "I have been at several crime scenes, but never a hanging. This is a first for me."

"Billy, you need to just take a look at the ground and see if there are any fibers or materials that don't belong. Tracks that aren't ours and anything else that looks strange. I know that is vague, but that's what we're looking for. Does Brian have his gloves on?" There were three other deputies as well as a highway patrolman guarding the perimeter, but only

Bobby, Billy, and Brian were inside the crime scene area."

"He's as ready as he can get. What time did the sheriff say the MBI would be here?" The Mississippi Bureau of Investigation was the investigation wing of the Department of Public Safety in Jackson. They were who you called in when you didn't want any foul-ups. Of course, they weren't perfect, which was the reason Sheriff Wactor had told Bobby to do some preliminary work. This was still their county and, when it got down to it, they would be the ones who would be doing the majority of the legwork.

"I heard my parents talk about things like this when I was a kid, but I never thought I would ever see it," Billy said as he looked at the rope lying on the ground. "I want to be the one who catches this joker. There probably won't be a need for a trial."

"Billy, keep your eyes on the job at hand. No amount of hate or anger is going to help you do your job. Only a cool, calm head, using all the faculties at your disposal, is going to make the difference. As far as those stories, I heard them too. Of course, I saw the work of the Klan first hand."

Billy turned and looked at Bobby. "What are you talking about, seeing the work of the Klan? You got some dark skin in your past?"

Billy and Bobby had been together long enough that either of them could make racial jokes at the other's expense without even thinking anything about it. It might not be good, but it was the way they lived and, as far as they were concerned, it wasn't anyone else's business what they did.

"I'm not sure of the answer to that question, but that isn't what I'm talking about. I was riding in the car with my uncle when they found that man beat to death over in Eddiceton. They had beat him and split his head open and dragged him behind the car before bringing him and throwing him out in front of his house. My uncle drove up and saw he was lying beside the well. He told me to stay in the car, but I didn't listen. I followed him and saw the body. That night, my uncle got a phone call. The person who called said the Klan could reach anyone and anywhere, so whatever he may have seen or may be thinking, he needed to forget it if he didn't want some of the same things to happen to him. I heard him tell my daddy that he thought he knew who the voice was, but I never heard him say the name. All he ever said after that was the Klan was not something to mess with. So, when the Sheriff's Department asked him if he knew anything the next day, he said he didn't. Which wasn't a lie, but he never mentioned to the authorities the call he got."

"Wow, I just thought the Klan went after black folks." Billy said.

"Now you know not to jump to any conclusions. Let's get Brian over by the tree line to see if somebody might have left a camera in a tree."

Billy stopped and looked at Bobby. "Why would anybody film a lynching?"

"They wouldn't. But this land is leased by some hunters from Louisiana, and they might have game cameras in the trees. Whoever did this might have been caught on a camera and never known it."

"I didn't even think about that. I guess I do have a few things to learn from you," Billy said.

"When can you positively ID the body?" Sheriff Wactor asked. The coroner was slowly getting prints and scanning them into the database.

"If this young man has any prior arrests, or if he was fingerprinted for anything for government use, that would help. It will only be a moment."

"Now, Chris, I know you are not profiling this young African American man by suggesting that he has a criminal record?" Reverend Matthews asked.

The coroner looked up from his computer screen and then over at the body. "Louis, I understand your concern, but when have I ever profiled a young person, whatever their color? I hate the loss of life greater than anyone."

"I know you do. I just don't know who would have done this. I know if this is Charles Baker's son, it will tear him apart, but Ms. Maxine will go berserk. She will be looking for someone to pay for this, and I don't know if I will be able to calm her down."

"Louis, you and I both know this is the worst thing that could happen, but I want you to try and keep the folks from doing something that they would regret. I have a funny feeling about this, and I don't know why," Sheriff Wactor said as he sat down at the desk.

"I have a funny feeling about it too, but my funny feeling and your funny feeling may be different."

At that moment, Sheriff Wactor's phone rang. Looking at the number, he shook his head. "It's the governor's office. I wonder how he found out? I am going to take this outside." As the Sheriff walked outside, Reverend Matthews came up and looked over the coroner's shoulder at the screen. The pictures and prints were filtering faster than he could follow them. "I'm sure Maalik got out a press release. If nothing else but to make himself look good." Louis Matthews tried to get along with everyone, but something about Maalik and his followers didn't sit well with him.

Suddenly, a bell rang and the computer stopped on a picture and a set of prints.

"Gentlemen," Chris said, "I told you it wouldn't take long if he was in the system. The prints belong to Marcus Baker."

"Are you sure?" Reverend Matthews asked.

"The computer says it's a ninety-five percent match, so yeah, I'm sure. Do you want me to print them out for you, Henry?" The sheriff had walked back into the room, but he didn't seem happy.

"Please Chris, if you don't mind. Louis, we need to go see Charles and Ms. Maxine. I need to officially tell her, and you need to be there to keep things from going sideways. The governor said that we should use everything at our disposal to solve this. He said that nothing within the law was off limits. Do you have any feel about how this is going to go within the black community?"

"How would you react if a young white boy was lynched? I don't think me or anyone else is going to keep this from being a full-blown racial problem. Especially if our friends from up in Jefferson County have anything to do with it."

Henry looked at the young man lying on the table. "I hate to bring this up, but as much as I respect you, Louis, you just categorized it as a racial problem. We have no information that this is racial. It may be, but I have to make sure it is not just a gang problem."

"All due respect to you, but Franklin County and Mississippi don't have the best record where it comes to racial incidents. But you are correct that it might be something else. I hope and pray it is, but whatever it turns out to be, we still have a young man who was murdered. That is not in question."

"That is how I am going to treat it, and I want you to believe that. I won't rest until we find out who killed this young man. They will be brought to justice no matter who they are or why they did this. You have my word on that."

Reverend Matthews walked over to the sheriff and put his hand out. "If I thought anything else, I wouldn't be here right now. But you have to keep me in the loop. I can't help you direct public opinion if I don't know what's going on."

Henry Wactor took the hand that was offered and smiled. "Louis, you know we are both getting too old for this."

"Speak for yourself old man, I'm in the prime of my life. And if we are going to tell Ms. Maxine her son is dead, we are going to have to be on our toes."

"Chris, you keep this silent until we get back. No leaks whatsoever. Is that clear?"

"Sheriff, I don't talk to anyone until you release the information. You have my word on

that."

"Chris, I have complete confidence in you and your skills. Louis and I are headed to this young man's parents' house. When we get back, I will go to the courthouse and have a press conference. By that time, all the major stations will be there anyway. I need a cause of death by then."

As they headed out the door, Henry's phone rang. Looking at the number, he almost ignored the call because it was from Ben at the newspaper and he would be wanting information. "Hang on a minute, Louis. It's Ben and I promised him I would talk to him."

"Just make sure you don't slip up and tell him anything. He's a good guy, but information is his business."

Henry accepted the call and put the phone to his ear. "Ben, sorry I haven't called you but it has been wild as you are aware."

"No problem, Sheriff, I just need something confirmed. Is the victim Marcus Baker?" Henry stopped walking. "How could you have guessed that? We just got the confirmation a few minutes ago. Did Chris send you a message? If he did, I may go back and strangle the coroner."

"No, nothing like that. Aggie was taking some pictures of the crime scene and I recognized the bandana the victim was wearing. I did a story on him a few months ago, and he said that he didn't go anywhere without that bandana around his ankle. He said it was his special thing. I knew there was something that I was missing, so Aggie and I downloaded the pictures and went over them. There was only one picture that showed the bandana, but I recognized it. I went back and found my picture from the article and it was a match. I just did some reporter guessing. Have you told his parents yet?"

"No, Louis and I are on the way right now. Ben, I need you to keep this quiet until the press conference. This thing is going to go viral quickly enough as it is. Can I depend on you to keep it under wraps for an hour?"

"I am a newspaper man, but I am not an idiot, Henry. I know you are doing your best, and I will let you do the announcing. I would like the first question at the press conference, however."

"That's a deal. If you don't mind, bring your podium over to the court-house and set it up on the front steps. You can tell the various media people where the press conference will be."

"I think I can find it. Henry. I am going to report this as closely as I can. I am going to hold this, but from here on out, I am going to cover this like it should be. No holds barred and no punches pulled."

"I can handle fair treatment. You do your job and I'll do mine. If we both do that, then everything should turn out fine."

"All right, we have an agreement. What time will you be at the court-house?"

"Let's say forty-five minutes. That will give me time to get my good uniform from the house."

"I'll handle everything till you get there." Ben ended the call and looked over at Aggie. "You were right. The victim was Marcus. I didn't see the bandana until you did. You have a good eye for these things."

Aggie smiled. It was nice to be appreciated for seeing something that a man with much more experience had missed.

"What is going to happen now? Will there be riots?" Aggie remembered seeing the riots in Camden, New Jersey, after a police officer had shot a young black man.

"No, I don't think there will be riots. There will be a lot of people coming in from all over the country. Many of them will want justice, but some will come here just to cause trouble. When we go over for the press conference, I will need you to help keep up with the various media members. I may need to get in touch with them during this, and I want to be on a first name basis."

"What will be the question you ask?" Aggie inquired. "The first question is sometimes the most important and best question that is asked. My professor told me that if you ask a good first question, every question after that is based off that first one."

"I am going to ask him if he thinks this is a racial crime. Unless he answers that question in his statement, which he very well may do. If he does, then I will come back with, have there been any racial problems in the last few months?"

"Have there been any problems?"

"No, but this will allow Henry to close off anyone who wants to say that Franklin County is no better now than it was fifty years ago. That is not true, and I won't allow outsiders to paint us as a bunch of rednecks who sit around and pontificate about how we miss the Civil War times. Those days are over, and I won't stand by and let that happen."

Aggie thought for a second. "But what if it is a racially motivated crime? What if that is exactly what happened? This African American boy might have spoken to a white girl or dared to ask her on a date and her daddy or brother found out and took care of him. Will you be just as vigilant to find out the truth then?"

Ben stood up and walked to the storeroom without saying anything. Aggie thought that he was mad or was ignoring her. When he came back, he was carrying a large wooden podium. "If what you asked is true, I will be just as vigilant to get the truth out, maybe more. I am very open-minded about many things, but that doesn't mean I am immune to the feeling of horror that someone in this twenty-first century might have lost their life because of his skin color. You have unbelievable perception for someone so young. I wish I had your mind when I was your age. You will be invaluable during this process."

Aggie smiled and accepted the compliment. Then suddenly the words "during this process," hit her. "What did you mean during this process? How long are you expecting me to be here?"

"Aggie, you came south looking for information to write an article that would get you a scholarship. God is giving you the opportunity to be involved on a level that most college students and the media in general would give their eye teeth for. I need someone I can trust to get this done. You need someone to train you and to give you real world skills. I can't see you leaving before this is completed."

"Ben, I have to go back to New York. You are right; I have a story to write. I have enjoyed the excitement, but I can't stay very long. I can stay over the weekend, but Monday I have to start home." The words were coming out of her mouth, but Aggie couldn't believe she was agreeing to stay over the weekend.

"Then you better hope this is solved and settled over the weekend. Let's go across the street and get ready for the biggest press conference to ever be held in Franklin County.

CHAPTER 7

Internet Sensation

Aggie couldn't believe that setting up a press conference could be this much trouble and yet so much fun. This was a tense environment, and she shouldn't enjoy the chaos, but she just couldn't help herself. She had gone around to all the news media outlets and gotten their information just as Ben had told her. She had gotten hit on by all the reporters, including one of the women. The only thing that was higher than her excitement, was the tension around the courthouse. What surprised Aggie was that it wasn't a racial tension, at least not yet. Everyone was milling around talking to each other. Yes, there were some young African American boys who were making remarks about what they would do to the crackers who did this. There were also some young white boys who were saying that if anything happened to any white people, then there were plenty of trees in Franklin County. A crude remark, but it was whispered loudly enough to be heard. The majority of the adults were very quiet.

Walking across the courthouse lawn, Aggie saw the clock on the bank sign say it was two- thirty. Ben was waving at her to come and stand beside him. As she walked over, a van drove up and parked almost on the sidewalk. Eight people, both men and women, got out and began to walk toward the throng. She saw that it was Aziz and his father leading the group. As they got closer, Aggie saw them disperse into the crowd, almost as if they wanted to be a presence in every quadrant of the courthouse lawn.

"Ben, did you see who just arrived?" Aggie asked when she got to Ben's side.

"I did, but I've been expecting them. I expected them to have already been here. I wonder what took so long?"

"How long until they get started?"

As she asked the question, a group of law enforcement officers led by Sheriff Wactor, walked out of the courthouse. They all stood behind in a line as Sheriff Wactor stepped up to the microphone. You could hear cameras begin to click and hum as they began to film. There were seven television stations on site. All three of the Jackson stations were here as well as CNN,

Fox, and two stations from Baton Rouge. Aggie didn't know how much coverage this would get but for this area, it was huge. There were also five newspapers as well as a representative from the Associated Press. Now they were about to hear what they were waiting for.

"Ladies and gentleman, my name is Henry Wactor and I am the Sheriff here in Franklin County. Behind me I have several law enforcement officers, both local and state. I would like to make a statement, and then Chief Deputy Bobby McCoy will make a statement as will Trooper Wiley Terrell with the Department of Public Safety. After these statements, we will try to answer any questions that we can, but some questions won't be answered because of the ongoing investigation."

He took a piece of paper out of his jacket pocket and put on his glasses. "This morning around nine-thirty, we received a call that there was a body hanging from a tree just off Union Church Road, or the Hospital Road as it is commonly known. Law enforcement was dispatched, and the body of Marcus Baker was found hanging from a tree. The coroner has determined a time of death to be between four and seven A.M. There is no motive at this time, and foul play is believed to be involved. The cause of death at this time is not officially known, but the preliminary report seems to be blunt force trauma to the head area. The Mississippi Bureau of Investigation will be assisting my department. Our thoughts and prayers go out to the Baker family during this trying time, and I would ask that everyone in our community allow the authorities to do their jobs. One other thing before I bring up Chief Deputy McCoy. This is a senseless act done by despicable people. My department and I will do everything in our power to bring this murderer or murderers to justice. At this time, Chief Deputy McCoy will come and make a statement about the crime scene.

Aggie watched as Bobby came up to the microphone. He didn't look nervous at all. The fact that he had never spoken about something of this magnitude before didn't seem to faze him. This side of Bobby impressed Aggie. Seeing him in his uniform in front of all these people made her forget that twenty-four hours ago he had put handcuffs on her and was about to take her to jail.

"Boy, the garden club ladies are going to freak out when they see what this crowd is doing to their new trees," Ben said.

"What trees and why aren't you listening to the press conference?"

Ben pushed his glasses onto the end of his nose and stared at Aggie. "Ms. Sharosh, I know what they are going to say better than they do. While you were getting the names of all the media outlets, I was in the sheriff's office writing the official statements. The only way I won't know what is being said is if they decide to not read the statement, and Henry threatened both of them with a slow miserable death if they deviated one word."

"How did you do that? Did he give you the details?" Aggie couldn't believe that the newspaper man had written the statement for the people he was supposed to be covering.

"I see a disapproving look on your face. Trust me, when the time comes, I will be right there nipping at their heels. Henry is not only my sheriff, but he is also my friend. If I can't help my friend when he is involved in the biggest case of his career, then I'm not very much of a friend."

"I guess that's the other way you get to ask the first question. You do favors and you get favors."

Ben looked at his watch. "Since you disagree with how close I am to the sheriff, I will let you ask the first question. I was thinking about letting you do it anyway. Now I think that it's a great idea."

"No way, I am not prepared. If you were going to let me do this, you should have told me in advance." Aggie was trying to keep the excitement out of her voice because, if Ben knew the truth, getting to ask a question at this press conference was exactly what she wanted.

"I'll bet you've already got a question ready, don't you? I recognize that look on your face. You would love to be the first person to try and grill the sheriff."

Aggie looked down at her feet and then back at Ben. "I guess I do have one question ready."

"Okay, when this state trooper gets through, Henry will step back up to the microphone. He's going to look at me and I will point at you. When he asks for questions, you raise your hand. It doesn't matter who else raises their hand, he will point to you. The only thing I will ask is that you speak clearly and say that you work for The Gazette. Other than that, you can ask any question."

Aggie looked up and saw that the state trooper was finishing his statement. Though she was excited to participate in the press conference, never in a million years did she think she would be able to ask a question.

"Thank you, Trooper Terrell. Now we will take questions from the press."

As Sheriff Wactor looked around, he found Ben. When their eyes made contact, Ben pointed toward Aggie. The Sheriff looked puzzled but nodded. While all the big-time reporters from all over Mississippi shouted to get his attention, Henry Wactor pointed toward a third-year college student from New York for the opening question. Aggie saw him point at her and opened her mouth but nothing came out. She felt the eyes of everyone focused on her and even noticed some of the cameras pointing toward her.

"Aggie Sharosh from The Gazette, Sheriff Wactor. Since the victim's face was beaten into an unrecognizable state, have you considered whether this might be a crime of passion instead of a hate crime?"

Everyone in attendance, both media and general public, stopped what they were doing and looked at Aggie. Even Ben looked over at her with a curious look on his face.

"Ms. Sharosh, I don't know what kind of crime it was, but it was definitely a murder." As he looked away to another reporter, Aggie felt emboldened.

"Sheriff, follow-up--but isn't facial destruction a sign of a close personal contact between the victim and the killer?" This was one of the things Aggie had learned in her forensics class. Until this day, she didn't know or understand why it was required, but she was so happy she took it and remembered something from it.

Sheriff Wactor turned back as did everyone in the crowd. "I don't know about that, but it is a great thought. We will take it into account in the investigation." He then turned to Bobby. "Take a look at that angle when you start your investigation." He looked back at the other reporters. "Now, next question."

For the remainder of the press conference, the questions all were slanted toward a crime of passion or if it was true the face of the victim was unrecognizable. When Sheriff Wactor finally ended the conference, Ben looked at Aggie.

"Young lady, I have never seen a rookie take over a press conference with one question. Where did you get that from?"

"I learned it in my forensics class. The only reason I remembered it is because I just took it this last semester."

"Let's head to the office. I'm sure Henry will be over in a few minutes to give me my interview."

"What interview? You wrote the statement that he read to the press. What could you possibly need a personal interview for?"

"Excuse me, Miss, could I get a word with you?" Aggie looked around to find one of the reporters coming toward them.

"Looks like you have made some news getting the news. I'll meet you in the office."

"This won't take very long," Aggie answered. "Don't do the interview without me."

As the reporter and his cameraman came over, Aggie wished she had a mirror. You never knew when you were going to be interviewed for television!

"Ms. Sharosh, my name is Curt Nelson and I'm with CNN's New Orleans bureau. I was wondering if we could get a word with you since you broke the theory that this might be a crime of passion. Is Aggie your name or just something you go by?"

"My name is Agnes, but I hate that name so please call me Aggie. And you can just hold on one minute," Aggie said. "I didn't break anything. I just asked a question."

"Okay, E.T. on me in three, two, one. I'm here with Agnes Sharosh local reporter for The Franklin County Gazette. Ms. Sharosh, you brought out the aspect that this might be a crime of passion instead of a hate crime. As a reporter, you are privy to many different things, could you expound on this theory that you put forward?"

Aggie started to argue and say that she hadn't broken anything or come up with any type of theory. But for some reason, she decided to answer the question. "In my experience I have found that tremendous facial beating and lacerations constitute a close personal connection between the victim and the perpetrator. Not necessarily a long connection, but something closer than just a random association with a person. If someone doesn't have a close connection, they do not continually beat a person after they are unconscious."

"We were told that you were one of the first people on the scene. Is this where you saw the evidence of the victim being beaten and then formulated this theory?"

Aggie didn't want to say that she saw it on one of the pictures she had taken after they took the cover off the body right before they set up the perimeter. She and Ben had found the picture when they were trying to figure out Marcus' identity. "Let's just say I saw how much damage was done and came up with this, might I say, unproven hypothesis."

The reporter looked from Aggie to the camera. "It may be unproven, but the sheriff told the lead investigator to include this in his investigation, so I would say you added something they didn't have. Thank you, Ms. Sharosh. Here in Meadville, Mississippi, I'm Curt Nelson."

He waited a few seconds for his cameraman to give him the sign that they weren't rolling anymore, then looked back at Aggie. "I don't know when this will show, but unless there is a major earthquake or terrorist attack, you should see yourself on CNN tonight. If you would like, I can send you a copy of the tape."

"Thank you so much, that would be great." Aggie wanted to have this for her reel in case she decided to go to work in television.

"I'll send it to the newspaper unless you have a card with your address? And thank you so much for your candor. Now I have to go get a report ready."

As Aggie walked toward the newspaper office, she wondered if anyone she knew would see the interview. *He was probably just kidding about it running tonight*, Aggie thought. *Probably thought I would be so overwhelmed because he was a television reporter that I would immediately invite him over for some quick appreciation sex.* Since her father owned several television stations, she had heard all the stories about reporters who make up stories to get women to go to bed with them.

"I saw you being interviewed. I guess you New York folks stand out around these hillbillies." Aggie turned to see Aziz walking toward her.

"He seemed to think that my question came out of nowhere. I guess there are enough people doing hate crime stories, and he is looking for something different. Either that or he was just trying to get me to swoon over him. I saw you and your father, but I didn't hear either of you say anything. After the things he said at the crime scene, I would have expected the two of you to be more vocal."

"My father is a very wise man. He knows that people here are not fond of him, so he keeps a very low profile. But trust me, when the time comes, he will be heard. When are you going back to New York?"

Aggie laughed, but not at the question. This morning, she had planned to be headed home by now. But with all the excitement going on, she couldn't just leave. Ben was right, but she didn't want him to know she knew it. "I am planning to leave Monday if everything goes well, but even if it doesn't, I have to start home. I have a great story to write and a scholarship to win."

"I wonder, what does the daughter of one of New York's richest men need a scholarship for? Your father owns many television stations and newspapers as well as several pieces of prime real estate in Manhattan." As he talked, Aziz smiled a very confident smile.

"How do you know anything about my family," Aggie asked? "I know that no one around here told you because no one knows."

"They have this little thing called the Internet. You can go onto this little-known website called Google and find out anything about anybody. I just typed in your name and away we went. And if you don't mind my saying, I like Agnes much more than Aggie."

"You are allowed to have an opinion. But since you have been checking up on me, let me ask you a question. Why would a person leave one of the most prestigious schools in the country to come back to Mississippi to finish his college career at Alcorn, I believe you called it? I'm sure it's a wonderful university, but there are few schools in the United States that have the standing among universities that Columbia has. Were you running from something or to something?'"

"From what I hear, he was not cutting the mustard at that big New York school and had to come back and slum around with the boys from Lorman," Billy said. He must have been listening from a few feet away, but neither Aziz nor Aggie had seen him.

"At least I have the benefit of a university education. Where did you matriculate from officer? Or are you a self-made man whose daddy got him a job in the Sheriff's Department?" Aziz's demeanor had changed dramatically with Billy's arrival. Aggie was taken aback at how quickly Aziz went from friendly to confrontational

"Oh no, I just have a little old BS degree in criminal justice from The University of Southern Mississippi. My father was a farmer and didn't even like the sheriff. Boy, to have all that information on Aggie, you don't know a thing about anyone else." Billy then turned his back on Aziz and looked at Aggie. "Thank you so much for giving me something else to look at. I couldn't believe it when the sheriff said for me to add your theory into my investigation. It must have struck a nerve with him, because he doesn't usually take theories from private citizens." When he saw that referring to her as a private citizen was demeaning to her, he quickly backtracked. "Not that you aren't a very accomplished reporter, but usually tips from non-law enforcement personnel are handled differently."

"Maybe he is trying to skirt the true meaning of the case by clouding everyone's thoughts with other things." Even though Billy had turned his back on Aziz, that didn't mean Aziz wasn't still involved in the conversation.

"Thank you, Aziz. I never thought you would try to cause trouble. Aggie, are you going? to stay at my sister's tonight?"

"I haven't thought about it because this morning I was planning on heading back home today. I may just stay in Brookhaven because I don't want to be a bother."

Before Billy could say anything else, Aggie's phone rang. She saw that it was a New York number that she didn't know. "Gentlemen, I'm sorry, but I have to take this call. It's from my father." Aggie couldn't believe that she was using her father as an excuse to get away from two men who both wanted her attention.

"Okay, I'll talk to you later. Aziz, have a good day. Make sure you obey all the traffic laws. I would hate to hear you were violating the laws that you and your father hold so dearly." As he said this, the contempt Billy had for the young man in front of him almost dripped off his words.

"You, too, Officer. I'm sure some African American teenagers are somewhere doing something they aren't supposed to. If I were you, I'd run right over and arrest them."

Aggie walked toward the newspaper office and answered her phone. If just for a moment, she was proud to be away from the brewing animosity between the two.

"Hello Dad, how are you?"

"I guess there is a problem. This is the first time you have answered my call. I have gotten used to talking to your answering machine."

"I've been busy today." Aggie didn't want to tell him about the murder. The less he knew about what she was involved in, the better she would be.

"Have you had any more run-ins with the law down there? Your Aunt Rachel said you called her last night."

"Yes, I did. I knew you were at the Oak Room and I needed to talk to someone. Is everything else okay at home?" Aggie didn't know how to do small talk with her father. Most of the time they spent their phone calls arguing, so this was something new.

"Everything is fine. I was just calling to check on you. I have a secretary who is waving at me that I have a meeting. Like I said, I didn't expect you to answer your phone. I will call you later this evening."

"All right, Dad. Bye." As usual, her father didn't say goodbye, he just ended the call.

When she walked into the newspaper office, Ben was hovering over his computer. "I hear you got interviewed by CNN. I didn't even get a 'hi how are you,' and I'm supposed to be the one with all the years of experience." As he said this, Ben laughed at the absurdity of the situation.

"I told you I was taught to ask a question that would make everyone else's question come back to your own. Do you think it's possible that this was something besides a hate crime?" Aggie sat down in the chair opposite and put her feet on the desk.

Ben looked up from his computer and frowned. "Please take your feet off my desk. I can handle everything in life except that."

Aggie quickly took her feet down. "Don't want to anger the more experienced reporter," she said with a smile. "What do we do now? Will you put out a special edition of the paper?"

"It won't be a special edition, but I'm going to move the delivery date up to Tuesday from Thursday so that I can get some traction off this story. That is one of the reasons that I wanted you to stay at least until Monday. I haven't done a hurried edition in years and, as you can see, I am very short staffed."

"What are you going to need me to do?"

"I will need a story about the killing and something about yourself for the people around here. Maybe you can do the one about Jughead. I was going to write it, but now that I think about it, you would do much better. Along with that, I need someone to help proofread everything. This will be the biggest seller in many years, and I want it to work. I have to get some more advertising this afternoon and tomorrow. That is another reason I need you. I just believe that God sent you here for a greater reason than you know."

"I'm not sure about what God had to do with me being here. I think it might have been just coincidence." At the mention of God, Aggie began to get that funny feeling again in her stomach.

Ben leaned back in his chair and looked over his glasses at her. "My young Jewish friend, let me tell you one thing that you should remember, if you don't remember anything else that I tell you. There's no such thing as coincidences with God. He has a plan for every person in this world, and he has a plan for you. I understand your unwillingness to believe that God is concerned about you personally. But I'm here to tell you that he is concerned with every aspect of your life, more than even your Father."

This made Aggie laugh. "I don't think God is as concerned with my life as my father is. He wants to interfere with everything I do and be involved with every facet of my life. Maybe that's not concern; maybe that's controlling."

"I know it seems that way. I had a Jewish father and I know how overbearing they can be. But I'm here to tell you that no one cares for you like Jesus does."

Aggie didn't want to have this conversation. Not because she didn't like Ben, but because she didn't like talking about God or Jesus like this. All her life she had been taught that God loved his chosen people, but he loved them from heaven. We were in charge of our own destiny and God watched us from above. As she sat trying to come up with a way to articulate her feelings, her phone rang. She was so happy that it rang that she didn't look to see who was calling. She just hit the button and answered. "Hello, this is Aggie."

"I know you are not thinking about spending the night anywhere other than my house. Besides, since I heard you are the big newspaper reporter who gets to ask the first question at the biggest press conference in the history of not only Franklin County but maybe southwest Mississippi, you need somewhere to hide out. Besides Archie wants to be able to spend some time talking to you without getting into trouble."

"Annette, I don't want to be a bother to you and take your southern hospitality for granted."

"You're not going to take anything for granted. When you get back here, I will make us a pot of coffee or maybe some tea. I'll tell you about my afternoon and what the Lord showed me when I was praying this afternoon. I think you'll be very surprised."

Aggie put her hand to her head and closed her eyes. Would these people stop talking to her about God? She wanted to shout it to Annette, but she couldn't be that arrogant. She took a quick breath to compose herself. "Okay, a pot of tea would be wonderful or maybe a glass of sweet tea. I am really getting hooked on that. As far as staying, thank you for the offer and I won't argue with you anymore. Tell Archie he and I will have some time tonight to talk about things."

When she hung up the phone, she saw that Ben was on his phone also. Maybe he would be focusing on the case and not about what he thought God, or Jesus or whoever else they knew about, was going to do. Since he was working on his story, Aggie decided to put some words on her computer while her thoughts were still clear. Her first journalism professor had been a stickler for getting words written before they got away from you. If he could see her now.

Across the street at the Sheriff's Department, Bobby was sitting in his office with the investigator from the MBI and Sheriff Wactor.

"Bobby, now that we are alone, I'd like to hear your plans, and do you have any idea which way you are going to go with this investigation?" Sheriff Wactor asked.

"Sheriff, I am going to look at every angle. What made you tell the world that Aggie's theory had merit?"

"Because it does have merit. I've lived in Franklin County all my life. I know there are some dinosaurs who don't like black people, but they are the minority in greater numbers than ever before. I know for a fact the Klan doesn't have a presence here now. I'm not saying this isn't a hate crime, but I am not going to say it was done because of skin color until I get all the information. Whichever way it comes down, we have to never forget, there is a young man dead before his time and a mother and father who are grieving. Whoever did this has to be brought to justice."

"When is Ms. Maxine going to hold her press conference?" Bobby asked.

"In about an hour, give or take. I asked Louis to take the lead because he's Maxine's pastor and she trusts him. Also, he can keep Maalik at bay. I don't trust him, and I don't know what his end game is. I called the sheriff in Jefferson County and asked if something was going on and Maalik was being pushed out. That would explain his foray into Franklin County. Sheriff Norman said he hadn't heard anything." He then looked over at the MBI investigator. "Wiley, what did your superiors tell you? How much leeway are they going to give you?"

"They told me to do whatever I had to do to help you solve this. We have an election coming up next year and our Public Safety Director has his eye on the governor's mansion. If you solve this with our help, or we solve it with your help, he will trumpet it as if he solved it personally."

"I know this is going to be a political hot potato, but I want everyone to know that as sheriff, all I want is to get it solved. The longer it goes unsolved, the more problems people like Maalik and his followers can cause. I also know that Louis is going to want results, because he won't put up with any dawdling, whether it's true or just perceived."

"I think we need to start with his family and go from there. They will know who he's been hanging out with and who his friends are. In my experience at the MBI, the family always knows more than you think."

"No offense, Wiley, but that's straight out of the how to be a detective playbook. It's the right call, but we are going to do that without your input. What we need from you Jackson boys is what we don't have, and that's deep undercover information on the gangs and drug runners in this part of the state. I know most of them, but I don't have tabs on everyone. I know for a fact that there's a room in the Public Safety building that has the names of every known gang member in the state of Mississippi. If memory serves me, they update that list every six months. I want to start eliminating suspects as quickly as possible."

"Sheriff we haven't heard about any gang fights in the last few weeks. Even the Roxie boys have been quiet since you broke up their three meth labs. Why are you focusing on gangs?" Bobby asked.

"Bobby, we know what we know. You and Billy have done a bang-up job with minimal resources. The problem is, if we knew everything, this would not have been a surprise to us. So that leaves us with three options. Either this is a gang killing involving someone that we don't have tabs on, or this is a racial killing, which I can't believe, or Aggie's idea about them knowing the victim and maybe a crime of passion could be true. Either way we are in a world of hurt. So, like I was telling Wiley, I want him to focus on what we don't know and can't do, and we will work on what we do know and what we can do."

"I understand where you're going, and I agree with what you're saying. I have some men and women that we use as CIs. Let me get their ears to the ground and see if we can find out what you don't know. But Henry, you've got to keep me in the loop. I can't sign off on this and you do your own thing. I know you got a raw deal out of the patrol, but please don't use this opportunity to rub our nose in it. Let's work together and get this solved."

"Wiley, you're right. I did get a raw deal from the patrol, but I got a better deal from God and he won't let me rub anybody's nose in anything. I promised him when I started preaching, and when I got this job, that I would never use either of my positions to get retribution against anyone. So far, I have held to that promise and I don't plan to start going back on my word, especially to Him."

Wiley stood up and held out his hand. "Henry, that's great to hear. How often do we need to meet on this?" Wiley asked as he shook hands with Sheriff Wactor and then Bobby.

"Bobby's still going to be my lead man on this. I want a daily status report from both of you until this is solved. A murder has been committed in our county, and with the good Lord's help, we are going to catch whoever did it. Bobby, you get started, and I'll go over to the Gazette and fulfill my promise to a certain newspaper man. I really wish I could write my own statements."

CHAPTER 8

Fame

"That should do it, Henry," Ben said as he turned off his tape recorder. "I'll get this written up for you and bring it to church on Sunday."

"Don't give it to me before church. I will have a hard-enough time keeping my focus on the sermon. I've got a real good one though. The Lord gave it to me two days ago and I didn't understand why."

"Don't tell me it's about thou shall not kill?" Ben said with a chuckle

"No, it's going to be out of James. I've titled it "Show me something Mister.""

"Catchy title. Good thing you got it worked out before this happened. You probably won't have much time for church work this weekend."

"That, my friend Ben, is where you are wrong. I've told you, I'm a pastor first and a sheriff second. If something has to take a back seat, it's this," Henry said as he tapped his badge. The entire time Sheriff Wactor had been giving his interview, Aggie had listened intently without acting like she was trying to listen. She was trying to hear something she didn't already know. Everything he said was pretty much what he had said in his opening statement, until just now.

"Sheriff, I have a hard time believing that." This so stunned both Ben and the Sheriff that they put down their cups of coffee and turned toward her.

"Ms. Sharosh, would you like to explain your tone and what you don't understand?" Sheriff Wactor asked.

"You have a murder happen in a community where you are the head law enforcement officer, and you are more worried about your job as a rabbi, I mean pastor. What happens if you get to the point where you have to choose whether to solve a case or do your job at your church? Is your job at your church really more important than your job as sheriff?"

"Aggie, I understand that you are emboldened by your performance this afternoon, but you may be stepping over the boundary with this line of questioning." The tone in Ben's voice changed ever so slightly. "You've been in

Franklin County for two days. I would suggest you get a lay of the land before you destroy some of the goodwill you have garnered in this short time."

Before Aggie could give a response, Sheriff Wactor held up his hand. "Ben, I can defend myself. Ms. Sharosh, I know you aren't from here, and I know you are of a different faith than I am. Ben said you are Jewish, right?"

"Yes, but my faith is not the question here." Aggie felt herself becoming defensive again.

"No, your faith is not the question, but to understand my faith and my way of thinking, you need to check your own. Have you gone to temple since you have been away from home?"

"I did the first Saturday, but I didn't last Saturday. I was planning on making it to Atlanta by tomorrow and finding a temple there, but that is out the window now. I guess I'll go to one that is close by. My father wants me to go, and I do too." Aggie hoped her words had more sincerity than her thoughts did.

"Why do you go to temple?"

"Because I'm supposed to. I was taught attending synagogue is the most important part of Jewish life along with a Kosher diet."

"But if your father didn't hound you into going, would you go on your own?"

"Yes, I would. I am proud of my heritage. We are God's chosen people. Why wouldn't I desire to go to temple?"

"Here is the difference between the two of us and Ben, too. You have a religion, but he and I have a relationship with Christ. There is a huge difference between those two things. I am able to say that my calling of God is more important than anything because I have a relationship with Him. I talk to Him daily and He talks to me. That may not answer your question, but that is the best I've got." As he got up, Henry turned to Ben. "Now Ben, don't you go misquoting me. If you do, I'll get someone else to write my statements." Both men laughed.

"How can I misquote you? Most of what you just told me was in my statement I wrote for you."

"Aggie, I would like to invite you to come to our church Sunday morning. I know Annette will invite you, but I wanted to do it first. Maybe you can add our church to your article you are writing."

"Annette goes to your church?"

"Yep, she's been there longer than I have. Anyway, those folks will be very kind to you and will welcome you with open arms."

"I don't think so, Sheriff, but thanks for the invitation. Now, if you'll excuse me, I have to get back to both my stories."

"No, you don't," Ben said. "You have to get over there and cover Ms. Maxine's press conference."

"Aren't you going?" Aggie asked.

"I have too many things to do here and you did great at the first one. Don't worry about asking any questions but get a feel for the people and what they are thinking. Maybe talk to a couple of them and see how much our Muslim friends have been able to stir up in this short amount of time."

"Where is it going to be held?"

"Henry, is it going to be at the courthouse?" Ben asked the sheriff just before he walked out the door.

"I just got a text a few minutes ago that said it was going to be at Louis' church in Roxie. He's getting it cleaned up now for all the cameras."

"Where is Roxie? Everyone needs to remember that I'm not from here." Aggie said. She was frustrated in a way, because every second she spent not writing her story was one more second that she was going to have to stay here. On the other hand, the first press conference went so well, a second one might be just as fun.

"I would say let Jughead give you directions, but that didn't turn out so well last time." They all laughed for a moment, then a hush came as Maalik walked in the door.

"Well, hello Maalik. I would have guessed you would be at Maxine's press conference."

"Thank you, Sheriff, for trying to meddle in my business. My son is going to the press conference, but I am going to stay here and allow this esteemed newspaper man to fulfill his promise to take my statement. You do remember that promise this morning, don't you?"

"Yes, Maalik, I remember. I didn't get to talk to you at the earlier press conference, so I didn't know if you were still in town or not."

"I was going to go to Ms. Maxine's home, but I was informed by several people that I wasn't welcome. I believe this came from the Reverend Matthews, but I can't prove that. Apparently, I'm going to have to fight both races to get justice."

"I don't believe you're going to have to fight anything. You just need to stop and let the law do its job," Ben said in his most condescending voice.

"Papa, I am leaving now. Do you want me to come back and pick you up?" Aziz said as he walked into the room.

"Yes, that would be perfect if you would do that. I don't know how long the press conference will last, but I'm sure it won't be long."

Aziz looked over at Aggie and nodded his head. "Are you going to the press conference?" he asked her.

"Yes, I am, but I'm not sure where this Roxie is. I guess I'll put it into my phone and follow the GPS."

"If you would like, you can ride with me. We can talk about New York and other things we have in common."

"I don't like to ride with other people that much. I like to drive myself when possible. My father taught me that whoever was driving was in control," Aggie said. She didn't want to ride with Aziz but didn't want to seem like a jerk.

"Since you don't know how to get to Roxie and I have to come back here, I'll just ride with you. That way you will be in control, and I can still get you there."

"I guess we could," Aggie said. She knew she had no defense except that she didn't want him to ride with her and that wasn't a real excuse.

"Then let's get to Roxie. The press conference starts in twenty minutes."

As they walked out to her car, Aggie expected some kind of wow reaction from Aziz upon seeing her Porsche. It might have been a little bit arrogant, but most everyone had that reaction when they saw her car. Aziz however didn't act impressed or awed. He just walked over to the passenger's side and waited for her to unlock the door. When she got in, Aggie started to regret this decision. There wasn't anything wrong with Aziz; he seemed like a very nice person. Maybe that was it? He was so nice. She didn't know what to think of him. If her father knew she had the son of a Muslim Imam riding in her car, he would probably have a major heart attack.

"If you need to move the seat back you can. The switch is on the side," Aggie said as she backed out into the street. "No one has been in that seat since Archie rode there yesterday, so I don't know if he adjusted it or not."

"Thanks, I'm fine." Aziz acted as if they were driving in a 1976 Chrysler instead of a seventy-thousand-dollar Porsche. Maybe if she showed him how well it handled and how fast it could go, he would be impressed.

When she turned out onto the main street, Aggie saw that there was still a good bit of traffic in town, so she couldn't open it up much. As she drove past the hospital, she saw an opening and made a passing move that would have impressed any race car driver. When she whipped back into her lane after passing three cars, she saw that she was about to come onto what constituted as a bypass between Bude and Meadville. *I wonder if he has ever gone this fast through here?* Aggie said to herself. Looking at the speedometer, it was headed past eighty and still had lots of room when Aziz patted her on the shoulder. "What is it? Too fast for you? You know these Porsches have more horsepower than most cars."

"No, you aren't going too fast, but while you were trying to set a new land speed record, you went past our turnoff for Roxie." Aggie began to slow down and tried to think of something smart and catchy to say, but nothing came to her as she turned around to head back toward her missed turn.

"You're right about how fast these Porsches go. My Lamborghini I had when I went to Columbia was the only thing that could stay with the Porsches.

Aggie was shocked. "You had a Lamborghini?"

"Yes, I did. I got rid of it when I came back to Mississippi because the roads around here are not good for a high dollar car like that. I got a Challenger that I drive now. Oh, and by the way, you just missed your turn again." Aggie had been so surprised that Aziz had a Lamborghini that she had forgotten to turn again. "Do you want me to drive? I know you are proud of this car, but if we miss that turn anymore, we are going to miss the press conference." Aggie spun around in the middle of the road and finally turned onto the on ramp.

"You just give me the directions and I will get us there. While I drive, you tell me what really happened in New York. Bobby came up and you didn't get to answer my question. I know I haven't known you for long, but I am a very good judge of people. You didn't leave because you weren't making the grades. Columbia doesn't accept people who can't make the grades. The only reason people flunk out of Columbia is because they start using drugs and become deadbeats. I have a few friends who went there. That's how I know these things."

There was a silence that came from the passenger's seat that was louder than any sound. Aggie looked over at Aziz and his head was bowed. "I'm sorry if I brought up a bad memory." Maybe Bobby had been right and Aziz was embarrassed.

"No, it's not a bad memory, but I don't really talk about that time of my life."

"If it is going to cause you to have bad thoughts, then we don't have to talk about it. Just forget I mentioned it."

"No, I'm going to tell you. I don't know why I'm going to tell you because no one in the tri-county area knows the real story. But since the two of us have very overbearing and powerful men as fathers, I believe we have more in common than we realize."

Aggie laughed. "If you have a father who wants to control every facet of your life and is happy when you fail and have to come to him then, yes, we are alike."

"My father is not happy when I fail. He wants me to be successful in every way. He wants me to succeed him and become a Muslim leader myself. I am slated to move to Shreveport next year to begin setting up my own Mosque."

Hearing Aziz talk about his own Mosque and the Muslim faith made the air in the car seem stuffy to Aggie. With her Jewish heritage and Aziz's Muslim faith, they should be at each other's throats. Unless he didn't know she was Jewish. "I don't know much about the Muslim ways," Aggie said.

"Of course, you don't. I don't know much about Jewish ways."

"You knew that I was Jewish?" Aggie asked as she reached to see if her star of David was showing.

"Yes, I told you that miracle of technology—Google--can get you any information about anyone. Besides, Sharosh is not a European name. I figured out your heritage before I looked you up."

Aggie knew that the key component of a good interviewer was to never let the person who was answering the questions change the subject.

"But you haven't told me why you left Columbia?"

"I didn't leave because I couldn't cut it if that's what you're asking. I left because my father thought I was losing my focus. I am to be his heir apparent when he retires, and he has a very strict regimen that he wants me to follow."

"But why go to Columbia to become an Imam? Aren't there schools in the Middle East that you go to for that?" As they drove, Aggie noticed that the landscape on the highway was not changing very much. That must mean that this Roxie town was not very large.

"Yes, but my family is from Jordan and they are very fundamental about the faith. I wanted to get an education in something real before I took my place."

"What were you studying at Columbia?"

"I was studying to be a doctor. I was in pre-med and I was going to go to Harvard Medical School."

"Wow," Aggie said. "The pre-med program is hard to get into at Columbia. One of my best friends scored in the top one percent in the country on her SAT's but couldn't get into Columbia's pre-med program. You must be extremely smart! Did you study pre-med at Alcorn?"

"No, after I left Columbia, I just took business courses. I wanted to get finished and get my degree. That was what my father wanted, and I didn't have the desire to fight him anymore."

"You said he was worried about you losing focus. How were you losing focus?"

"He found some literature my roommate gave me that I was reading."

"What was it, porn? I know some guys that haven't read anything but porn since the tenth grade."

"No, I could have probably survived being caught with porn. What he found was something that he said was the greatest threat to the Islamic faith. It was Christian tracts. My roommate was a Muslim who had begun dating a Christian girl during our freshman year. He had converted from Islam to Christianity our second year. He was telling me things and I was asking questions. The literature was not anything special, but it was enough for my father to bring several high-ranking Muslim leaders from New York to give me an intervention. He acted like I was on crack instead of just talking to a friend. Not only did he make me drop out of Columbia, but my roommate lost his scholarship and got a terrible beating. His family disowned him and he had to move to Ohio to live with some friend's family he had met in his church."

"So, you had to leave Columbia because your father thought you were going to convert from Islam? What did he say to you? How did he find the literature?" Aggie had many questions because, in a small way, she could understand Aziz's situation.

"He told me that he had never been so disappointed in me. He said that if I had followed my friend, he didn't want to think what would happen to me. He then took my credit cards and closed my bank account. Even if I had wanted to stay at Columbia, I couldn't have. I tried to explain to him that I wasn't going to change, but he didn't listen."

"What did your mother say about this?" Aggie asked with genuine concern.

"My mother spent most of her spare time solving disputes between me and my father. Most of the time it wound up being a bigger fight between the two of them than it had been between him and me. My mother would try to make the best of things because she didn't like friction in the family, but my father didn't care what she said. In our culture, the opinions of the women are not important. Now slow down."

"Oh, I guess because I'm a woman you think that you can just tell me what to do, is that it?" Hearing what he said about his mother had awakened a womanly passion in Aggie that she couldn't fight.

"No, but if you don't slow down you are going to miss the turn into Roxie and that will be the third turn you will have missed in the last twelve minutes."

"Oh," Aggie said sheepishly.

"This isn't much of a town," Aggie said as she drove through what must be the main part of town. There were several dilapidated buildings and a small park with a basketball court, but there were no basketball goals. "How do they play basketball without goals?"

"They had to take them down because the crowds on Saturday nights were too much. Turn left right here and the Church is on the right."

Aggie didn't need to be told where the church was this time because there were three television trucks and a large gathering of people standing around a makeshift stage.

"I don't see any parking places. Is there a time limit or a meter charge?" Aggie asked. Aziz looked at her and she realized how ridiculous that question

90

sounded.

"I don't think there is a meter, but if you want to give me two dollars, I will put it in my pocket."

The church wasn't extremely large compared to those Aggie had seen in New York, but it was not small either compared to the few she had seen the last couple of days. It had white bricks and a metal building alongside. When she stopped her engine, Aggie noticed that several young African American men were coming toward them.

"Did I park in someone's spot?"

"No, those are some friends of mine. You are perfectly fine where you parked."

"How many friends do you have in the church in Roxie?" Aggie asked as they got out of the car. "I didn't think you would be very welcome around here."

"I have friends in lots of places. The religion of Islam is not the boogie man that everyone thinks it is. I have to get people to believe that and being friends with other people who look like me and have similar interests is a start."

As Aziz began to meet with the young men, Aggie noticed how all of them were very respectful and didn't treat him as an equal. They treated him like he was "somebody."

"Excuse me, could I get a word with you?" A voice asked Aggie. When she turned, Aggie saw the CNN reporter she had talked to earlier.

"I thought you got enough words earlier, Curt?" Aggie wanted to remind him that she still remembered his name.

"I got plenty of words from a small-town newspaper journalist. I didn't get nearly enough from the daughter of Hyram Sharosh."

"How did you find out who I am?" Aggie mentally kicked herself for speaking defensively.

"We are very information savvy at CNN. We took your picture and googled it. I don't want to make your life difficult, but my producers want me to get a story out of you about why you're here. You haven't quit Rutgers, have you?"

"My God, how much time did you spend looking up my info? Do you have my blood type too?"

Curt laughed. "I don't know, but I'm sure my friends in Atlanta can get it for me. If you have time, what about sitting down with me for a few questions after this press conference?"

The overwhelmed feeling was beginning to subside, and Aggie began to get her bearings. Looking at Curt, she smiled her best smile. "I don't know where you went to school, but the story of a young man being hanged should trump anything you might want to know about me. Now if you would excuse me, I have a press conference to cover." Then with all the arrogance she could muster, Aggie walked away leaving the reporter standing alone.

The press conference went relatively quickly. Ms. Maxine and her husband along with Reverend Matthews made statements. They were extremely sorrowful but had complete faith in the law enforcement officers of the county and state. Aggie knew this had to be coming from Reverend Matthews. Even in a small town, the story line could be affected by those in power. Not that she disagreed with what was said, but Aggie wondered if this would have been the statement if Aziz's father was the one giving counsel. Aggie saw Curt looking at her one time, but quickly turned her head. Obviously, others noticed his interest.

"I don't know what you told the CNN guy, but he has been staring a hole in you since this thing started," Aziz whispered.

"Don't worry about him. He just did the same thing you did and googled my information and wanted to ask me some questions."

"Well, well, well, I guess I'm not the only person interested in getting to know the young lady from New York."

Aggie didn't say anything. Aziz's statement that he wanted to get to know her was not a surprise. "I saw your little posse come out to get you, then they just disappeared into the crowd. Were they here to keep the peace or to make trouble if it was needed?" They were back in the car headed east toward Meadville.

"No, they were here just in case the crowd was small. My father wants to make sure that every camera sees a large concerned and angry group of citizens. When I saw that there was going to be plenty of people, I told them to just be seen and not heard."

"Would you and your father be as excited if the young man had been white?" Aggie asked. She didn't know why she said this but seeing Aziz's

92

expression change made her reporter instincts begin to buzz. It may not have been instincts, but just sheer dumb luck. Whatever it was, she saw that the question made Aziz uncomfortable.

"I don't know. Sometimes I am uncomfortable with the double standards my father takes."

Aggie almost ran off the road when Aziz said this. "You were the most vocal of anyone at the crime scene. I thought you were going to cause a riot. Was that all for show or do you really believe it? If it's for show, you better be careful where you perform it. One day someone may call your bluff."

Aziz looked out the window at the school bus graveyard they were passing. "I believe it, but I don't know if I would believe it so passionately if it wasn't for my father."

As his voice trailed away, Aggie decided to just drop the subject. Besides, who was she to tell anyone about father problems.

As they drove back into Meadville, Aggie thought about Curt, the reporter from CNN. It wasn't that she was uncomfortable with anyone knowing who she was. Her father was well known, and she also because she was his daughter. She just never thought anyone would look her up while she was in Mississippi. All she came here to do was to get the rest of her information and get back home. Who would have ever thought she would get into something like this?

"Thanks for your directions," Aggie said as they pulled up to the newspaper office. "I hope I didn't offend you with my questions?"

"No, you didn't offend me. I don't know why I talked to you about all those things. I guess you're just easy to talk to. You will make a great reporter. Maybe I'll see you before you leave," Aziz said as he got out of the car. He had texted his father when they had gotten off the bypass, so Maalik was waiting when Aggie pulled up next to Aziz's car.

"I hear the press conference was very well attended," Maalik said as Aziz got out of the car. Aziz didn't say anything, just nodded his head.

When Aziz and his father drove away, Ben walked to the door and leaned against the frame. "I guess it shouldn't surprise me."

"What are you talking about?" Aggie asked as she walked toward him.

"The murder is the most important story, but you are in second place all by yourself."

"Ben, I don't have any idea what you're talking about. What do I have to do with 'second' place?"

"I got a call from one of the producers at CNN. They are asking a bunch of questions about you, and you'll probably get some air time tonight. I should have known that God had a special plan for you. I just didn't know it would happen all of a sudden."

Aggie put her hands on her head and leaned against the wall. "I didn't ask for any of this. I just want to help you cover this story and on Monday I am gone. Then all the problems of Franklin County and all ten thousand of its residents will just have to make it without me."

"There are eighty-five-hundred people in Franklin County."

Aggie looked at Ben and wanted to shout at him that she didn't care how many people lived here, but she saw something in his face that stopped her. She also realized his comment about God. "What could God possibly have for me to do here? Do you really believe that God has any concerns about me or Franklin County or any other place? I mean, really, doesn't He have more important things to concern Himself with than me?"

"Aggie, you and I have a special heritage that many people don't understand. Because of that heritage, I can talk bluntly to you. Our people don't understand the personal relationship God has with us. The reason they don't understand that is because they don't accept Jesus as the Son of God. I admit that I didn't for a long time but, when I did, it opened up my understanding greater than at any time in my life. Since then, I have been a different person."

"I really don't need to hear about your understanding right now. I need some time to think. If you want me to keep helping you, I will stay at the office and keep out of sight. I don't want to take away from anything, much less this story." Aggie wanted to steer the subject away from God.

"I don't think you're going to be able to do that. You and I are going to go out to the crime scene and take a look around tomorrow. After that, we have some stories to write. While we are talking, I want to discuss compensation."

Aggie was still trying to gather her thoughts. "Compensation? Ben, I don't want any compensation. I have plenty of money, and you can't be doing that well here that you can pay an additional reporter. If you could, you would already be doing it."

"I don't have anyone working for me because I haven't had anyone come into my office that was worth paying. Now, you are either going to accept compensation or you are going to accept compensation begrudgingly. Either way, you are going to get paid. If you want to get out from under your father's influence, you have to learn to work and earn your keep. I promise, in the next three days you will earn every penny. I'm thinking a hundred dollars a day plus mileage to be paid every afternoon." As he said this, he pulled out a money clip and pulled out a hundred- dollar bill. This was one of several that Aggie could see. She looked at the money and was almost entranced. This was her first reporting job, and her father had nothing whatsoever to do with it. She had come here of her own accord, and she was getting paid because of who she was and not because of her father. She reached out and took the bill.

"If that's the way it has to be, then I accept." At that very moment, Aggie felt great satisfaction and thought of her mother. What would she think if she could see her now?

Ben smiled. "All right then, I'll see you here in the morning at 7:30."

Aggie almost argued because she loved to sleep in on Saturdays. But the feel of the money in her hand and the pride it gave her quickly stopped her from saying anything. "Okay, boss, see you then."

CHAPTER 9

The Good and Bad of Video

"I can't believe things like this still happen in the world." Annette and Aggie were sitting on her porch drinking tea. Aggie didn't know how she would ever go back to drinking the unsweetened version.

"Ben and I both believe there's something fishy about this, but it's too early to tell what it is."

"Momma, where are my cleats?" Archie shouted from upstairs.

"They are wherever you left them after practice Tuesday. Don't make me come up there and find them," Annette shouted at the ceiling.

"What time is the game?" Aggie asked.

"The game times are five-thirty and seven-fifteen, but the first game never starts on time and it doesn't ever end on time, so the seven-fifteen game is usually starting around eight."

"Why don't they start the games on time? Don't they have anyone who keeps things on schedule?"

"Aggie, my dear, you've never been to a Little League game, have you?"

"No, I was an only child and the boys in my school played basketball and soccer. I really haven't ever watched any kind of baseball."

"Until you've been to the Little League field in Bude you haven't seen real baseball, and it's not as bad as it used to be. I have seen many times where parents threaten to fight right in the stands. There were a couple of times that the umpires and coaches almost fought. Bobby doesn't have many problems because they know he carries a pistol, and they aren't sure if he has it on him when he's working a game." Aggie smiled at the image of an umpire having to pull his pistol to keep order in some kids' game.

"I guess Bobby won't be umpiring tonight," Aggie said as she poured one more glass of tea.

"Why, did he tell you something?" Annette asked in an almost alarmed tone.

"I just thought that with the murder investigation, he would be working on it and not doing something that, in the grand scheme of things, isn't as important."

As she was talking, Annette took her phone out and began to make a call. "Bobby," she said into the phone, "Aggie said you weren't going to work the game tonight." She listened for a few seconds to his answer. "Okay, that's what I thought. Archie is getting his uniform on right now, so I'll see you at the field."

After Annette hung up, Aggie looked questioningly at her. "Did he say that he's going to be at the ballgame?" Aggie asked.

"Oh, yes. I didn't think he would miss tonight. He hasn't missed a game in several years."

"But he was put in charge of a murder investigation just a few hours ago. How can he justify not looking for the killer so that he can work with a bunch of children? No offense meant to Archie or any of the other kids, but I think the case should take precedent."

Annette smiled and rocked in her chair. "Aggie, I know this is a big thing, but I know my brother. If he's going to be able to do a good job on this case, he's going to have to be loose and clear in his thinking. Don't you fret about him. If there are any clues out there, he'll find them. Now you enjoy the view, and I'm going to go upstairs and find my son's cleats."

As she continued to sit on the porch, Aggie pondered why Bobby wasn't going to be putting his full efforts into finding the killer. In the television shows, you never saw the police taking a break to do anything except to find the killer. Of course, that might be because those were television shows and not real life. Besides, Aggie didn't want to admit it but she wouldn't mind seeing Bobby again. It was nice talking to him this morning and again this afternoon.

While she watched the shadows getting longer on the front lawn, her phone rang. Aggie saw that it was her Aunt Rachel. "Rache, how are you?"

"I was doing pretty well until I turned the television on and found out that I have a famous niece. Now I am doing spectacularly. Is there any possibility that the young policeman I saw at this press conference is the one you were talking about last night?"

Aggie almost dropped the phone. "Rache, how did you know about that?"

97

"Darling, it's six o'clock on the east coast and you were the second story on CNN. They

led with the hanging of a young black man in Mississippi, and the next story was about this young Jewish girl from New York who was down South working for a local newspaper. They said something about how you brought up an angle that no one had thought about. What did your father say about this?"

Before she could say anything, Annette came to the door. "Honey, you need to come inside and see this. I just got a call from a friend of mine that you were on television."

"I just heard. My Aunt is telling me about it now. I'll be there in a moment." Aggie couldn't believe what she was hearing. "Rache, my father doesn't know about this because I didn't know about it. How long was the segment?"

"I don't know, maybe forty-five seconds. They were interviewing you and then they pulled up a picture from somewhere. How lucky could you get to be involved in a hanging? Are you going to solve the crime? If you do, will that hunky police officer help you?"

"Rache, I'm not here to solve anything. I didn't know they were going to do anything about me. I thought the guy was just hitting on me." Suddenly there was a beep and Aggie looked to see who was calling her. The name said "home." "Rache, I've got to go, my father's calling me. When I get this sorted out, I'll call you."

"That's what you said last night. I'm still waiting to find out who put you in handcuffs. Bye love." When the call disconnected, her father's call connected automatically. Aggie could hear him shouting at someone.

"I don't care who you have to call. I want to know what is going on with my daughter. I would ask her myself, but she won't answer her phone."

"Hello, Dad," Aggie said.

"Agnes, what have you gone and gotten yourself into? First, you're almost arrested and now you're working for some small-town newspaper that's covering a racial lynching. I want you in your car and headed home in the morning if not sooner. You don't need to be involved in this in any way. Do I make myself clear?"

Aggie was thankful her father had taken a breath. "Dad, I'm not involved

98

in anything. I was at the newspaper office this morning when the call came through, and Ben asked me if I would like to go with him. I had no idea what the call was, but I am not involved."

"I would beg to differ. I just watched my daughter interviewed by a reporter from CNN who asked you some very pointed questions. They said that you even gave a different angle to the investigation. Did you go south and become some kind of crime solver?"

"No, Dad, but even if I did, what difference does it make? I'm going to write a tremendous story and win that scholarship. You will be so proud of me and my story."

"Agnes, you are going to be getting lots of bad publicity that isn't necessary. Trust me, those people down there have been fighting and killing each other since before this nation was founded. The blacks and whites don't like each other. The truth be told, the only people they like less than each other are the Jews, and that includes you." Hearing her father's argument, Aggie remembered him using that same phrase about the wars between Iraq and Iran. "Now please don't defy me. I'm asking you to pack up and come home. If you want to follow the story, I'll pick up a byline for some of my reporters and get them to do a follow up story."

"Dad, I don't know what you saw on television, but I'm gonna finish what I started, because I am a journalist and you taught me never to be a quitter. I'll call you tomorrow if I get a chance. Thanks for calling."

Aggie walked into the living room and dropped into the chair like she had been living there all her life. On the TV screen in beautiful high definition, she looked like a real journalist. "Why is my picture on there?" Aggie asked. The sound was down, but the words "Northern reporter comes South" were written under the name Agnes Sharosh. Aggie began to look around for the remote control so that she could hear what was being said. As she looked, she heard Annette talking.

"Yes, she's a wonderful young lady." There was a long pause as the person on the other line talked. Aggie couldn't understand what was being said, but whatever it was, Annette was just smiling and pointing at her. "Well, Myrt, I'll let you go because I think our star reporter is looking for the remote control to hear what's being said about her."

Aggie finally found the remote and began pushing the volume button. "Why won't this thing work?" Aggie asked as she began to get frustrated.

"Because my husband has a knack of breaking things and then fixes them differently from how they originally worked. Here give it to me and I'll show you." Aggie handed the remote to Annette but didn't say anything. "You see, he accidentally dropped it into a glass of Coke one evening watching the Saints play. But since he is such a technological genius, or at least that's what he calls himself, he quickly took it apart and dried it up. He couldn't make the volume button work, so he made the menu button become the 'up' volume button and the caption button into the 'down' volume button." As she said this, she pushed the proper buttons and the volume came up.

"Oh, no, I've missed it," Aggie said. They were showing a commercial for one of those water hoses you can put in your pocket.

"Don't worry your pretty little head. We may live in the country, but we do have automatic recording on our Snap channels. I can rewind and you can see everything from the beginning."

While watching the pictures rewind, Aggie saw several shots she recognized.

"Was that your parents who called?" Annette asked.

"One of them was my father. My mother died a few years ago. The other was my aunt."

"Were they proud to see you on the world's greatest cable news channel?"

"My aunt was, but my father definitely was not. He said I should pack my things and get home as soon as possible. He said that I'll get bad publicity. I don't want any publicity. Did you hear what they said?"

"I heard a little bit but had to turn it down so I could hear what Myrt was saying. She talks so low, and it's hard to understand. You weren't the first story, but that boy sure liked talking to you and about *you*. Let's see what they said."

For the next several minutes, Aggie watched as the pictures were shown of the press conference, both at the courthouse and at the church. If she was critiquing, she would have to say that the courthouse looked more professional, but the church press conference seemed more real. Probably because the parents of the victim were the main participants. Aggie saw herself standing in the front asking her question, but the reporter was talking over her. They mentioned the investigation was ongoing and had the highest priority among all law enforcement in the state.

"That wasn't so bad. The way Rache and my father described it, I was the centerpiece." As the program came back from commercial, Aggie's opinion changed. A picture of her was set on the screen and her real name was under it.

"While the hanging of a young man is a huge story, sometimes in an investigation, you find other stories. This young woman works for the local newspaper. This of itself would not be abnormal because many young reporters start their careers in small towns. But this young lady is not a native of Franklin County. She is the daughter of one of the richest men in the country, Mr. Hyram Sharosh, a New York billionaire who owns several television and print media outlets." They then showed a picture of her father taken from several years ago.

"I see now why he's so angry," Aggie said with a snicker.

"The fact that she came to Franklin County and suddenly the story of the year occurs is something that's unbelievable. That she came up with an investigation angle that none of the professional law officers had thought of is the stuff of legends. The residents I talked to say she just got into town yesterday, but no one knows why she came to this small rural area of Mississippi. I talked to her and here is the interview."

As Aggie watched the interview, she couldn't understand why she was being focused on now. Obviously, her father had hated being mentioned. Saying what she said at the press conference wasn't that much of a big thing. Why would they focus on her for any reason whatsoever?

Bobby sat at his desk and looked at all the preliminary evidence reports. From everything he saw, this was going to be a doozy to solve. He had just left the coroner's office, and he said that the state crime lab would conduct the official autopsy, but as he had told the sheriff, the young man's neck was broken from being hanged. Bobby believed that, but there was something else that was bothering him. Where were the markings from whatever he had been sitting or standing on? There should have been some holes or other indented spots. If they had used the back of a truck or a trailer, there should be tire tracks. As he looked at all the crime scene photographs, Bobby couldn't see any. Maybe going back to the scene would give him a little more insight. There were two reserve deputies on guard twenty-four hours a day for the next few days. Bobby didn't want anyone coming in and adding or taking away any evidence.

"Sheriff, I'm going to go out to the crime scene and look around again. I know this isn't going to be easy, but I need to look one more time today."

Henry leaned back in his chair. "Do you need me to go with you? Sometimes two sets of eyes are better than one."

"You can if you want to, but I need to get myself in the right frame of mind. Now that all the press coverage is over, I want to get started."

"No, I believe you misspoke. The press coverage is just beginning. Are you umpiring tonight?"

"Yes, Sir. Annette just called and asked me the same question. Do you think I need to skip it and work on the case?"

"No, I was going to tell you to not skip it. This case is huge, but it isn't going to be solved in one night. That being said, tomorrow's different. I want everyone in the office tomorrow at 7:30 a.m. and staff meeting at 8:00. You, Wiley, and I will meet after that. Now go out there and look around." As Bobby turned to leave, Henry called him back.

"This is a big case and you need to guard yourself. There are some people who would like nothing more than for us not to be able to solve this. Those same people will be looking for opportunities to get under your skin. You are a lead investigator not only because you are my best investigator, but because you are my most level headed officer. I don't want to hear anything about you cracking somebody's head because the pressure got to you. Are we clear?"

Bobby smiled and gave the Sheriff his best Tom Cruise look. "Crystal."

When he got to the crime scene, Bobby realized that from this day forward, he would never be able to drive by this spot without seeing that young man hanging from the tree. That was an image he'd never get over. As he walked toward the tree, he saw Wesley and Douglas standing looking at the woods. They were the two oldest reserve officers Franklin County had. There were even rumors that Wesley had once been a member of the Klan but had gotten out after his daughter was born. Douglas was the smartest person in Franklin County. If you didn't believe it, then you could ask him and he would tell you.

"You two are doing a terrific job," Bobby said as he walked up to them. "The only problem I've got is what happens if you go to sleep tonight?"

Wesley held out his hand to Bobby. "Young feller, I have stayed up all night more nights than you have been on this earth. I thought I might turn out my fox dogs and listen to them tonight."

"If he goes to sleep, I'll give him a little jolt with old Bessie," Douglas said as he patted his taser.

In Bobby's opinion, the best decision Henry Wactor had made since becoming sheriff was to take the pistols away from the reserve deputies and let them carry tasers. None had fired them yet, except at each other during training.

"As long as you keep old Bessie in the holster until I get out of here, I don't care. Has there been anybody around since y'all got here?"

"Only two cars came up, but I told them that Doug had the safety off old Bessie and they burnt their tires up getting out of here. What are you doing out here, Bobby?"

"I wanted to come out and get another look at the scene. You two aren't moving around anywhere except the designated areas, right?"

"We've been sitting right here or walking down the path Billy marked for us if we have to go pee. Are we really going to have to pull twenty-four hours out here?" Douglas asked.

"I have talked to Phillip and Rudy and they are supposed to relieve you at 12:30 tonight." While he talked, Bobby looked around for something that might have slipped past him earlier. His idea about the game cameras was still in his mind, the best hope for a quick breakthrough, but they hadn't found any yet. "Wesley, do you know who has the lease on that property?" There was a fence not fifty yards from the crime scene.

"I think that belongs to some folks from Louisiana. You don't think they were involved do you?"

"No, nothing like that, but I was wondering if they might have a game camera somewhere over there."

Douglas stood up and pointed. "Do you mean like that one up there?"

Bobby turned and looked in the direction Douglas was pointing. All the land had large pine trees on it, but where he was pointing was higher than where they had been looking.

"What are you looking at Douglas? I can't see anything." Bobby said as he kept trying to see what Douglas was pointing at.

"That's because he has almost x-ray vision when it comes to seeing things in the woods," Wesley said. "He's color blind to green and other colors, so anything that is camouflaged stands out to him like a pee hole in a snow bank. He's telling the truth. That box up there is flat against the tree and looks like it's orange.

"I can't see anything." But before he said anything else, Bobby saw the outline of something that was sticking out from the tree. It wasn't very wide and it looked like it was covered in camo tape or paint. Bobby began to walk around so that he could see the side of the tree. "Douglas, you don't know what you just did for me. That could close this case before the weekend's out."

"Bobby, I don't mean to tell you your business, but you are tromping through your crime scene. You've done knocked over five flags and some crime scene tape." Wesley had a hint of sarcasm in his voice.

"Wesley, if that camera is working, it won't matter about anything else. Have you got a ladder at your house?"

"You know I do. I've got anything you could ever think of to work with."

"If you don't mind, would you and Douglas please go get it and bring it back to me. I've got to call the sheriff and get permission to go over there and get that camera."

As he waited for Wesley and Douglas to come back with the ladder, Bobby wondered what kind of publicity he could get for solving this murder so fast. Sheriff Wactor had been almost giddy when Bobby told him that they had found a camera. Even though Bobby had assured him that he could handle things, the sheriff had insisted that he was going to come out and assist. He had also given Bobby the number to Judge Jordan who gave the authority to go onto the other property and get the evidence. The warrant would be signed in a few minutes, but since no one was there except law enforcement, there was no need for the warrant to be on sight. Bobby had not understood why the sheriff wanted Judge Jordan to give the go-ahead and sign the warrant until he remembered that the judge was Ms. Maxine's cousin. He would be willing to do whatever was necessary to find the killer of his cousin's son. That was one of the many things Bobby admired about Sheriff Wactor.

He was always thinking and looking at every angle.

When he looked at his watch, Bobby saw that he was not going to make it to the ballgame tonight. "Oh well, I believe solving this case is a little more important than umpiring a bunch of eleven- and twelve-year olds."

While he waited for the commissioner of the league to answer his phone,

Bobby decided to sit down in Wesley's chair. It was definitely not a regular fold out chair. It had a foot rest and a cooler underneath. Bobby moved the binoculars and reached in and got himself an ice-cold ginger ale. He knew Wesley loved those things, and if Wesley had a cooler, it was going to be full of ice and ginger ale.

Tim didn't answer the phone, so Bobby left him a message explaining that something had come up with the case and he was sorry about being so late in calling. As he put his phone down, Bobby saw something out of the corner of his eye. It was in the field about two hundred yards away. There was definitely some kind of movement, but he couldn't be sure what it was. *Probably just a deer or coyote*, Bobby thought as he looked over the area, but just to be on the safe side, he took out Wesley's binoculars. Scanning the edge of the woods, Bobby couldn't see anything out of the ordinary but, after this morning, what was ordinary anymore? Still, he kept scanning and looking for any sign of whatever caught his eye.

After forty-five minutes, Wesley and Douglas drove up and brought the ladder to the field. "I hope this is tall enough for you," Douglas said. "I tried to get him to bring the sixteen- footer but Wesley said this twelve-foot ladder was plenty tall."

"I'm sure it's tall enough. Just bring it over here and let's set it against the tree."

"Be careful Bobby. Douglas has to hold it with his left hand so he can keep the right one free. You never know when someone might come up and try to get the drop on us, ain't that right Douglas?"

"Wesley, you are the most incompetent deputy I've ever met. You don't ever think of the what ifs in this world. I like to keep my options clear and my right arm clear. Because of this, I'm better protected than you are. Bobby, you're a full-time deputy. Tell this goof ball I'm right."

"Technically you are right Douglas, but when we are in a field with a line of sight about two hundred yards behind us and fifty to seventy-five-yard ahead of us, I think if someone decided to come at you, you'd have time to put the ladder down and take care of business. So, in a sense, you're both right."

"By George, Bobby, you are going to be one heck of a politician. You just listened to an argument we were having and told us we were both right, and we were both wrong, and both of us are satisfied. That is the true sign of an old school political operative. How are you enjoying my ginger ale?"

"It sure tasted good. I knew if you had a cooler out here, it was going to be full of ginger ale."

Now that he knew where to look and what to look for, Bobby didn't have any trouble seeing the box on the tree. When Wesley put the ladder up against the tree, Bobby started to climb. After three steps, he heard a car drive up. Looking over his shoulder, Bobby saw Sheriff Wactor had parked his car and was getting out. Bobby had to give it to Douglas, the twelve-foot ladder was plenty tall enough. Though he wasn't scared of heights, looking at the top rung made him realize that twelve feet was still very high in the air.

"You better be careful up there, young'un," Wesley said. "If I'm not mistaken, that's a nest of some kind above that camera. I didn't see it till we got closer over here."

"What do you think is in there?" Bobby asked as he started to cut the zip ties that were holding the camera.

"It may be an eagle or it may be a hawk."

Douglas began to laugh. "I thought I had heard everything. An eagle nest out here, and we have never seen the eagle. You don't know enough about eagles to fill up the head of a pin."

"What do you think it is then since you are such an expert in bird nests?" Wesley asked with a hint of annoyance eat his friend doubting him.

"It might be a robin or something like that but nothing that'll hurt you unless there are eggs in the nest."

"The two of you can argue about who is the best bird watcher later," Bobby said as he took the camera loose from the tree. Right now, I've got to get down and get this to the office."

As Bobby took a step down the ladder, his foot slipped and he began to lose his balance. Since he had the camera in one hand, he only had one hand to hold on with. Any other time this would have been enough, but at that very moment, the parents of whatever eggs were in the nest right above his head returned. Though he was not disturbing the nest, the birds didn't understand that and began to fly around Bobby's head. This, along with the earlier slipping of his foot, caused him to completely lose his balance.

Henry Wactor was walking toward the tree listening to Wesley and Douglas argue about the birds when he saw Bobby slip. It looked like things were happening in slow motion as he saw Bobby try to regain his balance but lose it when the birds began to come around his head. As he fell, Henry opened his mouth to yell, but the sound of Bobby hitting the ground like a sand bag sucked all the air out of his body. Running the remaining steps, Henry knelt down beside his deputy.

"Sheriff, I couldn't do anything," Wesley said. "As he fell, the birds followed him down. Is he ok?"

"I'm not sure," Henry said. "But I think he's hurt bad."

CHAPTER 10

What Do You Do When You Can't Do Anything?

Nothing in her life could have ever prepared Aggie for what she was seeing right now. It seemed like the entire population of Franklin County, Mississippi, was attending a baseball game played by, not major leaguers, but ten-, eleven-, and twelve-year-old boys.

"I really can't believe that there are this many people here," Aggie said to Annette. "Is it like this every night?"

"Oh, no, it's not every night, just Friday and Saturday nights. When we were a dry county, this was the extent of excitement around here. That and the occasional celebrity from New York." Annette was giving Aggie a hard time because since they had been at the game. No fewer than fifty people had come over and told her they had seen her on the news. Several of the young girls had asked if they could take a picture with her. Jughead had been heard bragging that he was the reason she was still in Franklin County.

Aggie didn't mind the attention; in fact, she quite enjoyed it. Nothing about any of this was because of her father. It was because of what she had done and what she had said. Even the hundred-dollar bill sitting in her wallet was not because of her father. Aggie wasn't excited that someone had lost their life, but she was getting some publicity, and that couldn't hurt her in her desire to be her own woman and make her own way out from under her father's shadow. She just wished that Bobby had been able to come to the ballgame. He had called Annette and told her that he had a potential break in the case and had to follow up on it. Aggie couldn't hide that she was somewhat infatuated with the tall deputy. She had not followed through with the call to her Aunt Rache with all the information about Bobby, but she knew that when she got home, she would tell her all about him.

"What time does Archie's game start?" Aggie asked, trying to get the thoughts of Bobby out of her mind.

"According to the schedule on the wall over there, if he plays for the Pirates it will be another thirty or forty-five minutes," a voice said from behind her.

Aggie turned around to see Aziz standing there smiling.

"If you are following me, I must advise you that I have a very large security detail."

"No, Ms. New York, I'm not following you. I came to see my cousin play. He plays for the Giants, and they are playing the Pirates. Do you mind if I sit up there beside you?"

"I guess you can. I didn't see any reserved seating." Aggie felt some funny vibes coming from some of the people who were sitting below her. As she had been talking to Aziz, they had looked over their shoulders and then turned away. Their disgust was obvious. Aggie wondered if it was because he was a black guy, or because he was a Muslim, or both?

Obviously, he saw it also because the look on his face changed ever so slightly. "Maybe I'll just stand back here. Where is Deputy Bobby? He isn't umpiring tonight?"

"No, he had to work," Aggie said.

"I am pleased he chose to work on this high-profile case instead of coming to work at a youth baseball game."

When Annette heard her brother's name brought up, she sat up a little taller. "Young man, I hope you are not going to come around here and start trouble. You are welcome to stand behind me, but I won't put up with any negative comments about my brother. If you feel the need to say anything negative, I suggest you do it away from me."

Aziz opened his mouth to respond but apparently thought better of what he was about to say. "Ma'am, I meant no disrespect. I only meant that, never mind. I hope he is able to find the person or persons responsible for this heinous crime."

Aggie looked around and saw Annette's husband with several other men making their way toward the stands. Looking at the group, Aggie had the feeling of dread that there was no way this was going to end well. But as hard as she thought, nothing came to mind to diffuse the upcoming situation. While Aggie watched the group of men and the impending disaster she envisioned, Annette's phone rang. Aggie didn't pay any attention to the call until Annette screamed.

"What is it, Nette?" Aggie asked as she grabbed hold of her arm and Nette's husband came running over.

"Bobby fell out of a tree at the crime scene." Annette was crying now but

109

trying to regain her composure. "That was Sheriff Wactor. They're on the way to McComb to the trauma unit. Henry said he didn't know for sure, but from what he could tell, Bobby had no feeling in his legs and was barely conscious."

By now, the group of people who had been headed toward Aziz was surrounding Annette and had been joined by several others who had heard her scream.

"Grab Archie. We've got to go tell Momma, and then I'm going to the hospital," Annette said. "Everyone please pray for Bobby."

"Let's do it right now," someone said. With these words, Aggie saw something she had never seen before. All the people who were gathering around them began to grab each other's hands. Aggie looked at Aziz to gauge his reaction. He must have been able to recognize the confusion that was on Aggie's face. When she opened her mouth, he put his finger to his lips, telling her not to say anything. He then motioned for her to come over and stand beside him. Aggie turned, hopped off the bleachers, and stood beside Aziz. As she did this, a woman appeared out of nowhere and took Aggie by the hand. Aggie was beginning to get the gist of what was going on and grabbed Aziz by his hand. Everyone had their heads bowed and their eyes closed. Looking over at Aziz, she saw that his eyes were closed also, so Aggie closed hers, too. As she wondered what was going to happen next, someone in the group began to speak.

"Oh, Lord, we come to you asking for forgiveness of all our sins. We come to you knowing that without you, we are nothing. We come now joined together as you commanded us, uniting in prayer for our brother in Christ, Bobby, who has been injured. We don't know the extent of the injuries, but you do, and we thank you for what you are going to do in his life. We praise you for your goodness and ask that you bless Annette and her family. We believe that you know what is best and everything that happens is what you want to happen. So we trust and glorify you. Bless us to be closer to you in the future than we have been in the past. Thank you for each person who is hand in hand. Bless our community and bless our people, in Jesus' name, Amen."

Aggie realized that this was a prayer. Though she had heard many Jewish prayers, this one was different from any prayer she'd ever heard. This man whom she could finally see, and who didn't look like a priest of any kind, had jumped in and started to pray. What he had prayed had been so clear and concise, it was like he had it written down. But that couldn't have been true because he didn't know a prayer like that would be needed. As everyone

110

began to look up and turn loose the hands they were holding, Aggie noticed that most of them were crying. Aggie made her way back to Annette.

"Nette, is there anything I can do for you?" Aggie didn't know what to say but felt like she needed to say something.

"Just pray dear. I'm on the way to the hospital right after I go and tell Momma. You're welcome to go to the house. I didn't lock the door, so you don't need a key. I'll call when we know something."

"I don't know about praying, but I will definitely be thinking about you and Bobby." As she said this, for the first time, the true seriousness of what must have happened to Bobby hit Aggie. What if he died? Why did she care? Why did the fate of a man she had only met the day before matter to her?

"Do you need anything?" Aziz had walked up and was standing behind Aggie.

"I'm going to Nette's house. That's the only place I can go." Aggie was trying to get her composure. "Remember that I am not exactly a household name around here."

"You're welcome to come to my home if you don't want to be alone."

"No, I think I had better go to Nette's house. No offense, but I don't know you that well either."

"You're right on that point. I would offer to come and wait with you, but I'm not sure Annette or her husband would appreciate that either. If you need anything, don't hesitate to call me."

"Thanks, but I'm sure I'll be okay. Besides, I don't have your number."

"Yes, you do. I put it into your phone this afternoon on the way to the press conference."

"Smooth move. All right, I guess I'll talk to you later."

Watching Aziz walk toward the other side of the field, Aggie wondered about the young Muslim man. He was a completely different person when he wasn't surrounded by his father and all their followers. For that matter, she was a different person when she wasn't around her father and his lackeys. This was one of the many things Aggie was beginning to notice that she and Aziz had in common. That and the fact that neither one of them was very comfortable around these Southern Christians. During the impromptu prayer, she had opened her eyes and looked around. Everyone had seemed so sincere. When she looked at Aziz, she expected him to look as pessimistic as she was. The funny thing was, the whole time, he had his eyes closed and his brow was furrowed, almost like he was praying too. Aggie hadn't asked him about it because maybe that was how Muslims prayed, and he was just joining in the only way he knew how. All she knew was that Jews didn't pray like that, at least none of the ones she knew. Even her father didn't act like he could talk to God with such impertinence. Only the priests could talk to God. That was what she had always been taught, but for some reason Annette and these other people believed they could talk personally to God.

"Aggie, Aggie, I need your help."

Aggie turned around hearing Annette's voice. "What is it? I thought you were leaving?"

"I was leaving, but Jack has a flat on his truck and, since I rode with you, I don't have my car. Can Jack and I borrow you and your car? I don't want to waste any more time. I'm not even going to go to Momma's house. I'll call her on the way. Besides, I'm sure you and your Porsche can get us there faster than Jack's truck"

"No problem, let's go." Aggie felt a little exhilaration. She didn't know if it was the excitement of being needed, or the fact that she was going to be able to see Bobby.

Jack insisted that Annette sit in the passenger seat, and he would sit in the back seat with Jughead. Obviously, he had never been in the back seat of a Porsche. Even more obvious was the fact that he wasn't used to riding in the back seat at more than a hundred miles per hour. Annette was on the phone talking to her mother and trying to calm her down. Sheriff Wactor had called right after they got into the car and said Bobby was breathing on his own; but there were still some real worries about whether he had any feeling below the waist. Someone had called and said the ambulance had just arrived at the hospital, and they were taking him straight into surgery.

"This is awesome," Jughead said. "I can't wait to tell everyone how fast this car can really go."

"You won't tell anyone anything. I just hope we make it there in one piece. If we run over a nickel, it'll probably flip us," Jack said.

"Hush your complaining, Jack. I remember you and me going a lot faster than this in your old Nova when we were dating," Annette said as she put her phone in her purse.

"Yeah, but I was driving and that old Nova had more metal in the front fender than these cars have in their entire body. No offense, Aggie."

"None taken. I understand your concerns. I like to be the one behind the wheel also. How is your mother?" Aggie asked Annette.

"She's better than I am right now. Do you remember Brad from the dinner party? He's going to stay with her. He's my third cousin and the closest relative I could get hold of. Since he is a pharmacist, he will also have some happy medicine for Momma in case something happens." She turned and looked back at Jack and tears began to flow again. "What if he doesn't make it?"

Jack reached over the seat and put his arms around her. "Honey, we're going to trust in the Lord and the good doctors they have in McComb, but mostly the Lord. We asked Him, and He is going to take care of Bobby."

Aggie watched out of the corner of her eye and could actually see Annette take a deep breath and compose herself. "You're right. If I can't trust the Lord with this, what can I trust Him with?"

As Aggie listened, Jack and Annette continued to talk about what they were going to do at the hospital. Their dependence on prayers to do something was so foreign to her. She wanted to ask more questions but didn't think they needed her and her questions right now. As she focused on keeping the car under control, her phone rang. Since she was driving faster than was safe, Aggie didn't look at who was calling, but hit the hands-free button. "Hello, you are on hands-free." She said this just in case it was her Aunt Rache. Sometimes she said things that other people didn't need to hear.

"I'm relieved you are at least using the safe, hands-free option on your phone, Agnes. At 110 miles per hour, you need all your focus on the road, even if it's on a four-lane highway. Where could you possibly be going that requires you to travel at that speed? Haven't you had enough trouble with the law?"

Aggie couldn't respond to her father's voice. Nothing came to mind that she could say to him. The deafening silence in the car proved that Annette and Jack were also shocked into silence. "Daddy, how are you," Aggie finally managed to say.

"I am fine, but you didn't answer my question. What could possibly be so important that you have to travel in excess of 100 miles per hour? Well, at least you are slowing down now." Aggie looked down and saw that she was down to 85 miles per hour and slowing.

"I'm on the way to the hospital. My friend Annette's brother had an accident and he's at the hospital. They had a flat tire on their truck and asked if I would get them to the hospital." As she talked, Aggie was getting her bearings. "How in the world could you possibly know where I am and how fast I'm going?"

"I had a GPS tracker installed on your car. Just in case I had to come down south among all those Neanderthals and get you. Did all the tires on their old pick-up truck go flat? Is that why you are endangering both you and your, and I use this term loosely, friends' lives?"

"Daddy, I don't know what you are thinking, and though I appreciate your concerns for me, I will go and have this GPS tracker taken off my car as soon as I get home. And since I am on hands-free, I would appreciate you not making disparaging remarks about my friends. We are on the way to the hospital, and if there is anything else you need, please text me."

"Mr. Sharosh, this is Annette Walker. I apologize for your daughter scaring you, but my brother is a deputy sheriff and he was injured on the job. I will be tremendously in your daughter's debt. I am truly believing that the Good Lord sent her. I don't know what He has in store for her, but I'm excited to see."

"This deputy, please tell me he is not the one who tried to arrest my daughter. I talked to some young man who told me the police were arresting her."

"Yes, Sir, that was me you talked to," Jughead said from the back seat. "But Bobby didn't arrest her because Sheriff Wactor showed up and cleared everything up."

"Archie, shush," Annette said.

"Daddy, I'm going to hang up now. Thank you for embarrassing me. Have a good night." Then, as if he could see her, Aggie punched the disconnect button as hard as she could. She then gave the car more gas. The Porsche had plenty of power left and quickly got back up to 105.

"Aggie, you need to slow down. We're almost to the interstate. Even though this thing probably banks a curve as well as anything with wheels, I don't want to be a smear on the bridge," Jack said. Hearing Jack scared from the backseat broke a little of the tension that was still in the air from her phone call.

"I understand, Jack. I wouldn't want you to leave this world all folded over in my backseat."

"Aggie, honey, I don't mean to intrude on you and your family business, but what is his deal? I understand he doesn't understand a lot of southern ways, but I could sense a genuine disdain and arrogance toward us, and he's never even met us! It was a hatred for someone he has never seen that I've never experienced before."

"Nette, you have to understand my father. He's a true believer in the idea that the Jewish people are the chosen people. Also, he feels that everything he has seen about the South on television is a true rendition of Southern people. If it makes you feel any better, he feels quite superior to everyone, not just Southerners."

"I guessed that. I started to say something more, but I'm sure that would have been counter-productive. Is that the reason you came down here, because your father hates the South so much?"

"Like I said, it's not that he hates the South, my father doesn't have any great feelings for

anyone who isn't Jewish." Aggie wanted to tell Annette that she should try living with her father if she wanted to truly experience a counter-productive attitude but, before she could, Annette's phone rang.

Aggie was thankful for the moment's respite so that she could get her own thoughts together. She hadn't been kidding about getting rid of whatever GPS bugs her father had installed on her car. If it became a problem, she would just give him the car back. As she thought about this, she reached up and rubbed the leather console and felt the finish on the steering wheel. *But I really love this car*, she thought.

"That was Sheriff Wactor. Bobby is going into surgery right now. They were going to send him to Jackson, but the surgeon didn't want to wait any longer. He said that every minute they waited was a minute more toward complete paralysis. Aggie, we are on the interstate and about fifteen miles from McComb. Get us there as fast as you can."

CHAPTER 11

Is This Where Healing Comes From?

In Aggie's opinion, just like most of the things outside of New York, the hospital in McComb was very small. Of course, her idea of hospital size came from her untold number of visits to St. Luke's when her mother had been there. Aggie stopped in the middle of the street as she realized that she hadn't been in a hospital since her mother died. She hadn't come to visit a friend or other family member or anything else. She'd gone through six months of therapy after the funeral, but that had been at the doctor's office. When she told her father, she didn't want to go anymore because she felt like she wasn't still grieving, he had agreed, and she hadn't gone back. Unfortunately, she hadn't been completely truthful with her father. Her grief hadn't gone away but having to talk about it to a stranger had made her more and more miserable. Both she and her father adjusted to their grief in different ways. He had gone deeper into his business interests, and she had decided she was going to become her own woman without her father pulling strings and making a way for her. The sound of a horn blowing brought her back to reality. That along with Annette calling her name several times.

"Aggie, come out of the road. Even though you aren't at home, there's still traffic here. I can't handle something happening to two people I care about tonight."

Aggie looked at the car that had blown its horn at her. "Sorry," she said as she walked toward the emergency room. "I was daydreaming."

"Annette, here we are," a voice called out. It was Sheriff Wactor and Ben.

"Where is he?" Upon seeing Henry and Ben, Annette's composure began to crumble. Being a pastor, Henry recognized this and put both his arms around her in a hug that was all about compassion. He then took one of those arms and wrapped Jack and Archie up in the hug. Finally, they separated and Annette began to wipe her eyes.

"He's in surgery now. I don't know how long, but the nurses are going to call me at the halfway point."

"You said he was numb. Is he going to be paralyzed? What happened to him? Where were you when this happened?" Annette's voice was changing

116

from fear and sadness to an angry tone.

Once again, Henry's pastoral experience kicked in. He put his hands-on Annette's shoulders and smiled. "Nette, I don't know if he's going to be paralyzed. He fell off a ladder getting a camera that we think may have pictures of who killed that young man. I was walking up when it happened, but Wesley said a bird flew out of a nest on the tree and startled him and he fell. This is the best trauma surgery center in Mississippi. The doctors are going to do all they can. We just have to pray for them to have strength and wisdom."

"A lot of good that'll do." Aggie didn't mean to say that out loud, but she had just blurted it out. Even though they were all standing outside with the sounds of the night, everyone heard her and turned.

"What do you mean, Aggie?" Ben asked. He had been standing over to the side talking to Jack and Archie.

"I mean praying for someone in the hospital hasn't been very successful for me." Even as the words came out of her mouth, Aggie was kicking herself for voicing what was in her head.

"Henry, take Annette, Jack and Archie to the waiting room. Aggie and I will be there soon." Everyone walked toward the front door. Ben walked over to Aggie, put his hand on her

arm and smiled.

"Okay, young lady, let's you and I have a little talk." The volume of Ben's voice was not loud, nor was he menacing in any way. However, Aggie knew that he was serious, and she didn't argue.

"Aggie, I'm not your father. In fact, we have not known each other very long at all. That being said, I also feel that you and I are kindred spirits in that we were both raised in the Jewish faith. Because I'm a very good judge of character, I know you are not a bad person. So that little outburst toward Annette was more about something that's bothering you than what is bothering her." Aggie opened her mouth to begin her defense, but Ben held up his hand and motioned for her to wait. "I'm not through, so please listen to me. I sense in you a battle that you don't know how to fight. Before you start to defend anything that you have said or thought, why don't you tell me what it is that you're angry at God about."

Aggie had opened her mouth, but this time she didn't stop because Ben had stopped her. She stopped because of what he had said. "Why didn't God make my mother well? Why should I pray to someone or something that

117

doesn't do what I asked Him to do? Why couldn't He have taken my…" but she stopped before she said it and broke down and began to sob. She didn't just cry but sobbed harder than she had since her mother died.

Ben reached out and put his arms around her. "Come on, and let's get this out of your system, then you and I can talk about how to go forward."

"What is there to go forward with? I don't have a mother and my father put a tracking beacon on my car."

"Your father seems like a very loving and caring man, and if I had a daughter who was going from here to New York, I would probably put a tracking beacon on her car also."

"You would do that to your child? I thought you had a bigger heart than that!" Aggie stated.

"A father does that because he has a bigger heart. I know most Jewish men aren't very big on talking about their feelings, but I would be willing to bet that your father isn't the ogre you make him out to be."

"What about my mother? I spent more time at the temple while she was sick than I did in my entire life and you know how much it helped? None at all. She still died and left me. She left me, and God didn't do anything to stop it. Or is he really your God since you have left the faith?" Aggie was trying to stop crying and regain some composure. She hated other people seeing her tears, and she also hated being told how wrong she was.

"Aggie, I won't say that I know how you feel about your mother's death. I lost my mother, and there is no way in the world that anyone ever hurt as badly as I did that day. What I will tell you is that God doesn't do things just so He can make us feel bad. He is a loving God and He just wants to have a relationship with us."

"How can He have a relationship with someone who doesn't believe in Him anymore and I don't know if I really ever did? You said your mother died, but weren't you angry at Him? Or are we just wasting our time believing in something that is supposed to love us, but really doesn't care or maybe doesn't even exist?"

Ben sat back and looked curiously at Aggie. "I don't think you believe that. I believe you are trying to justify your continued anger at God. I believe you know there is something better out there, and you are just too scared to face it. You are blaming God for your mother's death, but you don't want to form a true relationship with Him."

"I have the same relationship that my father has. I have been to every service he's been to. I've been through every ceremony there is for Jewish girls. I've done everything that they have told me to do. I have had it beaten into my head that I am one of Yahweh's chosen people, but I still don't have a mother. My father has more money than he will ever need, so I guess that is why he believes; but I don't have to believe."

"But still, you don't have happiness?" Ben asked. "Still, you don't have a piece that passes all understanding. You are spiritually miserable and you don't understand. That's the Holy Spirit convicting you and dealing with you. I'm here right now to show you the way to salvation and a new life with Jesus, but you are the only one who can accept this. If you turn it down, I don't know how many more times that the Spirit will deal with you, but I know this is one of those times."

"How can you know this? Did you have some kind of epiphany?" As she said this, Aggie took out her compact and looked at her eyes. Her mascara was running like she was in a death metal band. Seeing this, Ben reached into his pocket and handed her a handkerchief. "Don't worry, I haven't used it, so it's clean."

"Thanks," Aggie said as she began to wipe under her eyes.

"Aggie, I argued with God just like you are, but I used different arguments. I told Him that I was happy and that I was always right. I was able to argue with everything except His words in the Bible. I couldn't argue with them."

As he was about to continue his argument, Billy walked into the emergency room waiting area. "Ben, where's the sheriff.? I need to talk to him immediately."

"He's in the back with Annette, but I don't think he wants to be disturbed. Right now he's got his preacher hat on. What's so important?"

"Kenneth was able to pull some pictures off that camera Bobby was getting when he fell. I was on the way here when they called and told me. He said the sheriff wouldn't answer his phone, so I told them I would come and tell him."

"Do they know who did this?" Ben asked as his reporter switch came on.

"There hasn't been any identification but, from what Kenneth said, the pictures are very clear. With a little work they should be able to put them through facial recognition and get the people responsible."

"How many was it?"

"Kenneth said he saw at least four, but there could have been more. The one thing he did say that has me worried was that at least two of them were wearing those hats that those guys from over in Jefferson County wear. Those Muslim hats like Jim Brown wears. I want to tell Sheriff Wactor personally and find out how he wants to handle it."

"Wait a minute, do you mean to tell me that you think some of Aziz's people were involved in the murder?" Aggie asked. She had begun to compose herself and had walked over to hear what Billy was saying.

"Ms. Aggie, I really can't discuss this with you." Billy was kicking himself for letting her hear what he considered classified information. Especially since he had seen her riding with Aziz at the press conference earlier this afternoon. "For that matter, Ben, I don't need to be discussing this with you either. If you will excuse me, I have to talk to the sheriff."

"What do you have to talk to me about?" Henry had come out the door on the other side of the room and no one had noticed. "Billy, what have you got?"

Billy was determined not to make the same mistake twice. "I think it's best if we talk in private, Sheriff. This is sensitive information." When he said this, he looked toward Aggie.

Henry understood the gesture. Even though he had confidence in Aggie, he'd just met her only a couple of days before. "Ben, if you and Ms. Sharosh will excuse us."

"That's fine, you can tell me later what is going on, but how is Bobby? What did the doctors say?" Ben asked.

"He's in surgery now and they're waiting. I came out here to get some fresh air and try to get some power from the Lord. Annette is not taking this well, and the strain's starting to show on Jughead. Aggie, if you don't mind, would you go back there with her. I don't know why, but women seem to be comforted better by other women sometimes. Annette's going to let me send Jughead back with whichever deputy goes back home, and he is going to stay at my house with my wife. In fact, Billy, why don't you send Michael back right now. He can take care of any patrolling that needs to take place and get Jughead home to get some rest. Then come back up here and you can update me." Billy agreed and went to get Jughead to tell him to go with Deputy Michael.

120

Aggie wanted to say something smart about already knowing what Billy was going to tell him but decided against it. "Yes sir, I would be happy to." As she walked toward the back door, her mind began to piece together the puzzle of whether or not Aziz's father's people might have been involved in the murder. Even if what Billy said was true, that wasn't ironclad proof. Aggie knew what kind of hat Billy was describing. They were very popular in New York, and she had also seen them in other larger cities over the years. Just the hats wouldn't be enough to get an indictment, even in Mississippi, but it was very damaging evidence.

Walking down the hall, Aggie realized that she had not asked where she could find Annette and her husband. Even though this was a small hospital compared to what she was used to, it was still large enough to get lost in. As she looked down the hall, she saw a sign that read CHAPEL. *That's probably where they are*, Aggie said to herself.

When she reached out to open the door, Aggie felt a strange sensation. It wasn't a bad feeling, but it was different from anything she had ever felt before. It was so different that she stopped and just stood outside the door. If she had to describe it, it was like a warm ocean breeze that washed over her. There was also a feeling of peace that she couldn't explain. Aggie looked around to see if there was an air vent blowing warm air, but the ceiling and floors were both smooth with no vents in sight. For a few more moments, Aggie just stood at the door. She didn't know whether to go in or run away. The feeling was still washing over her as she stood with her hand on the knob.

Aggie didn't know what she was going to see, but she was trying to be prepared for whatever was in the room. The chapel looked like it had once been a waiting room but had been remodeled. There were several chairs and a small stage with a podium. There was what looked like a small electric piano in the corner and several shelves with books, but the lights were dimmed down so that she couldn't see clearly. What she could see clearly, and what caught her totally by surprise, was Annette and Jack lying down on their faces on the stage. Aggie listened and heard Annette's voice. Obviously, she was praying, but it wasn't what Aggie had expected. The voice didn't sound angry or upset.

Aggie remembered all the times when she tried to talk to God and asked Him to make her mother well and He had not heard her. All those long nights of crying and begging this God that her father said was the leader of their faith, and He did nothing for her mother. It had not helped Aggie at all, except to make her bitter. But here was a woman who was talking to her God

121

and didn't sound angry at all. She didn't sound upset or sad either. As she listened, Aggie heard Annette's words. She was telling God how great He was. She was thanking Him. How stupid was that? Her brother was in surgery and might be paralyzed or even die, and this woman was telling her God how good He was. Why wasn't she telling Him how good *she* was and how good her brother was? That would have made more sense to Aggie. As she listened to this prayer, none of it made any sense, but Aggie couldn't force herself to leave. Though she didn't understand why Annette was doing this in this way, something about the prayer deep down gave Aggie hope. Something about Annette's calm and smooth way of talking made Aggie feel this might not be a hopeless case yet. Besides, that warm feeling that she had felt outside the door was even stronger now that she was in the room.

What was it that Annette had that made her talk and act like this in a situation where everything looked so bleak? Why not go down and talk to the doctors? Why not talk to the nurses? Why was she doing this? Aggie decided to sit down and wait them out because, even if she didn't understand what was going on, she didn't want to be a disturbance. Both of them deserved that privacy.

Driving always gave Aziz time to gather his thoughts. When he had been summoned back to Mississippi from New York, he had insisted on driving instead of flying. It took most of the twenty-two-hour drive for him to come to the conclusion that his father was only doing what he thought was best for him. Now as he drove toward McComb, Aziz wondered why he was doing this. The only reason to go was because of Aggie. She was the one thing that he was concerned about. Since he had seen her at the crime scene, he had been able to think of little else. The way she acted around the deputy sheriff should have given him reason to forget these strange thoughts, but it did little to affect his feelings. His feelings were as clear as this stretch of highway was empty without anything else in sight. When his phone started to vibrate, he initially didn't realize it because he wasn't expecting anyone to be calling him. When he finally noticed, he saw that it was his father. Pushing the button on the steering wheel was so much more convenient than having to pick up the phone. "Hello, Father, why are you not in bed?"

"Where are you right now?" Maalik Saalam was not a man who gave in to emotional outbursts, so the anxiety in his voice was particularly offsetting to Aziz.

"I'm out riding. Why, is there something wrong?"

"You wouldn't be on Highway 98 headed toward McComb by any chance, would you?" Aziz looked into his rearview mirror to see if his father had

122

suddenly come up behind him.

"Yes, I am. How did you know this?"

"I am your father and your Imam. You are my son and my heir. I make it a point to know where you are at all times. Why are you going to McComb? Is there some business there you need to take care of at this late hour?"

"Father," Aziz was struggling to come up with a suitable story. If he told his father he was going to check on the Jewish girl and the injured deputy, he might explode. Then again, the one thing he hated was for someone he trusted to lie to him. "I am not going to McComb. I am going to a club in Summit." This meant he would have to go to a club to make the lie true, but it would be worth it.

"I need you to do something else for me. You will go to the hospital and talk to the receptionist in the emergency room. She heard something very troubling, and I want someone I trust to hear it firsthand instead of over the phone. You never know when a conversation may be recorded." Aziz smiled at the luck he was given.

"I will do as you ask, Father. But first, I must know. How did you know where I am? I told no one of my plans."

"I could lie to you and tell you that Allah told me, but you are too smart for that. Let's just say I have my ways. The woman is awaiting your appearance now. Do not bring attention to yourself. Try to have a reason for being there that has nothing to do with us or our people. Can you do this?" Aziz wanted to laugh at the question. His true intentions and reasons for coming to McComb would serve as a cover for whatever his father wanted him to find out. Truly, Allah must be looking out for him. But even as the thought came across his mind, Aziz questioned if he believed that at all.

"I believe I can make anyone who asks me believe I am there for anything except to talk to the receptionist."

Sheriff Wactor and Billy sat in an office just off the hall connecting the emergency room and the hospital. They were facing each other and the door was shut. They had to use the hospital phones because there was no cell signal in this part of the building. They were also using a computer and apparently searching the Internet. Billy had been completely blown away that his sheriff had convinced the on-call administrator to allow them to use the hospital communications equipment without a question.

"Kenneth, I need you to go back in and check to see if there are any pictures of these people walking out of the field."

"Sheriff, isn't this enough? You can clearly see five people half dragging, half carrying a young man toward the tree. What else could you possibly need? All we need is to get warrants to go out to that Muslim mosque and find our murderers."

"Kenneth, I thank you for getting these pictures, but I really wish you would leave the police work to me. Explain again to me why there aren't pictures of them leaving but there are pictures of them arriving?"

"Because, Sheriff, when Bobby fell, the camera fell also. This was an old camera with a limited amount of memory. It was set to only record when it sensed motion. Unfortunately, the fall from the tree damaged the camera almost as much as it damaged Bobby. I was lucky to be able to get those pictures."

"So, this is all we have." Henry took off his hat and rubbed his forehead because he could feel the tension headache coming on. "It's a start, but it's nowhere near enough. Kenneth, I'm giving you carte blanche to work on this all night if you have to. I want you to tear that camera apart and put it back together as many times as you have to, but I want the other pictures. I want to see them walk away without him and I want to be able to recognize something besides the dead boy and those two Muslim hats." Call me here at the hospital when you get something."

"Yes, Sir, Sheriff."

Henry was running on very little rest and it didn't look like he was going to get very much tonight. "Billy, what do you think? Do you believe Maalik and his people had anything to do with this boy's murder?"

"Sheriff, I don't know. I do know that they are hard-core. If somebody got out of line, then it's possible they could go to that extreme. But I have never heard of Ms. Maxine's son being involved with them. Anything's possible, but it doesn't make sense."

"Billy, beating someone to death or hanging a person by their neck until they die doesn't make sense either. Who did it is important, but we need to figure out why if we are going to find out who did this? I want the lid closed on this. No one but you and me and Kenneth are to be told of this. I don't want anyone knowing about this and alerting Maalik, whether he is guilty or not. Have you told anyone else?"

Billy grimaced at the answer he was going to have to give the sheriff. "I

124

told Ben and maybe that Aggie girl heard me, but that's all. They were the only two people in the room except for the receptionist and she was too far away to have heard anything."

"Billy, you are a good cop, but sometimes that hole under your nose gets you in more trouble than it should. I'll handle Ben and Aggie. You make sure no one else hears about this. Is that understood?" Henry stood up and twisted his back left then right, popping it, and making a sound like there were firecrackers going off.

"Wow, Sheriff, how can you walk after that?"

"That's the *only* way I can walk sometimes. You go out front and make sure that the receptionist didn't hear you. I'm going to go see if there's any word from Bobby's surgery."

The funny thing about her current situation was that Aggie hadn't gotten up and walked out. Though she didn't believe in the kind of praying that Annette and Jack were doing, something was keeping her seated with her head bowed. There had been no reaction when she had come in, so obviously Annette and Jack didn't know she was there. But that feeling of warmth and whatever else was still making an impression on her. Then it hit her. Maybe the reason she had not gotten up and left was because she didn't want to lose this feeling. Was this the only place you could feel it? Was there some kind of magic warmth spot in this hospital? Thinking back to what Ben had said, tears began to well up in her eyes again.

"Aggie, how long have you been here?" Annette asked. She and Jack were standing right in front of her now. How did they get there without her noticing it? Realizing that she was crying again, Aggie kept her head down while she looked in her purse for a tissue.

"Oh, I was trying to be quiet. I didn't disturb you, did I?"

"Aggie, why are you crying? What can I do for you?" Annette sat down beside Aggie and put her arm around her.

"Why are you worried about me? Your brother is in surgery fighting for his life and you are worried about me? My problems are nothing compared to that." As she kept talking, the tears kept coming.

"Jack, go see if there is any update from Bobby. I need to talk to Aggie."

"No, Nette, you go with your husband. I'll be fine."

"Aggie, I just spent almost an hour talking to God about Bobby.

125

Everything is going to be fine. You on the other hand are in need of help, too."

Aggie looked up at Annette and saw that she was smiling. "How do you know Bobby is going to be all right? Did you see some great flash of light that I didn't see? Was there a ball of fire that came out of the sky? How could you possibly know this?"

"I didn't say Bobby was going to be all right, I said *everything* was going to be all right. Because God told me, I am going to have faith and believe that He knows what is best for Bobby and me. I am going to believe Him because He has never let me down. He also told me that there was someone else who needed my help. I was assuming it was Jack until I got up and saw you in here. Aggie, I don't know what problems you are having or what you have against God but accepting Christ as your Savior is the only way you are going to be able to get to God."

"I don't need any help getting to God. I don't even know that there really was a Jesus." Aggie was quoting one of the lessons her teachers had taught about Jesus, that he might have been a good man but that was all he was.

"Aggie, you are lying to yourself and you are never going to be happy like you could be. I might not know much about your faith, but I do know about mine. I have a relationship, not a religion. Jesus knows my name and He talks to me. You don't know what a great feeling it is to know that the God of the universe knows you by name."

Before Aggie could come up with more of her argument, Jack came back into the room. Even in the limited light, Aggie could see the despair in his eyes. She could see that there wasn't any good news. "Nette, there have been some complications in the surgery. The doctors came out a few minutes ago and said they are going to just stop and wait, but it doesn't look good. They said you can come and stand outside the surgery center and the doctor will give an update or let you know." Jack hesitated because he didn't want to tell his wife the doctor would come tell them if her brother passed away.

Annette reached up and wiped a single tear from her eye and then looked up to Heaven. "Okay, Lord, I take you at your word. It's going to be all right. I'm going to go down here and see what you're going to do."

Aggie stood up to go with them, but Annette stopped her. "You stay right here. I'll let you know when we hear something. You talk to God and see if you can get right with Him." Arguing about religion was almost a talent with Aggie, and she was about to explain to Annette why she didn't need to do

126

anything, but the look on her face made Aggie stop.

"Ok, I'll stay here, but it won't do any good."

"We'll see. Come on Jack, you are going to have to show me where surgery is."

CHAPTER 12

The Fireworks Begin

"I could get away with anything in Franklin County tonight," Aziz thought. There were two deputy cars not counting the Sheriff's Escalade in front of the McComb hospital. "I guess everybody is here."

Since it was after 11:00 p.m., Aziz didn't bother with the main entrance. He knew they closed it at 9:00p.m. Besides, he had a mission that must take place in the emergency room. As he walked across the street, Aziz began to consider how he was going to explain his presence to all the white officers. It had seemed a simple thought when he was explaining it to his father, but now that he was almost face-to-face with the situation it didn't seem so simple. He knew he had to talk to the receptionist, but his father had been explicit that he was not to let anyone know that was why he was there. Telling everyone he was there to check on Aggie was all the reason he had, and now it seemed a little weak. Not to mention the idea that he was a black Muslim man coming to check on a young white girl still wasn't widely accepted in this part of Mississippi. The idea that she was a Jew wouldn't be that much of an obstacle. In fact, most people probably didn't know she was Jewish. Either way, it was too late to back out now. He had a job to do, and Aggie was going to be his cover. At least that's what Aziz told himself.

He saw the deputy named Billy as soon as he walked through the automatic doors. Even though he was one of two black deputies in the sheriff's department, Aziz knew there was no love lost between the two of them. Aziz's father said that any black man who had animosities toward him was either jealous or was of the Uncle Tom variety. Aziz tried every day to keep his father's prejudices from allowing him to make uninformed decisions about people. But in Billy's case, he was going to guess that the two of them would never be close.

"What are you doing here?" Billy asked with much more ferocity than Aziz expected.

"Hello, Deputy. I didn't know you owned this particular hospital. Did I need permission to come here?" Aziz didn't need much incentive to put up a fight when necessary. Truth be told, he actually enjoyed a little back and forth. It helped him relieve tension. As he looked into Billy's eyes, Aziz saw something that caught him completely by surprise. There was almost a hatred in his eyes.

"I don't own this hospital, but I own enough authority to arrest you for being a complete jerk wad. How about that? Or maybe I'll just pound you into the ground and call it resisting arrest."

Aziz didn't know what was going on, but he knew his rights. He also knew that this was Pike county and, though some law enforcement officers felt differently, a Franklin County deputy had no authority here. As Billy walked forward, Aziz had no choice but to meet his attitude with one of his own, but for the life of him, Aziz couldn't understand where this was coming from. Then if there wasn't enough tension, another deputy came around the corner. Recognizing the aggressive stance Billy was taking, he immediately assumed there was an incident about to erupt.

"You need a hand Billy? This guy looks like he's ready to take a swing at you."

"Naw, I've got this. You just stay ready in case he's got some of his thugs with him. Of course, if he doesn't have more than six or seven, I won't need any help."

"Why would I bring any help to a hospital?" Aziz asked? "I just came to check on Aggie and you two storm troopers come at me like I'm some kind of criminal that can't come to a hospital. Every time I think you guys are going to change, you do something to dash that hope." Aziz was talking clearly and not just because it was what he did best. Several times over the years he had seen unruly crowds confront his father. Every time they looked like this, and if there had been an altercation, it would have been awful for all sides. That was why Aziz was looking for a peaceful solution. Especially since he didn't have any backup at all.

"Billy, you and Rusty need to go down to the surgery area. The sheriff is down there and he wants y'all to come and pray with him. It doesn't look good for Bobby. Aziz, what are you doing here?" It was Ben walking into the waiting room and, at that moment, Aziz was never happier to see him.

"I came to check on Aggie. She seemed very upset at the ball field, and I wanted to make sure she's all right. I know what it's like to be in a strange place with things going crazy around you. Where is she?" As he asked the question, Aziz casually looked around the room to see if he could find the receptionist.

"Annette told me she is in the chapel. You're welcome to go there, but I wouldn't suggest you go any farther. Bobby and Rusty and the rest of the family are standing outside the doors to surgery." As Ben talked, Aziz watched Bobby and Rusty walk away. They were still staring at him even as retreated.

"Where is the chapel? If you don't know, I will ask the receptionist." It was a little clumsy, but at the moment, it was all Aziz could think of to get his mission started.

"You will have to wait a while. She left a few minutes ago to go get something to eat. She said something about being back in an hour."

Aziz mentally kicked himself because he had stopped and gotten something to drink before coming to the hospital. Those few minutes might be what cost him now. "Where could she be eating in McComb at this hour of the night?"

For just a fraction of a moment, there was a questioning look on Ben's face. Obviously, he was wondering why Aziz was so agitated about a receptionist going to get something to eat.

"If you want, I can take you down to the chapel. That way, I can buffer between you and the other guys and keep any bad feelings from flowing over. But there's one thing I've got to know. Does your father know you are here to see Aggie? I know he wasn't very excited about the two of you going to Roxie together this afternoon. Now you're driving all the way to McComb to see her. I don't claim to know a lot about him, but I do know that Maalik would not approve of you running after a young Jewish girl."

Aziz knew that what Ben was saying was probably true. Though there was a motive from his father for his being here, the truth was that he would have been here no matter what.

"Mr. Ben, please trust me. I am doing exactly what my father wants me to do. If you will just give me directions to the chapel that will be enough. I promise not to go past it."

Ben rubbed his chin for a moment. For those closest to him, they knew this was his gesture when he thought something wasn't quite right. "Go down that hall and it's the second door on the right."

"Thank you so much."

Aggie had moved down to the front row of chairs in the chapel and was looking up at the cross and the image of the man who was hanging there.

130

The feeling of warmth that she had felt earlier was still there. Something in this room was speaking to her, but she didn't know what it was or what it was trying to say. The entire time she had listened to Annette and Jack praying, she had wondered what it was that she wanted. Looking down, she saw a book sitting beside her on the seat. Picking it up, she thought it was some kind of song book. Turning it over in her hand, she saw Holy Bible written on the front.

"So, this is what one of their Bibles looks like?" Since she was alone, Aggie felt comfortable talking out loud. "What is in here that I haven't already heard about?" As she asked this question, she opened the book. When she did, she noticed there was a bookmarker of some kind. "I guess they have it marked for you to read what they want you to. But what do they do about it being dark?" Aggie said this because she didn't expect to be able to make out the words, but when she looked down, she was able to see and read the words clearly. There was a section highlighted in pink. "Well, since I'm this far, I might as well read what they have highlighted for me." *For God So Loved the World That He Gave His Only Begotten Son That Whosoever Believeth in Him Should Not Perish But Have Everlasting Life.* "What does that mean? I have heard of Christians dying every day. Bobby may die tonight."

"It means that God knew that there had to be a perfect sacrifice for our sins."

Aggie jumped up from the chair when she heard the voice. Looking back, she saw a woman standing in the door. She was an older woman, but her hair was not grey. She had on glasses, a shirt, a black vest and blue jeans. Nothing about her attire seemed special, but the clothes weren't what Aggie saw. This lady was smiling at Aggie like they were long lost friends.

"I'm sorry to have startled you, but I was walking by and heard you talking and asking questions. Can I talk to you and try to give you some answers? My name is Joan, what's yours?" It seemed that in the last few days she was speechless more than at any time in her life.

"My name is Aggie Sharosh. I didn't realize you could hear me outside the door. I must have been talking louder than I thought."

The lady walked down and sat beside Aggie and took the Bible from her hands. "Were you looking at John 3:16? Was that what your question was about?"

"Ms. Joan, I don't understand how you can believe in something that must not be true. I just read that if you believe in Jesus then you won't die. I know

131

lots of people die, and I'm sure many of them are Christians. How does a Christian believe anything?"

"Aggie, you are trying so hard not to believe. That verse you read means that you won't spend eternal life in Hell. We all have to die, but where we go after we die is what that verse means. Have you lost someone close to you?"

"Who are you and how do you know this?" Aggie was getting freaked out and was beginning to wonder if she had become part of some crazy religious reality show.

"I know this because I recognize the signs. I recognize the anger at God for allowing your loved ones to die. I recognize this because I have been there and done that. The one thing you have to realize is that you are not in charge of anyone but yourself. You are the only person you can do anything about. That verse you just read means that if you accept Jesus as your savior, he will save you from eternity in Hell as well as live inside of you for the rest of your physical life. You won't have to face anything alone for the rest of your life. No, it won't always be easy, but God's peace through Jesus is the greatest thing you can get. If you'll admit it, you have been looking for something like this for a long time. Why don't you just give in and accept what Jesus is offering you?"

Aggie began to cry. It seemed she had cried more in the last few hours than in her entire life. But this time it was different. Different from earlier with Annette. Different from all the hours of tears and therapy she had undergone after her mother's death. "What do I do to get this? I want this. Can you give it to me?" Aggie asked between sobs.

"No, I can't give it to you. I can only tell you about it and show you the way. You have to admit to God that you are a sinner and need a savior. Getting saved is the easiest thing in the world. Living saved is a little harder, but let's take one step at a time."

"Do you have something written down that I need to say? I've heard that you Christians make people say certain words. Do you have them with you?"

"Aggie, have you ever heard a true Christian pray?" Aggie thought for a moment and then remembered hearing Annette praying.

"Yes, I heard the woman I came here with earlier. But I don't really think she was praying right. She was praying like she was talking to a friend instead of talking to God. She said that was how she prayed, but I don't understand. How can you talk to the almighty God like that?"

"Aggie, Christianity is a personal thing. It's something between you and Jesus. You bow your head and you pray and ask for His forgiveness and tell Him you want Him to come into your heart. How you pray is left completely up to you.

Aggie stared at this strange woman who was talking to her. How could she do this to her family? How could she go completely against everything she had ever been taught? But right now, at this very moment, she was sure that was what she had to do. She needed this peace in her life. She wanted to know the kind of peace that Annette had and this woman had. "I just bow my head and talk?" Aggie asked one more time just for assurance.

"You just bow your head and talk. Actually, bowing your head isn't mandatory, but it's what most people do. One thing I can promise you, when you ask him to come into your heart, God hears you no matter what your eyes are doing. The only requirement is that it come from the heart."

Since bowing was something she could understand, Aggie decided to bow her head. As she wondered what her next words should be, Aggie decided to just open her mouth and see what came out. "Jesus, I don't know how I got to this place. I don't know why I'm here or what I am going to do. All I know is that I want what Annette and this Joan lady have. I want to stop hurting and missing my momma. I want to know that when I die, I know where I'm going to go. If what she said is true, then I accept you. I accept you, and I want you to be my God and my Savior."

As the words left her mouth, Aggie felt an even greater feeling of warmth than before. It felt like the weight of the entire world came off her shoulders. There were no tears. There wasn't any sadness. Only peace and a contentment she had not felt since she was a child sitting in her mother's lap. "Oh, Ms. Joan, you are right. I do feel different," Aggie said as she raised her head.

"Who are you talking to and who is Joan?" Aziz said. He was standing just inside the door with a perplexed look on his face. Aggie looked around the chapel, but she and Aziz were the only two people there.

"Aziz, you'll never believe what I just did."

CHAPTER 13

And Then This Happened

As she explained to Aziz everything she had just done, Aggie wondered if this was how all Christians felt. "Aziz, I feel better than I ever have. Ms. Joan was exactly right. I just opened my mouth and talked to Jesus. Are you sure you didn't see her walk out? She had to have walked past you."

"Aggie, I'm telling you that there was no one else in the room with you. When I came in, you were sitting there with your head down saying something. Now you are telling me that you have become a Christian. I know you, and I've talked about a lot of things regarding our parents, but have you even considered the repercussions from your father when he finds out? I was only *talking* to a *Christian*, and I got called back from college and almost exiled from my family."

"I don't know what my father will say, and I am not going to worry about that. I have become a new person and everyone is going to have to deal with that. Come on, let's go check on Bobby."

"I don't think you want to do that. I heard the other deputies talking about how it didn't look good."

"I don't care. I need to check on him. Also, I need to tell Annette what I did. Are you coming?" Aggie was already walking toward the door.

"I don't know that I'm welcome by the other deputies. I'll let you go talk to Annette. I need to talk to someone, but when you find out something, come to the front and let me know." During all of Aggie's excitement, Aziz had forgotten why his father wanted him to come to the hospital in the first place. Now that he had made contact with Aggie, his story was iron clad.

"Okay, but after a while, I want to talk some more to you about this choice I made." Aziz noticed that there was definitely something different about Aggie. Maybe it was just her voice, but something definitely changed. "I look forward to it."

Aggie knew that she was walking down the hall because she was moving, but if someone had told her she was floating, it would not have been a

134

surprise. Never in her life had she ever felt this free. Each breath she took seemed to be sweeter than any she had ever taken. As she turned the corner, she saw Annette standing against the wall. She was not looking at the doors to the operating room. In fact, to Aggie's surprise, she was looking directly at her. Without thinking, Aggie picked up her pace and almost ran to where Annette was standing.

"How is Bobby?" Aggie asked.

"The last thing we heard from the doctors was that he is partially stabilized, but he isn't out of the woods yet. If he comes out of this, he may be paralyzed, but we are hanging on." As she was talking, Annette began to stare at Aggie. "Aggie, what's going on with you? Did someone do something or say something to you?"

Knowing that this was a very tense situation for the family, and though she wanted to joyfully exclaim the decision she had just made, now just didn't feel like the time. "We'll talk about it later. I just want to be here to help in any way I can."

Annette still looked puzzled. She opened her mouth to say something but decided not to and just put her arm around Aggie and smiled.

Sitting at the receptionist's desk, Aziz wondered how long it took for someone to get something to eat this time of night. He had expected the receptionist to have returned when he walked back from the chapel. Unfortunately, the only other people in the waiting area were a couple of men who looked like they were homeless and were settling down to sleep for the evening. It was hard for Aziz to think that in a town as small as McComb, there were people that didn't have a home. Of course, compared to Fayette and Meadville, McComb was a metropolis. As he continued to think, a woman walked through the doors and headed toward the desk. Aziz thought she looked familiar. Apparently, she recognized him immediately, because she hurried over to the desk and began to apologize for being late.

"I am so sorry. My car wouldn't start, and I had to get my brother-in-law to come over and jump start it. I didn't realize that they were going to send you."

"Who did you think was coming?" Aziz asked.

"They just told me that someone would come and that I should wait to tell that person what I heard. I am so unworthy for the son of our Imam to be here with me."

This was not the first time that someone had showed him such respect, and it would probably not be the last, but that didn't make it any easier for him. Something about this kind of adoration made him feel uncomfortable. His father, on the other hand, seemed to revel in it. Thinking about his father made Aziz remember why he was there. Contrary to his true feelings, he was there to find out what this woman had heard.

"I understand your feelings, but time is of the essence. I would rather the sheriff's department not know you overheard anything. Tell me what was said by the officers."

"I heard that other black deputy come in and tell the white guy and the young lady that they had pictures of the people who murdered that poor young man. He also said that two of the people in the pictures wore those Muslim hats that they wear in Jefferson County. When he said this, I almost went over there and gave him a piece of my mind, but I decided that I could do better if I just listened and found out what they knew. When they went back, I immediately called a friend of mine, and he was the one who told me someone would be here. What are you going to do?"

Obviously, she expected Aziz to handle this in the same way his father would handle it. If that was what she was thinking, then she was going to be extremely mistaken.

"I'm not going to do anything right now. Your wisdom and loyalty, however, will be dually noted; and I am sure there will be a special recognition given to you. Did you hear them say anything else?"

"No, they began to whisper and then walked away. You don't think anyone in our community would be involved in killing another black man do you? Don't you think this is just some kind of trick to get people to not look at those rednecks?"

"I'm in agreement with you about anyone in our group being involved. But you can't be heard making statements about it being a cover up or a conspiracy until we have some proof. For now, I need you to just remain calm and keep your ears open." Reaching into his wallet, Aziz took out his personal card. "This is my card with my cell number. If you hear anything else, call me. That way someone else doesn't have to call me and you can speak directly to me."

When he handed her the card, she looked at it like it was engraved in gold. The look of excitement in her eyes matched her earlier adoration. "I won't let you down. I am supposed to get off at 5:00 a.m., but I can stay over if you think I should. I'll make up a story that I have some filing to get done. The early morning shifts love when I stay late."

"No, I don't think that will be necessary. Like I said, the authorities don't need to know that you overheard any of their discussion. Probably they will all go home once they find out how the officer's surgery ends up."

"Then they are going to be very upset. Before I went on my break, I talked to one of the nurses, and she said that if he made it through the night, it would be a miracle."

"Can you call down to surgery and find out how he is?"

"I can't call down there, but I can walk down and ask. There usually isn't very much going on at this time of night."

Aziz didn't want to leave the hospital without knowing what was going to happen but something told him to make his way home. Now that he knew why there was animosity coming from the deputies, getting back home seemed the prudent move. Even though he and Bobby didn't get along, there was still a human concern, and surely there would be an update on social media. The other reason he might considered staying, even though he didn't want to admit it, was that it was exciting that Aggie was worried about him. Thinking about Aggie made Aziz remember what she had told him in the chapel. She had made some kind of Christian conversion and, whatever it was, he could see it. How could she turn her back on her heritage? How could she think that her father would allow this? Where could she get this kind of courage? As he walked toward his car, Aziz thought about everything that might happen to Aggie, and another question came into his mind. Could he ever do something like that? As he got into his car, the ringing of his phone brought him back to reality. "Hello, Father. I was just getting in the car to come home."

"Did you talk to the receptionist? Did she corroborate her story from earlier?" Again, the anxiety in his father's voice was a strange thing for Aziz to hear.

"Yes, apparently some of the people involved in the young man's murder were wearing Muslim head covers. She said that the faces were not clear but, in my opinion, that alone may be enough for them to make some wild accusations against us." There was silence from the other end of the line.

"I agree with what you are saying, but I want to see what the officers do. Did you say you haven't left yet?" Aziz smiled as he remembered just a few hours earlier how his father had told him exactly where he was.

"I am about to pull out of the parking lot."

"No, stay there. Can you see the other sheriff's department cars?"

"Yes, I can. I see one cruiser and the sheriff's SUV. Apparently one of the officers left because there were two cars here when I arrived."

"I want you to call me when Sheriff Wactor leaves. If they are going to do anything tonight, he will do it himself. Can you follow him back to Franklin County?"

"I can, but again, how can I explain myself if he were to figure out that I am following him to Franklin County. I wouldn't go that way to come home."

"I am sure you'll come up with something. Obviously, you came up with a good reason for being at the hospital. I trust your experience. Don't forget to call me when you get back to Meadville."

Aggie looked at the assembled group of people and saw the grim determination on each face. Sheriff Wactor had found a couple of chairs and gave them to Aggie and Annette. Aggie had tried to argue with him, but the look he gave her squelched any more comments on her behalf. No one was really saying anything, so neither did Aggie. But the feeling in her heart and mind felt like fireworks going off. Even though she had told Aziz about her change, she wanted to tell Annette and everyone else, but it still didn't feel like the right time.

"Here comes Dr. Stephens," Sheriff Wactor said. He was standing the closest to the doors and could see through the windows.

"Does he look sad?" Annette asked.

"Can't tell, but he's walking pretty quickly."

Aggie and Annette stood up and watched as the automatic doors opened. "Dr. Stephens, how is he?" Annette blurted out, unable to wait.

"He's going to be in ICU for the rest of the night, but I think the major danger is over." The collective sighs of relief from the people standing in the hall could have blown out all the candles on twenty birthday cakes.

"You said the major danger. What is the minor danger?" Annette asked as Jack put his arm around her.

"The life-threatening danger is mostly gone, but there is some paralysis. It could be temporary or it could be permanent. We won't know for a day or two. Now I know you are all concerned, but it would be in your best interest to get home and get some rest. He is in the best hands possible and is going to be sleeping for the next several hours. I am going to keep him off limits to visitors, so staying here will do nothing for him except make you feel worse. We have the numbers of his next of kin, and we will be in touch if anything changes."

"Thank you so much," Annette walked over and hugged the doctor. "I don't like the idea of paralysis, but I like it better than the idea of death. Besides, I serve a healing God, and He is not impressed with paralysis."

"I believe in that same God, so I will be praying along with you, but I will also be praying for mercy for each of you no matter what God decides."

"Thank you so much Doc. I think we will all take your advice, won't we Annette?" Sheriff Wactor said as he looked at Annette.

"I am going to make sure she does, even if I have to pick her up and tote her to Bude," Jack said.

"No arguments from me," Annette said.

"Let's pray now and thank God for what He has done and what He is going to do." As Sheriff Wactor reached out, everyone took each other's hands. Aggie reached out and took Annette's hand and also Billy's hand. As Sheriff Wactor began to pray and thank God for taking care of Bobby, Aggie felt different from the other time at the ballgame. As she listened, Aggie felt like she was part of the prayer, even though she wasn't saying anything. This Christian thing was going to be something to get used to. Finally, Sheriff Wactor finished and everyone began to hug. Annette turned and looked at Aggie.

"Aggie, are you alright? You look almost radiant. For this time of night, that's very impressive."

Since she didn't know for sure the proper ways to talk about her new conversion, Aggie smiled and put her hands-on Annette's shoulders. "Why don't we go get in the car and I'll tell you and Jack all about it?"

Annette had convinced the doctor to let her walk into the ICU ward to look into Bobby's room. After she saw him, she turned and said, "Let's go. I want to see Archie now." With that, they all walked out of the hospital in a much better frame of mind than when they had walked in just a few hours earlier.

When they got into Aggie's car, Annette let Jack sit in the front and she sat in the back. Since they weren't in as much of a hurry as they had been on the way out to McComb, Jack had suggested that they take the shorter two-lane route back home. When they pulled out onto the interstate, Annette leaned up between the seats. "All right Ms. Aggie, what is going on? What did I miss out on?" Aggie looked into the rearview mirror and smiled at Annette.

"After you left the chapel, a lady named Joan came in and talked to me. She talked to me clearly and explained the idea of becoming a Christian. We talked for a while and I accepted Jesus as my Savior." Out of the corner of her eye, Aggie could see the look of disbelief on Jack's face. That didn't compare to the smile on Annette's face.

"Oh, Aggie, that is the greatest thing I have heard since the day Archie got saved. I am so proud for you. I have got to call Archie and tell him."

"Where is Archie? I guessed somebody took him home, but I didn't ask."

"Deputy Michael came and told me that he was going to get Archie and take him to Henry's house. At the time, I didn't know what was going to happen to Bobby, so I guessed that was the best thing. Even if he's asleep, I've got to tell him about you getting saved."

Aggie didn't know what she meant when she said getting saved, but guessed it was some way of talking about being a Christian. Suddenly a phone began to ring in the backseat. Annette laughed as she held up Archie's phone.

"I guess we won't be telling him anything. He must have left it in here when we got out of the car. That right there proves how worried he was. He never goes anywhere without this thing. Oh well, I'll see him in a few minutes. Why don't you tell me some more about this Joan lady?"

CHAPTER 14

Nothing Makes Sense

Archie felt his head fall over and the motion woke him up. For a moment, he didn't remember where he was. Seeing the examination room, he was reminded that he was still at the hospital. Deputy Michael had wanted to take him home, but Jughead didn't want to go, so he told him that his mother had changed her mind, and he could stay at the hospital. Before he could check to see if what Jughead was saying was actually true, he got a call on the radio about a wreck on Highway 98. After he had gone, Jughead didn't want to go back and explain to his mother why he wasn't gone, so he decided to just sit in the empty examination room and wait on something to happen. Somewhere in the last while, he had decided to get up on the table because it was more comfortable than the chair. Sitting on the table had led to lying down and lying down had led to sleep. Since he was like most kids and didn't wear a watch anymore, he reached into his pocket to get his phone. When he didn't feel it, Jughead remembered that he had left it in Aggie's car because he didn't want it to go off in the hospital. He had convinced himself that if anything happened to his Uncle Bobby, they would say something over the loudspeakers in the ceiling.

That was the reason he had chosen this room--because he saw speakers in the ceiling. Since there had been no calls for someone to come to surgery, in his mind everything was all right. Hopping off the table, he decided to go down and check on things. He really didn't think his parents would get mad at him for his little lie. Especially since he lied so he could stay close in case anything happened.

As he walked out into the hall and began to make his way toward the operating room, Jughead noticed there wasn't anyone standing around like there had been before. When he turned the corner, he saw that no one was there. Turning around and retracing his steps, he found the chapel and went into it, expecting his family to be there praying. Unfortunately, there was nothing in the chapel but empty chairs. "Where is everybody?"

Aziz waited until he saw what he thought was the last car to leave. His father had been very clear that he was to stay and watch until everyone, including all the law enforcement officers, had left the hospital. He had slid down in the seat when Aggie and Annette and her husband had driven by because he didn't want them to think he was spying. Even though he was, it wasn't on them. Looking at the clock on his dash, Aziz began to dread getting up in the morning for early prayers. If the truth was known, he had been known to fall asleep during the early prayers. If he didn't hurry up and get home, he might do that again.

As he pulled out of the parking lot and onto the street, Aziz began to think of all the repercussions that would happen to Aggie when her father found out about her new conversion. Before any of the words he would use came to his mind, Aziz saw a young man walk out the front doors of the hospital. Something about him was familiar. Slowing down, Aziz saw that the young man was Annette's son. What was he doing here alone? There was no way that they left him to stay with Bobby. Since it was so late and there wasn't any traffic around, Aziz stopped and backed up the street. As he came closer, the young boy started to walk toward him.

"What are you doing out here, young man?" Aziz asked as he rolled the window down. "I saw your parents drive away."

"Well, at least you saw them. I was beginning to think that the rapture had come and I missed it." The mention of this rapture sent a chill through Aziz that was completely unexpected. Though he had heard his friend Keith talk about the Christian rapture or flying away, the mention of it had never really affected him until just now.

"Are you listening to me?" Archie asked. "You look like you saw a ghost."

"Yes, I'm sorry go ahead."

"I tried to find somebody to tell me what was going on, but there wasn't anyone to ask. By the way, who are you?" Jughead thought this man looked familiar but didn't know him.

"My name is Aziz. I am a friend of your…" but he stopped before he said his parents because, as far as they were concerned, he was the enemy. "I'm a friend of Aggie's."

"Do you have a cell phone? I must have left mine in Aggie's car. I am going to be in big trouble if they get home and I'm not there." Jughead paused and shook his head. "Nope, I'm going to be in big trouble no matter what happens. You say you are a friend of Aggie's?"

"I guess so. I, like you, just met her. I have her number in my phone. If you would like, I can give her a call and tell her you're with me. Then we can meet and you can get back with your parents." Jughead didn't really trust this guy, but something told him that everything was going to be all right.

"I guess that will do." Jughead opened the door and got in. "Can this car go as fast as Aggie's Porsche?"

"I don't think it will go that fast, but for an American-made car, it's all right."

As they pulled back out onto the street, Aziz began to look for Aggie's number. But before he could call her, he got another call. It was his father. Aziz reached down and took the phone off speaker mode and answered.

"Hello, Father, everything is fine here." This was a code his father had taught him that if it wasn't safe to talk, that was the phrase he was supposed to use.

"All right, son, I was just calling to check on you. You don't require any assistance, do you?" This was the other phrase they used.

"No, but when I get home, I will tell you all about it." This was the completion of the code that there was no danger, just someone was listening who didn't need to hear them.

"Very well, I look forward to hearing your report. Have a safe trip."

"Wow, your father still calls to check up on you, too? I thought that was going to end when I went off to college." Aziz looked over at the innocent young man sitting in the seat beside him.

"When a parent loves their children, they don't stop loving them after they are older. You will understand when you get older and have children of your own."

"Do you have children of your own?" Jughead asked innocently.

This made Aziz chuckle at the inquisitiveness of this young man. "No, I don't have any children, but that is what my father has told me over the years. I hope to have children one day."

"Do you have a girlfriend?" Instead of answering, he deflected. He didn't know why he didn't answer the question, but he didn't. "Let me get Aggie on the phone."

When he found Aggie's number, Aziz felt a small sense of excitement. Was it the thought of hearing her voice again that excited him? "Hello, this is Aggie, who's calling?" Since her number seemed to be known by more people in Mississippi than she knew, seeing another Mississippi number come up was not so surprising.

"Hello Ms. New York, this is Aziz. Do you have Ms. Annette in the car with you?" Aggie could feel the anger begin to boil from the backseat.

"I'm here, but if you have called to say anything about my brother, I promise, you will regret it," Annette added. Though her voice didn't raise in volume, the implication was clear. Aziz chuckled to himself at the immediate angst his call had brought.

"No, I'm not calling to do anything except to find out where you are so I can bring you a package that is in my possession. I'm sure you would like to have it."

"Aziz, what are you talking about?" Aggie asked. "I hope this isn't some kind of joke."

"No joke. Say hello little package."

"Hello, Mom," Jughead said rather sheepishly. "I guess I missed you leaving at the hospital."

Hearing the voice of her child changed the direction of both Jack and Annette's attention

from Aziz to their baby. "Archie, what are you doing? Didn't I send you to Sheriff Wactor's house?"

"Yes ma'am, but I didn't want to be gone, just in case something happened to Uncle Bobby. I told the deputy that you had changed your mind, and he got a call on the radio and left. I was scared you would get mad, so I went and sat in one of the exam rooms. I must have fallen asleep because, when I woke up, everyone was gone. By the way, is my phone in Aggie's car?"

"Yes, it is, but I promise you won't need it for a long time. When I get my hands on you, I may break it over your head." Jack, realizing the fragile state of mind his wife was in, reached into the back seat to calm her down.

"Jughead, we will take care of this later. Mr. Aziz, where are you right now?"

"We are about to pull out beside the mall. I haven't had anything to eat, so I'm going to get something in the drive through. If you're almost home, I can bring him to your house. It isn't really out of my way and you wouldn't have to come back to McComb." Annette started to say something else, but Jack held up his hand.

"That will be fine. Jughead can give you directions to the house. Thank you so much for picking up our child. This is the second time he has gotten in the car with a stranger. After I get through with him, I'm going to believe it will be the last."

Aggie hadn't said anything because this was something between parents and their child. It was strange that once again both she and Aziz were involved in a chance meeting. What was her life going to consist of?

After hanging up the phone, Aziz looked over at Jughead. "I think you are in a world of trouble, my friend."

"Yeah, it looks like it, but that seems like my life these last few days. Did you say you were going to go through a drive through? I haven't eaten tonight either. I was going to get something to eat after the game, but we left. I don't have any money with me, but I will get some from my dad when we get there."

As he pulled into the twenty-four-hour drive through, Aziz took out his wallet. "Don't you worry, this is my treat. You probably won't get any treats for a very long time after this."

"I may beat him to death," Annette said as she walked into the kitchen. "How can he do this? I specifically told him to go home. Now because he disobeyed me, he is in the car with someone who hates our family, and I am obliged to be thankful to this person. Jack, you better get to him before I do." Jack laughed at his wife which infuriated her even more.

"I agree he should be punished, but this guy was willing to pick up our child and bring him home to us. He could have been left alone at the hospital. Aggie, you have had some interaction with this young man. Is it safe for us to let him bring Jughead home? If you think he's crazy, I will go meet them." Aggie thought for a moment.

"No, I don't think Archie's in any danger. Aziz seems to be a nice person. I rode to Roxie with him this afternoon. He and I have some things in common when it comes to our fathers."

"Only in my life would I get involved with a Jewish girl and a Muslim guy. Do you want me to fix something to eat? When I get upset, the best way for me to calm down is to cook. Jack what can I make for you?" Annette waited for his answer.

"I would love one of your awesome omelets. What about you Aggie? Wouldn't you like one of Annette's awesome omelets?"

"If they are so good that you call them awesome, how can I turn it down?" As Annette began to get pans and things out to cook, Aggie got an idea. "I'm going to go wash my hands. I'll be right back to help you, Nette."

"Go ahead, I've got enough nervous energy going, I might just put out the 'open for breakfast' sign and feed the entire town of Bude."

When she shut the door behind her, Aggie began to think about everything that had been going on. There was one thing that she had forgotten amidst all the excitement. It was what the other deputy said about Aziz's father's followers maybe being involved with the lynching. She had faith in Aziz that he was not involved, but did she really know him? The real reason she had taken a moment alone was so that she could contact Ben and find out what was going on. She started to send a text message but decided to call him. Texting would take too much time. The phone only rang once before Ben's voice came over the line. She could hear the exhaustion in his voice. "Ben, it's Aggie. What have you found out? Did they get anything from the video?"

"I am riding with Henry now. He talked to Kenneth and they said it definitely was some of Maalik's crowd. If they had been that sure, Henry might have detained Aziz at the hospital. By the way, did he find you? When I saw him, he said he was there to see you and to check on Bobby."

"Yes, he found me. Do you really think he had something to do with that murder?" Aggie couldn't believe it, but she didn't know if it was because the facts didn't line up or she was not thinking clearly when it came to Aziz.

"I wish I knew where he was now," Sheriff Wactor said in the background.

"If he wants to see Aziz, tell the Sheriff to come over to Annette and Jack's. Aziz will be here in a few minutes." As she said the words, Aggie wished she had kept her mouth shut.

Ben didn't miss the importance of what she said. "Henry, get over to Annette and Jack's, Maalik's boy is going to be there."

Aggie could hear the sirens go on and the Suburban go into overdrive, even over the

phone. "What happened?" Aggie asked.

"Why is he coming there? Isn't it a little late for a date?"

Aggie didn't like what Ben was alluding to. "Ben, for your information,

146

Aziz is bringing Archie home."

"What do you mean bringing Archie home? He went home with Deputy Michaels. I was there when Henry told him to take Jughead home."

"Apparently Jughead is more persuasive than you might think. Archie convinced him that

his mother said it was all right to stay at the hospital. She and Jack are going to take care of that when he gets here, but until then I'd appreciate it if you would give me some benefit of the doubt."

"I'm sorry Aggie. You're right. It is none of my business and I jumped to a conclusion. How long until he gets there?"

"I talked to them about ten minutes ago. He was going to get a take-out burger and head this way. He shouldn't be very far behind you."

Aziz was only a half mile or so behind the sheriff's car. Looking down at his speedometer, Aziz wondered why the sheriff needed to be going more than a hundred miles an hour. Archie was enjoying the ride and eating his hamburger like it was the best one he ever had. Aziz had almost forgotten that his father told him to follow the sheriff from the hospital. When he remembered, he was already in the drive through line. Apparently, the sheriff had stopped also, because Aziz had caught up with them right outside of Summit. Now, he was pushing his car to stay within eyesight and still not look like he was following them. *I wonder what made him take off so fast*, Aziz thought to himself.

"Billy, I need you to pull off the road and wait for a car when we pass the Franklin County line. Look for a black Challenger. When it comes by, tail him. Run the tag, and if it's that boy of Maalik's, follow him. If he turns off the highway before you get to Bude, pull him over and detain him and call me. Read him his rights, but don't give him any information. I want to talk to him. Also be careful because Jughead's in the car with him."

"Freddie Michaels took Jughead home. Did this guy kidnap him?"

Henry couldn't help but smile at the irony of Jughead being presumed kidnapped twice in two days. "No, Freddie didn't take him home, and I will deal with him when I see him. Right now, all I need you to do is follow his car if he turns off Highway 98. He will probably be speeding, but don't do anything. When you get behind him, radio MHP not to stop him if he meets any troopers."

"Sheriff, I'll do whatever you say, but I don't understand."

"When you get to the office in the morning, I'll explain everything."

"I hope you're right, because a black Challenger just came by me doing every bit of a hundred miles per." Even though sheriff departments couldn't run radar in Mississippi, Sheriff Wactor required all his officers to take a course in speed determination.

"Then get behind him and keep me posted. I want to be here when he arrives."

Billy pulled out and immediately put the accelerator to the floor. Even though the car was equipped with the police package, he was going to have to push hard to keep an eye on that Challenger.

Aggie was once again amazed at how quickly Annette could put a meal together. In less than fifteen minutes, she had prepared and cooked a meal and they were eating it. "I have to hand it to you; this is the best omelet I've ever had. Jack, you were right to call them awesome."

"You should try her Mexican chicken. Everyone says it's the dish they look for when we have dinner on the ground at church."

"Speaking of church, this situation with Archie has interrupted all the facts you were telling us about your good news. Are you going to tell your father in the morning?" Annette asked between bites.

"I don't know when or if I will tell my father. He didn't like it when I went to Rutgers instead of going to college in the homeland. When I tell him about this, he will probably disown me."

"Don't worry about the world," Annette said. "You tell everyone because that's what Jesus saves us for, to tell the world about Him. You may be the only person who can reach your father."

Aggie thought for a moment and for the first time a sad realization hit her. "If I tell him, I may no longer have a father."

CHAPTER 15

The Unexpected Call

It doesn't take long to go thirty-three miles at the speed Aziz had been traveling, even though he had slowed down when he crossed the Franklin County line. He could have sworn that a police car of some kind was following him, but he couldn't be sure. Either way, he had decided to slow down. Though his father had tasked him with following Sheriff Wactor to find out what he was planning, Aziz didn't want to take a chance with the safety of his passenger, who was still nibbling on his fries.

"I don't know if this car is as fast as Aggie's, but I sure like it," Archie said.

"Thanks. I am very proud of it myself." Aziz was about to ask Archie if he liked Aggie and why they called him Jughead, when his phone rang. Looking at the number, he was surprised to see that it wasn't his father or any of the other brothers. The number looked familiar but wasn't in his phone as a contact, and it had an area code that he did not recognize. Since it wasn't a known number, Aziz decided to pick it up instead of using the hands free, just in case it was someone Archie didn't need to know about.

"Hello. This is Aziz."

"Hello, my friend. I don't know what time it is in Mississippi, but I couldn't go back to sleep without giving you a call." Hearing the voice made Aziz consider pulling over. It was Kareem, his former roommate. That was the reason the number looked familiar, but it wasn't in his phone. His father had made sure the number was deleted from the phone when they brought him back to Mississippi.

"Kareem, how are you? It has been too long since we've spoken."

"I am well. I'm living in Cincinnati, Ohio, now."

"What are you doing in Cincinnati? The last time we spoke, you were living near Cleveland." Aziz felt a small amount of guilt that he had completely removed himself from the best friend he had ever known, simply because his father had threatened to cut him completely off and he would be in exile from his family and everything he had ever believed in. Was that enough to forget someone like Kareem?

149

"I am working in a church here. I'm the assistant youth pastor, and I have a job at a hardware store owned by one of the members. I have never been happier in all my life. How are you getting along? Are you still stuck in the life we were born in?"

"I'm doing well." Aziz didn't have to go into much detail with Kareem. He was raised a Muslim and knew the rules. He also had a hard time believing that Kareem was doing so well working two jobs. His family was very wealthy and, until his conversion, Kareem had lived a life of luxury and never needed anything. Now he was working two jobs, disowned by his family, and he said he was happier than he had ever been. That just didn't seem right.

"Well, enough small talk. I can see the wheels turning in your head from all the way up here. The reason I called should be simple, but I'm not sure it will be. I need to ask you a very important question," Kareem said, his mood and voice were much more serious. "Right now, at this very moment, are you alright? Do you feel like you are in quicksand and are being dragged under? I guess the real question I have to ask is, are you still sure the Muslim way is the only way?"

"Of course, I believe the Muslim ways are the only way. I thought we covered that the last time we spoke. I know I asked you some questions about Christianity, but I chose to follow my father. Why would you call all the way from Ohio at this hour to ask me that?" Aziz was acting indignant, but inside he was trembling. Was he trembling in anger or fear? Fear of what the question was or what his true answer might be?

"Aziz, let me explain. I was asleep until a few minutes ago. I had a dream that you were stuck in a large hole of quicksand. You were slowly sinking, but you weren't crying out for help. Since you weren't calling out, no one would help you, even though you were about to go under. Then out of the blue, a woman dressed in a blue shirt wearing a red apron threw you a rope and pulled you out of the quicksand. But before you could get all the way to safety, your father came up out of the quicksand and tried to pull you back in. When your father grabbed you, you began shouting out for someone to help you. The part that drove me crazy was that all I could do was watch. I was totally helpless and I hated that. It seemed like the struggle went on for hours, but it couldn't have been but a few seconds. Suddenly I woke up and I was sweating. I have had dreams about you and me before. Sometimes it would be a memory or just us hanging out in the apartment, but never have I felt like I needed to call and talk to you. What are you involved in? What can I do to help you? I know you chose to continue in the Muslim faith, but I want you to know that it's not the only way. I'm telling you this because I care for you and I want you to have what I have."

Aziz wanted to berate his former roommate and friend about the choices he had made. He wanted to explain to him how his father had made him realize that Islam was the true way. How he was driving a brand-new car and had a future that was bright. Aziz wanted to do this, but for some reason he couldn't. Was it because he didn't really feel happy? Why were all these questions coming up now?

"Kareem, I'm proud you are happy, but I am happy also. I was not cut off from my family and my faith. You can be happy with your choice, but I really wish you would respect my choice and allow me to live my life." Aziz stopped talking because it was getting hard to breathe. In fact, his breathing was almost ragged.

"Are you okay?" Archie asked. Aziz had almost forgotten he was there

"I am fine. It is just an old friend of mine calling."

"I don't know, you're breathing hard and it looks like you're sweating."

Aziz reached up and felt his forehead. It was wet like he was sweating off a fever. Why was he sweating? Kareem was talking, but Aziz was not listening. "Kareem, I'm sorry, but I have some things I need to take care of tonight. Is this your number? Sometime next week I will call you and we can talk about old times. Have a good night." Then before his friend could say anything else, he hung up the phone.

"Who was that?" Archie asked. Aziz was still so disturbed by Kareem's call that he didn't answer Archie's question. "Whoever it was, he must have given you some really bad news. I've never seen anyone's face change from happy to sad as fast as yours did."

"What do you mean?" Aziz asked when Archie's question finally hit him.

"I mean that you were smiling and happy when you first answered the phone, then you sounded really nervous and scared. Did he tell you something that scared you?"

"I don't want to talk about it. I just want to get you to your house and get this day over with." Aziz knew his tone was gruff, but at this moment discussing what Kareem was talking about was not what he wanted to do.

As they turned off the highway, Aziz didn't think he had ever been as happy to see Bude as he was now. "Where do you live, my drive-through friend?" Aziz wanted to try and make Archie forget his gruffness by assuming a lighter tone.

"You turn right here on the next street and then we are the fourth house on the left." If Archie was angry, he wasn't showing it.

As they drove along, Aziz realized he had never been on this street even though Bude was an extremely small town. Probably because this was the white part of town. Or maybe it was because he lived in Fayette and this wasn't his town. Either way, Aziz knew he wanted to drop Archie off and get alone for a few minutes. When things got heavy in his life, Aziz always got alone and worked it out in his mind. Hopefully, there would be enough alone time on the drive back to Fayette. As they pulled up into the driveway of the fourth house, Aziz noticed that parked alongside Aggie's Porsche was the sheriff's SUV.

"What is he doing here?" Aziz asked.

Not only was the sheriff's car in the driveway, another sheriff's department car, that had apparently been following them, pulled in and blocked Aziz from leaving even if he wanted to, and right now he desperately wanted to leave.

Looks like I have driven into an ambush, Aziz thought. *What am I going to do?* Before he could think any further, something came into his line of sight that made all the air leave his body. If he had been looking in the mirror, he would have seen all the color go out of his face. Walking out the door with a very determined look on her face was Archie's mother. Her determined look and the man walking behind her were not what was most surprising, however. What took Aziz's breath was the fact that she was wearing a blue shirt and a red apron over it--just as Kareem had described. Where was the quicksand?

"Archie Walker, you get out of that car right now," Annette said as she walked up to the passenger side of the car.

"I guess I better get out and face the music. Can you unlock the door, Aziz?" Archie asked.

"Oh, yeah, sure." Aziz was still stunned that this woman was wearing the exact same outfit his friend had described in his dream just a few moments ago. Did Kareem have a vision? While he was looking at Archie, Aziz didn't notice that Sheriff Wactor had walked up to his window and was standing and waiting patiently.

"Archie, why didn't you do what I told you to do? Do you know that you could have been hurt?" She then looked in the car at Aziz. "Thank you so much for bringing my little con artist home. You and I may not agree on some things, but tonight you have my gratitude."

"Aziz, could you and I have a few words?" This came from Sheriff Wactor. He must have gotten tired of waiting. Aziz hit the button and let his window down.

"Sheriff, it's very late. What could you and I possibly have to talk about at this hour? I hear your deputy is doing well. I really want to go home and get some rest, unless you are going to arrest me for doing a good deed without a license." Another trait Aziz had was that when he got worried or scared, his tongue became sharp and biting. None of his words seemed to affect the old sheriff and preacher.

"No, I'm not going to arrest you. I just want to talk to you about the murder this morning. We can do it here, or we can go down to the courthouse and make this an official talk."

"I suggest unless you want to arrest me that you should talk to me right here, because the only way I am going to go to the courthouse is under arrest. And I don't think you want to have to deal with another racial incident, especially two in two days."

"Sheriff, I can arrest him right now for driving more than a hundred miles per hour. I followed him and clocked him." This was coming from the deputy that had pulled up behind him.

"No, that won't be necessary Billy. I just need to speak with Aziz. "Billy nodded but didn't change his aggressive stance.

"Aziz, I'll make you a deal. We just got here, but I would be willing to bet that Annette

has some coffee she can make or already has made. We will go inside and have a cup of coffee and talk off the record, just you and me. Then there will be no threats of arrest or anything else that is unpleasant. How does that strike you?"

Aziz knew that he was in a very strong position right now. Not only did Sheriff Wactor not have anything he could arrest him for, but Aziz felt like he knew everything the Sheriff knew. His father would probably counsel against this, but there was also the woman in the red apron. Aziz had to find out if there was something about her that would impact him or if it was just

153

a wild coincidence.

"I agree to your terms, Sheriff. Let's have some coffee."

CHAPTER 16

Honor Thy Father and Mother

"I hope you like it strong," Annette said as she handed the cup to Aziz. "Now if y'all will excuse me, I'm going to have the second heart to heart talk with my son in the last two days. Henry, you take all the time you need."

Aziz took a swallow of the coffee and almost spit it back into the cup. She wasn't kidding about it being strong. But he wasn't going to let them think they had anything he couldn't handle, including their coffee.

"Here, put some more cream in it," Sheriff Wactor said as he slid a pitcher across the table. "Annette's family is from down around New Orleans, and she gets her coffee made with double chicory. I'm scared to spill it because it might eat through the table." This brought a chuckle from both Aziz and Ben. Apparently, Ben was also going to sit in on this conference. It took four spoonfuls before the coffee began to change to a lighter shade of black. Aziz guessed that was as good as he was going to get it.

"Sheriff, I appreciate all the pleasantries, but I would really like to know what this is all about. Though I am a young man, it's very late, or very early, whichever you choose. I am also going to tell you that if this gets confrontational, I will politely get up and go to my car and go home. If you don't like that, then I guess you or the other deputies will have to go ahead and arrest me."

"Aziz, I don't think there's any need to arrest you. But make no mistake, if I feel there is a need, I won't be intimidated." As he said this, he smiled, but there was no humor in the sheriff's eyes. Aziz knew he was serious. Though some of his father's friends thought the Franklin County Sheriff was just a country bumpkin, neither Aziz nor his father did. In fact, Maalik spoke to Aziz of Sheriff Wactor in a very complimentary way. That didn't mean the two men were going out to a movie together, but Aziz knew his father's respect wasn't given easily or very often.

"Why is he in here?" Aziz asked pointing to Ben. "I don't want to see any of this in the newspaper."

"Ben is here strictly as a witness that I don't do or say anything untoward to you. Now, I want to discuss the murder."

"You want to discuss the murder with me? What could you possibly want to talk about with me?" Aziz was trying to talk and formulate a plan of attack. His father always taught him that it was important to not only know what you were saying at the moment, but also know what you were going to say next to counter what your opponent might say. He called this chess conversation.

"What I am going to tell you is completely off the record. No one knows this except my department and Ben." Aziz wanted to laugh at the idea that this was some secret that no one knew, when in fact he was sure his father and his other advisors were working on a plan to dispute the findings that were on the camera.

"Oh, and I'm also sure your father knows as well as his other folks that work for him. That was the reason you were at the hospital tonight wasn't it? Supposedly, you were getting secret information from the receptionist and relaying it to your father, weren't you?" Aziz had heard of being hit with a ton of bricks, but it was never as real to him as it was at this very instant. Obviously, it showed, because Sheriff Wactor picked up his coffee and nodded over to Ben and both men had a look of satisfaction on their faces.

"Oh, I know you think that you are slick, and I would tend to agree, but I have been in the investigation business for too many years not to see the copy of the Quran on that woman's desk. Then Billy tells me that he might have said something in front of that woman, and the next thing we know you're there. It really wasn't hard to put two and two together. What I need to know is, are you going to cooperate with me and help me or are we going to have to do this the hard way?"

Aziz was not as skilled as his father in getting back onto his feet after being knocked down. "How can I cooperate on something I don't know about? All I did was listen to someone and then told my father what she told me."

The Sheriff reached into his pocket and took out his phone. "I have the pictures right here. I had Kenneth send them to me, and I want you to look at them and see if there is anyone you might recognize."

"I am not going to turn on anyone of our followers," Aziz said. Sometimes anger helped him to get his bearings, and he needed some righteous anger right then.

"I don't want you to rat on anyone. I just want to know if you know any of these people." As he reached over to hand Aziz his phone, he stopped and took the phone back. "You have got to be kidding me."

"What's wrong?" Ben asked. "You get a call about another major crime?"

"No, I took my phone into the hospital and didn't let it charge. Then when I got in the truck, I forgot to charge it. Now it's dead. Have you got a smart phone?"

"I just got rid of my rotary dial phone a few years ago. I am a long way from having a smart phone."

"You can give me your email address and I can look it up on my phone," Aziz offered.

"No offense, but I have too many things on my email that I don't feel confident letting you have the password to."

"I think Aggie has an iPad," Ben said. You can get Kenneth to send them to her and we can look at the pictures on it. You can get a bigger picture and can zoom in closer also."

"If she's still awake, that will be fine."

Not only was she awake, but Aggie was talking excitedly to Annette about being a Christian. The time spent on the road from the hospital had done little to dispel any of Aggie's excitement. "But have you ever heard of this Joan lady?" Aggie asked. "She acted like I was her best friend, and I believe she may have become my best friend tonight, even if I never see her again."

"Aggie, I've heard many stories about someone at that hospital talking to a patient and telling them that it was going to be all right, and the next day the nurses say that there is no one by that name working for the hospital. I also know that God is in the saving business and some people require greater shows of miracles than others. Are you going to be baptized?"

"What does it mean to be baptized? Does that mean I have to be a Baptist?"

"No, baptism is a representation of your accepting Christ and taking part in his death, burial, and resurrection. When you are baptized, you are showing the world what you have done and whom you are going to serve. I think you can talk to Henry later today and he will give you some pointers and ask you some questions."

"What kind of questions do you want answered?" Sheriff Wactor asked. He had walked into the room and neither Aggie nor Annette had heard him.

"I wanted to tell you earlier, but Aggie accepted Christ tonight at the hospital. She's been dealing with a lot of things, and a lady named Joan came to her and helped to lead her to Christ."

"That's a great and wonderful thing. I wish we could talk some more, but I really have to ask a favor of you Aggie. Can I get Kenneth to send you some photos onto your iPad? My phone died and I need to let Aziz look at some pictures."

"Not a problem," Aggie said as she pulled out her iPad. "Do you need my email or my phone number?"

"I'm not sure. Annette, can I use your phone to call Kenneth? He has the pictures and I don't want to miss this opportunity."

"Go right ahead. It's on the table behind you. Just call whomever you need."

As Sheriff Wactor walked into the other room to call and get the pictures, Aziz saw Aggie and Annette sitting on the couch. "Ben, I am going to stretch my legs a little bit if that's okay?"

"Aziz, you are not in custody. Even if you were, I don't have any jurisdiction over you. You're a visitor in Annette's home. She's the only one who has the legal right to tell you what to do at this moment."

"Then I think I'll make my way into the living room and make some conversation with her and Aggie. No offense against you and the sheriff, but they are much more pleasing to look at."

"You'll get no arguments about that. When Henry gets back, I'll come get you."

"You don't mind me coming in here for a few minutes, do you?" Aziz asked the ladies. "That room feels too much like an interrogation room."

Aggie turned around and smiled at Aziz. "You're welcome to come in here. Annette was just telling me about getting baptized."

"Oh yeah, you made the big conversion tonight didn't you. I was thinking maybe after

everything that has happened that you were just confused. But, please, don't let me put a damper on your transformation."

"Aziz, I am a very good judge of character." As she said this, Annette looked Aziz directly in the eyes. "You are struggling with something also, and

I don't think it has anything to do with this case."

"I struggle with the same thing everyone faces. Unlike what most everyone thinks, we Muslims are people just like you are. We have turmoil and troubles in life." Aziz was talking as smoothly as he could, trying to assuage any questions Annette had.

"But Aziz, I'm going to ask you a question. Do you still think the Muslim way is the only way?" Apparently, tonight was the night for Aziz to be completely caught off-guard. Despite his best efforts, every question that was asked of him in the last few hours were questions that he was not prepared for. This question was asked for the second time in the last hour, and in the same form.

"Why would you ask me that?" Aziz was looking at the red apron that Annette was still wearing.

"You may think this is strange, but something in my spirit told me to ask that question. From your reaction, I'm guessing it is a very real and pertinent question."

"Aziz, I don't know what you are feeling, but I promise, you've never had the feeling of

peace I have now, "Aggie said. "You and I are two people from two totally different religions, but both of us have been wondering if there was something else. I found out tonight that there is. I found out, and my life will never be the same."

"Aggie, did you tell her anything that you and I discussed today? Is that where this question came from?"

"Aziz, you may not believe this, but God has His ways of getting people to that special moment in their life. Sometimes if we turn it down, He gives us other chances, but He is not obligated to. This may be your only chance to get out of the quicksand you are in and accept Jesus as your Savior."

There was that word quicksand again. "Why would I accept someone as my savior whom I know nothing about? What has this Jesus ever done for me? The Quran speaks of him, but he is just a good man." Aziz was fighting to hold it together, but something was burning in his heart that, somehow, he knew was always there. Something that had been there since Kareem first began to talk to him about Christianity. He felt tears coming down his face. Why was he crying? What was going on?

159

"Aziz, you are at a very important point in your life. Let me show you something." Annette got up and walked over to the desk behind the couch and brought back a book. Aziz had seen enough of them to know it was a Bible. "I want to show you something." She then flipped to a page like she knew exactly where she was going. "This is the most important verse in the Bible for salvation. It is John 3:16. I want you to read it out loud to Aggie and me."

"I really think I need to get back into the other room. Come to think of it, I need to get home." Aziz was feeling a flood of emotions, but for all his words, he couldn't get up off the couch.

"Just read these words. Then I've got a couple of other verses for you to read. If you want to leave after that, then I won't stop you." Aziz took the book and looked for the chapter and verse. *For God so loved the world that he gave his only begotten son that whosoever believeth in him should not perish but have everlasting life.* As he read the words, Aziz felt a warmth begin to come over him.

"Now, I want you to read two other verses." She took the Bible and quickly turned to another verse. "This is Romans 3:23. Read this to me and then one more." Aziz had no control of his emotions anymore. He couldn't have gotten up if someone had held a gun to his head. *For all have sinned and fallen short of the glory of God.*

"Okay, now one more verse and you are done. Its Romans 10:23."

Aziz didn't have to be told to read it. He wanted to read it to see what it said. Also, he wanted to find out what this warm feeling was. *That if you confess with your mouth the Lord Jesus and believe in your heart that God has raised him from the dead, you will be saved.* After he read this verse, Aziz didn't say a word.

"Aziz, you have an opportunity right now greater than any that you have had or will ever have. But only you can take it. I can't take it for you, and neither can Aggie. This is something that you have to do yourself. I can help you, but you have to make the decision."

"Aggie, did you feel a warm feeling? Do you still have it?"

"Yes, Aziz, I did. I don't know how to explain it, but it's greater than anything I've ever known."

"Yes, I want this Jesus as my savior," Aziz said. "What do I do? Aggie, what did you do?" Aggie who had been sitting back watching in complete amazement had not said anything, mostly because she didn't know what to say and was afraid to say the wrong thing if she did say something.

"Aziz, Ms. Joan just told me to talk to Jesus like I was talking to my friend because that's what He is, the best friend I'll ever have."

"That's exactly right," Annette said. "There are some people who tell you there is a certain prayer, but I'm telling you just like Aggie did. Just talk to Jesus like you are talking to your friend."

"But what if he knows I am Muslim. Will He talk back to me?"

"Aziz, Jesus knows everything about you already. He's just waiting for you to accept Him."

Aziz wanted to ask more questions but couldn't think of any. Since he had heard Jesus was in Heaven, Aziz decided to look up at and talk to Him. "Jesus, I don't know anything about your life, but these people tell me you know everything about me. My friend, Kareem, called me tonight and asked if I believed the Muslim way was the only way. Then this lady Annette asked me the same thing. Also, she was dressed in the red apron Kareem dreamed about, and she said I was in quicksand. I don't know everything, but I do know that all this isn't a coincidence. I guess what I mean is I want this warm feeling I feel right now to last forever. I want to know that there is something else when I die. I also want what Kareem has. He was willing to walk away from his entire life just for this Christian thing. I want that too so, whatever it takes, I want to become a Christian, Amen." As he said these words, Aziz felt like the weight of the world was lifted off his shoulders. If life as a Christian was going to be like this, Kareem's decision was easier to explain.

"Aziz, do you feel better? Have you ever felt like this before in your life?" Aggie asked.

"I can't say that I have. Annette does it always feel like this?"

"Well, it isn't always easy, but the peace of God is always with you. You are now my brother in Christ just as pure as Bobby is my brother." Annette reached over and wrapped both arms around his neck. "I know it's strange for you, but I have to admit this has been the most overwhelming two days I've ever seen."

"I finally got the pictures to come through," Sheriff Wactor said as he walked back into the room. Even though this was the breakthrough that this case needed, and Aziz might be able to break this murder investigation wide open, Henry had been in too many spirit-filled services not to recognize the presence of God's spirit. "Okay, what happened while I was gone?"

"Aziz asked Jesus to come into his heart. Isn't that amazing?"

"I know you said Aggie did, but Aziz did, too? This is the kind of revival that no one will believe. Congratulations Aziz and you too Aggie. You just made the greatest decision you will ever make. I can't imagine the courage it took. I will be there if you ever need me. All you have to do is call."

"Thank you, Sheriff, I'm not sure how my life is going to go after this, but I'm ready for whatever happens I think." Aziz wanted to call Kareem right now and let him know the good news. "Is there any way I could make a phone call? I have a friend who should know what happened."

"I think that would be a great idea," Annette said. "Telling the world about your experience with Jesus is the first sign of true salvation. Aggie can profess to that, can't you, Aggie? You couldn't wait to tell me about what you did."

Aggie smiled as she remembered the moment just a little while earlier. "The funny thing was, the first person I told was Aziz. He walked into the room just after Ms. Joan left. He was actually the first person I told. Now I get to see him make the same decision just a few hours later. This is a great night."

"You are very welcome to call your friend, but before things get too much out of hand, and I know this is going to be a buzz kill, I need you to look at these pictures. If you can identify anyone in them, it would go a long way to solving this investigation and getting on with our lives."

"Do I have to look at the pictures now?" Aziz asked. "It can't wait for a little while?" "No, the pictures are very clear, and every minute we go without knowing who these people are, the more time they have to possibly get away." Henry didn't want to say that since Maalik already knew they had these pictures, and if he was somehow involved, he would have these guys on a fast plane out to somewhere else before the day was out. That meant every moment counted. Of course, Aziz becoming a Christian was something that Henry had not expected. Henry realized what a huge decision this was for him and, even if Aziz wasn't thinking about it now, Henry knew what a drastic change it was going to be in Aziz's life. But right now, he needed the people in these pictures identified.

"Just take a look and see if you recognize them. If you do, then let me know who they are and where we can find them. If you don't, then you and I are done with the sheriff's part of my job, and I can put on my preacher's hat on and try to answer any questions you may have."

162

"Can you answer my questions, too?" Aggie asked. "I've got tons of them."

"I'll take both of you into a full-blown counseling session but let's look at these pictures first."

Aziz didn't say anything but held out his hand for the tablet. Henry handed it to him and stepped back, not wanting to pressure the young man in any way. As the pictures appeared on the screen, Aziz saw the background very clearly. He hadn't expected it to be this clear. Closing his eyes, Aziz hoped that the people in the pictures would not be anyone he knew. Being familiar with this iPad model, Aziz knew he could pull in a close up of each face. That way he could look at them one at a time instead of all four at once. This probably didn't make a difference, but he wanted to do it like this. The first man was not known to Aziz. He was of medium height and weight with no distinguishing features. *One down, one to go*, Aziz thought to himself.

The second man was taller and had a tattoo on his right forearm. Aziz didn't recognize him or the tattoo. Neither of the first two had been familiar to him, but neither of them had been wearing the hats. Those he saved for last because, in his mind, they would be the faces he would be most likely to know if he knew anyone. As he moved his hand down the page, he noticed that the time in the corner said 4:45. He had not known it was that late.

"You doing okay?" Aggie said from behind him. She had come over to offer support because she could see the turmoil on his face.

"I'm fine. I didn't know the first two, but now I am going to look at the other two." Looking away from the tablet, Aziz saw Sheriff Wactor, Ben, and Annette's husband talking in a corner. They were too far away for Aziz to hear, but they also couldn't hear him as he whispered softly aloud to Aggie. "Can you believe what we have done? I have been battling this for so many years and I never thought I would ever go this far. I have to be honest with you now. My friend Kareem almost had me to this point at Columbia. I was planning on attending a revival service with him the day my father and his friends showed up. I tried to tell my father that I was just humoring him, but deep down, I knew that I was searching for something. When I saw the picture of Kareem after his family had him beaten, and everything he owned was taken away from him, I decided that whatever he found in Jesus wasn't enough for me to go through that. So, I asked my father for forgiveness, and I immersed myself in the ways of Islam. I tried to become so proficient that nothing would ever make me question it again, but there was always that hint of doubt. Then, tonight, after Kareem called, I started wondering once more."

"You recognize anyone?" Sheriff Wactor asked. "I don't mean to hurry you, but time is of the essence. Aggie, I know you and Aziz have a lot to talk about, but I don't think you will know anyone."

As Sheriff Wactor was talking, Aziz began to scroll down to the other pictures. Aggie, though a new person on the inside, was still a stubborn person on the outside and didn't like being told what to do. Before she could inform Sheriff Wactor that she was just trying to be a friend to a friend, something caught her eye. "Hey, I recognize him." Everything in the room came to a complete halt.

"Aggie, I don't want to doubt you, but the odds of you recognizing someone from around here with your limited exposure are almost impossible," Ben said.

"I'm telling you that I recognize this guy in the brown shirt. He was at the funeral in Roxie yesterday. He came out to the car and met Aziz and me. Aziz, you said he was one of your friends who came to make a good showing of the crowd. Remember?"

Unfortunately, for Aziz, he did remember. He did recognize Gerald. The hat he wore was common among Muslim men, and Aziz knew that Gerald had one, but he didn't wear it very often. Why would he be involved in a murder? The question Aziz had but didn't want to ask was who else could be involved?

"Aziz, is this someone you recognize? If you can identify him, please do so. Unless he is proven to have been the ring leader, I will try to help him all I can. I just need you to tell me who he is and where he lives." Henry had taken off his preacher's hat and put his sheriff's hat back on.

"I am not sure it is the person Aggie thinks it is. He looks like someone I know, but I am not sure." How would the God whom Aziz just asked to come into his life take it if he lied about this?

"Aziz, that's the guy. He was the first one to meet us at the car at the funeral. I know I can't be that crazy. If he was involved with this murder, you have to tell them where to find him. He may not have done the killing, but he was definitely involved somehow. No amount of friendship can keep you from turning him in."

Aziz sat there holding the tablet. The warmth of just a few moments ago was still there. Would it stay there if he didn't do the right thing? For the longest of seconds, Aziz considered his options. This would be his first ever decision outside the Muslim faith. Even now, he could tell his father that he was just stringing along the sheriff. He could tell him that all the things he said were just a ruse to get into their inner circle. His father would believe it and would commend him for it. But deep down, Aziz would know that it wasn't the truth. The decision he had made to follow Christ was real, and it was his life from now on.

"His name is Gerald Johnson, but his Muslim name is Gedaliah Abdim. He lives on Two Bridges Road just outside of Fayette. He drives a blue Pontiac Grand Prix." He had said all this without looking up from the screen. Slowly he looked at Sheriff Wactor. "Is there any way this can happen without anyone knowing that I was the one who identified him?"

"As far as I'm concerned, a confidential informant with the Franklin County Sheriff's department identified him. If it ever got to a court and I had to produce that witness, I would produce Aggie. She actually identified him first, and she has no ties whatsoever to your father or his followers. How's that for covering yourself?"

"But won't that put Aggie in danger? I know my father, and he will hate her forever if he ever found out."

"Aziz, she is a Jew and he is a Jordanian Muslim. Unless Jesus changes his heart, he will hate her forever no matter what. Now, I'm going to get all my ducks in a row with the sheriff in Jefferson County, and we are going to arrest Mr. Johnson, or Abdim, or whatever his name is. All of you need to go get some sleep because it is almost the dawn of a new day. For you two," he pointed at Aziz and Aggie, "it is the beginning of a new life in Christ."

Watching the law enforcement vehicles drive out of the yard, Aggie wondered what was going to happen next. She wanted to get involved with people of like mind that she now had--even though she wasn't sure what that mind was. She needed to talk to Ben, because he was the only person she knew who had gone through the same situation she just did. Of course, Aziz had also, but she guessed he was as emotionally confused as she was.

"Why don't you go get some sleep, Aggie," Annette said. "I just talked to the hospital and the nurse told me Bobby was resting comfortably. I'm going to get a couple hours of sleep, and then I'm going back to the hospital. Aziz, you are welcome to get some shut eye on the couch."

"No thank you. I have to go home or my father will have someone out looking for me. I'm sure since he has a GPS tracker on my car he knows exactly where I am."

Aggie gasped. "My father has one on my car also. When did you find out, because I found out earlier tonight?"

"I found out earlier tonight also." As he said this, the details of the night before became so blurred, but the details of his conversion tonight were still crystal clear in his mind. How he was going to handle this with his family wasn't so clear, however. That was why he had to get home. He had to get home and begin to make a plan.

"I understand about being a father," Jack said. "As mad as I was at Jughead, I still love him more than life. I will be praying for you and your father."

"Thank you. Thank you all for this night. I don't know what's going to happen, but I want each of you to know that I count you among my friends. I wouldn't have said that twenty- four hours ago."

Annette walked up and put her arms around Aziz and hugged him. "Don't worry about it, I felt the same way about you twelve hours ago. Isn't it amazing the difference Jesus makes? Now you get on home. Please text Aggie's phone so that I will know you made it safely. I know I'm not your mother, but I need to know you are alright."

Aziz laughed. "I will do that. Aggie, are you going to be busy tonight?"

"I don't know, what did you have in mind?"

"I thought maybe I could come back here. And, Annette, you could help us, or at least me with a little understanding."

"I would be happy to. What about around 7:00? That'll give me time to get back from McComb and rest a little."

"One other thing," Aziz asked as he turned before going out the door. "Do you think God will get mad if we keep this our secret until I figure out what to do?"

"It's okay, Aziz. I don't think God will get mad. I'll look up some scripture and we'll talk about that tonight."

As he got into his car, Aziz thought he saw a familiar car parked around the corner. When he looked back, it was pulling away. "Probably just my imagination." The Challenger cranked reliably and, as he pulled onto the street, Aziz asked himself the question he hadn't considered because he dreaded the answer: What was he going to tell his mother?

166

CHAPTER 17

The One Who Plans or The One Who Makes it Happen

Henry Wactor was not as young as he once was. That was why he had let Billy drive when he asked. Even though he had gotten as much sleep as the sheriff, which was none, a cup of coffee and that young man was ready to go. Henry remembered a time that he could stay out all night either coon hunting or working and come home, get a shower and something to eat, and go back to his regular job at the tire plant. Those days were long gone and a good thing, because if he had to pull many more of these all-night excursions, he might not make it. But this morning was the beginning of a great day. The warrant for Gerald Johnson was signed and all the proper law enforcement authorities had been informed.

Now as the small caravan of state and local police headed toward the address Aziz had given them, Henry wondered if this young man would even be there. Since Maalik knew they had pictures of the men involved in the murder, there were some things that were quite obvious. If Maalik was somehow involved, then all four of the suspects might be long gone. The pictures of the other three were being sifted through the various data bases searching for facial recognitions. Depending on their results with Mr. Johnson, all the pictures would be released and warrants on them as fugitives would be issued. If any of them were already in the system, it would be easier. But if they had never been arrested and had no record, then the process would take a little longer. If Maalik wasn't involved, but his followers were, then Henry didn't know what tack Maalik would take. He was very loyal to his followers and even to those who weren't his followers, if it was to his advantage. The only thing they could do is play it out and continue to try and stay a step ahead. The finding of the camera was a great coup which had impressed all the MBI people. Henry could read between the lines. They were impressed that a little bohunk county like Franklin could actually find clues to solve a crime without the help of the great and mighty state officers.

"Sheriff, we are a half mile from the turn off. According to the Google Earth picture, the house is only a hundred or so yards after the turn. What do you want to do?"

167

"Let me have the radio," Sheriff Wactor said. "Gentlemen, remember that this young man is a suspect in a murder investigation. He is still just a suspect, so we treat him as such. That means no unnecessary force from anyone. If you feel your life is threatened, make sure to protect yourself, but only if your life is threatened. No one gets out of the car without their body armor. I have the warrant. MBI, I need you to get out at the end of the road and make your way to the back of the house. Key your radio one time when you are in position. I will lead the way from the front. Wactor out."

Billy admired the position the sheriff just took. He told everyone that the man was innocent until proven guilty, but also let them know to protect themselves at all times. That was the sign of a true leader and the kind of man Billy wanted to become as a law man.

Pulling into the driveway, the house was no different from a thousand houses in Southwest Mississippi. There were a couple of cars parked around beside the house that obviously were never going to move again unless they were pulled by a wrecker. The yard needed cutting, but it would be hard with all the various piles of trash. The house had one window covered with ply wood. The storm door was wide open, but it looked like it could fall onto the ground at any moment. The only thing that looked like it worked in the yard was the four-door car with a green paint job and what looked like twenty-two-inch rims which were probably worth more than the car. Billy recognized all this because the house he was raised in looked a lot like this one. It was the home of someone caught in a cycle of poverty. A cycle that they either couldn't or didn't want to break out of. He knew a person could get out of this cycle because he was a living example.

"Ok, Billy, when MBI is out back, you come up behind me. The JCSO guys are going to stay as our backup. Their sheriff said he was totally in support of us and would do whatever he needed to, but if we could handle it without him getting involved it might help him at election time. So, they are going to hang back at the cars to cover us. I guess it's you and me at the door." Right then, a microphone was keyed signaling that the MBI folks were in position. "All right, let's do this."

"Right behind you, Sheriff," Billy replied.

Coming up to the steps, they heard the sounds of a dog growling but didn't see one. "Sheriff, if that dog comes at me, I'm going to shoot him."

Henry laughed because it was well known in the department that Billy was deathly afraid of large dogs. "Calm down, Billy, if he was gonna come out at us we would have already seen him." Henry looked at each window, wary of the shadow of a muzzle being pushed past the blinds. "Gerald Johnson, this is the Franklin County Sheriff's department. I have a warrant. Please come out."

Billy noticed that, though he had all the authority in his voice and in his hand, Sheriff Wactor didn't stand in front of the door. He knew if a gun was discharged, that door wouldn't stop a bullet. They waited fifteen or twenty seconds and he knocked again. When nothing happened, Henry signaled the Jefferson County deputies to come on up onto the porch. That was the other part of the agreement. If the door had to be kicked in, the local deputies would do the kicking.

"Wylie, any movements out back?" Henry asked over the radio.

"Negative Sheriff. Nothing back here but a couple of them wiener dogs. They came out from under the porch when you walked up on it."

Henry had to stifle a snicker. He then looked over at Billy. "Good thing those vicious dachshund dogs didn't make you shoot them."

"Sheriff, that ain't funny." Even in this tense situation, Billy couldn't suppress a smile.

The JCSO deputies looked at Sheriff Wactor. "You ready?"

"Okay, go ahead. But why don't you try the door knob first, just in case it's already open." Reaching down, the deputy turned the doorknob and the door opened. When it did, there was a noticeable droop in his shoulders. Apparently, he had been fired up about kicking in that door. "Okay Billy, let's go."

As they walked into the room, Henry saw the living room of a young single man. There was a couch and a recliner with a flat screen television and one of those multi-player games playing on the screen. On the coffee table there were several cans of soda as well as a half-eaten sandwich. Henry saw that in one corner of the TV screen it said "paused."

"He may be in the bathroom." He then called out again. "Mr. Johnson, this is the Franklin County Sheriff's department. We have a warrant. Please come out with your hands up." When again nothing happened, everyone began to make a sweep of the house. Henry and Billy took the bathroom, and the other deputies worked through the other rooms. Henry could hear the shower running and pushed the door open. It was then he pulled his pistol.

"Gerald, can you hear me?" Reaching out, Henry quickly pulled back the shower curtain only to find it empty. "Clear in here. Anyone else got anything?" The sound of gunshots from behind the house answered that question.

"Everyone down. Take cover!" Henry shouted, though it was probably a wasted effort because the sound of people hitting the floor was echoing over the sound of the gunshots.

"MBI, what is your status?"

"Come on out, we've got a young man fitting the description in custody."

"Did he fire at you?" Henry asked as he got off the floor.

"No, we fired right over his head. He decided that no matter how fast he ran, he wasn't going to outrun those bullets, so he surrendered very quickly."

"Where did he come from?"

"He came out from under the house on the back corner. Maybe a trap door or something like it, because I don't believe he was under there when we got here."

Henry turned around and went back into the bathroom. Now that he was focusing on something other than getting shot or what he was going to find in the bathtub, his eyes were able to see things clearly. There was a box on the floor, but nothing was in it. Walking over, he tried to push it with his foot, but it didn't move. On a hunch, he reached down and grabbed the corner of the wooden box. Instead of coming up straight, the box pulled at an angle and the floor came up showing the trap door.

"You've got to give it to him, he was ready to get out in a hurry," Billy said. "He just didn't think we would come with this many people."

"Why don't we get him back to Franklin County and ask him all these questions, what do you say?"

"Sounds good to me, Sheriff. I don't like the way this house feels. It brings back too many memories."

Aziz woke up with a start. Looking at his watch, he saw that he had been asleep four hours, but it felt like he had just closed his eyes. When he got home this morning, he had slipped into the house as quietly as he could. He didn't want to answer any questions or go through any type of interrogation. The ride from Bude had been uneventful but was the most exciting drive of his life. Even though it was early in the morning, he had tried to call Kareem to tell him the good news, but he didn't answer. The rest of the drive consisted of asking God questions and wondering if now that he was a Christian, God would speak to him like in the movies. Aziz had seen "The Ten Commandments" movie where God supposedly spoke to that guy out of a bush that was on fire. His father had caught them watching the show and had given him and the other kids a beating. But now that he thought about it, that image of God was always in the back of his mind. Aziz turned over and almost jumped out of his bed. Sitting in a chair beside him was his father. "Good morning, Son. You didn't wake me last night when you got in."

"I had been up all night and was very tired. I didn't want you to be tired also." Aziz had rehearsed this initial conversation in his head when he drove into the driveway earlier. "I didn't call you anymore because I didn't know what your status was with that little boy. How long were you at his house?"

Aziz believed that his father knew exactly how long he had been at the house. He knew, not only because of the tracker, but that car that Aziz had seen was probably one of the security men from the mosque. That was why Aziz recognized it. Aziz knew right then that this was going to be a test from his father. Since he obviously knew that Sheriff Wactor was there, he was going to see if Aziz was going to tell him or not. He also would be wanting to know what he might have told the sheriff.

"When I got there, Sheriff Wactor was waiting on me. I don't know how he knew I was going to be there, but he was waiting. He threatened to arrest me and take me down to the jail, but I called his bluff and told him he didn't want another racial situation. He agreed and asked if we could go inside and talk. I guessed you would want me to go and find out what else he might know, so I agreed. We went inside and drank coffee and talked for most of the time. You are right about him. He is a very wise man and not one to be trifled with. But of course, I told him nothing that he didn't already know."

"I know Henry Wactor is shrewd. I also know that he plays the part of country sheriff very well. There have been many people who have underestimated him to their detriment, but I am not one of those people. What I want to know is what did you tell him without knowing you told him? Did your story of why you were at the hospital hold up? Did he believe you?"

"I told him that I was there to check up on Aggie, to make sure she was alright. He seemed to understand, but I don't think the other deputies liked me being there for her." This wasn't exactly true, but his father knew how most people in Franklin County felt about inter-racial couples; it would be a good nugget to toss out.

"Yes, I can understand how that would be a problem for them. Did he mention the pictures they have?"

"Yes, he did. He said that he had pictures of four or five men coming and going with the body of the young man." Aziz left off the bombshell that Henry knew that he knew about the pictures.

"Did he show them to you or ask you to identify them?"

"Yes, but he didn't show all of them to me. The only pictures I saw were the ones of them from the back." This was a very big lie, but it had to be told like this for Aziz's story to be believable. "I'm guessing they have pictures of them from other angles, but I didn't see them."

"Probably because he didn't expect you to identify anyone. In fact, I believe that the entire episode was done to see how much you were willing to divulge. Did you make any rash statements or do anything that I need to know about?" Aziz froze for just a moment, wondering what that question meant. When he was a child, sometimes his father would ask if there was anything he wanted to admit to. Most of the time, it was just a bluff. Was that what it was this time? Though he was older and wiser, Aziz still didn't have a real ability to read his father.

"Nothing rash. I acted like I cared about their investigation, and I let them know that you and I would be on them until they solved this crime. But Father, two of the young men were wearing Muslim head wear. Since we are the only Muslim group in the tri-county area, is it possible that someone we know who was involved?"

"I am in the process of finding out now. I just received a call telling me that Gedaliah has been or soon will be arrested for suspicion of murder. Apparently, someone identified him from the picture. I haven't confirmed it, but I've been told that it was some informant who saw the picture and made the identification. Did they mention if anyone else was looking at the pictures?"

"When I looked at the pictures, I asked him if anyone else was going to look at them. He didn't mention anyone, but I could be wrong." Aziz knew he was moving dangerously close to the line when his father could tell he was lying.

"Are you still tired? If you are, I will let you get back to sleep. You have had a long and successful night. I have some investigation to do of my own. First and foremost, I need to find out who else was involved with Gedaliah."

"I am definitely tired. I think a couple more hours would be nice. When I get up, I will call you if you aren't home."

As he watched his father walk out and close the door behind him, Aziz began to ponder the fact that his father said he was going to investigate who was involved but not why they did it.

Aggie awakened to the sound of her phone ringing. She knew it wasn't her alarm because she hadn't set it. She tried to get her eyes to focus and saw that it was Ben calling.

"Hello," Aggie said trying to not sound like she just woke up.

"What kind of reporter are you? The first arrest of the subject happened a few minutes ago, and he is being transported to Franklin County as we speak. I need my new reporter down here right now."

Aggie threw the cover off and sat on the side of the bed. "He was there? They got him without any problem?"

"I don't know the details, but I do know that they are on the way. We need to be there for the perp walk, and then I can ask Henry a few questions. No one from anywhere else will be there, so we will have the scoop. By the way, how was your first night's sleep as a Christian?"

"I slept better this morning than I have since before my mother got sick. I feel great, and I don't ever want to have that fear again."

"Don't think it will all be wine and roses but, trust me, you'll have a better life than you used to. Now get off the phone and get down here to the office."

Aggie dressed quickly and brushed her teeth. She was glad she had taken a shower the night before after everyone had left. When she opened her door, Archie was walking past. "Good morning, Archie. How are you this morning?"

"I'm good. We're headed out to the farm to work on the barn. At least that is what we are telling Mom. If I know my dad, we will do more fishing than working. Telling her that we are working on the barn gives us some cover. I don't think she believes it, but it's our game we play. Where are you headed?"

"I'm going to the newspaper office. Ben has some work for me to do. You go and do lots of work on that barn. Where's your mother?"

"She left about an hour ago headed to the hospital. Oh, yeah, I was

173

supposed to tell you that Uncle Bobby is doing better. His vital signs are strong, and they hope he will wake up later today. I gotta go before it gets too hot to fish…I mean work."

She studied this young man who had begun this little escapade with her as he left to meet his dad. Aggie envied the relationship he had with his parents. Though they were angry and wanted to punish him for what he had done, he still knew that they loved him no matter what. Aggie knew that about her mother but wasn't sure about her father. Since her mother's death, their relationship had gotten even more toxic. Her turning her back on Judaism wouldn't help. In fact, it would probably be the death knell for their relationship, what there was of it. Walking through the kitchen, Aggie looked around to see if there was some kind of snack on the counter. She then stopped in the middle of the kitchen and laughed at her situation. If her friends from Rutgers could only see her now. She was in the home of a family that three days ago she didn't know at all. Now she felt so comfortable in their home, she was looking for snacks on the counter like it was her home. The kind of friendship that Annette and Jack offered her here was rare and non-existent in her life prior to coming south.

When she got to her car, there was a piece of paper under the windshield wiper. "Aww, I'll bet Nette left me a note," she said aloud. Pulling it out and opening it, Aggie immediately saw that it was not handwritten. How it was written was not what took her breath away but *what* was written. Even though she had been mugged once and had been around and seen her share of criminals, never had a chill of fear ever come over her like the one she experienced as she read the note: *You are a foreigner in a foreign land. You need to make your way back to New York before something happens to you like what you came to write an article about. Your choice.*

CHAPTER 18

Even Good Decisions Have Consequences

"Who do you think put that on your car?" Ben said as he laid the note on his desk.

"It has to be Aziz's father's people, wouldn't you think?" Aggie had driven straight to the newspaper office after she found the note because she knew Ben would know what to do.

"No, it doesn't have to be them. They would be a good suspect, but I don't think they are the only suspects. You can't have many enemies. Most folks have to stay in Franklin County for months before people are ready for them to leave. You got the royal treatment in less than three days. Congratulations."

"Ben, this isn't funny. That's a threat on my life. What could I have possibly done to anyone that would make them threaten my life? For that matter, how many people know why I'm even in Franklin County. There can't be many, so that should lower the pool of suspects."

"Aggie, you were on national news. CNN did an interview with you, and I'll bet everyone Googled your name. Your story is not well known, but it *is* known. I'm going to say something that may burst your bubble. I'm not sure this had anything to do with you. I think it may have had something to do with Aziz. There was a strange car parked up the street from Annette's house last night. It had Jefferson County plates, so it might have been some of Maalik's people. Maybe, and this is a big maybe, Maalik doesn't like his son cavorting around with a young Jewish girl. Trust me, worse things have happened around here when people of different social, ethnic, and economic backgrounds started to seem too chipper together."

"But Aziz and I are just friends. He and I share a tough family life, and we have both accepted Christianity over our families' religious beliefs. But there isn't anything romantic between us." As she said it, Aggie wondered if she really believed it.

"It may not be from your end, and I'm not going to bet the farm on that, but it probably is on his end. Enough about this. We'll get with Henry after he gives me the inside story on the arrest. They should be through with the

175

preliminary questioning by now. Let's go over and see what he had to say."

"What is the preliminary questioning? Are they going to work him over with a garden hose, or beat him with a stick through a phone book?"

"Aggie, you watch too many movies. Even if this was thirty years ago, this case is too high profile for this Johnson fellow to have anything he could say that would get him off the hook. I promise you Henry is handling this exactly by the book."

The knock on the door was as expected as the person who was doing the knocking. "Aziz are you awake?"

"Yes, Mother come in." Aziz was sitting at his desk trying to come up with a way to embrace his newfound religion without destroying his family.

"Do you want to come and have some lunch?" Kadeera Salaam was not a very large woman, but she wasn't that tiny either. She never talked about her family back in Jordan, but Aziz had seen some pictures and all of them were well-built and proud looking.

"Yes Mother, please. Where did Father go?"

"I don't know and he didn't tell me. I did hear him say that he might have to go to Franklin County and help bail someone out. Do you know what he was talking about?"

"I believe he said that Gedaliah was arrested today."

"I do not know his family. I would be heartbroken if you were ever arrested. Did he say what he was arrested for?"

"Something about the young boy who was killed a couple of days ago."

"I would reach out to his mother, but I don't believe they are members of our faith." Aziz thought to himself, *neither am I*, but kept this to himself. Then he had another idea.

"Mother, what do you think of people in different faiths?"

"I do not think anything of them. The Quran teaches that anyone who doesn't believe is

an infidel. I live among them, but I do not think anything of them. Why do you ask?"

"No reason, I was just wondering."

176

"Why don't you come to the kitchen while I prepare your lunch? Don't wait long or it will get cold."

"Yes, Ma'am. Let me get a shower and I'll be right there."

Aziz took his time in the shower as he tried to adjust to the new feelings he was having about his life. As he got dressed, he wondered if he looked any differently. When he began to put his shoes on, his phone rang. It was Kareem. Aziz walked over and looked down the hallway to make sure no one was there before he answered the phone. "Hello, Kareem, my friend," Aziz said as he tried to hide the excitement in his voice.

"Hello, Aziz. I'll be honest, I didn't expect to hear from you ever, much less within a few hours of our conversation last night. You didn't leave a message this morning. Is everything all right?"

"Kareem, do you remember the night my father showed up at Columbia?"

"That is a night I will never forget. I got a beating like I have only seen on television, and you were taken away in a black Mercedes."

"Do you remember where we were going that night?"

Kareem was quiet for a moment. "I think I was trying to get you to come to a revival service with me. I had thought you were actually considering going."

"I was considering it, but when my father showed up and I saw what happened to you, I forgot any thoughts of going and instead came home and immersed myself in Islam. But Kareem, last night after you called, something amazing happened. I accepted Jesus as my savior. Not only did I do this, but a young Jewish girl from New York did too. That is what I called to tell you." All Aziz could hear from the other end of the phone was sobbing.

"Kareem, are you ok? Why are you crying? Didn't you hear what I said?"

"Aziz, I am crying for joy that is unspeakable. The only one who's salvation I am more pleased about is my own. I would have never thought that you would ever believe the truth. Have you told your father?"

"Let's take this one step at a time. I hope I learned from your experience that just walking in and telling him cold turkey is not the best idea. I'm going to tell him, but I have to work on the timing and how. I want to come up and visit with you very soon. When will you have a free weekend?"

"I will have to look at my schedule. Let me go to the church and look on my computer. I will call you back in an hour, and we will come up with a time where we can truly celebrate the greatest decision of your life."

"All right, I'll talk to you soon." Aziz ended the call and threw his phone on the bed. What a great feeling he had. He hoped his life as a Christian would always be like this. All of a sudden, he heard a crash. Turning around, he saw his mother standing in the door. The plate of food she had made, along with the tray she had carried it on, with were both on the floor.

"Do you know what you have done?" Kadeera asked. "Do you know what your father will do when he finds out?" Aziz just stood there in the middle of his room. He knew he needed to say something, but words would not come out of his mouth. "How could you do this to your father? You will refute whatever you think you did and we will never speak of this again. Is that understood?"

"Mother, I can't do that." As he began to speak, the warm feeling came over him. "Mother, I found something last night that was more real than anything I have ever experienced in Islam."

Kadeera walked over and took Aziz by the hands. She was crying and shaking. "Son, I know you and your father have not always gotten along. I know that you resented being brought back from Columbia, but this is not the way to get back at him. You were to be his heir apparent. He has spoken to those above him, and you will take his place when the time comes. All your dreams and hopes will be thrown away, for what? For some religious feeling that will eventually disappear? I heard you say something about a girl. Was she the reason you did this?"

"No, Mother, please understand. I have been searching for the truth in Islam for a long time, but I have not found it, only a bunch of rules and laws that are almost impossible to fulfill. Last night, I..."

"I don't want to hear any of it. You will stay in this room until your father comes home. Then you will recant. Do you really think your father will allow his son to convert to Christianity? The damage to his reputation would be irreparable. Don't you love your father and me?"

Aziz knew that he loved his father as a son should, but the love he had for his mother was even greater. "Mother, I love you, but this is something that I have to do. It is nothing against you or Father. It is something for me and me alone."

"That will be something for your father to decide. I'm going to call him now." She then did something Aziz didn't expect. She reached over onto the

178

table beside the door and grabbed the keys to Aziz's car and shut the door.

"Mother, this isn't going to stop me. I've made my decision." But his words echoed down a lonely hallway.

Aziz knew he had to get out of the house. If she was able to contact his father, he would have men coming immediately to detain Aziz until he returned. Maybe somewhere in the back of his mind, Aziz knew a day like this might come. This must have been the reason he had gotten the spare key. After the incident at Columbia and the taking away of his car, Aziz promised himself that he would always have a way out. When his father had given him the Challenger, Aziz had gone the next day to Natchez to the dealership and gotten a spare key made. It had cost him two hundred dollars, but right now it was worth its weight in gold. Reaching into his bookshelf, Aziz took out the wooden box that had held his pen and pencil set someone had gotten him for graduation from high school. Underneath the pen and pencil was a black key. Taking the key, Aziz walked to the door and listened. He could hear his mother pushing the buttons on the wall phone and then hanging up and doing it again. Apparently, she wasn't able to contact his father. Knowing that she would do everything in her power, including grabbing him, to keep him in the house, Aziz decided he must go out the window. As he opened the window, he saw a car coming down the drive. It wasn't his father's car, so she must have called someone else. Either way, they would try to keep him here. Aziz hopped out his window and ran to his car. He was relieved he had remembered to grab his cell phone. When he cranked the car, he saw his mother come to the door. She was waving at him, but Aziz knew better than to let her slow him down. The other car was almost there, and he didn't want to be blocked in. He threw the car into drive and hit the gas, throwing up a cloud of dust that covered the entire yard and house. For a moment, whoever it was that was coming down the drive lost sight of Aziz, until he went by them like a gazelle being chased by a cheetah. When he had turned onto the main highway, a question came to Aziz. Where was he going?

"Sheriff, I don't know what you think you're doing, but this young man doesn't have any counsel present, and anything he says is inadmissible in any court of law, including these kangaroo courts you have here in Franklin County." Maalik was not yelling because he only did that when he thought it would do some good. He was, however, talking in an agitated tone. The more his phone vibrated, the more agitated he became. He knew it was coming from home, and they knew that if he didn't answer the second time, they were to stop calling. Now that the phone was ringing for a third time, Maalik assumed that it was Aziz calling. He knew the rules, but sometimes he seemed to ignore them. He would speak to his son about the rules when he returned

179

home.

"Maalik, the prisoner has been read his rights and he signed a consent form to talk to us without a lawyer present. I have been in touch with the DA in Natchez, and he has been informed of everything we've done. This young man is willing to talk to us, and we are willing to listen. I would appreciate it if you would take all the other folks you have with you and wait in the lobby. When I am done, I will come and talk to you, but not a moment before."

"You won't be talking to me. You will be talking to Billingslee Stovall."

"Maalik, I don't care if I'm talking to Ben Matlock or Perry Mason. I am going to do my job and do it the right way. You do what you have to do."

Henry Wactor knew that he had to handle this one carefully, and until now, everything had gone better than he could have hoped. Gedaliah or Gerald had not said much on the way to the jail. They had read him his rights at the house, and Henry had expected a quiet trip. About half way to Meadville, he had begun to talk about how he would tell them whatever he knew, if he could get a deal. Henry had not promised him anything but had texted the DA what the prisoner had said. He had immediately sent back that if Gerald would identify the other three men, he would make sure that he would not be charged with murder; and if he identified the murderer, then he might be able to get his charge moved down to involuntary manslaughter and only six months in jail. Henry didn't tell Gerald this because he wanted the young man to sweat a little. He also knew that he had to do everything by the book so that any testimony he gave would be admissible. Now that Maalik was here, Henry was glad he had taken his time.

"What did Maalik have to say?" Ben asked as Henry came back into the booking room.

"Exactly what you would expect him to say. Billy, have we heard how long until the DA gets here?" Henry had fibbed a little bit to Maalik, because Gerald would not talk until he had a deal in his hands. Even though Henry knew he was within his authority, he wanted that document signed before Stovall got here. He was widely assumed to be the best defense attorney in Mississippi from either side of the racial divide.

"I just got off the phone with LV. He said that he was outside of Roxie and was going as fast as his car would go."

"Is there any possibility that Aziz's father is involved?" Aggie asked.

180

"I don't know for sure, but my gut tells me that this is just a face-saving attempt because this young man is a new Muslim. Maalik and I don't believe the same about very many things, but I don't believe he would be involved with murder."

"Would he be involved with intimidation?" Aggie asked, as she took out the note that had been on her car.

"What is that?" Henry asked.

Ben looked at Aggie with a hint of agitation, because he had told her they would talk about this when the Sheriff had fewer things on his mind.

"It's a note that was on my car when I got to it this morning."

"Ben, why haven't you mentioned this to me before now? Whoever left this note might have done it while we were there last night."

"It's my fault, Henry. I told Aggie that you had enough on your plate and didn't need anything else to worry about."

"I understand, but this is not a subtle threat. This is a deliberate threat against someone who may or may not be involved in a criminal investigation." Henry then took his phone and began to look for a number. "I won't allow this to become an intimidation situation."

"Who is he calling?" Aggie asked Ben.

"I have no idea."

"Yes, this is Sheriff Henry Wactor of Franklin County. I would like to request twenty-four-hour security for a possible witness. Yes, immediately. I can keep her here at the sheriff's office until the units arrive." Henry then listened for a few moments and began to smile. "That's fine, I'll be here when they arrive."

"Sheriff, I don't want security. I'm leaving on Monday if at all possible. I can take care of myself until then."

"No, Aggie, that is where you are wrong. You may leave Monday, or you may not. But what you are not going to do is take care of yourself. I will do that and you will accept my protection. The only reason I asked for help from MBI was because when Gerald names all the men in the picture, I will have to round them up, and then I will be too busy to take care of you. This is not negotiable or questionable. Is that understood?"

Though Aggie had many questions and many arguments she kept them to herself, because she knew they would fall on deaf ears with this man. Also, she knew that he was taking care of her, and she didn't mind that. If the truth be told, she was very nervous about the note anyway."

"Sheriff, I don't want to drive that fast ever again," a tall man said as he walked into the meeting room. I think I've arrived only about five minutes before Billingslee. Where is the suspect?"

"Good to see you," said Henry. "L.V. Jarrett, this is Aggie Sharosh, and you know Ben."

"Aggie Sharosh. Is this the young woman from New York that CNN was fawning over last night? Nice to meet you Ms. Sharosh. I would introduce myself more formally but, as I said, I am about five minutes ahead of Billingslee so can we get this deal done."

"Come on L.V. He's in the holding cell. Ben, you stay with Aggie back here until those guards arrive."

As they watched the Sheriff and Assistant DA walk out of the room, both Aggie and Ben looked at one another, neither knowing what to say or do. "You got a deck of cards with you?" Ben asked.

"How can he do this? I am perfectly capable of taking care of myself."

"No, Aggie, you aren't. I don't know if this has anything to do with the murders, or your

friendship with Aziz, or just that someone might not like Jewish women, but this is not something to take lightly. By the way, have you heard from Aziz?"

"No, I haven't. I tried to call him earlier when I was headed down here, but he didn't answer the phone. I don't know why."

The reason Aziz didn't answer the phone was because he had thrown it out the window. That was just another way for his father to track his whereabouts. At this very moment, Aziz was looking under the trunk for the GPS tracker his father had on the car. If he could get rid of that, then he could move without being found. He knew the car didn't come with an onboard GPS system, so it had to be something that was added. Aziz knew enough about these things because one of his friends at Alcorn had majored in electronics and had told him all about getting a tracking unit and putting it on his girlfriend's car. He had ordered it online and installed it one day while she was in class. It had a magnet, and he had wired it to the taillights so that he didn't have to take it off and recharge it. He could pull it up on his computer or phone and know her exact location and everything. That had to be what Aziz's father put on the car. All he had to do was find it. While lying on the ground with his hand searching under the car, Aziz wondered if this was really what he wanted. But the thought went away in just a moment, because he knew that when he accepted Christ he'd gone all the way. Trusting in Him was all he had now. "Now God, I just need you to help me find this GPS unit," Aziz said aloud. No sooner had the words come out of his mouth than his hand bumped into something. It felt like it wasn't part of the car and had a wire running from it. That had to be it. Pulling the rectangle block loose, Aziz saw that it was exactly as his friend had described it. Now all he had to do was cut the wires and tape them up. Aziz didn't want to take a chance on blowing a taillight and getting pulled over by the local cops. He knew that his father would eventually have them looking for him.

As he taped the wires, Aziz realized that he had found the box immediately after asking God to help him. In all his years as a Muslim, he had never heard of anything like that happening to someone much less it happening to him. How could he have missed this Christian thing all these years? How could he tell other people about it so they wouldn't miss it?"

CHAPTER 19

The Picture Becomes Clear

"Gerald, why would you and your friends murder this young man?" Henry asked. "You've given us the names, but I need a reason. Are these guys going to tell us the same story that you did?"

"He can't say what anyone else will say. The only thing my client *can* say is that he is telling the truth. Even though he has signed this deal, I am advising my client not to answer until I have had time to review the document. Gedaliah, would you please listen to me?" Billingslee Stovall was definitely flustered, but he maintained his composure. He had to try and earn his money, probably from Maalik, who would most likely be paying for his services.

"No, I'll answer. I've done been to Parchman one time. I didn't like it then and I don't like it now. That's why I made this deal, so that I won't have to go back there. I don't care what the other three guys say; I know what the truth is. As far as what happened to Marcus, he said he wanted to convert to Islam then changed his mind. He said that his momma wouldn't like it. It's like that song where you can check out anytime you like but you can never leave."

"Who gave the order to kill him? Was it Maalik or one of his underlings?" Henry wanted to know if Maalik was involved while he was still in the building. Subjects were always easier to arrest when you didn't have to go around and find them.

"No, our leader had nothing to do with this. He didn't even know about it, though I'm sure he would have agreed with us."

"I highly doubt that," Henry said. "Did you intend to kill him?"

"No, Kenny and I were just going to work him over and remind him of his promises, but he decided to fight against us. I guess we got a little too rough with him, and he fell and hit his head on the concrete. David had the great idea to make it look like a lynching. Who would have thought some crazy redneck would have a camera on a tree?"

"Sheriff, can I have a few words with my client?" Billingslee Stovall asked.

"No problem, Billingslee. LV., do we have anything else to cover?"

"No, only to reiterate that if he changes his story, or if it proves to be untrue, then this deal is null and void, and we will charge him with First Degree Murder as well as the others. Also, I will make sure that whatever jail time he does, whether it be one week or the rest of his life, it will all be spent at Parchman." L.V. Jarrett had heard how much Gerald didn't want to go back to Parchman, so using it to reinforce the deal was a smart move.

As he walked down the hall from what had been the best interrogation he had ever been through, Henry Wactor reflected on what would happen next. Billingslee Stovall would be a pain, but if everything Gerald told them turned out to be true, then this case was solved. Henry didn't care what happened in the courtroom, or how much time any of them got. The case was solved and a mother and father could have some closure.

"Henry, you got a minute?" Ben was looking out the door of the office.

"What's going on?"

"I just got a call from Annette. Bobby woke up."

"That's great news. I mean that's wonderful news. For this weekend to have started so badly, it's definitely getting better by the minute."

"Not only is he awake, but he has feeling in all his extremities. It's almost like he was never injured. Annette said he was going to be moved out of the ICU this evening. If I know Bobby, they will have a hard time keeping him any longer than necessary. Annette was crying so hard I could barely understand her. She was completely overwhelmed by God's intervention."

"Let's go into my office so I can sit down. All this sudden good news combined with the fact that I haven't slept since Thursday night is hitting me like a ton of bricks." Once they were seated, Henry realized just how tired he was.

"I've got to know. Did Gerald give up the names of the others?" Ben asked. "When I saw Stovall come in, I wondered if he was going to be a fly in the ointment. Did he keep anything from happening?"

"No, Gerald had already signed the agreement and had started naming names and telling us where he thought they might be. I told Billy to get some help down here and to go get them. I know Billy is as tired as I am and, with Bobby out of commission, we are already short-handed. I am going to

185

depend on our friends from the state police. MHP should be able to take care of these boys, since only one of them is in Franklin County. The other two are from Hazlehurst, so I am going to let the boys from Copiah County do some work. To tell you the truth, I am running on my last fumes. Where did they take Aggie?"

"Those MBI boys came and I suggested they go to McComb, but Aggie wouldn't hear of it. She said that she was going to stay at Annette's. She couldn't stand being in a strange motel room with a bunch of strange people. I agreed with her, so they are going to have one person in the house and two cars outside. She's also going to start working on a story for me for the paper. I figured I should get as much out of her as I can, because she is probably not long for this area. She'll be back in New York very soon."

"What about Aziz? Have you heard anything from him? Even though Aggie got a threatening note, he's the one I think is in more danger. If Maalik ever realizes what he did, he will blow a gasket."

"Are you sure you heard him say that?" Maalik asked his wife. He had ignored her calls for the entire afternoon because he was worried about Gedaliah. Though he had nothing to do with the murder of that young man, Maalik couldn't allow him to be steamrolled. That was the reason he had brought in Billingslee Stovall. If there was anything that could be done, he would do it. Now Maalik was being told that his only son had forsaken his birthright and supposedly become a Christian.

"Yes, I heard him talking to his friend Kareem. He is planning on going to visit him. I took his keys to keep him here, but he must have a spare. He left before I could get someone to guard his room. Do you know where to find him?"

"I have a way to track him. I will find out where he is and go talk to him. Do not talk to anyone about what you've told me. Who did you have coming to guard him?"

"Manu, but I didn't go into any specifics. I just told him I was having a disagreement with Aziz. Just as he got here, Aziz was leaving. I told him that Aziz was angry and wanted to get away for a while. What are we going to do?"

"The Quran tells us what to do when someone leaves our faith. My son can be no different, but I must talk to him to make sure he is not just brainwashed. I will call you when I've found him." Without saying goodbye, Maalik ended the call and looked out the window. Suddenly, the situation of

Gedaliah and his cohorts was not as important as it had been just a few moments earlier.

"Can I look at your gun?" Archie asked Keith Coffey, the lead officer. Keith was the officer stationed in the house.

"Jughead, would you please leave the officer alone," Jack said. "You've seen guns before. His gun is not a toy to amuse young men." Though he didn't say anything, having armed guards in and around his house was clearly disconcerting.

"Don't mind him Mr. Walker. I have two sons myself, and I understand their curiosity. It is a fine weapon," Keith said as he took his pistol out of the holster. He then removed the clip and took the bullet out of the chamber. "I'm sure your father has already told you this, but as a certified firearm instructor, I always tell young people this. You never give someone a loaded weapon. If they are going to shoot it, then let them reload it. It is impossible for an accidental shooting to happen with an unloaded weapon." He then handed the pistol to Archie.

"Wow, this is lighter than your gun Dad." Even though he knew the gun was not loaded, Archie made sure not to point it at anyone. "What kind is it?"

"It is a 40-caliber Sig. It is one of the finest pistols made. It's the same kind the secret service uses to protect the president."

"Aggie's being protected just like the President. That is way cool," Archie said. "Where is she?"

"I think she went upstairs to her room. She said she was tired."

Aggie was exhausted, but she wasn't able to go to sleep. She was sitting on the bed thinking about everything that had happened. The best news was when Annette called and told them that Bobby was awake and alert. The worst thing was that there were armed men standing in the kitchen and sitting in two different cars outside. They were there because Sheriff Wactor thought they needed to protect her. Looking up at the ceiling, Aggie wondered if this was how her life as a Christian was going to be. On the bedside table, Aggie saw a Bible. She had noticed it the day before but, now as she looked at it, she realized that book meant something totally different to her than it had before. Taking it in her hands, Aggie didn't know where to look or what to look at. It was a big book and, as she turned the pages, she began to understand why it was something special to Christians.

"I guess there's no better time than the present," Aggie said to herself. She had considered starting at the beginning, but decided to trust fate, or whatever Christians trusted. There was a ribbon marking a page and someone had highlighted a verse. It said "Proverbs." The words that were highlighted were from the fifth and sixth passages. They said, "Trust in the Lord with all your heart and lean not unto your own understandings. In all thy ways acknowledge him and he will direct thy paths." *That answers all my questions,* Aggie thought. *How did I come to that exact place at the exact time?* She read and reread the highlighted words. Each time she read them; she became more emotional. *If ever there was someone who doesn't understand, it's me.*

The ringing of her cell phone brought her back to reality. The number displayed a 601-area code which she now knew was Mississippi, but the number wasn't in her phone. The area code also meant it wasn't her father. It was late in the afternoon, and he hadn't made any attempt to call today. That was a first. He must really be angry after last night. "Hello," she said very cautiously.

"Hello, Daughter. So nice of you to take my call. Are you on your way back home like I asked you to do?"

"You should know, don't you have a tracking device on my car?"

"Yes, I do, but I don't have access to a computer at the moment. Am I to believe that you aren't on your way back?"

"No, I'm not on my way back. I am currently sitting in the bedroom of my friend Annette."

"Where does this person live? Is it in this Franklin County place?"

"Yes, she lives in Bude. I was planning on coming home Monday, but there have been some difficulties, and I have to wait and see if they get handled."

"Does it have something to do with this murder investigation you were involved in? Does it have anything to do with the fact that someone found film of the suspects? Does it have anything to do with you at all? Does it have anything to do with the fact that you have special officers standing guard over you because you were threatened? Please tell me when I get warm."

Aggie sat there with her mouth open in complete disbelief. "How can you know all of that?" was all she could manage to say. "No one knows about any of this. It hasn't been through any media outlets. The only people who know about this are local law enforcement." Then out of the blue, it hit her.

The call came from a 601-area code. "You're, here aren't you?"

"If you mean am I there with you, obviously not. But if you mean am I in Mississippi then, yes, I am. I am currently at the Department of Public Safety building in the office of Mr. Rusty Osborne of the MBI."

"Rusty Osborne, with the MBI? How could you possibly know him?" Aggie asked this, but she should have remembered what a man of her father's means could do.

"Because the people I know put me in contact with him last night. I flew in this morning and have been briefed on the details. I want you to come meets me this evening. Though we have spoken on the phone several times over the last couple of days, I haven't seen you in several weeks. As your father, I still feel responsible for you, and if you will not come home, I had no other recourse but to fly down and make sure you are alright. Despite what you think of me, I do care about your well-being."

"Dad, you didn't have to come down here. I know you don't like to leave the city."

"Nonsense! What use is having a plane if you don't use it. Besides, Mr. Osborne is a fine upstanding Jewish man. He has been very helpful in my understanding of this state and the people in it."

"I am not able to come to Jackson tonight. I have an article to write and, as you said, I have some protection issues. You don't have to worry about me. Why don't you take the plane home and I'll see you when I get back?" Aggie knew she wasn't making a lot of sense, but she couldn't think of anything else to say. What was he doing here?

"I understand you don't care to see me, but just hearing your voice helps to ease my anxiety. Officer Osborne tells me that they have found the killers of that young boy who was found lynched."

"That's news to me. When I left the courthouse, they were still interrogating him. Why is this Osborne guy telling you all these things? Isn't he supposed to keep this quiet?"

"His oath to his office is important, but his support of his people is also important. I didn't realize how few of our faith there are in Mississippi. It is a shame how few people know about our religion here."

"They may know more about our faith than you realize," Aggie said looking at the Bible sitting in her lap.

189

"I highly doubt that. If you aren't interested in seeing me, and you are not in danger anymore, then I will make my way back home. But please, I implore you, hurry home. You and I have many things that we need to discuss."

"You don't know the half of it," Aggie said. "Thanks for being concerned, Dad. I'll talk to you later." As she put her phone back onto the bed, Aggie felt pangs of guilt because there was a huge decision in her life that she hadn't shared with her father. No matter what their relationship was, he was the only parent she had left.

"So, let me get this straight," Bobby said as he took a drink of tea. "Aggie, the Jewish girl from New York and Aziz, the Muslim gentleman from Fayette, both accepted Christ last night while I lay paralyzed in ICU? What kind of parallel universe did I wake up in?"

Annette laughed at the statement. Not only because of the look on Bobby's face, but also how totally unbelievable it truly sounded. "Yes, that's in essence what happened. I've never been a part of anything like this in my life. This could be the beginning of a revival like none we have ever seen."

"But what's going to happen when both their fathers find out about their decisions? I'm pretty sure they are not going to take it lying down, especially Maalik."

"I have worried about that some myself, along with worrying about whether or not you were going to be alright. But I do have to say, God had given me a peace about you, whatever is going to happen. When I called our mother and told her you were alright, do you know what she said? She said of course he is; he's a child of God. Our mother is a great woman of faith."

"I wasn't really paying attention when the doctor was in here after they brought me out of ICU. When did he say I could go home?"

"He mentioned something about tomorrow or Monday. I'm not a doctor, so I'm not going to argue with him. So, if I'm not going to argue with him, *you* are not going to argue with him, is that understood?"

"Yes, I understand. Was Aggie concerned about me?" Bobby asked, almost sheepishly.

"She was distraught in a way I wouldn't expect from someone who just met a person. She drove that Porsche hard getting us here last night. I have noticed you have been paying attention to her, too."

"I didn't think a lot about it because she won't be around for long, and you know how I am with long-distance relationships." Annette knew all about the pains in Bobby's life from his long-distance relationship with his high school girlfriend after she went off to college in Georgia. He had tried hard and driven many miles to see her before it had begun to affect his own education. That was when their parents had sat him down and explained that if he was going to follow after something that most likely wasn't God's choice for him, then he was going to have to finance his own college. At first Bobby had been angry and said that if they didn't care about who he loved, then he would take care of himself. He had then gone to Atlanta to be with his one true love to only walk into her dorm room to find her with another guy. Though he was a Christian at that time, Bobby had gone into a week-long depression fueled by alcohol and pity. When he had finally gotten over his embarrassment and come home, their parents never mentioned it again. But the girls Bobby dated after that were all within a few blocks of wherever he was living. Unfortunately, none of them had lasted.

"This girl is definitely different from any one you have ever had any dealings with. Besides you have never had a relationship with anyone you put handcuffs on."

"Yes," Bobby smiled at the memory of Aggie in handcuffs. He had been so scared that she was some kind of human trafficker. Her beauty had not even registered until after Sheriff Wactor had arrived. "When are you going back home?"

"In just a little while. There are going to be a couple of your deputy friends who are going to stand guard outside your room. With the threat to Aggie, they don't want to take any chances."

"What threat to Aggie?" Bobby almost jumped out of the bed. "Who threatened her and what does that have to do with me? Was it something to do with the murder? If I need to go, I can be ready in ten minutes."

"Bobby, don't you even think about getting out of that bed. If I have to get them to knock you out, I will. I don't think that it has anything to do with the murder, but I haven't heard and they aren't sure. There are MBI agents at my house now just in case. When you get home, we will worry about how to take care of you. Now you get to healing and I will see you in the morning. I really need some rest and you do, too."

"Don't skip church tomorrow checking on me. Like you said, I'm gonna be fine. Besides, if everything you say happened last night, what might happen tomorrow at church?"

"Bobby, I think you may be right."

CHAPTER 20

The Ultimate Choice

The back roads of Southwest Mississippi are many, and most of them look the same. It doesn't matter whether you are outside Natchez, which is the largest and oldest town, or around Meadville, which is the smallest town. Aziz was keeping off all the main roads because he knew by now his father was aware of his decision. He also knew that the law enforcement of Jefferson County would be looking for him. There were at least three Muslim policemen in Natchez and a couple in both Amite and Claiborne Counties. The only place Aziz knew his Father didn't have a lot of sway with the law enforcement was Franklin County, and it was there that Aziz was headed. Looking at the phone he had picked up at the dollar store, Aziz wondered who he could call. When he threw his phone out the window, he had forgotten that all his numbers were in the phone. He couldn't call Kareem or anyone else because he didn't have their numbers. He didn't even know Aggie's number. The only thing he knew to do was go to Annette's house.

He had listened to the radio to see if there was any information about the murderers being arrested, but the stations he listened to hadn't mentioned anything. What would Annette and Aggie say when he drove up? Annette did tell him he could come back tonight, and she would talk to him about the Bible and how to live like a Christian. Just the words alone seemed strange, though they were only in his thoughts. Still, though the words might seem strange, there was no doubt about the change in his heart. He hated the fact that his family might never accept him, but he knew he had done the right thing. It wasn't anything he could touch, but it was definitely something he could feel.

Another downside of having a cheap throwaway phone was the lack of a map app. Aziz was struggling to find his way out of the woods he was in and was looking for a sign he might recognize. The sign he saw ahead said New Hope Road, but Aziz didn't have a clue where that was. As he came around a curve, he saw a church on the right. The sign out front said that it was New Hope Baptist Church. Underneath the name of the church, it said "Henry Wactor, Pastor." Aziz stopped in the middle of the road and backed into the parking lot of the church.

"So, this is your church?" Aziz said to the air. He wondered if the doors were open. If this was going to be his faith, he would like to see what a Christian church looked like. As he got out of the car, Aziz thought about what he was doing. Though he was not doing anything wrong, and it would be harmless to look in the windows, he decided against it. The sight of a black man looking into a predominately white Baptist church might be construed as something besides trying to get closer to God. Probably a better idea was to go to Annette's and talk to them. They were the only people he trusted to guide him on this new path. He just had to figure out how to get to their house.

After driving for what seemed like an hour, but was actually fifteen minutes, Aziz started to recognize some landmarks. When he came to a four-lane highway, he finally knew where he was. In fact, he had come out only a couple of miles or so from Annette's home. Aziz drove down the road he had just driven down last night. The feeling of comfort along with the weariness he still felt dulled his senses just enough that Aziz didn't see the brown car sitting on the side of the street. Since he didn't see the car, he also didn't see the young man walk into the middle of the street until it was almost too late. Slamming on the brakes, Aziz looked to see if maybe he had run over the man. Jumping out, Aziz ran to the front of the car to see if there was a body. His heart almost jumped out of his chest when he saw a young man lying on the ground.

"Oh no. I can't believe I did this. Hey, brother, are you alright? Can you hear me?" As Aziz leaned over to check and see if he could feel a pulse. He couldn't get his own heart to slow down. He was so consumed with concern that he didn't see the other two people coming up behind him.

"Who are you?" was all he got out before one of them took out an iron pipe and hit him on the side of the head. Aziz fell like a tree that had been struck by lightning. Before he lost consciousness, Aziz saw another car drive up. Though his vision was cloudy and blood was beginning to run down into his eyes, he saw the most peculiar thing. The car looked exactly like his. The next thing he saw was blackness.

One night when he was at Columbia, Aziz had gone to a party thrown by the Omega Psi Fraternity. Even though he only drank one glass of punch, he had woken up the next morning with a headache that made him swear off parties, alcohol, and anything else that might cause his head to hurt. That was the way his head felt right now. He was sitting in a chair, but he didn't know why or where he was. Opening his eyes was what he wanted to do, but he feared the pain that would come. First, he decided to put his hands up to his eyes to block out any light that might be shining. But when he made the effort to move his arms, he realized that either he was paralyzed or he was tied up. Since he could feel his arms starting to tingle, he knew he wasn't paralyzed. That meant he was tied to a chair. Slowly opening his eyes, Aziz saw that he was sitting in a bedroom, but the bed had been moved. There was a chest of drawers and a closet and a bedside table. There was a window, but it looked like there was a trash bag over it. Standing against the wall were three of his father's security team. When they saw him open his eyes, one of them took out what looked like a walkie talkie and said something that Aziz couldn't hear.

"Hey guys, could someone tell me what's going on? I like a good practical joke, but this is going a little far, don't you think?"

"You will get your answers when Imam Maalik gets here."

"Okay, could you maybe loosen these ropes, or whatever they are?"

"I can't help anyone who is not a true follower of Islam. You're an infidel now. I don't know what Imam Maalik will do, but I know what I would like to do."

Before Aziz could come up with a witty comeback, Maalik Saalam walked into the room. "Leave, please, and could one of you please release my son?"

The one who had been doing all the talking, Aziz remembered, was named Baaly. He came over and cut what must have been zip ties off Aziz's hands and feet and one that must have been around his chest. After the three had gone, only Aziz and Maalik were in the room. It was like each one was seeing the other for the first time. Aziz knew that he was looking at his father differently than ever before.

"I talked to your mother. She told me that she heard you telling Kareem that you had forsaken Islam and become a Christian. If you tell me this is not so, and your mother didn't hear correctly, then I will apologize to you and we can go on with our lives. Is that what it was, my Son?"

There it was. Aziz knew that his father was not one to beat around the bush. He knew that his wife had not misunderstood, but he was giving Aziz the chance to recant and forget the whole thing. It would be blamed on the woman and everyone would accept that. All he had to do would be to tell his Father that he didn't convert to Christianity. That was all he had to do. With the pain that was still pulsing through his head, Aziz knew they were not kidding.

Before he spoke, Aziz took a deep breath and then looked his father squarely in the eye. "I know that you are disappointed, but I can't recant anything. What Mother heard was exactly what she thought she heard. I found something real last night. It's the same thing I was looking for when I was at Columbia, but I wasn't able to find it before you arrived. This time, you can't convince me of my error."

"Do you remember what happened to your friend Kareem at Columbia? Do you remember how he was beaten, and how lucky it was that he was allowed to remain alive? His parents disowned him and took everything from him. His father is wealthy beyond anything Kareem could ever realize, but he has changed his will and Kareem will get nothing. I have spoken to Kareem's father, and he says that he hasn't spoken to him since that day. Do you want to get nothing? Do you want to be cut off from your mother and me? Is this the last time you want to speak to me?"

"I don't know what is going to happen to me, but I can't turn my back on Jesus. What I felt last night is something that I have never felt before. I have never seen nor heard of anyone of our faith having the things happen to them that have happened to me. You speak of life, but everything in Islam seems to be of death and destruction. I want to believe in something that focuses on life."

"You are just confusing coincidence with providence. We receive what we make of a situation. You are what you make of yourself. Allah will give you what you need to take care of you. Do not make me do what Allah commands." Maalik was trying to scare his son, but inside his heart he was begging him to recant what he just said. Because if he didn't, then Maalik knew the consequences. If his followers ever thought that they could come and go with impunity, then the Quran and its laws would be of no importance.

"Father, I of all people know what you are facing. You have taught me the punishments of leaving Islam and even showed them to me. But what I found last night, and what I feel, is worth any punishment you could give."

"If you know the punishments, then why would you ever consider it? Has someone confused you and made you do something you don't want to do? Is that it? Are you being blackmailed?" Maalik was grasping at straws, and he knew he was running out of straws.

"I was not blackmailed. I did this because of the feeling in my heart." Aziz didn't go into Kareem's phone call about what he had dreamed. One reason was because he didn't think his father would believe him and another because it was still a little freaky, even to him.

196

"I will take no pleasure in what is about to happen, but if this is what it takes for you to see the true way, then I will be happy. Amaal, come in here." Aziz knew who Amaal was. He was termed the enforcer for his father. He was the one that was sent when there was a problem that couldn't be handled with just a phone call or threat. Aziz had gone with him a few times to intimidate someone.

"Amaal, this gives me no pleasure, but you know what must be done. There is no one who is above Islam, not even my son. Do what must be done."

Aziz didn't know what to say as he watched his father leave the room. At that moment, he felt more alone than at any time in his life. But since his hands and legs were untied, Aziz knew he wasn't completely helpless. As he tried to plan how he would attack Amaal, three other people appeared in the room. They were not known to Aziz, but they immediately put an end to his ideas of escape. That didn't mean he was going to go down without a fight. Looking at the smallest of them, Aziz dove at him with the idea of driving through and getting out the door. Apparently, this was expected because the smaller man, instead of fighting with Aziz, just grabbed him and held on until the other three could come help him. They held his arms and legs and no amount of struggling could help. They punched and kicked him several times until he stopped struggling. Then they put him back into the chair and secured his arms and legs.

"Amaal, you and I have shared many times together. We have been friends for many years. Do none of those memories matter?"

"I don't have a friend who ignores the true religion. I only follow my Imam's wishes. That is something you used to do, and what I hope you will return to when we are through." And with that, Amaal hit Aziz in the face harder than he had ever been hit. Even the blow from behind at the car didn't seem as hard as Amaal's punch.

"Jesus, if you can, I really need your help," Aziz said under his breath.

"Oh, now you are crying out to your god. There is no god other than Allah. You have left the true god and now you have to pay the price."

Aziz blinked and tried to clear the fog in his mind from the first of what he expected to be many blows to the head. Watching Amaal putting on a pair of leather gloves, Aziz just closed his eyes. This might be the end, and he didn't get to live a Christian life. Maybe he would see the Heaven Kareem had talked about. The loud bang of an explosion shocked Aziz. There was also a bright flash that Aziz saw through his closed eyes. Immediately after the bang and flash, there was a flurry of movement. Aziz opened his eyes, but the bright light was all he could see. He could hear shouting and someone said "police." The tumult and excitement ended as quickly as it began. Aziz felt someone cutting the zip ties off his arms.

"Who is it," Aziz asked. His vision was slowly becoming clearer, but the face in front of him was still unrecognizable.

"Son, its Commander Wiley Terrell. I have seen you, but I don't know your name."

"My name is Aziz Salaam."

"Salaam--you mean Maalik Salaam's son?" Obviously, this was a very big surprise to the officer. "These people were all associates of your father. Why did they have you in custody?"

"They were going to bring me to my senses by beating me until I recanted. But what I want to know is who in this room was involved with the murder? I didn't see any of them in the pictures." When he said this, Aziz didn't think anything about it, but unfortunately for him, his captors were not out of the room yet.

"You saw the pictures? You didn't call anyone and tell them? Truly you are an infidel to your faith." Amaal said before one of the troopers gave him a little tap in the gut.

"Get these four out of here," Wiley said. He immediately realized what had just occurred. Henry had told him that there was a confidential informant who identified one of the suspects, but never in a million years did he expect the informant to be Maalik Saalam's son.

After the other men were led out, Wiley started thinking of a course of action. "Aziz, we have got to get you into protective custody. I have a detail looking after that Sharosh girl already. I guess we can put you two together since the same people probably want to hurt both of you. But first, we need to get some of these cuts and bruises cleaned up."

Aziz knew he must look a mess after the earlier beating he had gotten from Amaal's goons, but that didn't matter to him now. "Aggie is in danger? Why would anyone want to hurt her?"

"We don't know, but she is being guarded and you will be, too. Where did they pick you up?"

"I was on my way to Annette's house and there was a car in the road a couple of blocks

away. I got out to check on this guy I thought I had hit and someone knocked me on the head. When I came to, I was here."

"Wait a minute. Do you mean to tell me that you were only a couple of streets away from Annette's home when you were abducted?" The distress in both Wiley's face and in his voice startled Aziz.

"Why is that such a surprise to you? I guess they knew I was going to eventually come to Annette's and they just waited on me."

Wiley didn't answer the question. He took out his phone and made a call. The words he spoke made Aziz almost lose his breath. "We need to move our perimeter out to four square blocks. We've had an incident only two blocks away. Inform Sheriff Wactor that we are going to move our principle to a safer more defendable position. Also inform him that we will be adding more protective custody since we have another person to protect."

Driving down the highway, Maalik Saalam tried not to look down at his phone. Amaal had orders to contact him as soon as Aziz recanted. Although he knew the rules and orders of Islam, Maalik also knew that he couldn't be there when they began to punish his only son. He knew it was required, but he couldn't do it. The urge to get involved could be more than he could bear. Hopefully, Aziz would realize what he was doing and what he would be giving up and return to his faith. That was what Maalik hoped, but there had been a completely different look in his son's eyes. Maalik actually thought that, given the nature of the offense, his son would never dishonor his father or his faith.

Over the years, there had been those who claimed that they wanted to leave Islam but would quickly change their minds when shown the error of their ways. Though he hadn't heard from Amaal, Maalik didn't expect his son to recant anything. Though he was his Imam, Maalik was also Aziz's father. He knew how stubborn his son could be when he made up his mind, but this was something completely different. That boy Kareem had also failed to recant, but Maalik had just chalked that up to an inability of his parents to do what needed to be done. Now he was faced with a similar situation. Kareem's parents had stopped short of the ultimate punishment because they believed their son would come back. The years had gone by and, from what his sources told him, Kareem was doing well. Now Maalik had to ponder the decision to give the go ahead for the ultimate punishment. Could he truly give the order to kill his son for the good of Islam?

CHAPTER 21

Choices Are Hard, Especially When They're Personal

For the last two hours, Aggie had watched the number of cars appearing in Annette's yard continue to increase. Along with the four that had originally arrived, three more highway patrol cars and the lone Bude police car were also there. This much excitement in a town like Bude was bound to bring out the people to see what was going on. Several were beginning to stand on the sidewalks; and every time a squad car arrived, it seemed more people showed up.

"Aggie, do you want some of this chicken?" Annette asked from the kitchen. "You get to pick out your piece before the police get theirs."

"What kind of chicken is it? Is it Kentucky Fried?"

"No darling, this is Gas Lane chicken. Now you come in here and eat. I don't know what's going to happen tonight, but after last night, I don't want to miss a chance to eat. You never know when the next time will be."

Aggie walked into the kitchen and sat down. The curtains were closed and the blinds pulled down because the police didn't want to take any chances. Something must have happened that they weren't talking about, because she had heard whispering about getting more security and getting them moved to a more defensible place. When they said this, Aggie assumed they were talking about Annette and Jack and Archie. "Does this chicken have spinach in it?" Aggie asked as she fixed her plate.

"Typical Yankee," Jack said. "This chicken is better than anything you can get in New York, unless you go to my grandma's, that is."

"Bobby would love to have some of this," Jughead said as he sat down at the table. "When is he coming home?"

"Hopefully tomorrow or Monday. I'm just amazed at how he has come back to himself. I was sitting there in the room and we were talking normally, and I just began to cry because God did such a wonderful miracle. I was crying because less than twenty-four hours earlier, I was thinking my brother was going to die or at the very least be paralyzed. Now everything is back to normal. On top of that, we have a new brother and sister in Christ." Annette reached over and squeezed Aggie's hand.

"We've got a black car coming onto the street," the radio blared. The officer fixing his plate dropped it and ran to the door.

"Oh no, is this what I have to look forward to? I don't think I can deal with this."

"Don't worry, Aggie. They have a perimeter set up around us. No one is going to get onto this block without someone knowing about it. I also heard them say that the safeties were off, so they are authorized to shoot if the need arises."

There was a tense fifteen or so minutes until the trooper walked back into the dining room. Everyone noticed that he had a comical look on his face.

"What is it, Keith?" Aggie asked as he began to re-fix his plate. Before he could say anything, there was a knock on the door.

"Who is that?" Jack asked. "Is it okay to answer the door?"

"Go ahead, you'll be surprised."

Jack got up and went to the door. Even though the officer said it was okay, he wasn't going to take any chances. Opening the door, Jack couldn't believe what he was seeing. "Bobby, what are you doing here? You're supposed to be in the hospital."

"I heard they were going to need some more officers for security duty. I told the doctors I wasn't going to sit in the hospital while World War Three broke loose. Especially involving people I care about."

"I didn't know you cared so much, Bobby," Aggie said with a smile on her face. The thrill that he was here and wanting to take care of her was hard to suppress.

"I did want to take care of you, but there's someone else, too. Come on in, Aziz."

Bobby being there was a shock because he was supposed to be in the hospital. Aziz was a shock because he had such a scared look on his face as well as several cuts and bruises.

"Aziz, you look like you have been to hell and back," Annette said. "Get in here and get some food in that stomach of yours. I have never seen anything that a little fried chicken and some Jesus couldn't fix."

"I think I will take you up on that chicken," Aziz said. "After everything that has happened, I need some energy."

202

"What are you talking about, Aziz?" Aggie asked. "Did someone find out that you were the one who identified the murderers?"

"No, I don't think I have been linked to that, but I will be. My mother heard me talking to my friend Kareem about my accepting Christ, and she tried to take my keys and lock me in my room. I got away and was headed over here when I was ambushed by some men. When I woke up, I was in a room tied to a chair. My father was there and he wanted me to recant my Christianity. I told him I couldn't and he made several threats."

"Did he touch you in any way?" Bobby asked. If he was the one who did this to you, we could file charges against him immediately even though he is your father."

"No, he never touched me. He called Amaal into the room, and I knew what was going to happen. They were going to beat me until I recanted." He reached up and touched his swollen face and winced. If it hadn't been for the police, I don't know what they would have done. Amaal did find out that I had seen the pictures though. That's why I said I will be linked to the them."

"That and Wiley's report are the reason for all the added security. We are going to move both of you to a safer and more defensible position. Sheriff Wactor says he has a farm house that belonged to his parents on a dead-end road. One way in and one way out. We will hole up there until the judges decide what's going to happen. I am just waiting on the go-ahead from Henry."

"Bobby, do you truly think I'm going to let you go do any kind of work after what you've been through?" Annette said.

"Sis, I love you very, very much, but this is not your decision. I am feeling fine, and I am not going to let this happen without me. So, the best thing you can do is get me a plate and let me have some of that chicken."

"Got another car coming," someone said on the radio. "Looks like a limo." They knew that if the car had made it through the first perimeter, then there was no danger. Whoever was in the car had some connection to the house.

"Who in the world has a limo in Franklin County other than the funeral home?" Jack asked.

"I don't know, but whoever it is, they let them through as they must have a reason to be here." Keith was standing at the window watching through binoculars as the car pulled up close the house and the doors opened. "Do any of you know anyone who wears a bowler hat and uses a cane?"

Aggie almost fell out of her chair. "Did you say a bowler hat and a cane?"

"Yeah, is that someone you know?"

"It's my father."

Annette began to laugh. Jack was caught off-guard by her laughing. "Is it that funny?"

"Jack, don't you see God is doing some mighty work around here. I don't know what is going to happen, but I do know that only God could orchestrate something of this magnitude."

As they heard footsteps coming onto the porch, Aggie wanted to run out the back door.

Not because she wasn't happy to see her father, but because she didn't know what she was going to say to him. When the door opened, HyramSharosh walked in and, just like he always did, he owned the room. It wasn't that he was especially good looking or had an overpowering physique. It was his presence and confidence that few people could match.

"Hello, Agnes," Hyram said as he walked toward Aggie. Aggie knew he was purposefully ignoring the others in the room, because to his way of thinking you always greeted the most important person first. In his eyes, that was Aggie.

"Hello, Daddy," Aggie said as she got up and met him. Aggie was surprised that instead of the usual touching on the shoulder, her father gave her a full-on hug. Only very few times in her life could she remember him doing this. The last time had been at her mother's funeral.

"Thank goodness you are alright. I have been told that there is a threat against you and some other young man. I have come, even though you told me not to, to get you and take you home. The plane is waiting in Jackson at the airport, and we can be gone from here in less than two hours. I have arranged for a security detail to meet me whenever I call them, and they will escort us to the airport." It was like he didn't see anyone else in the room except for Aggie.

"Daddy, I appreciate this, but I can't leave my friends yet. There are lots of things going on and I can't just leave them."

For the first time he began to acknowledge the other people in the room.

"Ladies and gentlemen, I apologize for my short sightedness, but my concern for my daughter overrode my manners. Whose home is this?"

"It's ours," Jack said as he stood up. "Your daughter has been staying with us for a couple of days." Though he understood the love of a father for his children, Jack also remembered the vile way this man had talked about them the night before. He was not going to take that in his home from anyone.

"Thank you so much for your hospitality to my daughter. Was it you that was with her last night? I know I may have said some things that would seem inappropriate to you, but you have to understand my concerns are always for Agnes and her safety. If I offended you and your wife and child in any way, I apologize."

"We completely understand," Annette interjected. She knew the look on Jack's face was not one of admiration no matter what this man said. "Would you like to sit down and have some supper?"

"No thank you, Madam, but Agnes and I must be going."

"Daddy, you're not listening to me. I am not leaving. There is too much going on, and I am involved in a lot of it. I am perfectly safe, and you don't have to worry about me."

"No daughter of mine is going to be threatened while I just stand around and do nothing. You policemen, what are you doing to protect my daughter, other than sitting around at the trough?"

"Sir, we are doing everything possible to make sure that these two are safe. If you are not happy with the arrangements, you are welcome to make your way back to New York and file a formal protest." Keith apparently didn't like the derogatory tone of HyramSharosh either, but before the situation could escalate further, the door opened and Henry Wactor walked in. Since this wasn't his first rodeo, Henry recognized the aggressive stance and the tone that was almost palpable in the air.

"Goodness gracious, are we about to have a scrum right here in these people's home? Hello Sir. I'm Sheriff Wactor. From your dress and the fact that no one in Franklin County has a matching hat and cane, you must be Aggie's father."

If HyramSharosh had an overwhelming personality, Henry Wactor's was almost as imposing. Just his presence alone brought down the hostility factor in the room. Aggie watched as her father realized that he had met someone who commanded authority as well as he did. She could see in his eyes the admiration he had for Sheriff Wactor, just from the few seconds of meeting him. "Sheriff, I am pleased to meet you. I have been told by the directors of the state police that you are one of the finest law officers in the state."

"I don't know about that, but I do the best I can with what God gives me. I feel like I'm a better preacher than I am a sheriff, but sometimes the tools of one job help with the tools of the other. Keith, what is the ETA for getting out to the farm house?"

"Sheriff, we are waiting on a confirmation on Aziz's father's whereabouts, and then we are going to head out."

"Why do you want to know about my father's whereabouts?" Aziz spoke up for the first time since Aggie's father had entered the room.

"Because, if what you told the officers is true and your father was willing to beat you, then we need to talk to him and let him know that you are off limits now."

"You don't know my father. You won't intimidate him with threats. He doesn't care about anything but Islam. When I turned away from that to Christianity, I became nothing to him.

"Your father is Muslim and you became a Christian?" Hyram asked. "That's two religions I don't understand and both of them hate Judaism. I would shudder to think that anyone in my family turned from the religion of their forefathers to something as unbelievable as Christianity. Not accepting that kind of betrayal is likely the only thing I would have in common with your father."

Aggie and Annette both looked at each other and both saw Aziz look at them as Hyram made this statement. Aggie didn't know what she should do. Her father just said that he didn't believe in Christianity and would not accept it if his child turned from Judaism. Before she could say anything, a voice came from the radio.

"Hey, everyone, we don't have to look for Maalik. He just drove up to the outer perimeter." Aziz stood still and wondered what was going to be the next move. He didn't have to wait very long for the answer. "He says he wants to see his son. What do you want me to tell him?"

Sheriff Wactor picked up the radio. "Tell him that I'll be right out." Looking over at Aziz, Henry smiled. "Do you want to go out there with me? I'll be right beside you, so he can't do anything that you don't want him to do."

"I will go and you can go with me, but I don't want anyone else. My father and I have to have a talk man-to-man while I am not tied to a chair."

"I must say, this is something I would love to see," Hyram said.

"With all due respect, I want you to sit right down at that table and don't go anywhere. You are a guest in this house and in this county, but if you try to involve yourself in any official business, I will arrest you and hold you for whatever I deem necessary."

The sheer audacity of the statement so overwhelmed Hyram that he did nothing but sit down and watch. No one had ever talked to him in this way, but Sheriff Wactor had been so clear and firm that there was nothing else left to say.

"Okay, Aziz, let's go see your dad."

As they walked across the lawn, Aziz wondered if he would ever take a longer walk. His father's car was pulling in and was parking a few feet away from Aggie's father's limo. What a contrast between the two men. HyramSharosh arrives in a chauffeur driven limousine and Maalik Saalam drives himself in a brown Audi. As they walked up to his car, Maalik got out.

"Hello, Henry. You and I are meeting more than I ever thought we would. I hear you have solved your murder investigation. Though I feel the young man was coerced, I applaud you on your effectiveness."

"I thank you, but having good people is the true difference in any situation. As far as you seeing me yet again, I didn't expect to see you again this week either. Of course, that was before you had your people kidnap beat your own son."

"Are you trying to say something, Sheriff? I haven't heard my son say anything. I haven't done anything to endanger my son. The only person who might say that would be my son, and I don't believe he would. Are you accusing me of having someone attack you, Aziz?"

Aziz knew what his father was doing. Neither Amaal nor any of the other three men would say anything implicating Maalik, so that meant that the only person who could give a testimony against him would be Aziz. Maalik knew this and knew what he was doing. He was intimidating his son without saying a word.

Henry Wactor also understood what was going on. "I don't know if Aziz is going to implicate you or not. What I do know is he is under my protection now. If you have a problem with your son, then you need to realize that *you* have that problem. He is over eighteen and a legal adult of the United States. He doesn't have to bend to you or anything you have for him. I can also promise you that if something happens to him, I will be at your door with an arrest warrant that I can make stick because of the people who heard Aziz's account of what happened to him. That is why I am here. I'm also here to let the two of you talk without any interference. I don't want to hear what you are saying, but you won't threaten him in any way."

"Henry, intimidation is not your usual way of working. Are you sure this is the road you want to travel?"

"It is the road we are all going to travel." Henry looked over at Aziz and nodded. "Do you want to talk to him or do we go back to the house?"

"This is something that he and I need to work out together. If you will give us some room, I believe we can do that."

"All right, it's all yours." Henry walked away, but knew Aziz was in no danger. Though it wasn't a completely secure area, there were too many law enforcements eyes on Maalik for him to do anything besides talk.

Aziz walked toward his father but this time was different from earlier in the day. Now he was the one with the upper hand. He was the one with the numbers supporting him. But somehow his hands were still sweating.

"I guess you feel confident now, don't you?" Maalik said. "Do you really think the decision you have made is the right one? You have chosen these people who would not have given a care about you just a week or even a day ago, over your own family. Over your own people who have been there for you no matter the situation? Don't think about me, think of your mother. The woman who gave birth to you. Does she not matter to you anymore? Have you rejected her as well as Islam? What will you do with your life now that you have nothing?"

"I don't know what I am going to do; but I have made my choice, and I won't be swayed by your threats. You will always be my father, and I will always love you and Mother, but I have found something that Islam could never give me--I have found peace. But there is a question I have to ask you. Have you rejected your son over his choice? Do you love Islam more than you love your own flesh and blood? Why is it that I have made a choice that is inconceivable, but you are making a choice that you think is without question? Have you ever truly questioned what you are giving up? I do not hate you or Mother. I have made a choice, but that choice doesn't include me

208

hating you. The religion I have chosen does not require me to hate you. Why should you continue in something that requires you to hate your own flesh and blood?"

For the briefest of moments, Aziz thought he saw a glimmer of doubt in his father's eyes. As quickly as it appeared, the doubt disappeared, and what replaced it was pure disdain bordering on hatred. "I know one thing and one thing only. I serve Allah, and from this day forward, I don't have a son. Never contact me or your mother ever again."

"I guess I just wait for you and your goons to come and kidnap me again, is that it?"

"No, neither I nor anyone affiliated with me will ever bother you again as long as you do not attempt to subvert Islam. You and I are done, and I do not care if I ever see you again. If you should decide to change your life, I will decide if you are allowed back."

"Father..."

"Do not call me that. I am not your father and you are not my son." With that, Maalik signaled to someone in the passenger's seat of the car. The man who got out and started to walk toward them was Amaal's father Anon. He was Maalik's closest of aids. "Since you and I are no longer a part of each other's life, I will take my property with me. Please give Anon the keys to my car and the phone I pay for."

Aziz had expected this eventually but didn't think it would happen this quickly. Reaching into his pocket, he took out his key and handed it to Anon. "I don't have the phone anymore. I threw it away."

"That is fine, I will have the line suspended just in case." Without another word, Maalik walked over and got back into his car. Anon got into the Challenger and followed Maalik out of the yard.

As he watched the man he had idolized all his life drive away, Aziz felt the pressure of being truly alone. Slowly he felt an arm come around his shoulders. It was Sheriff Wactor, and he had tears in his eyes. "Son, I don't pretend to know or understand anything you are feeling right now, but I promise you one thing. Only God can love you more than anyone else. You have put your trust in Him and He will take care of you."

As the tears began to stream down Aziz's face, he watched his father's car and the car he used to call his, go around the corner out of sight. "I guess God is the only family I have now."

Aggie couldn't make out what was being said, but with Annette's binoculars she could see that Aziz's father was very animated in how he was talking. Aziz, on the other hand, was very calm and quiet. Aggie wondered if when the time came, she could be as quiet and calm talking to her father.

"I wonder how that young man feels?" Hyram said to no one in particular, but Aggie knew it was said for her benefit.

"What are you talking about? How is he supposed to feel? His own father had him threatened and beaten. If the state police hadn't arrived, they might have killed Aziz like they did that other guy."

"I don't agree with anything involving Islam. I believe it to be a religion of barbarians, but for him to forsake his father is something I would hope you would never do. I know we have had our disagreements, but how we look at God is something we should always be able to agree on.

"Look, he's leaving and someone is taking Aziz's car," Bobby said. "I guess he's going to take everything away from him that he can." Everyone went to the windows and strained to see what was going on except Aggie. She was standing silently looking at the table.

"Can I see those?" Annette said as she took the binoculars. "I want to see if he leaves or tries to double back."

"He won't double back, I promise that." Bobby said.

"How do you know, Bobby? Do you have some kind of police instinct?" Annette asked.

"No, but we'll be watching him for the next few days. Maalik is said to be a smart man. If he's as smart as they say he is, he'll lay low and stay away."

Annette was scanning the area like a spotter for a sniper. "Henry has his arm around Aziz. Apparently, the discussion didn't go very well."

"Father, what did you mean about that not happening to you? What would you do if it did?" Aggie was extremely scared, but then she realized that sometimes the best way to get a band-aid off was to just go ahead and rip it off.

HyramSharosh was sitting at the table drinking coffee. He was sitting there because he wasn't sure he could move around without this sheriff's approval. "I mean that whatever happened with this young man is a sign of someone who has been corrupted by outside forces, present company excluded of course, into turning away from his birthright. I despise the Muslim

147 faith, but you have to remember that Abraham is the father of us all."

"Father, what if I told you that a couple of hours before Aziz became a Christian, I accepted Christ?" Aggie looked her father directly in the eyes as she said it because she didn't want there to be any misunderstanding.

It was a tie between Annette and Aggie's father for who had the most stunned look. His-- because he never expected this, and hers--because she hadn't expected this to happen now.

"That can't be true. Agnes, you have rebelled against me since your mother died and several times before that. You will never make me believe that you accepted something that is not in your bloodline. Something that hasn't been passed down to you and is blatantly untrue. We are God's chosen people and we will always be. Our people have endured for generations against the worst kind of oppression you can imagine, and you want me to believe that you are going to turn your back on that? I don't believe it."

Aggie knew that her father was not exaggerating. Why had she done this now? Why hadn't she just waited until she got back to New York? It had to be because now she had some support, and there she would be completely alone.

"Daddy, last night I felt something that I have never felt in all my years of temple. I felt something come over me when I accepted Christ. When Ms. Joan explained it to me, I truly understood why those people in Iraq and Syria are willing to die instead of convert. Because they have something inside of them and now I have it, too. You can hate me all you want, but it won't change me or what I have done."

Hyram calmly took a drink of his coffee and stared into the cup. Annette looked over at Jack to see what she should do, but the look on his face showed that neither of them had any idea.

Suddenly, Aggie's father got up from the chair and picked up his hat and cane. "I guess you need some time to assess the decision you have made. I am going back to Jackson, and I will leave in the morning. If you are not on that plane with me, then I will believe that you do not desire to remain my daughter and, in so doing, do not desire my money or my lifestyle. I do hope you think long and hard because, contrary to what you think, I am here and this Jesus you have chosen is not."

Annette started to speak, "Mr. Sharosh, I don't..."

"Ma'am, I do not wish any confrontation with you or your family. I thank you for the coffee and the hospitality you have shown me and my daughter, but let's not get into a theological argument. I bid you all a good day." He then looked over at Aggie as he put on his hat. "I will expect your answer in the morning."

As he walked to the door, Sheriff Wactor and Aziz opened it and came in. "Sheriff, it was a pleasure to meet you, good day."

"Nice to meet you, Mr. Sharosh," but the words were spoken to Hyram's back because he was walking toward the limousine.

Seeing the amazed looks in the room, Henry took off his hat and scratched his head. "I'm guessing she told him the good news, too."

CHAPTER 22

The Enemy of My Enemy is my Friend

The drive to the safe house/hunting lodge wasn't very long. It belonged to a group of churches that allowed underprivileged and physically challenged children to come and hunt for the weekend. Aggie was following Sheriff Wactor who was following Bobby who was following two other highway patrolmen, and there were two patrolmen behind her. It was actually quite an impressive caravan, but Aggie wasn't thinking about them. She was wondering what it was going to be like without her car. The car which her mother had made her father promise to buy for her when she graduated. Any time she drove it, she felt like her mother was there with her. Now, if she didn't go home with her father and disavow her new commitment to Christianity, then she was going to be homeless, penniless, and carless. If that happened, she and Aziz would have something else in common. He was riding in the car with Sheriff Wactor, even though he had asked if Aggie wanted some company. When she said no, he had acted like he understood. But after everything that had occurred in his life over the last few days, his mind had to be in turmoil.

While they had sat at Annette's and Jack's table, Aziz had described the feelings he felt as his father drove away. The loss of the car had been painful, but the impending loss of the relationship with his family was definitely the thing that Aziz felt the most. Even Jughead had been amazed that Aziz's father was so hard and unbending. Aggie didn't add a lot, but she knew that there wasn't very much difference between the feelings of Maalik and her own father. She knew that he was not making idle threats about what would happen if she didn't meet him in the morning. She knew this, but she also knew there was no way she could turn away from her new Christianity. Though she didn't completely understand everything she had accepted, she knew that she couldn't turn her back on it no matter what.

As they turned onto a gravel road, Aggie laughed. Since Thursday when she got to Franklin County, she had driven on more gravel roads than at any time in her five years of driving. This was just another little tidbit she would be able to tell her grandchildren. Suddenly the little caravan stopped, and Aggie immediately thought that the people who wanted to hurt both her and Aziz had decided to do something. Picking up her phone, she dialed Sheriff Wactor.

"Don't panic, Aggie," Henry Wactor said, almost as if he was reading her mind. "There's a locked gate up ahead, and we are waiting for them to open it. You okay back there?"

"I'm fine. Sheriff, what am I going to do? If I don't meet my Father at his hotel in the morning, I won't have anything. I think I know that Jesus loves me, but what do I do if I don't have anything but Him?"

"Aggie, you and I are going to sit down and have a long theological talk, but I'm here to tell you on the authority of God that if you have Jesus, you have everything. I also assure you that you have all you need. I have been telling Aziz those very same things. I don't pretend to understand how the two of you wound up in the same place at the same time with both of you searching for something that your respective religions didn't provide. This is something that people will be talking about for years to come. Now follow me and let's get you two into this cabin so we can all get some rest. I still have to somehow prepare a sermon for the morning."

"I meant to ask you about that. Do I go to your church tomorrow? I have never gone to temple on a Sunday, so this is another thing that I am not used to."

"Let's get you settled in and we will discuss what tomorrow holds."

As they started forward, Aggie wondered what her father was doing at that very moment.

"I am able to get the personal phone number to the President of The United States and you tell me that you can't get me the phone number to a Muslim Imam living in Mississippi? I am beginning to wonder why I pay you as much as I do." Without waiting for a reply, HyramSharosh slammed the phone down. That was a feeling you could never get with a cell phone. Sitting in the Presidential Suite of the Edison Hotel in Jackson, Hyram never felt so helpless. The last issue of Forbes listed him with the top one hundred richest men in America. With over nine hundred million in cash and assets, you would think there was nothing he could want or get if he decided to have it. Agnes coming to him and telling him that she had forsaken the religion of her forefathers was something he never thought he would ever see.

All the way back to Jackson from Bude, Hyram had wondered what his wife would have done. She was always the one who took Agnes' side. He sometimes wondered if she loved their daughter more than she loved him. Her death had almost destroyed him. He couldn't afford to show that kind of weakness. Sure, he loved his wife, but he was a businessman and countless numbers of people depended on him for their livelihood. Other people could mourn, but he had an empire to run. If it hadn't been for Agnes, Hyram might have fulfilled his lifelong goal of moving to Tel-Aviv and getting back to his ancestors' homeland. With the amount of money he had spent, there ought to be a small city somewhere in the area of Israel named after him. As he looked out at what little skyline there was in this so-called capital city, the phone rang. Since few people knew he was in Mississippi and even fewer knew where he was staying, Hyram felt sure he knew who was calling.

"Louis, I hope you have what I asked for because if you don't, there is going to be hell to pay when I get back."

"Mr. Sharosh, I have been told that you would like to speak with me."

Hyram was taken aback because the person on the other end wasn't his executive assistant. "I'm sorry, I don't know to whom I am speaking."

"This is Maalik Saalam. Since I have met your daughter, I am giving you the courtesy of calling you and hearing whatever it is you have to say. However, I don't know why a man who hates me and my people would be wanting to talk to me. I have done some research on you in the last hour and I must say, you are a very vocal man about your disdain for the Palestinians and Muslims in general. So, I have no idea what the two of us would have to talk about, but after the events of the last two days, anything is possible. What can I do for you?"

"Mr. Saalam, you and I may be at odds, but we have much more in common than you could ever believe. Did your son's conversion to Christianity make you wonder where you went wrong with your child?"

"I guess your child told you about this." Maalik tried to sound confident, but he knew that only six of his trusted followers knew about Aziz's betrayal and none of them would ever talk.

"No, my daughter didn't tell me about it. In fact, I was there today when you confronted your son."

"So that was your limousine. I thought maybe the governor had come down to talk to Sheriff Wactor about solving the murders. Once again, I missed a vital piece of information. Yes, my son's betrayal gave me pause, but I have taken every earthly thing from him that I can. If you were indeed watching, you know this." Then suddenly it hit him. "Your daughter converted to Christianity also, didn't she? That explains this call and gives me a little better feeling about Aziz."

"How could this give you a better feeling about your son?"

"Mr. Sharosh, surely you have seen young men do stupid things to impress a girl. Obviously, your daughter fell victim to someone who tricked her, and she did the same thing to my son. He must have thought this was a way to get your daughter to be with him."

"Let me tell you one thing you, Muslim heretic. If there was anyone who led someone astray, it was your son. Agnes didn't tell me anything until you and your son had your little talk this afternoon. And if you ever disparage the honor of my daughter again, I will make sure that you find yourself dead from an unknown sniper bullet, is that clear?" Never in his life had he ever threatened another person with deadly harm, but at this moment HyramSharosh didn't care.

There was a long pause between the two men. It was Maalik who broke the silence. "Mr. Sharosh, I apologize for intimating that your daughter was anything but a pure flower. My mind is not functioning clearly as I'm sure yours is not either. I am grabbing at straws, and obviously I grabbed at the wrong straw. Back to your comment, the two of us definitely have more in common than I realized. I am almost to Vicksburg and I can be in Jackson in an hour. Why don't the two of us meet and talk face to face? Maybe between the two of us, we can figure out a solution for both of our children.

HyramSharosh was starting to see a little more clearly as Maalik talked. Whether Maalik knew it and backed down or he was truly sorry, Hyram didn't know. "I would be happy to sit down and discuss the situation with you. I would like for it to be just the two of us. Since this is your state, where do you suggest we meet?"

"There is a truck stop in Pearl. The restaurant is open twenty-four hours, and we can find a room in the back that will give us privacy. Let's meet there in an hour."

"I will be there when you arrive." As he hung up the phone, Hyram began looking through his special book that held all the names of former Moss ad officers who could be hired in case this meeting didn't go as he wanted it too. He would never trust anyone of the Muslim faith, and that was never going to change.

Maalik also began to make plans after he got off the phone. He knew that this man was wealthy beyond anything he could fathom; and if he wanted someone killed, he had the money to make it happen. He wanted to kick himself for saying what he was thinking out loud, but just the slimmest

216

possibility of Aziz's conversion being something that wasn't genuine was something that made him lose his composure. Now he had possibly made an enemy that he didn't need to make. Never did he ever think he would have to make a call to this number, but he couldn't be too careful now.

"Good evening, Sir, I hate to call you at this hour. How are things in Gaza?" "I have heard of hunting in comfort, but this is really going above and beyond. Who did you say owns this place?" Aziz asked.

"On the deed, it is owned by a group of churches, but the real owner is a friend of mine who made a pile of money in the oil business. Not only did he make a pile of money, but he sold all his wells and equipment two weeks before the bottom fell out of the market. God has blessed him because he blesses so many other people." Sheriff Wacter led them inside.

"I guess all Christians aren't broke then," Aggie asked. "That Mother Theresa lady was broke and died of starvation after giving all her food to others. I was hoping that wasn't what I had to look forward to as a Christian."

"What you have to look forward to as a Christian is living a life knowing that God is and will be taking care of you. You and Aziz are both worrying about things that are out of your control, but they are completely in God's control. Now, before I leave, let me give you the situation. I don't expect any trouble tonight or any other night. However, Aziz, since you were assaulted and threatened with being beaten because of your decision, I am not going to take any chances for a few days. Aggie, you were threatened by the same people but for a different reason. There will be two guards in the house and four patrolling outsides. This is as secure as you can be in this world."

"There will be three guards in the house, not two," Bobby chimed in.

"Bobby, I am strongly considering ordering you to go home."

"Sheriff, don't make me quit the job I love. I am well and recovered by the grace of God.

I am not going to sit this one out. Besides, Annette told me that the video they got off that camera solved the murder. I've got to have a few brownie points after that, don't I?"

"I give up. Bobby, if you are going to be stubborn and stay here, I am putting you in charge of this detail. You text me with a full report every two hours. Don't make me put my pants on and drive out here in the middle of the night. Is that clear?"

"Yes, Sir, Sheriff, that is clear. Of course, if I happen to sleep through one of my check-in times, please call me before you drive out."

"If you sleep through your check-in time, I will drive back out here and put you back into a coma. But each of you realize, tomorrow morning, church is not optional. I am not one of those people who think going to church makes you a Christian, but when you become a Christian, you want to be around other Christians, and this is something other Christians need to hear about."

"I'm not sure you want me to go to church tomorrow, because I don't have anything to wear besides what I have on my back. When I say that, I am being the most truthful I can be. I have no clothes and no home." When he said this, the weight of the situation finally struck Aziz and he fell on his knees and broke down. This was different from back at the house, because now he had to face life as it came without his parents or their possessions. Both Bobby and Aggie started to walk toward Aziz, but Sheriff Wactor beat them to him.

"Aziz, I know I have told you a lot of things in the last few hours, so now I am going to let God tell you something. Take that Bible I gave you in the truck and read Matthew, Chapter 6, Verses 25-26. That will answer your questions about what you are supposed to do about clothes or food or anything else that you may not have at the moment." He then looked over at Aggie who had come up and put her hand on Aziz's shoulder. "That goes for you too, young lady. You are going to have a decision to make in the morning also. You have already chosen Jesus, so choosing to stay with Him shouldn't be that difficult. I want you to read that verse also."

"I don't have a Bible. Nette said she was going to give me one, but I left the house before she could."

"I've got one in my patrol car that you can have; just let me go get it," Bobby said as he walked toward the door.

"Sheriff, thank you so much for all you are doing for me," Aziz said. He was regaining his composure slowly.

"You don't worry about what I do. You just keep your focus on God and what He wants to do with you and your life. That goes for you too, Aggie. Since you are here on private property, your father can't do anything, but you will have to make a stand somewhere along the way."

"I know I will. I have watched what Aziz has gone through; and if a weakling like him can make that transition, then so can I."

218

For the first time since they had gotten to the cabin, Aziz laughed. "Any other time I might have argued with you, but right now I am feeling a little puny."

"Here you go, Aggie," Bobby said as he walked back into the living room. "That one was given to me when I graduated from the police academy."

Aggie took the book and looked at it. The cover was slightly worn, and it looked like something had been spilled on it. As she flipped through it, she saw that Bobby had used it a lot. "I will give it back to you tomorrow," Aggie said.

"Oh, no you won't," Bobby said. "The greatest gift you can give someone is to lead them to Jesus. The second-best gift is to give a copy of God's word. I will get another Bible, but I want you to have that one as your first Bible."

"I don't know what to say. Thank you so much, Bobby." Aggie didn't know what else to do, so she gave him a big hug. Bobby didn't know what to say either, but he knew he liked being that close to Aggie; so instead of ruining the moment, he just let her hug until she let go.

"Okay, folks, I've got to get out of here. Bobby, you keep them safe."

"I will, Sheriff. You get some rest."

Each person stood in the living room and watched Sheriff Wactor drive off. After his lights were gone down the road, Aggie and Aziz looked at each other.

"I am going to go outside and set the perimeter," Bobby said. "Aggie, your room is the first room on the right at the top of the stairs. Aziz, you are downstairs over beside the pool table. We felt it would be best if the two of you were separated so that there won't be any talk."

"But there is no one out here but us. Who could talk?" Aziz asked.

"Obviously, you haven't been around the Franklin county tongue wagers much. They don't have to see anything to talk about it. We are just doing things so that when we tell the stories, they will be true. They taught me in college that if you tell the truth, you don't have to remember what you said."

Aggie yawned and stretched. "I really don't think I could care any less about anyone talking about me right now. I just want to get some sleep. Just a few minutes ago, I realized how little I have slept in the last three days. What about you, Aziz?"

219

"I agree. I'm going to look up that scripture Sheriff Wactor was talking about and see what it says to me. Bobby, where are you going to sleep? You were in the ICU last night, and I would hate for you to relapse."

"Thank you for your concern Aziz, but I am going to be just fine out here on the couch. As far as being in the hospital last night, I've never felt better in my life. Annette said there were lots of people praying for me, and I am an example of what happens when God's people pray. I'll check in on both of you when I come back in."

"Bobby, I've got to ask you, do you think any of this is necessary? I mean four armed guards outside and one inside? I know my father is capable of many things, but I don't think he would do anything to me now."

"Aziz, you are probably right, but why take any chances. This is an un-precedented situation, and we are going to handle it the best way we know and let the Lord handle the rest." As Bobby walked out the front door, a figure clothed completely in black stood beside a tree less than three hundred yards away. He was wearing an earpiece, so he only had to hit redial on the phone to make contact with his superiors. They picked up on the first ring.

"I am standing outside the perimeter less than three hundred yards from the cabin. There are at least four guards in sight, but there may be more. All well-armed and very aware of their situation. Odds of an assault being suc-cessful are less than twenty percent. What are your instructions?"

Hyram looked at Maalik sitting across from him and wondered whose phone call was so important to interrupt this most important meeting. Speak-ing into the phone, Maalik said, "Apparently Sheriff Henry is not going to take any chances. I guessed he wouldn't, but I had to see for myself. At least we know where they are being kept, and they will probably be there for a while. You are released for the evening, and we will make new arrangements tomorrow."

"I hope you don't mind that I was listening to your conversation."

Maalik smiled. "I am at your table so listening to the conversation was your
prerogative. The important facts are that the topic of my conversation was of importance to both of us."

"Then you know where they are being kept? Were you considering cap-turing your son?"

"I think capture is a strong word. I was looking to bring my son home to his mother to see if she and I could make a change in him. If not, then the Quran is very clear about how to handle situations like this. If I had been able to capture my son, as you say, would you have wanted your daughter also?"

Hyram took a swallow of what passed for coffee in this restaurant. The lack of a decent cup of coffee did nothing to raise his opinion of this small rural state.

"I have left the decision up to her. If she is on the plane with me tomorrow, then everything will be done. If, however, she chooses this foolish path, then I will be forced to make changes to our relationship."

"Do you think she will be willing to change her mind? I do not know much about her, but in our limited conversations, she seems to be very strong-willed and capable of making it on her own."

"You are very perceptive. My daughter as well as your son have many of the same qualities. You could have given me a thousand guesses, and I would have never guessed a child of my loins would succumb to this Christian way of life. What about your son? Was this a complete surprise to you?"

"My son went off to college to become a doctor. My plans were for him to get his medical license and open a clinic that we could use to help people and to grow Islam in the surrounding area. He was gone for a year when I heard from people in New York that there were Muslims who had converted to Christianity on the Columbia campus. I didn't pay any attention until I found out that one of these young men was my son's roommate. I contacted this young man's parents and informed them of what I had found out. They immediately went and confronted their son. When I got to Columbia, I confronted Aziz. He told me that he had no desire to convert to Christianity, but I didn't want to take the chance. So, I made him come home to go to college where his mother and I could keep our eyes on him. That was a big decision for Aziz, but he seemed to want to please me. In hindsight, maybe should have seen it, but my son is very confident and a very persuasive person, so I guessed that I had gotten to him in time. Apparently, the seed was planted but took longer to come to fruition. But enough about my family. You asked for this meeting, and I feel like all the pleasantries are over with. How do you suggest we handle this situation with our children?"

"As I said earlier, my daughter will make her decision tomorrow morning. I have contacted a company to take her car if she chooses unwisely. After that, I will begin to change my financial situation with her. I saw you take your son's car, and I assume you have closed his bank accounts and still he chooses to spit in your face. You were even going to go so far as to torture

221

him until he was rescued. I do not see where either of us has any real ability to do anything else."

"You may be true with that statement, but I won't give up on trying to reach my son. But it's not because of my undying love for him, although I love him very much. If my followers see that it is this easy to move away from Islam, then I will see a dwindling of my influence."

Looking at his watch, Hyram decided that he was not going to get any more information from this man. Though he seemed cordial enough, Hyram knew Maalik was a man who possibly hated Jews as much as Hyram hated Muslims. Sitting here any longer was detrimental to his own mindset.

"Maalik, I wish you well in your endeavors." He then pushed his card across the table. "Here is my card and my private number in my office. If you hear anything, or if there is some change in my daughter's mindset, please let me know. I will have investigators looking in as well and will give you the same courtesy."

Maalik took the card and then slid his own across the table. "Here is my number also. I will be in touch if there is any information."

As the two men stood and shook hands, they both had a wry expression on their faces. It was Maalik who spoke first. "If the two of us can come together without anger and fighting, why can't our respective people do the same?"

Hyram nodded. "I feel the same way. You never know. The two of us may have started a blueprint for a roadmap to peace."

When he was back in the car, HyramSharosh took out a bottle of hand sanitizer. They may have shaken hands, but there would never be a day that he ever appreciated any of the Muslim people. As he looked up, the driver held out a note. "This is the name and address you were looking for, I believe."

"Can you take me to this address and also inform Mr. Paul to meet us there?" Hyram asked as he looked at the name on the piece of paper.

"Yes Sir, if that is what you want to do. But if I may remind you, that you just left from that area this afternoon and are leaving for New York in the morning. Wouldn't you like to get some rest tonight?"

"Driver, you go where I tell you to go and I will worry about where I have been." Then he raised the glass between the two compartments, put the note in his pocket, and sat back for the drive south. There was always a traitor in the midst. You just had to know where to find them.

As he pulled away from the truck stop, Maalik took a sanitized wipe and wiped his hands.

CHAPTER 23

The End of The Beginning

Aggie sat on the couch and looked at the television. Bobby and Aziz were watching Sports Center, but it had no effect on her at all. They could have been watching a documentary about the rituals of rhinoceros mating and she wouldn't have cared. All she could think about was *what now?* She knew she couldn't go back to what she was, because as Bobby had described it, she wasn't the same person. She had given her life to Christ and she would never be the same. Any other time in her life that would have been the scariest thought imaginable, but now it was the only thing that made sense. Looking down at her phone, she wondered how long it would stay active. "I better make a few calls while I still can," Aggie thought. "Guys, I'm going to go upstairs and make a couple of calls and get ready for bed. You boys don't stay up too late. We've got to go to temple tomorrow."

"Not temple," Bobby said with a chuckle. "We are going to Church tomorrow. In fact, we will go to Sunday School before we go to Church, so you both can get the full effect."

"I've always heard if you are gonna do something, go big or not at all," Aziz added. "I'm guessing we are going to need lots of Sunday School."

Aggie laughed at the comments thinking how much she had to learn about her new religion. "That's even more reason for me to get some rest. I'll see you guys in the morning"

"Goodnight, Aggie," Aziz said.

"Goodnight, Agnes," Bobby said mockingly.

When she heard Bobby, Aggie turned on her heels and walked straight up to him. "Bobby, I am a good person, and I am now a Christian, but if you call me Agnes one more

time, I might do something I will regret."

Bobby leaned back in mock fear, but he saw the twinkle of humor in Aggie's eyes. "Yes ma'am, Ms. Aggie. I apologize for angering you. Did you hear that, Aziz? Does that go for Aziz too? I don't want him to accidentally call you the wrong name."

224

"Don't get me involved with this. She already told me she didn't like the name Agnes and I sure don't want her getting on me."

"Now that we have that settled, I'm going to bed. Goodnight." As she walked up the stairs, Aggie thought about Bobby and how he liked to aggravate her. What were her feelings for him? For that matter what were her feelings for Aziz? Before she could answer her own question, her phone began to vibrate. "Please don't be my father," Aggie said to herself. When she saw the number, a smile came to her face. It was Rachel. If ever there was a time that she needed her Aunt Rache, now was it. Even more than a couple of nights before. Aggie walked into the bedroom and closed the door before she answered.

"Rache, I am so glad you called."

"I'll bet you are glad. What in the wide, wide world is going on with you? Your Father called me a little while ago and told me that if I had anything, I needed to say to you, that I should do it in a hurry because your phone was about to be disconnected. When I asked him what was going on, he said that you chose some southern religion over Judaism, and he was going to cut you off. Aggie is any of this true or is your father just being dramatic?"

"No, he is not being dramatic. In fact, the only thing he told you that wasn't completely correct was that part about the southern religion. I chose to accept Christ as my savior and become a Christian. He told me that I had until the morning to join him on his plane or he would take everything of mine that was his."

"Wow, you really were serious the other night when we talked. How did they get their claws into you? You have always been a good little Jewish girl. What changed? This woman, Annette, was her argument that compelling, or did your policeman bat his eyes at you and you agreed to anything? I know *I* might convert for something like that."

Aggie laughed at her always hormonal Aunt. "No Rache, this has nothing to do with Bobby or Aziz, or anyone. I have been looking for something to believe in that felt real. Annette, the woman I have been staying with, talked to me some about it and so did Ben, the publisher of the newspaper I have been working for. But Ms. Joan, the lady at the hospital, really explained it to me. She told me that accepting Christ was the easiest thing in the world, and she was right. She also said that living for Him might be a little harder, but He would help me through that, too. She left before I got a chance to thank her, but I will find her eventually."

"Hospital? Why were you at the hospital? Did something happen to you?"

"No, not to me. Bobby fell out of a tree while getting some evidence in a murder investigation. They thought he was going to die but somehow, he pulled out of it, and I believe that God did it. I don't know if it was just for him or for Annette, or someone else, but I know that the doctors gave him little hope last night and tonight he is downstairs helping to guard me and Aziz."

"Hold the phone. Why do you need guarding? Your father didn't mention anything about any danger you were in, and who is Aziz? That's the second time you have mentioned his name tonight. Who is he?"

"Aziz is the other guy I have met here. He is a Muslim and he also accepted Christ last night."

"What kind of worm hole did you fall into down there? Let me get this straight. You, a devout Jew, who has been raised a Jew from birth, and a Muslim male who I am sure was raised the same way in his culture, both became Christians on the same day? There has to be something strange going on down there. One of those things happening would be strange and unexpected. Having both of those things happening on the same day in the same place has to be something controlled by a higher power. Is this Aziz's father one of the richest men in America also?"

"No, but he is an Imam." When she said it, Aggie could understand why the shear incredulity of this simply floor anyone who heard it.

"Where are you right now? Are you near an airport? If you don't want to come home with your father, why don't you come and see me. I really want to help you, and you know I will do anything I can for you."

"I know you will, Rache, but I'm not coming home right now. When, or if I do, I will probably have to stay with you until I get ready to go back to college."

"You know you are welcome here anytime. If you need some money or anything, you let me know. Your father may have lots of money and influence, but you are my sister's only child, and I won't let you be destroyed because you chose to live your own life. In fact, when you do come back to New York, I want to hear about this Christianity. Anything that can change two people with such different backgrounds is something that might need to be heard about."

"I would love to share that with you. I want to tell everyone, because if

226

this makes me feel this good, then I want everyone to feel good."

"My favorite niece, I look forward to getting together with you. I'm not sure I agree with what you are doing, but I applaud you for being willing no matter what the cost. Anything I can do for you now?"

"No Rache, I don't think so. I go to their church for the first time in the morning. I'll call you and let you know how that goes. I don't know if they do the same kind of service that the priest does at temple, but I'm ready to find out."

"I'll look forward to hearing everything. Tell that young policeman and the new Muslim Christian I said hello. You really ought to think about writing a book when all this is over. No one will believe it's the truth."

"Thank you Rache. I'll talk to you tomorrow." Just hearing her aunt talk to her and not chastise her made Aggie feel so much better. If her aunt could accept her, then maybe everyone could. At least everyone but her father that is. Speaking of writing, Aggie had not even thought about what had brought her to Mississippi in the first place. She needed to put down some notes for her story and also work on the story for Ben. Maybe she wouldn't get to sleep as early as she thought. As she took out her laptop and her notebook, Aggie thought about Ben and his conversion experience. What a man he was and what a mentor to her he could be. Maybe tomorrow after this church service, she would go by and talk to him.

Ben sat in his chair and tried to study his Sunday School lesson for the next day, but for some reason he couldn't focus on it. The last twenty-four hours had been possibly the best hours of his life. Not because of anything that had happened to him, but because of what he had seen God do. Two young people had accepted Christ against all the odds in their lives. Not only that, but a murder had been solved, and a family who had lost a son could at least have some closure in knowing who did it and why. To top it all off, Ben knew that he might have found his heir apparent at the newspaper. Aggie might not know it, but she was just the type of person he was looking for to train and eventually inherit the Gazette. He didn't have any children of his own, and he really didn't want to sell the paper to some larger syndication who would get rid of all the local news and just repeat everything that came over the associated press web site. It used to be the AP wire, but the Internet had taken the place of the teletype machine.

Outside, he heard a dog barking and cars driving down the main street in Meadville. The dog wasn't out of the ordinary because there were several stray dogs that wandered around town. Cars driving down the main street at this hour was a little strange, but perhaps not really. Nothing about Franklin County compared to his time when he was a young man in New York City with all the traffic and excitement. Seeing Aggie had brought back a lot of memories of his younger days. He hadn't been back to New York in twenty years and then only for his father's funeral. The family had treated him like a leper, and he had flown out right after the service.

A knock on the door downstairs brought him back to the real world. Who in the world would be knocking on his door at this time of the night? Ben checked the clock on the wall and saw that it was almost midnight. Many years ago, when someone knocked on his door, Ben would have gone with his pistol drawn expecting someone angry over his coverage of some racial problem. Now, getting his pistol didn't even enter his mind. The knocking continued as he walked down the stairs and across to the door. Another proof that he had lived in his own little paradise for too long, because he didn't even look out the peep hole to see who it was. He just reached out and opened the door to reveal two large men standing there.

"Can I help you?"

"Are you Benjamin Burgdorf?" The man on the right asked.

Even though his senses were somewhat dulled, they weren't dead; Ben immediately realized that this could be a dangerous situation. Wishing he had come to the door with his pistol, Ben answered so that they would not think anything suspicious. "I'm him, can I ask who you gentlemen are?"

Without saying a word, the two men moved aside and another man stepped in-between them. "Hello, Benjamin, I am HyramSharosh. I would like a few moments of your time, if that isn't too much to ask?"

"Mr. Sharosh, I am honored to talk to you, but at this late hour, I would have appreciated a little notice or maybe even an appointment. I'm sure a man of your stature and prominence would not accept anyone who just showed up at your door around midnight without prior knowledge. I know I'm nothing but a small-town newspaper editor, but I assure you, to me my time is worth just as much as yours." Though he was not raising his voice, it didn't take long for Ben to get back into the flow of talking to someone who thought they were above him.

"I assure you that I agree with what you have said, but I must insist on speaking with you. It concerns your newest employee, my daughter, and quite possibly a business venture."

"Since it involves the newspaper, I will be happy to meet with you on

228

Monday at 9:00 a.m. If that is all, I have to prepare a Sunday School lesson." Ben began to shut the door, but quickly realized this conversation was far from over. The large burly gentleman on the right grabbed the door and pushed it back open.

"I am afraid neither I nor my associates are going to take no for an answer."

It was then plainly obvious to Ben that this meeting was going to happen no matter what time it was. But he still was not going to allow them to have complete control. "Alright, Mr. Sharosh, you can come in, but I will ask that your men or associates or whatever they are, remain outside. If this is a business conversation, then I see no need for anyone else but you and me to be involved."

"That is more than fair." He then turned to the man who was still holding the door. "You two wait in the car. Mr. Burgdorf and I can take it from here."

Ben could see that the two men were not expecting to be left outside, but neither of them offered any resistance. They knew who was paying their salary.

"May I offer you something to drink?" Ben asked as they walked into his office. "I have a blend of coffee that I am sure would be suitable to your palate."

"No thank you. If I drink much coffee after dinner, I have a hard time going to sleep, and I have already had too much. If you have a glass of water, I would appreciate that."

Ben got up and walked over to the fridge. He always kept a pitcher of water in there for visitors who didn't want their water coming from a plastic bottle. As he took the glass out of the cabinet, Ben watched his visitor in the reflection off the glass. He was immaculately dressed and had an air of affluence that couldn't be bought. You either had it or didn't. Ben still didn't know what the real reason was for this meeting, but he guessed that would become apparent very soon. The fact that he mentioned Aggie gave Ben a good idea what it might be about.

"Here you are, Mr. Sharosh," Ben said as he handed him the glass. "Now, what is so important that you need to talk to me tonight at this hour?"

"Since you and I are both near the same age, please call me Hyram."

"Alright, Hyram, and you may call me Ben. Now what couldn't possibly wait until Monday that you had to strong arm your way into my home?"

"I like a man who is willing to get to the point. I agree that my manners may not be where they need to be, but I am in a very untenable position. My daughter is working for you, correct?"

"Yes, she is. I hired her Friday, and things have been popping faster than ever around here. I won't say she is the reason for all the excitement, but it has been non-stop since she got here."

"I am sure you are aware that she has disavowed the religion of her fore-fathers and has become a Christian of some kind."

"Yes, I am aware of her decision to become a Christian. But pardon me for asking, what does that have to do with her working for me? You said this conversation was about her employment and a business opportunity."

Without saying anything, Hyram reached into his coat and took out an envelope and slid it across the desk. "What is this?" Ben asked.

"That is the business opportunity I mentioned, but please let's discuss Agnes first. As I said earlier, you and I are roughly the same age. Since you run this paper, I am sure you are more familiar with the Internet than I am. However, on the way down here, I was able to find out some very interesting facts about you online. The most intriguing of them was that you and I attended the same synagogue as children. There were several young boys my age, but I seem to remember you as a very soft-spoken person who wasn't very outgoing. Was that you or did I Google someone else and just add them to my memories on my own?"

"No, we did attend the same synagogue and, yes, I was very soft-spoken as a child. My parents moved away from Manhattan when I was twelve right before my bar mitzvah. I lived in Hoboken, New Jersey until I graduated high school and came back to New York to go to college."

"How did you wind up in this god forsaken state? A smart young man like yourself should have had no problems going anywhere and doing any-thing."

Ben didn't know where Aggie's father was trying to lead him, but he de-cided to stop being led and take control of the conversation. "Hyram, are you going to ask me why I became a Christian and if I had anything to do with your daughter's conversion? That is what you came here to ask, isn't it? Or did you come here with these two giant men to try and intimidate me? Or maybe you have some blackmail information in this envelope. If it is the latter, I assure you that intimidations as well as blackmail have been tried on me many times and with no success. However, if you want to know about Christianity and my experiences, then I have all the time you need."

If the change in tactics had thrown Hyram off, he didn't show it. "Ben, you have correctly guessed my intentions, but you are wrong about the contents of that envelope. That is a formal offer to purchase this newspaper from you. As you know, I have a very large network of television stations and newspapers. I want to purchase this newspaper to give me another area to venture into. I would like for you to continue to work for me as editor. Your compensation package will be completely separate from the purchase price."

Ben took the envelope and slowly opened it. All the while he tried to put together his thoughts and his remarks. There was no question that this was no more than a bribe of some kind to put him under HyramSharosh's thumb. Ben knew he would never be a stooge for someone like this man, no matter how much he offered--until he saw the amount written on a slip of paper. Even with his years of perfecting his poker face, Ben's breath was definitely taken away.

Hyram saw this and smiled. "I want to know how my child can do something that is completely unsatisfactory to me or her family. I want to know why she would throw away everything I have to offer her for something that is just a pipe dream and nothing more. I want to know if you had a hand in this. If you and I can come together as partners, I need to know what kind of man I am getting."

"I don't know which question you want me to answer, so I will ask you a question. What did your daughter tell you? Isn't she the one you should be having this conversation with?"

"Agnes told me that she was happy and she had never felt anything like this in our Jewish faith. I don't believe this because I choose not to believe it. Since you are her most trusted confidant here in this hovel that is called a town, I would like for you to talk to her and tell her that she needs to think about her future. If she will reconsider, I will allow her to come back occasionally and work with you. Possibly, when you get ready to retire, she can come and take over for you."

"I have heard of sheer audacity before, but I have never experienced it. Hyram, you are most likely a good man. I even believe that you love your daughter, but your actions this evening are not those of a gentleman but of an insolent, arrogant, hate monger." He then took the envelope and offer and tore them into pieces. "I believe that you have been able to bully and

231

persuade people over the years by force of personality and money, but this is not a battle you can win. You are fighting against your own child and calling it love. You can take away everything you have ever given her, and she will still not return to you or your faith. This is not because of anything I did, because I am not capable of convincing someone to walk away from everything in their lives. Only God can do that. There really isn't any difference between you and the Muslims when you think about it. Especially since you came to my home with two thugs. Did Maalik give you their names or did you get them yourself?"

"You are an insolent man to think that I would do anything that would be any way encouraged by those malcontent killers of women and children. I love my daughter and I love my faith. I came here in hopes that you would be reasonable. I realize I was wrong on that account."

"If you love your daughter so much, why don't you want her to be happy? Let me give you a story from the Bible. I would read it to you, but I am going to paraphrase it because my Bible is beside my bed, and I don't want to walk up the stairs. Besides, I don't believe you would appreciate it anymore, whether I read the story or tell you the story."

"If the story is from what is called the Old Testament, I have probably heard it. However, if it is out of this New version, then I most likely haven't heard it."

"Ok, that's great. I'm a pretty good story teller, so I'll try to be concise. Peter and John, were two of Jesus' most trusted disciples. After Jesus' death, they went daily into the temple and taught about Jesus and his resurrection. One day, the chief priests and the scribes brought Peter and John and the other apostles and put them in prison. That night an angel let them out of prison and told them to go into the temple in the morning and to preach and teach as before. When the priests and the scribes found out that the apostles were not in prison but standing in the temple teaching, they commanded them to be brought before the entire council. When they asked the apostles why they did this and reminded them they had forbidden them to teach in this way, they responded that they were supposed to obey God and not man. So, this really angered the priests, but one of their own, I think his name was Gamaliel, stood up and spoke to them. He said that there have been lots of men who came claiming to be sent from God or claiming to be someone important. But each time, after a little while when the leader was killed or jailed, the group would disband. But these men speak with power and honor. If they are just men, then they will come of naught and will eventually disband and go away. But if they truly are from God, do you really want to go against

God? After they listened to Gamaliel, they beat the Apostles and commanded them not to speak in the name of Jesus anymore. But the Apostles rejoiced even more and greater because they were worthy of suffering for Jesus' name. And do you know what they did the next day?"

"I am tingling with excitement," Hyram answered sarcastically.

"They went and taught in the temple just like before."

"Thank you so much for this wonderful story, but what does any of this have to do with my daughter and her current situation? For that matter what does it have to do with anything pertaining to me?"

"Mr. Sharosh, you are a Jew's Jew. You have kept the faith and studied the Torah and done all the things that you believed a good Jewish man should do. Your daughter has chosen a way that is contrary to what you have lived. I chose a different way from my family also. What you have to realize is that if this Christianity is not everything it is supposed to be, then she will go away from it and come back to you and your faith. However, since I know what she became is real, and you do believe in God, do you really want to be someone who fights against God? You can take away all the things of this world from your daughter, and it will hurt her physically and financially. But what she has accepted in her life and into her heart is so much greater than anything you have. And by the way, I have googled you also, and I know how much you have. My suggestion to you is to not sever the ties you have to your daughter. She is your only child, and she will always be that no matter what faith she is. You are a good man from all I can tell, but you need to realize that everything you have believed is false about Jesus, and if you don't accept him, then you will spend eternity regretting that decision."

"Well, Ben, you left out one small option. You said that even after the priests listened to Gamaliel, they beat the men and sent them on their way. I gave you an opportunity to become a very rich man. I didn't have to do this, but I did it out of respect for what your family is and who they are. Since you have chosen to reject my monetary offer, I will make another. If my daughter doesn't deny this religious choice she has made and come home with me, I won't blame her because she is a young person and prone to make mistakes. What I will do is blame anyone I think helped her make this decision, and the main person will be you. So, as I leave, I want you to remember those men outside. If my daughter doesn't come to Jackson with me in the morning and go back to New York, then you will see them again. I promise you, that meeting won't be as cordial as this one."

Then without another word, Hyram got up and walked out the door. Ben

233

heard the car crank and drive off, but he was unable to say anything. After a few moments, he shouted as loud as he could. He didn't care if it woke up the entire town of Meadville. He had been threatened with physical pain and violence if he didn't convince someone to turn away from Jesus. In just the tiniest way, he felt the elation that the Apostles must have felt. He, Benjamin Burgdorf, humble and faithful, was worthy to be threatened about the name of Jesus.

While Ben was reveling in being persecuted for the faith, Aziz was just beginning to make his way to his bedroom. When he shut the door, he realized that he didn't have anything to sleep in.

"I guess I'm sleeping in these again," he said as he looked down at the only clothes he had to his name. When he did, he saw something hanging off the chair beside the bed. Folded neatly over a pair of sleep pants were a white tee shirt and a pair of socks. On the table were several toiletry items that he hadn't thought about, but obviously someone had. Once again, when he thought he didn't have anything, out of the blue his needs had been provided. There was no way anyone could describe this as chance.

"I wonder if I will ever get used to God doing great things for me?" Aziz said as he began to change into the sleep clothes. After changing, he went over and brushed his teeth and looked at himself in the mirror. At 6'2 and 190 pounds, he was not a small person by any stretch of the imagination. Many times, in his high school days, coaches had wanted him to play football or basketball or run track. He had always declined because he had Quran studies he had to do and, in his father's eyes, nothing could interfere with those studies. If he had known what he knew now, he might have given sports a try.

As he got into bed, Aziz looked at the ceiling and closed his eyes. "God, it's Aziz again. Thank you for the clothes or whoever you told to bring them to me. I know I have a lot to learn, but I am willing to listen and do good for you. Amen." It wasn't a prayer like the ones Sheriff Wactor had prayed or like Kareem had prayed when they were in college, but it was from the heart and Aziz figured that was what God considered important.

CHAPTER 24

Ignorance Knows Many Forms

The alarm went off and Aggie turned over and looked at the window to see a bright sunny day. In fact, it was the first Sunday that she ever thought of as really important. She had set her alarm for 7:30 because she didn't know what to expect and wanted to be ready. Going to church, as they called it, was going to be a new experience on so many levels. Getting out of bed, she walked over to the window and looked out expecting to see her car gone. When she saw it still there, she breathed a sigh of relief. She didn't know why, because she knew her father was a man of his word if he was anything. If she wasn't on that plane at 9:00, then he would probably have someone on standby to come and pick it up. But he hadn't gotten it yet, so maybe there was still hope. She could hear movement downstairs, so someone must be awake. She stepped out of her room and could smell something that she recognized from yesterday at Annette's house, but she didn't know what it was.

"Good morning, sleepy head," Bobby said when he saw her coming down the stairs. "Did you sleep well?" He was standing in the kitchen putting food on plates while two of the state policemen stood there chatting and drinking coffee. They all looked like they hadn't had any sleep the night before, and it made Aggie feel a little self-conscious about being so refreshed.

"Yes, I slept very well. What is that you are cooking? Is it deer sausage? Jack made some yesterday, and I didn't know what it was, but I really liked it."

"No, I don't have any deer sausage. But I do have some eggs and biscuits and some bacon, grits, and fresh figs. Actually, I can't take credit for the food. Annette brought it over about fifteen minutes ago and gave me some relief."

"I thought you said I was your back up," Jughead said from the couch.

"Relief and backup are the same things in this context," Bobby said laughing.

"Well hello there, Archie. Why are you up at this time of the morning?" Aggie was really beginning to like this young man. Something about him was special because, if it hadn't been for him, none of the things that had

235

happened up until now would have happened.

"If you must know, I am in charge of getting the two of you to church this morning. You see Sheriff Wactor called Daddy this morning and told him that Bobby was to stay at the cabin and rest. They are sending two other officers to escort us, while these guys get some sleep. He asked if I would be able to ride with you and Aziz and give you directions to the church since neither of you have ever been there and neither have the troopers."

"I have been to Sheriff Wactor's church," Aziz said. He had also smelled the food and made his way out of the bedroom. "I found the church yesterday when I was riding around looking for Annette's house."

"But do you know how to get there from here?" Jughead asked.

"You've got me there. I don't even know if I could get out of here by myself. But enough of this talk. What did you say Ms. Annette sent us for breakfast? I don't think I have ever been this hungry in the morning."

"We've got eggs, biscuits, bacon, and grits and jelly."

"I guess this Christianity is going to be full of new things every day," Aziz said.

"I know what you are talking about," Aggie said.

Bobby smiled as he realized what Aziz was alluding to. He wasn't talking about new experiences. He was talking about pork.

"Aziz, you don't have to do the bacon if you don't want to. I know that is a very taboo thing to all Muslims. Why don't you get some biscuits and eggs and let's go for the bacon next time? Sometimes we have to take baby steps in everything."

"Thanks for your understanding, Bobby, but as they say, there's no better time than the present."

"Well, get over here and dig in because you two have to meet with the sheriff, I mean the Reverend, at 9:30."

All his life he had been told that pork was an abomination, and anyone who touched it was defiled. After taking his first bite, Aziz couldn't understand how anything that tasty could be bad for anyone. He and Aggie were both attacking their food as if they'd been starved.

"What do you think about that bacon, Aziz?" Bobby asked.

"I think that I have been missing out on some good tasting things by not eating pork. I hope everything I eat tastes that good."

"I think you will find out that from this day forward, air is going to taste better. Did you find the clothes laid out for you last night?" Bobby asked as he put some more figs on his biscuit.

"I did find them. I thought I was going to have to sleep in my clothes. Where did they come from?"

"I would like to take responsibility for it, but I can't. Sheriff got hold of Kevin from the Baptist association, and he brought them out. In case you didn't look in the closet, he also brought some dress clothes for you to wear today. I didn't see them, but I am willing to bet that they are the perfect size and fit."

"Why would you be so sure about that?" Aggie asked as she finished off her eggs.

"Because Kevin is one of the smartest people I know. Lots of people dismiss him because he doesn't talk very much, but if you give him a general description of someone, he can match their sizes without ever seeing them. We have used him in a couple of cases where we didn't have a drawing of the perpetrator, and he was able to make a mock drawing of the person on the computer. He's not a forensic expert or anything, but he is as close as we have. Plus, he loves the Lord and that is a big plus. Are you two finished eating?"

"I am," Aggie said. "If you can get your backup to clean up, I will go get ready for church. She put emphasis on the word "church," taking great pleasure in using it in relation to herself.

"I should be a busboy as much as I have cleaned off tables in the last few days," Jughead said, as he began to take the plates away.

Aziz wiped his mouth and handed Jughead his plate. "I need to get ready also. I just wish I could call Kareem and talk to him about all that has happened. He is the only person I know who's gone through something like this."

"Why don't you call him?" Aggie asked. "You own your phone, so you can call whomever you want."

"Yes, but when I got rid of my other phone, I also got rid of all my contacts. I don't have his number, and there is no way for me to get it."

"Update your new phone on the cloud," Jughead said. "All you have to do is login with your password, and your phone will automatically download all your contacts as long as you have the same type of phone you had."

"Jughead, that is a great idea. For a young man, you are much wiser than you seem."

"That's because he has such a wise uncle," Bobby chimed in. "You can use my computer if you need to update your phone. Annette picked it up at my house and brought it to me this morning."

"Thanks, Bobby, I really appreciate it."

It only took ten minutes for the contacts to download onto his phone. Aziz decided to call Kareem immediately, because since Cincinnati was in the eastern time zone, he didn't know if he was busy with his church work yet. The phone rang several times before a voice picked up. "Hello?" The voice on the other end sounded weak and tired.

"Kareem, it's Aziz. I am sorry I haven't called you back, but since I talked to you, things have really taken off. How was your night?"

"Aziz, it's so good to hear your voice. I thought they may have gotten you." Even over the phone, Aziz could hear his friend's labored breathing.

"What do you mean they got me? How could you know anything about what has been going on?"

"Last night I got a visit from a few Muslim gentlemen. They grabbed me on the way home from the store and gave me a beating comparable to the one I got at Columbia. I spent the night in the hospital."

"I am so sorry, Kareem. Why would they do this now? I thought your father had disavowed you, and you weren't in danger anymore."

"Let's just say someone told them that you left Islam, and that I had something to do with it. They told me that I was unworthy to die, but I deserved everything I got. They told me that I should stop trying to convert other Muslims and, if you called me, I was to tell you that Christianity was not worth what would happen to you. Did you tell anyone about our conversation yesterday?"

"Kareem, I am so sorry. I have told no one about you because I have been almost fighting for my own life. I have been kidnapped myself and been under guard all night. I don't know how they would have even known that you and I were talking." Then the answer came to Aziz. "I know who it was! My mother heard me talking to you yesterday. She heard my end of the conversation, but she knew I was talking to you and what we were talking about. She must have told my father and he sent word to some people up there."

"Aziz, don't you worry about it. I have read the Bible from cover to cover and this is one of the things the world does when Christians start to win. They try to intimidate and beat the Gospel out of people, but they don't realize you can't beat something out of someone's heart. I will be fine and all my bruises will heal. Tell me all about your experiences."

For the next ten minutes, Aziz shared the story of his time with his friend. When he got to the part about going to church this morning, Kareem clapped and Aziz laughed saying, "What are you clapping about? Did you need to turn your light off?" This was a joke from their days at Columbia because they had a clap on light in their dorm room.

"No, I don't need any light. I am clapping because you are going to church immediately. Will you walk down the aisle today? You need to be baptized as soon as possible so that you can testify to your new faith for everyone to see."

"I don't know," Aziz answered honestly. "All I know for sure is that we are supposed to meet Sheriff Wactor at 9:30 this morning, and he is going to talk to us."

"You said us. Is the Jewish girl you mentioned yesterday going with you also?"

"Yes, she and I are staying together. Wait a minute! I didn't mean we are staying together. I meant that we were in the same house last night with armed guards inside and outside."

"I knew what you meant my friend. Once again you have called and made the pains in my body begin to feel much better. I am chosen to be beaten for the cause of Christ and because of my witness for Him. I am unworthy, but I am so thankful. Is this your new number? I tried to call the other number last night, but it said it was disconnected."

"Yeah, I threw the phone away so that they couldn't track me, but they found me anyway. This is my new number for the foreseeable future."

"Great. I should be released from here this afternoon, so when I get back home, I will call you and see how things went."

"That will be great. Again, Kareem, I am sorry that you were hurt because of me. I never thought that they would go after you since the two of us have not seen or spoken in so many years. How did they know where you were anyway?"

"Who knows these things? All I know for sure is that God is good and He is going to take care of me and you both. Tell this young lady that I am proud of her and for her decision also. I've got to go now. A nurse has come in and wants me to take a bunch of horse pills. I will talk to you this afternoon."

"Good bye my friend," Aziz said and ended the call. Looking at his phone, Aziz could picture his friend lying in a hospital bed. What he couldn't picture was a hatred so great that someone would order a completely innocent person beaten because of a choice that he, Aziz, had made. Without thinking about what else he could do, Aziz decided to go to the root of the problem. He looked at the favorite's list and hit the number for his father's phone. He answered on the fourth ring, most likely because he didn't recognize the number.

"Father, I understand that you hate my decision, but why would you take it out on Kareem? He hasn't done anything to you. You may not have touched him, but every injury on his body, you are responsible for. If I could prove it, I would make sure you were prosecuted. If you gave the order to attack Kareem, then how do I know you didn't give the order to kill that young boy?"

"Good morning. Since I recognize your voice, I know who you are but I would appreciate it if you would refrain from calling me Father or any other parental name. I no longer have a son, because if I did, he would not reject my life's passion. I would also appreciate it if you didn't make unsubstantiated charges against me."

"All right, since I can't call you Father, then I will call you by your name. Maalik, I want you to leave my friends alone. Your problem is with me not them."

"I didn't know you had any friends. I have no idea what you are talking about but, I appreciate your call. Now that I know this number, I won't be answering it again. If you wish to return to your life's calling, you know where I am. I have nothing else to say to you."

The end of the call was abrupt, but not unexpected. Aziz didn't know whether to stay angry or be sad. All he knew for sure was that the die was cast and, whatever happened, he was going to trust God to take care of him.

The first way he was going to do that was to get ready and go to church.

Aziz sat and waited on the couch. He looked at his watch and saw that it was 9:07. Bobby had said that it was a fifteen-minute drive to the church. If they were going to make it by 9:30, they needed to hurry.

"Aggie, are you ready yet?" Bobby shouted up the stairs. I can't get any rest until y'all are gone."

"I'm almost done. Give me two minutes," a voice called down.

"I have heard these stories about women not being ready for church, but this is the first time I have ever witness edit," Bobby said as he plopped down in a chair.

"You should see how Dad handles it," Jughead said. "He goes out to the truck and gets in and blows the horn. I don't think it makes Mom go any faster, but I think it makes him feel better. It sure does make the trips to church entertaining."

"Maybe I should go out and turn the siren on in one of the patrol cars. Do you think that would…" but before Bobby could say anything else his eyes were drawn to the top of the stairs? The girl with a ponytail he had handcuffed only three days earlier was a far cry from the one standing here now. She was wearing a maroon dress that wasn't tight, but snug enough that you didn't have to wonder if she was a female. Her hair was completely different from an hour earlier when she had sat at the table eating breakfast like she hadn't eaten in days. The only thing Bobby could think of was that he was looking at the prettiest girl he had ever seen.

"See, I told you I wouldn't be long," Aggie said. "What? You guys haven't ever seen a girl dressed up and ready to go to church?"

Aziz hadn't missed the change either. "Does everybody who gets ready for church look like *that*?"

"Not at our church, but this one will be a first. Aggie, you look wonderful," was all Bobby could say.

"Let's go, Aggie. I don't have all day. I am supposed to be getting my classroom ready for some kind of game we are playing after the lesson. If you would come down here, we can leave." Obviously young Jughead was still immune to the powers of a beautiful woman.

When she got downstairs, Bobby could see both of the new state troopers who had come to relieve them standing at the windows looking in. "I hope

I'm not overdressed, but I want to make a good first impression." Aggie wasn't stupid and she knew what she was doing. She knew that even though she was new to Christianity, she was not new to public perception. She wanted everyone to know that she was there. Hopefully, that wouldn't make God angry.

"You better take some more clothes if you don't want that dress to get wet." Jughead said. "I like it, but I don't think you will like wearing it for baptism."

"What do you mean? I thought you only had to be baptized if you had either touched a dead body or were converting to Judaism. Do you do this also? We Jews call it tvilah, but I've never experienced it.

"You have a lot to learn about Baptist baptism," Bobby said. "Jughead's right. You need to take extra clothes for the baptism." He then looked at his nephew and smiled. "Good call little man. You may make a decent backup yet."

"Do I need to take more clothes also?" Aziz asked. "I have not seen any of these baptisms, so I am completely clueless. Kareem mentioned it, but he didn't go into any detail."

"You better get some clothes," Aggie said. "If I have to change for this baptism, then you do too."

"Fine. There is another pair of pants and a shirt in the closet. I was going to save them for tomorrow, but I guess I can wash and dry them, wherever we are tonight. By the way Bobby, you were so right about this Kevin guy. He got my clothes and they fit perfectly. Even this sports jacket fits well. He could make a great living as a shopper or a tailor."

"You can thank him when you get to church. He will be sitting there in the third row reading his Bible."

"He doesn't need any money, and he is perfectly happy helping people. Some folks are just good in that way. Now if you three are ready, I am going to go and take a nap in your room Aziz, if that's okay. I don't think the princess here would appreciate me sleeping in her room." The surprise at how beautiful Aggie was had worn off a little, and Bobby was able to deflect his uncomfortableness into a little good-natured ribbing.

"I don't care what you do. I won't be able to sleep this afternoon anyway, and I was able to sleep last night because I knew you were here. You get all the sleep you need. You deserve it."

"I would normally go with you, but I am worn out, and if you two are going to be here tonight then so am I. Have a good church service, and I want both of you to know that I am so proud to have been able to see something like this with my own eyes. It's something that you hear about but never expect to see for yourself. Now get out of here."

At 9:20, after five minutes of Aggie complaining about what she was going to have to wear to be baptized in, the convoy headed out with one trooper in front, Aggie, Jughead, and Aziz in her car and another trooper behind. Jughead had taken over and told the lead car that they would flash their lights when they got to the road to turn onto, and then Aggie would lead the way with Jughead giving directions.

"My father had some men attack and beat up my friend Kareem," Aziz said as they turned off the highway onto the local road.

"Oh no, Aziz, I'm so sorry. How did he know anything about him?"

"I was telling Kareem about becoming a Christian yesterday and my mother overheard me. I'm guessing she told my father and he did the rest. I can't believe that he was hurt because of something that I did."

"That kind of gives you something in common with Jesus," Jughead said. "He was hurt because of something that we did. He was perfect, but He had to be punished for our sins."

"Are all of the young men in your church as smart about the Bible as you are?" Aziz asked. "That is very insightful and from everything I have seen so far, it sounds feasible."

"I wish I could say that I am a great Bible guy, but that is the lesson we are studying today. I usually don't read it before church, but I did today."

Aggie thought for a moment. "I know my father is crazy, but I can't believe that he would ever hurt someone I knew because of something that I did."

As they came around the curve, they saw a car on the side of the road. The road was wide enough for two cars but just barely. Aggie slowed down and looked because the car seemed familiar. When they had pulled alongside, she saw Ben sitting on the road in front of the car. The two state police cars didn't immediately realize what was going on and initially just maintained their distance.

"Oh no, it's Ben," Aggie shrieked. She quickly pulled her car over and

243

they all got out. The two troopers recognized the situation and got out with weapons drawn.

As he saw them coming, Ben laughed at the irony that was taking place. "I knew you didn't get on that plane, but I never in a million years would have expected you to be the first person I saw when I came to."

"Mr. Burgdorf, what happened to you?" Aziz said as he helped him up.

"Let's just say that being a friend to Ms. Sharosh is a very dangerous but rewarding situation." There was a small cut on the side of his head and a bruise was beginning to form on his face. "I stopped to help what I thought was a young lady whose car had broken down. When I walked up to her door, she rolled down the window and asked if I could look under the hood. I guess I am getting senile, because this is the second time in the last twelve hours that my inner radar hasn't gone off. I raised the hood and leaned over to look, when someone came up behind me and put a bag over my head."

"Did they say anything?" Aggie asked.

"Yes, the person said, 'She's not on the plane.' Then they hit me with something, and I went unconscious for," he looked at his watch, "twenty minutes. I had made my way over to the car when you drove up."

"We have to get you to the hospital," Aggie said. "You may have a concussion or even worse."

"Young lady, you will do no such thing. I have been threatened and now assaulted for the cause of Christ. A hundred mules couldn't keep me away from church. I will go to God's house and praise His name and you will come with me. I think I will leave my car here though. Officers, do you mind if I ride with one of you? We are all going to the same place."

"Will you let us fill out a report?" Lieutenant Gilbert asked.

"After church you have my complete attention," Ben assured him. "In fact, I will give you a copy of the story I am going to write for next week's paper. All the necessary facts will be in there if I leave anything out this afternoon."

"Okay, let's go, but I promise you this. If anyone tries anything now, I am going to shoot first and ask questions later." Though he didn't sound tough, the steel in his words made everyone realize that Lieutenant. Gilbert wasn't kidding.

"Lieutenant, you have my permission to shoot anyone who threatens any of us, and I will defend you to my last breath. I don't think they would be crazy enough to stay around here, but the car she was driving was a white Honda. Now let's go to church. I'm excited to see what God has in store after the way this morning has started."

CHAPTER 25

Church is a Building but a Revival is Life

"Okay, I want you two to stand outside and patrol," Henry Wactor said to the state troopers. Don't shoot anyone, but if you get into trouble, hit the siren and I will come running. If he had ever been angrier than he was right now, he didn't remember when. "I won't have some well-to-do man come into my county and try to ride rough shod over me. No offense to you or your family Aggie, but when we get done this afternoon, I'm going to contact the New York Attorney General's office and have charges filed against Mr. Sharosh. Then I am going to fly up there and personally extradite him back to Mississippi."

"That may be a problem," Aggie said from the corner of Henry's church office. She along with Aziz, Ben, Annette and Jack were all sitting down discussing the assault on Ben. Aggie wasn't hurt by the feeling toward her father. She wasn't surprised in the least that he tried to strong arm someone to do what he wanted them to do. Though she had never heard of him ordering someone to do physical harm to another person, she knew it wasn't out of the realm of possibilities for him. She was also the only person in the room who knew how politically powerful her father was.

"What do you mean that may be a problem?" Henry said. "I may not be a lawyer, but I know the law and if someone makes a threat and someone else carries it out, they are both guilty of carrying out the attack."

"I'm not arguing about that, but I'm saying that the Attorney General of New York is a personal friend of my father's, and I don't think you would get anywhere going through him. As a matter of fact, the District Attorney of New York City and my father play golf every Thursday morning." Aggie wasn't bragging about her father, but she knew how powerful he was in New York political circles.

Henry was about to make another argument when Ben held up his hand. "Henry, I don't want to be a stick in the mud, but while you were ranting, I read the bulletin. What is your sermon topic for this morning?"

"It's titled, 'Vengeance is God's that He will repay.'" As he said this, Henry got a little quieter and finally sat down in his chair. "Wow, God knew what was going to happen before I did and made me prepare a sermon for myself when I thought I was preparing one for everyone else. He is *really* something. Okay Ben, thanks for helping me get my priorities in order. Aziz and Aggie, are you ready to walk down the aisle and be baptized?"

"Jughead mentioned something about that, but I'm not clear on what that entails," Aziz said. "My friend Kareem told me that I should be baptized as soon as possible, but I didn't know it would be today."

"Me neither. Bobby told me that I didn't need to wear this dress when I was baptized. He wouldn't go into any details about it. Can you explain it to me?"

Henry laughed again and all the tension of the previous few minutes went away. "After I get through preaching and offer the invitation, you two will walk down one at a time and I will talk to you. Then we will announce that you have accepted Christ as your savior and that you would like to be baptized. Since I knew this was coming, I had James David come and fill the baptistry last night. He remembered to put the heater in, so the water is warm and ready."

"Wait a minute, do you mean you have a bathtub somewhere in here?" Aggie asked.

"It's not a bathtub, it's a baptistry. When we leave out of here, I'll show both of you. Now, like I was saying, after I explain to the congregation, you two will go to the rooms on each side of the building and change into some clothes and the robes I have laid out for you. Aziz, since Aggie is the lady, she will go first. I will go back also and change into my jeans and a tee shirt as well as my robe. I will step into the water, and then, Aggie you will come down into the baptistry with me. Then when you have been baptized, you will walk out and Aziz, you will come down and you will be baptized. Any questions so far?"

"I've got a million questions, but I'll save them for another day," Aziz said. There is one thing I'm concerned about."

"With everything that has gone on, if you only have one concern, I'll take that. What is it?"

"I haven't seen a lot of black people here today. I wasn't expecting any, but this is Mississippi and up until yesterday some of these people probably would have considered me a Muslim terrorist. Will they have a problem with you bringing me up front and baptizing me?"

"Aziz, I wondered about that this morning. I know we have some deep

Southern people who go to this church, but I can't believe that they will have any heartburn over someone coming to know Christ, no matter what color they are. I'll tell you this much though, if they stand up and say something derogatory or say that you can't be here, then you and I will leave together and they can explain their attitude to God. How's that to ease your mind?"

"I'll take it, and I won't worry anymore."

"Henry, I am going to go wash some of this blood off my face and make sure there isn't any on my shirt. Aggie, would you help an old man?" Ben was talking a good game, but he still seemed uneasy on his feet when he stood.

"Since you got that way because of me, and because you are my boss, it's the least I could do. Lead the way."

The church was filling up with the usual late arrivals. Since Henry Wactor had become pastor, the membership of New Beginnings had quadrupled. They now had an average of one hundred students in Sunday school and two hundred for morning services. There were several older couples, but most of the congregation was between twenty-five and fifty, with several youth and younger children. Aziz and Aggie were sitting with Annette's family in the second row from the front. There was plenty of room in the pews in front and behind, but it looked like they were trying to jam people in on the back pews.

"Bunch of back row Baptists around here," Annette leaned over and told Aggie. "Some of them are scared if they get too close to the preacher. Something he says might hit them and God might actually call them to do something."

Aziz was quiet but smiled at Annette's statement. There had been several people who came over, shook his hand and welcomed him and Aggie to church; but there were several of those in the back and he could feel them staring a hole in the back of his head. Obviously, they didn't have a lot of black folks in their lives.

"I sure hope Sheriff Wactor is right about these folks. I think I saw a few of them sharpening their knives when I turned around a few minutes ago."

"You don't worry about them. We have come too far and done too much to let a group of hillbillies scare us off." Aggie noticed that a couple of the people who had come to welcome them were much more friendly toward her than they were to Aziz and it angered her. If Annette had acted like this toward Aziz, he would have never accepted Christ.

The entire church service took almost an hour. There were several songs sung and a group of children had come down front for something called Children's Church. Both Aggie and Aziz were impressed by how everything had a time and a place, and everyone who was involved seemed to be genuinely happy with being a part of the service. After Sheriff Henry had preached his sermon, which both Aggie and Aziz enjoyed very much, he came down to the front and said they were going to have a time of invitation. He had both of them walk forward and then turned them toward the congregation.

"Ladies and gentlemen, I don't know if any of you have ever seen a miracle in your lives but standing beside me are two people who are both miracles and a great example of God's love for us. Aggie Sharosh, whom most of you may have seen on CNN Friday night, was born into the Jewish faith, and Aziz, whom most of you know is from Fayette, was born of the Muslim faith. They both come here today to let you know that they have accepted Christ as their Savior and want to be baptized. They have rejected everything they have ever been taught, because they realized Jesus is the way and the truth and the light and no man comes to the Father but by Him."

For just a moment there was silence, and Aggie thought that maybe the people were going to reject the idea. Then someone in the back stood up and shouted and the entire crowd of two hundred or more people stood up and began to clap and shout. They were saying things like "Hallelujah," and "Praise God." One woman, who was sitting in the same row they had been in but on the opposite side of the church, began to dance. The feeling of excitement and joy in the room was overwhelming. Annette and Jughead were both standing and shouting. Annette was crying, but none of the tears were tears of sadness, only joy.

"I think you got their approval," Sheriff Wactor said. "Now, let's go get baptized."

The baptism had been anticlimactic after the celebration of sorts that took place when Sheriff Wactor made the announcement. Both Aziz and Aggie were put under the water, first Aggie and then Aziz. When Sheriff Wactor prayed and put them under the water, they each came up shouting. Aggie had never shouted anywhere but at a Rutgers football game, but she shouted as she came up out of the water, praising God and thanking Him. For his entire life, Aziz, who had seen videos of other Muslim men shouting about Mohamed and promising to kill all infidels, also came up out of the water shouting, but it was nothing about Mohamed or Allah. It was all about Jesus.

CHAPTER 26

Jesus Plus Nothing

"That has to be the prettiest baby I have ever seen," Annette said. "She is gorgeous."

"Um, don't I count?" Jughead asked. "I've seen my baby pictures and I am just as gorgeous now as I was fourteen years ago, I'm just taller and weigh a little more. In fact, I may be even more gorgeous now."

"I believe you are more gorgeous today than you were that fateful day you got in my car three years ago," Aggie said. "Of course, I believe little Angelica is going to have first place in my eyes."

"Mine too," Aziz said as he took his little girl from her mother and sat in the rocking chair beside her.

Annette and Archie were the second group of people to come and visit the new parents and their baby. The recently retired Reverend Wactor, along with his replacement, the newly elected Sheriff Bobby McCoy, had come earlier in the day along with Bobby's wife Zoe who was expecting their first child in a couple of months.

Everyone in the room was focused on Aggie and Aziz's baby, and none of them were paying attention when the door opened. Aggie was lying in bed, so she was the first to see the man walk in. The gasp of breath she took was so sudden that it shocked everyone. Aziz, who since the day he turned from Islam to Christianity stayed on alert to any spark of danger, immediately stood up and took a defensive posture over his wife and child. When they looked at Aggie's face, they turned and saw someone they had not seen since he drove away from Annette's house three years earlier. It was Hyram Sharosh.

"Daddy," was all Aggie could get out before she began to cry. She had not spoken to her father since that day. No phone calls or letters or anything. She had even sent him an invitation to the wedding and asked him to walk her down the aisle, but the letter had been returned unopened and Ben had walked her down the aisle. Now he was here and words were hard to come by for everyone.

"Archie, you and I need to leave and let this family saga take its course. Mr. Sharosh, it is a pleasure to see you. Archie, let's go." Annette then leaned down and hugged Aggie who was crying now. "God brought him here despite himself. Don't forget that," she whispered. She then walked around and kissed Angelica and then hugged Aziz. "God's got this," she whispered to him.

When Annette and Archie had walked out of the room, Aziz looked at the man he had only seen once in person, and that was as he was walking out the door.

"Would you like to hold your granddaughter, Mr. Sharosh?"

"I would like very much to hold my granddaughter." The arrogant man who had walked out of their lives years earlier was not the same man standing before them now. This was someone else. Aziz stood up and walked over and handed an old man his first grandchild. As he held the child, a single tear came down his face.

"I have to talk to the two of you, but especially you, Agnes. I have tried for these three years to stay away because of your decision to leave our faith. I have tried to hate you also because of your choice to marry someone who was born a Muslim, and I succeeded most of the time. But when your Aunt Rachel told me that you were going to have a baby, I couldn't hate you anymore. I don't agree with your decision, and I will never agree with it. But I can't hate anyone who would bring into the world something beautiful that was part of my family. You both are doing well I hear?"

"Yes, we are," Aggie said. "Ben made me the managing editor of The Gazette, and Aziz is the assistant administrator at the hospital. We are also youth ministers at New Beginnings Church, but I would be willing to guess that you already knew that, didn't you?"

"Yes, Agnes, I did. Like I said, I have hated everything you did, but I couldn't hate you forever. I tried and I tried, but I couldn't do it. I won't be involved with your beliefs, but I would like to be involved with the lives of you and your husband as well as the life of my granddaughter."

"Daddy, that is all I ever wanted. I gave my life to Jesus, but I will always be your daughter."

"Were you still my daughter the day they came and took your car? I really thought I was getting the best of you that day. Now I look back at it and I agonize. I don't think I was a very good father to you. No, I know I wasn't a very good father, especially after your mother died. What I want, and the reason I have come here today is the opportunity to become a good grandfather, because this little one is worth swallowing my pride. Also, will you allow me to make an amends for the last three years financially also? There is a car that has been in storage for three years that I would love to return to its rightful owner."

"Daddy, I would get up and hug you but the doctors don't want me to get up very much yet. I might tear out my stitches. Could you come over here?"

"I would, but if I do, I might have to put this little one down and I don't know if I can do that."

"I'll tell you what," Aziz said. "why don't you give her to me for a moment and I will give her back to you when you are done?"

Hyram handed the child to her father and then moved over beside the bed. "I know you have hated me, but I can't live with myself anymore. If you will let me, I want to treat you differently." Aggie grabbed the man that she had despised as a teenager and pitied after she became a Christian. All the prayers she had prayed were coming to pass, and she couldn't do anything but cry and hug him.

Since he knew everything was going to be all right, Aziz walked out into the hall with his new daughter to give them some privacy. When he turned to walk toward the nurses' station, he saw a woman dressed in a Muslim head scarf. She had her back to him, but something about her was familiar.

"Mother," Aziz said. The woman heard the voice but didn't immediately turn around. "Mother, is that you?" Aziz said again.

When she turned toward him, Aziz saw that it was the woman he had last seen walking out of his bedroom door three years ago. "Aziz, is that your child? I was trying to look in the nursery to see if I could see her without you knowing I was here."

"Yes, it is your granddaughter. Is Father here with you?" Aziz asked. If Aggie's father could come, anything was possible. "No, he doesn't know I'm here. I came because I saw on Facebook that you and your wife were going to have a baby, and they were asking people to pray for her because of some possible complications. Is she well?" As she talked, Kadeera Saalam was walking toward him. Finally, they were face to face and Aziz couldn't hide his joy.

"Aggie is fine and so is the baby as you can see. Mother, I have missed you so much. Look how beautiful your granddaughter is. Would you like to hold her?"

Looking down at the precious child, there was no way for Kadeera to hold back the tears. "No, my son, I can't hold her because if I held her, I would not be able to let her go, and that is a battle I am not ready to fight. This is a beautiful child and you will have a beautiful family."

"Please mother, come and see my wife. You've never met her." Aziz knew he was stammering, but the answer to both of their prayers on the same day was something that would take the words from the strongest Christian.

"Aziz, you know that I can't be part of your life. But know that no matter what your position in life, you will always be my son, and this will always be my grandchild. Perhaps one day we will be able to reconcile something."

"What about Father? Could you and he come over and talk to us? I haven't spoken to either of you in over three years."

"Aziz, your Father is a very sincere man about Islam. I don't know what he would do if he knew I was here, so do not ever mention it to me or him." Kadeera leaned over and gently kissed the cheek of her grandchild. "I must go, but I have done everything I wanted to do. Have a good life my son." Without another word, she turned and walked away, the head scarf barely covering the tears coming down her face. Aziz wanted to run after his mother but knew that he was holding his daughter, and she was very still very fragile. Instead he turned and walked back into the room to his wife.

Hyram Sharosh stayed for thirty minutes more and then left. His reasoning was that the baby needed rest and so did the mother; however, he did promise to come visit soon after they were home and to bring a different car since the Porsche wasn't conducive to a family lifestyle. He also made Aggie promise to bring the child to New York so that everyone could see that there was something more important money in his life. Though this wasn't funny, it was a good sign to hear him be self-deprecating. After he left, Aggie couldn't believe that was the same man who raised her and walked away from her three years ago. If she thought that was strange, she would have been completely flabbergasted when Hyram walked into the hospital stairwell after leaving them.

"Was the child perfect?" Maalik asked.

"The most beautiful child I have seen since her mother was born. There's something I still don't understand. You came here, but you would not see your son, daughter-in-law, and your granddaughter. I'm a stubborn man, but I am getting older. What do I have in my life as important as that child?" Hyram sat down on the step beside Maalik and looked at the man whom he still didn't like or trust. "For that matter, what do you have in your life that is more important than that child?"

"I have Islam. Isn't your Jewish religion important to you? Aren't the beliefs of your forefathers worth more than anything?"

"It's important to me, but I have spent three years trying to convince myself that it was more important than my daughter and her family. That family includes your son, and I really don't understand why they are together. But when I heard there was going to be a child, I decided to try *not* hating something. That is the reason I called you. You and I are the most valiant of adversaries, but we have a common bond in that little baby. If you were going to sit in the stairwell, why did you accept my offer to come here?"

"Because the desire to know that my son and his child are safe is important to me, but I can't allow anyone else to know this. I also have tried to hate him, and I succeeded for several months. When you called, I couldn't think of any reason not to come here, but I couldn't think of any reason to go in. I don't expect you to understand, but that is how I feel."

"I don't expect either of us to understand the other. Still, isn't it amazing that our people hate each other so much, and the only thing we can both agree on is that we both hate Christians? Yet Christianity is the one thing that has brought our people together, even on an individual scale. That is a question I don't have the answer to." Hyram then stood up and brushed off the back of his tailored suit. "If you are not going to go see the baby, we should leave. I'm not sure it would be any good to either of our reputations to be seen together very much." "Did you take a picture of the child with your phone?"

"I do not have a phone, but I did bring my camera." Hyram took the camera out of his pocket and handed it to Maalik. As he looked at the little girl Aziz was holding, Maalik had no expression on his face. He then got up and handed the camera back to Hyram. I hope they are happy with their choices. Let's go."

As they walked down the stairs, Aziz stood at the door of the stairwell and watched them walk away. He had gone after Aggie's father to thank him again for coming when he saw him go into the stairwell. Since he didn't take the elevator, Aziz had not immediately followed him but instead looked through the window. Seeing his father, he had fought the urge to go and confront him, but instead he had listened to the entire conversation.

"No, Father, I hope you are satisfied with *your* choices."

ABOUT
KHARIS PUBLISHING

KHARIS PUBLISHING is an independent, traditional publishing house with a core mission to publishimpactful books, and channel proceeds into establishing mini-libraries or resource centers for orphanages in developing countries, so these kids will learn to read, dream, and grow. Every time you purchase a book from Kharis Publishing or partner as an author, you are helping give these kids an amazing opportunity to read, dream, and grow. Kharis Publishing is an imprint of Kharis Media LLC. Learn more at https://www.kharispublishing.com.

CPSIA information can be obtained
at www.ICGtesting.com
Printed in the USA
BVHW051415210821
614413BV00009B/26